These two wo...

U...

Suspicion

from the very men they hoped would be much, *much* more than just good friends...

Renowned authors
Elizabeth Bevarly and
Bronwyn Jameson show that
even rugged, handsome heroes
can make mistakes!

Dear Reader,

Welcome to the sexy world of Desire!

We have three lovely volumes for you this month starting with two intense reunion stories in **Even Better Than Before** which features Anne McAllister's *A Cowboy's Promise* and another tale in BJ James's MEN OF BELLE TERRE miniseries called *The Redemption of Jefferson Cade*.

Our two heroines are **Under Suspicion** by rugged heroes in Elizabeth Bevarly's *The Secret Life of Connor Monahan* and Bronwyn Jameson's *Addicted to Nick*.

Finally, we have two wonderful stories with a fairytale twist in **The Nanny and the Boss** featuring *Wyoming Cinderella* by Cathleen Galitz and *Taming the Beast* by Amy J Fetzer.

Enjoy!

The Editors

Under Suspicion

ELIZABETH BEVARLY
BRONWYN JAMESON

™ SILHOUETTE®
DESIRE™

*Silhouette, Silhouette Desire and Colophon
are registered trademarks of Harlequin Books S.A.,
used under licence.*

*First published in Great Britain 2002
Silhouette Books, Eton House, 18-24 Paradise Road,
Richmond, Surrey TW9 1SR*

UNDER SUSPICION © Harlequin Books S.A. 2002

The publisher acknowledges the copyright holders of the
individual works as follows:

The Secret Life of Connor Monahan © Elizabeth Bevarly 2001
Addicted to Nick © Bronwyn Turner 2001

ISBN 0 373 04764 9

51-1002

*Printed and bound in Spain
by Litografia Rosés S.A., Barcelona*

THE SECRET LIFE OF CONNOR MONAHAN

by
Elizabeth Bevarly

ELIZABETH BEVARLY

was born and raised in Louisville, Kentucky, and earned her BA with honours in English from the University of Louisville in 1983. When she's not writing, the RITA-nominated author enjoys old movies, old houses, good books, whimsical antiques, hot jazz and even hotter salsa (the music, not the sauce). She resides with her husband and young son back home in Kentucky.

For Dad

One

One

Winona Thornbury was up to her elbows in trouble, and, ever the optimist, was trying to assure herself that things couldn't possibly get any worse, when, naturally, things got worse. Really worse.

The up-to-her-elbows-in-trouble part came in the form of a large chocolate bombe she had fashioned for the evening's dessert at her self-named restaurant, Winona's. She was putting the finishing touches on said bombe—a delicate ring of ripe, red raspberries—when one of her waiters came scurrying into the kitchen much too fast, and careened right into her back. And before she could say *"Pardonnez moi"*—not that *she* had done anything for which she needed to say *pardonnez*—Winona was biceps-deep in chocolate bombe, something that did nothing to enhance the once-white chef's jacket that had been so crisp and clean when she had donned it earlier that afternoon.

Wonderful, she thought as she extracted her arm from the icy confection. Now what was she supposed to serve for dessert tonight? Although her restaurant was famous for its delicious and innovative sweets, Winona was reasonably certain that chocolate-bombe-with-arm-hole wasn't going to go over well with her patrons, even with the ring of ripe, red raspberries. It would probably be even less popular with the Bloomington, Indiana, health department. Fortunately, she had experimented with cheesecakes earlier that afternoon, some of which had turned out surprisingly well. They would just have to do.

However, no sooner had she settled that problem than did the things-got-worse-really-worse part arrive. It came in the form of a request from the hostess stand, a request her waiter had been about to relay before he stumbled into her. The message itself went something like, "Oh, my God, Winona, come out here quick. Hurry, hurry, we're in big, big trouble." Doing her best to wipe what she could of the chocolate bombe from her sleeve—which, unfortunately, wasn't much—Winona went rushing from the kitchen forthwith.

It was seven o'clock on a Friday night—a lovely September evening with just a hint of autumn in the air—and Winona's was packed, now that classes were back in session at the nearby Indiana University. Even the bar was full—either with people who were stopping in for a cocktail on their way home from work or class, or with people who were waiting for a table to open up so that they could dine.

The restaurant's regular patrons were an eclectic assortment of pin-striped local businesspeople and casually dressed teachers and students—mostly graduate and postgraduate. History and English majors in particular seemed to favor Winona's. But that was probably because of the decor as much as it was because of the menu and extensive wine list. Being something of a romantic person—actually, being a fanatically romantic person—Winona Thornbury tended to live quite shamelessly in the past, and everything about her reflected that. As a result, her restaurant was a very accurate reflection of turn-of-the-century America.

She had purchased the big Victorian house three years ago with her half of a modest inheritance that she and her sister, Miriam, had received from an elderly aunt. Winona, being thrifty and talented as well as romantic, had then completed the bulk of the renovation work and decoration herself while working full-time as a pastry chef at another local restaurant. She'd spared no expense—or elbow grease—in turning the dilapidated building into a show-place, comparable to any Tuxedo Park estate circa 1900ish.

In fact, the restaurant's decor very much resembled a turn-of-the-century luxury hotel, quite elegant, quite opulent, quite abundant. Lace curtains and silk moiré draperies framed the floor-to-ceiling windows in every room, and more lace and moiré covered each of the tables. The color schemes varied from room to room, but Winona had opted mostly for dark jewel tones and contrasting color schemes throughout. The main dining room was ruby and emerald, the smaller salon dining room was sapphire and topaz, while the patio dining room was amethyst and coral.

Her slogan for the restaurant was "At Winona's everybody feels at home." And, indeed, anyone who dined there would agree with the statement wholeheartedly. Less than a year after opening, Winona's was *the* place to dine in Hoosierland—because there was nothing in Winona's that wasn't finely crafted and genuinely beautiful, not to mention extremely tasteful. Including the food. Especially the food. That, primarily was what brought her patrons back again and again.

Well, that, and the telephones.

Because somewhere along the line, before opening her establishment, Winona had come up with the idea of putting an antique telephone at the center of each table, all of them wired together within the restaurant, so that patrons could telephone each other from one table to the next. Elaborately calligraphied numbers hung above the antique lamps that hovered over each table, and by dialing that number from one's own table, one could contact whomever was seated elsewhere.

So far, the telephones had proved to be great fun and good conversation starters. There had even been one or two romantic entanglements that had resulted from the gimmick. In fact, one couple was renting out Winona's this month for their wedding reception, specifically because they had met while flirting over the telephones on opening night. Winona had been delighted when the couple had called to make the arrangements, and had found the whole idea to be enchanting.

Tonight, however, she wasn't delighted *or* enchanted. Because tonight, for the first time since she had opened the restaurant, *nothing* was going right.

Her head chef had called in that afternoon with something highly unpleasant and even more highly contagious, and Winona hadn't been able to find anyone who could come in to cover for him. As a result, she was trying to complete the work of *two* chefs tonight, in addition to her owner/manager duties. Ruthie, her expediter, was working with a bad ankle, thanks to a hiking accident the day before, making her anything *but* expedient. And Winona had discovered earlier that morning that the alleged organic farmer from whom she had been purchasing alleged organic produce—and specifying, *not* alleging, on the menu as such—was, in fact, using chemicals on his decidedly unorganic harvests.

And as if all that weren't enough, when Winona left the kitchen to go to the hostess stand and uncover whatever *else* was about to go wrong, she discovered the most troubling thing of all.

He was here again.

And as troubling as his appearance was, a little thrill of excitement shimmied right up her spine to see *him* sitting there, gazing at her in his usual way—as if he wanted to make *her* his dessert tonight.

Actually, if she were honest with herself—and truly, Winona did always try to be honest with herself—she would be forced to admit that, normally, his arrival wouldn't necessarily be something she considered to be going wrong. Because, normally, she liked seeing *him* in the restaurant, even if his…attentions…were just a *tad* forward.

Then again, normally, when *he* came to the restaurant, Winona wasn't frazzled and high-strung and overwrought, not to mention bedecked in once-white chef's togs that were now splattered with 99 percent of the evening's recommended selections—never mind the chocolate sleeve. The last thing she needed or wanted was for *him* to see her like this. Even if she had no idea who *he* really was.

She did know, however, that he was exceedingly attractive. His jet-black hair and ice-blue eyes made for a combination Winona had never been able to resist, and his features were almost blindingly handsome. He easily topped six feet, his broad shoulders and back straining against the seams of his expertly, and expensively, tailored dark suits. His silk neckties, clearly expensive, and his understated—but likewise expensive—wristwatch suggested he came from a moneyed background, and he fairly oozed wealth and success and refinement.

Winona suspected he was a newly transferred executive who had come to work in a regional corporate office of some kind. Perhaps he even lived as far away as Indianapolis. She was fairly certain, at least, that he wasn't a native of Bloomington. He just didn't seem to have that local air about him. But for the past few weeks, he had been coming in for dinner once or twice a week. He always arrived alone. And he always dined alone. And he always left alone. And he always seemed to be watching Winona *very* intently.

It was just too bad that he was so young, she invariably

thought when she saw him. Not that she had a problem with such age differences—not for other people at any rate. She herself, however, already suffered from a significant generational disadvantage—namely that she had been born about four generations too late. It was something that made her soul, at least, more than a hundred years old.

The mysterious stranger, on the other hand, must be at least ten years younger than her own thirty-eight, temporally and chronologically speaking at any rate, because he couldn't possibly have yet hit thirty himself. And in addition to his young age, he was clearly upscale, trendy, hip…and thoroughly modern. He was all those things that Winona herself most certainly was not. Which made all the more puzzling his interest in her. Because clearly, he *was* interested in her. Because, clearly, he *did* watch her very intently whenever he dined at her restaurant.

Just as he was doing tonight.

Winona did her best to avoid his attention as she skirted the edge of the main dining room, hoping to keep a low profile—she didn't want *any* of her patrons to see her bedecked in chef's-previously-whites-with-a-chocolate-sleeve. She had won herself a reputation for being tidy and well organized, in addition to her proudly worn mantle of nice, old-fashioned girl, and she never appeared in her restaurant in, shall we say, dishabille. No, whenever Winona made an appearance in the dining room, she always made sure she looked as if she had just been cast as an extra on the set of the movie *Titanic*.

Tonight, however, she much more resembled a chip of the iceberg. A very messy chip at that.

"What's the problem?" she asked Laurel, her hostess—who, like the rest of the staff, *was* dressed as if she'd just been cast as an extra for the movie *Titanic*—when she arrived at the hostess stand.

"It's the Carlton party," Laurel said.

"What about the Carlton party?" Winona asked. "They're not coming until tomorrow night."

Laurel shook her head. "No, they're here tonight."

Winona gazed blankly at her hostess, certain she'd misheard. "But they're not supposed to be here until *tomorrow* night," she said again. "They made a reservation for *tomorrow* night. Saturday night."

Winona knew they had, because she'd taken the reservation herself a month ago and reconfirmed it just the week before. Granted, she may have uttered the date of the reservation when doing so, as opposed to the day of the week, but that was beside the point. Either Edna Carlton's calendar was wrong, or Winona's was. And with all due respect to Mrs. Carlton, Winona was certain she herself had, as always, recorded the correct date and time. She simply did not make mistakes like that.

"That's not what they're saying," Laurel told her. "Mrs. Carlton insists the reservation was for tonight. And she's brought the entire party. And they want to be seated. Now."

"All *twelve* of them?" Winona asked incredulously. "They want to be seated *now?*"

"Actually, there are fourteen of them," Laurel told her. "Mrs. Carlton decided at the last minute to invite another couple, because she was sure you'd be able to accommodate them. And yes," the hostess added, "they want to be seated *now.*"

Winona eyed the other woman with much panic. "Oh. No."

Laurel nodded. "That was pretty much my reaction, too."

Winona thought fast. "All right. We can handle this. We can. We'll just…"

Run away, was her initial reaction. But she quickly saw the inappropriateness of that. "We'll just…" she began again. "Just…just…" And then she brightened. "We'll seat them upstairs, in my dining room."

"*Your* dining room?" Laurel echoed with disbelief. "But you *live* upstairs. Those are your *private* quarters."

"Not anymore, they're not," Winona told her. "Now they're our special party room. Find Teddy and Max and tell them to run upstairs and set the table for fourteen." Thank goodness her table sat that many, Winona couldn't help thinking. And that was the maximum limit. "And tell them to use my china, crystal and silver that's in the bottom of the china cabinet," she continued hastily. "They'll have to mix and match, but it will be faster that way—they won't have to lug anything up the stairs. Then tell Teddy to give his tables down here to Max and Stephanie, and take the Carlton party himself."

She thought for a few minutes more, to see if there were any problems with the plan. And although there were indeed one or two—or fourteen—they were nothing she couldn't handle. Probably.

"Yes," she finally said with a decisive nod, "that should work out just fine."

Except that the service wasn't likely to be up to snuff, Winona thought. Not for the Carlton party, and not for the main dining room, either. And having such a large party was bound to slow up the food preparation for the other diners. Then again, if she opened a couple of cases of champagne and had the servers present each of their tables with complimentary glasses…

Maybe, just maybe, all would be well.

Winona spun back around to return to the kitchen, only to find herself staring at *him* again. And, drat it all, he was staring back at her. Very intently, too. Worse than that, he was running the pad of his middle finger slowly around the rim of his wineglass, and somehow making the leisurely journey seem inexplicably—and profoundly—erotic.

For one brief, electric moment, their gazes held firm, and

Winona felt a shiver of something inexplicable and unwarranted—and very, *very* warm—go shimmying right down her spine. Her reaction made no sense. She had no idea who or what the man was, or why he kept coming into her restaurant.

But there was something in his eyes in that scintillating moment, something fierce and knowing and determined and…and…and—*oh, my*—and *hot,* that told her it wouldn't be long before she found out.

Battling a sudden fever that seemed to come out of nowhere, Winona fled to the kitchen and tried to forget about the handsome, young, mysterious—hot—stranger. Somehow, though, she knew he wasn't likely to stray far from her thoughts.

Detective Connor Monahan fastened his gaze to the fleeing backside of Winona Thornbury as he lifted his glass by the stem to sip carefully—and only the smallest amount—from the ruby liquid inside. But his reaction wasn't due to the fact that her backside was an especially pleasant thing to gaze upon, though indeed it was quite pleasant. No, the real reason Connor watched his quarry with such interest was that he was wondering how much longer it would be before he finally nailed the woman for her numerous and colorful crimes.

He'd worked some interesting cases since being bumped up to the Vice Squad nearly a year ago, but never one like this. Never such an elaborately organized and stealthily operated prostitution ring, and never one that worked out of an allegedly respectable establishment like this one, with an allegedly respectable proprietress like Winona Thornbury. Because in spite of her alleged respectability, Winona Thornbury was, in a word, very luscious.

Okay, so that was two words. Sue him. One word just didn't seem like enough for a woman like her.

Though, granted, tonight she didn't seem to be quite up

to her usual very luscious standards. Where before she'd always been dressed in some kind of turn-of-the-century getup that made her look like a nice, old-fashioned girl— yeah, right—tonight she looked more like a chef-in-training. A chef-in-training who wasn't training particularly well, at that. Not unless one chocolate sleeve and a long, bedraggled braid was all the rage for chefs in the know.

Usually, though, she really did look like a nice, old-fashioned girl—*as if*—with her pale gold hair all piled atop her head, and wearing antique-looking dresses that she might have found in her great-great-great-grandmother's hope chest. Or else she wore a white embroidered blouse with a high collar and a million buttons up the back, coupled with some long skirt that swished around button-booted ankles.

But no matter how much she buttoned herself up and battened herself down, no matter how nice and old-fashioned her clothes were, Winona Thornbury couldn't hide her lusciousness. Because even whalebone couldn't restrain the curves that woman possessed.

But then, of course she was luscious, Connor reminded himself. She was a high-class madam who ran one of the most exclusive—and elusive—call-girl rings in Indiana. As such, she'd almost certainly started off her career as a call girl herself. And only the most luscious call girls made enough money to go into business for themselves.

And what a business. Oh, sure. Winona's might look like a legitimate four-star restaurant on the outside, but the interior fairly shrieked *brothel*. Hell, the furnishings alone had probably started off life in some house of ill repute. What person in their right mind would furnish a place like this, if not because they wanted to evoke a certain, oh…mood? And what woman dressed like that, if not to hide what she really was?

And why would a restaurant have telephones on the table, for criminy's sake, he thought further, if not to make illicit assignations? Sure, it might look like a cute gimmick, but Connor Monahan—along with the Bloomington PD and the Indiana State Police—knew better.

There was all kinds of evidence to indicate that a ring of call girls was working out of Winona's. All Connor and his colleagues had to do now was find the person in charge. Or, at least, uncover solid evidence against the person in charge. Because Connor, for one, knew it was Winona Thornbury masterminding the operation, even if some of his colleagues had their doubts. Even if some of his colleagues were convinced that, although there was most certainly a call-girl ring operating out of the place, Winona Thornbury herself was oblivious to the fact.

Hell, those guys were just smitten, that was all, Connor thought. They'd just fallen for the nice, old-fashioned girl—oh, sure—routine. Not that he could much blame them. If he wasn't such a pragmatic guy—not to mention if he wasn't totally mistrustful of women in general, and luscious women in particular, though not without good reason, dammit—he'd be smitten, too. But he knew better. He knew Winona Thornbury was guilty of pandering, and he intended to prove it. Once he had that solid evidence in hand, then they could bust some lamb chops.

By now Winona Thornbury had disappeared into the kitchen, so Connor glanced down at the menu that lay open on the table before him. Hmm, he thought as he perused the selections. The lamb chops *did* look rather nice this evening....

But then, everything in Winona's looked nice. Especially Madam Winona herself.

Oh, it was going to be such a pleasure to bring that woman down, he thought. And he tried not to think about how *bringing down* Winona Thornbury suddenly took on an entirely different connotation than the one vice cops traditionally entertained.

Pushing the thought aside, he gazed at the telephone on

his table and silently willed it to ring. *Ring, dammit,* he commanded. Why didn't it ever ring for him? He and the boys on the Bloomington PD had been staking out Winona's for three weeks now, and they had yet to get a nibble, even though they knew—they *knew*—there was a ring of call girls working out of the place. Connor had been chosen among the men to be the bait, because he'd seemed the most likely to carry off the charade of successful businessman. And also because, he'd assured the others, there wasn't a woman on the planet who could resist him.

Okay, so maybe he'd been lying about that last part. *Most* women couldn't resist him. Well, several, anyway. He could think of at least three, right off the top of his head. So why wasn't his telephone ringing? he wondered. Why hadn't it rung any of the half-dozen times he'd come into the restaurant over the last few weeks? Why did it always just sit there, mocking him?

He couldn't blame it on faulty wiring, because he'd sat at different tables on nearly every occasion. And as he gazed around the room now, he saw a number of patrons chatting amiably on their phones, some of them seated at tables he'd occupied himself on previous evenings. So why wasn't anyone calling *him?*

As if jarred by his mental meanderings, the telephone on his table did suddenly ring, jarring him from his mental meanderings. Immediately Connor snatched up the receiver and placed it by his ear. Leaning forward, he forced his voice to remain steady and calm as he spoke into the mouthpiece. "Hello?"

There was a slight pause from the other end, then a man's voice said, "Oh. I'm sorry. I seem to have the wrong number. I was trying to reach the redhead at table fifteen."

"No problem," Connor muttered irritably into the mouthpiece. All for nothing. Because the man had already hung up.

He turned his attention to table fifteen then, which was

immediately to the left of his own. Sure enough, a rather breathtaking redhead was seated there—alone.

Hmmm, Connor thought.

As he watched, her telephone rang, no doubt due to the gent who had just erroneously called Connor. The redhead answered the telephone with a low, throaty greeting, then smiled and began to murmur something he couldn't hear into the phone.

Connor sighed. Damn. That was probably one of the very illicit assignations he was supposed to be halting being arranged right there under his nose. Because the redhead certainly had the look of a high-priced call girl. Meaning that she was dressed in an elegant, and very modest, black cocktail dress, with understated jewelry and makeup and simply arranged hair.

That was the problem with call girls these days, he thought. They all looked like debutantes and corporate interns. She was probably a student from the university. An economics major, he couldn't help thinking further, making a few extra bucks on the side.

Man. What was the youth of today coming to?

Within moments of hanging up her telephone, the redhead was joined at her table by a man old enough to be her father. Connor watched to see if maybe she'd slip up and do something incriminating—like loudly demand cash up-front for very specific sexual services she would render right there at the table for all to see—only to have her and her companion open their menus and peruse the evening's selections.

Well, of course, he thought. What woman was going to give it up without getting a steak dinner out of it first, even if she would be paid handsomely for her efforts at evening's end?

Connor sighed his frustration and willed the telephone on his table to ring again. But it never did. Not even after he'd ordered dinner, and not even after he'd finished eating the dinner he ordered.

The only thing that kept him from sinking into a totally black humor was the fact that, eventually, Winona Thornbury appeared in the dining room again. She was still dressed as a chef, but had changed into a clean jacket. And she must have taken the time to rebraid her hair, he noted, because the length of gold that fell to her waist now was much tidier than it had been before.

All in all, Connor thought, she really did appear to be harmless. Of course, he'd had the same thoughts about other women of his acquaintance—one in particular—and look how that had turned out.

Maybe it was time for him to stop waiting around for something to happen with this case and take matters into his own hands, he thought. Not that he wanted to skirt the edge of entrapment or anything, but maybe a nudge in the right direction would get things rolling.

Like maybe, he thought as he watched Winona Thornbury make her way to the hostess stand, it was time he paid his compliments—among other things—to the chef.

Two

By midnight Winona was ready to collapse—such had been the evening's toll on her. Only one more hour, she told herself as she carried the bar and restaurant receipts and cash register drawers up the stairs to her office. You can last one more hour. On weekends the kitchen closed at precisely eleven o'clock, the bar followed at precisely twelve, and, usually, all of her employees were gone by precisely 1:00 a.m. Laurel, or whichever of her other hostesses or hosts was working on any given night, would take care of winding things up downstairs while Winona did the numbers work upstairs. It was a system that generally worked very well.

Tonight, however, all Winona wanted to do was escape into sleep. To nestle herself down into the feather bed that lay atop her regular mattress, and snuggle under the cool, lavender-scented cotton sheets, and lose herself in sweet slumber until dawn crept over the windowsill tomorrow. Instead she groaned with much feeling when she passed by her miniscule kitchen on the way to her office and beheld the mess that awaited her there.

She had told Teddy to simply clear away the dishes from the Carlton party as he would any other group of diners and leave them in her kitchen, and then to return to work downstairs the moment the party left. She hadn't wanted to disrupt the flow of the restaurant's pace any more than she had already by robbing it of one of its servers, and at the time Winona hadn't minded performing the cleanup herself. Now, however...

She sighed heavily. Now the last thing she felt like doing was hand washing and drying all the fine crystal, china and silver left over from fourteen people. But she couldn't very well put her antique serveware in the restaurant's hobart, could she? The delicate pieces would fairly dissolve under the strength of the water pressure and detergent. And she wasn't about to ask Teddy or any of the others to wash them after the exhausting night they'd all just survived.

No, this was Winona's responsibility, and one which she would dispose of forthwith. Because there was no way she could go to bed knowing what clutter and squalor remained in her kitchen. The very thought of sleeping with all that in there sent a shudder of distaste winding through her entire body.

With another heartfelt sigh she went to her office to lock up the night's receipts—she could do her numbers work tomorrow morning. Then she went to her bedroom to shed her stained and bedraggled chef's togs and slipped on an ankle-length, sleeveless, embroidered white cotton nightgown in its place. To protect her sleepwear from the mess she was about to assail, she tugged a long, flowered cotton robe over it, then tucked her feet into a pair of tapestry slippers. Then she wound her braid around the top of her head a couple of times, headband fashion, and pinned it in back, to keep it out of her way.

There. That was better. No one would be seeing her for

the rest of the night, after all, so she could, as they said in the old movies, slip into something a little more comfortable. Except for Laurel, of course, who would come up later to tell Winona that all was well and that she would be locking up on her way out. Winona herself always performed a final check of the premises before turning in, but for now, she could relax.

Relax and wash dishes leftover from fourteen people.

She sighed yet again. Ah, well. There was nothing else for it. She made her way to the kitchen, shoved up the sleeves of her robe and went to work. She had finished scraping and had just submerged the first stack of plates into the soapy water of her old-fashioned porcelain double sink when she heard a soft whuffle of sound coming from nearby and turned toward it.

And then she gasped when she saw *him* standing framed by her kitchen doorway, one forearm braced on each side, his entire body leaning forward. His dark hair fell recklessly over his forehead, and his ice-blue eyes were fixed on hers, blazing with much…with much…much…

Oh, *my*.

Winona swallowed with some difficulty as an eddy of heat purled through her midsection, but somehow she remembered to breathe. For the life of her, though, she couldn't move a muscle, couldn't so much as bat an eye, so enthralled was she by his mere appearance.

He was still wearing his dark, elegant suit, but he, too, had clearly made himself more comfortable some time ago. Now the jacket hung open casually, and the silk necktie dangled unfettered from his collar. The top two buttons of his white dress shirt were unfastened, revealing a strong column of tanned throat, and a hint of the dark hair that must be scattered richly across his chest.

Winona felt herself blush at witnessing such a thing, harmless though the vision might seem to most people. After all, men revealed more than *he* was revealing now at the beach or swimming pool, didn't they? Then again, she had always avoided swimming pools and beaches for that very reason—she simply was not comfortable being around people who were only half, or less, clothed. And now, to see *him* in such a state...

Well. It simply ignited her imagination in ways she would just as soon not have it be ignited. Because suddenly, her imagination was filled with visions of *him*. Worse, it was filled with visions of *him* and...*her*. And they were doing things no one in Winona's imagination had *ever* done before.

Not that she was a complete innocent—oh, no. By some standards she was a vastly experienced woman. Like, for example, by a four-year-old's standards. But Winona did know what went on between a man and a woman. Fairly well, actually, in spite of never allowing the lights on when that man-woman thing went on. She had been engaged once, after all. She wasn't a virgin. Not quite.

But that was all beside the point now. The point now was that *he* was standing in her private quarters, in a state of dishabille. Worse than that, *she* was standing in her private quarters with him, in an even greater state of dishabille. And Winona had no idea how to react to such a development. It had been years since she'd been in a state of dishabille with a man. And she'd certainly never done so with a man whose name she didn't even know.

Thinking for a moment that she must only be imagining *him* here, she closed her eyes briefly and counted to three, as if doing so might magically dispel the vision. But when she opened her eyes again, there he still stood, gazing at her in that maddening way he had of gazing at her—as if he wanted to consume her in one big, voracious bite.

"Hi," he said. And not at all voraciously, Winona couldn't help remarking. No, his was a simple how-do-you-do sort of greeting, totally lacking in intent. Realizing that, however, did nothing to ease her concern.

She blinked her confusion and replied automatically, "Hello." Then, kicking herself into gear again, she added, "Can I help you?" The question felt a bit odd, all things considered, because the last thing Winona wanted to do was help a total stranger with questionable intentions who had invaded the privacy of her home. But she was, above all things, courteous, and she didn't wish to come across as a harridan on their first meeting, even if that first meeting consisted of him having invaded the privacy of her home.

Not that she wanted to imply, to herself or anyone, that there would be a *second* meeting, she quickly qualified to herself—especially if that meeting, too, involved violating her privacy. In any case, implying such a thing would be much too forward. Still, she did want to be polite.

Plus, she knew that if she screamed at the top of her lungs right now, however frightfully discourteous that might seem, someone downstairs was bound to hear her and come rushing to her aid. Probably. So there was that.

And she was considering doing just that, in spite of its discourtesy—and she was also considering whether or not she should hurl herself out the window and onto the fire escape, again at the risk of seeming impolite—when the man smiled.

And oh, *my,* if she had thought him handsome before, when he smiled the way he did then, he was…he was…he was…

Oh, *my.*

"I was, um… I was just looking for the men's room," he said with a self-conscious shrug. "I spilled something on my jacket," he hastened to qualify, pointing to a small stain just above his left pocket. "Guess I took a wrong turn, huh?"

She nodded slowly, still too entranced by his smile and the way it seemed to soften his otherwise rugged features, to have her full wits about her. "The facilities are downstairs,'' she told him. ''In the restaurant. I'm afraid this is a private residence.''

His mouth—that generous, beautiful mouth—dropped open a bit, and he emitted a single, nervous chuckle. ''Oh, man, I really am sorry. I saw a big party of people come down the stairs earlier, and I just assumed there was more of the restaurant up here. When I couldn't find the… facilities—'' he smiled a bit indulgently at the word, almost as if he were mocking her, Winona couldn't help thinking ''—downstairs, I assumed they were up here.''

She smiled, albeit a bit anxiously. His explanation made perfect sense and offered a reasonable excuse for his appearance. Why, then, was she having so much trouble believing him? Why did she feel as though he was acting out some kind of charade? Why did she get the impression that he wasn't being honest with her? Because for some reason, she didn't think he was being honest with her. She had no idea why.

''Well, there *was* a large party of diners up here this evening,'' she conceded. ''But that was due to special circumstances. Normally this part of Winona's is off-limits to patrons.''

She was about to conclude with a very meaningful, very adamant—but very polite—*Good-night, sir,* but was halted by his expression. It had changed dramatically the moment she'd uttered the words, *special circumstances.*

Then, ''Special circumstances?'' he repeated avidly. He punctuated the question by arching his dark eyebrows, and his blue eyes fairly twinkled with his—rather extreme— interest. She had no idea why he should be showing such an inordinate amount of attention to the Carlton party, and she had no idea how she should reply.

So she only nodded warily and told him, ''Yes. Special circumstances.''

''What, uh…what kind of special circumstances?'' he asked, still seeming far too interested in such a simple thing. And he actually seemed to be awaiting her reply with his breath held.

"It was a large party for whom I was unprepared," she told him. "The facilities downstairs wouldn't have adequately accommodated their needs."

But even that didn't seem to satisfy the man's curiosity, because he grew even more avid. "Unprepared?" he echoed. "Wouldn't have accommodated their needs?" He tipped his head forward, now clearly very interested. "In what way? Just what kind of *needs* did they have?"

What on earth was going on? Winona wondered. Why was this man so fascinated by the Carltons? Were they in some kind of trouble? But that was ridiculous. The Carltons were one of Bloomington's oldest, finest and most upstanding families.

"In the way that I didn't have room for them," Winona told him cautiously.

"Well, just what kind of room did you need?" he asked.

She narrowed her eyes at him, with much of her own interest now. Just what was he up to? "Not that it's any of your business, Mr...."

"Montgomery," he replied without compunction. His smile suddenly dazzling. "Connor Montgomery."

She dipped her chin deftly in acknowledgment. "Not that it's any of your business, Mr. Montgomery," she began again, "but there was some confusion with a reservation, and, unexpectedly, I found myself with need for a table to accommodate fourteen people, at seven o'clock sharp. I didn't have that downstairs, so I seated the party up here instead. It was the best I could manage on short notice."

He gazed at her intently for a moment, as if he were taking great care to process that information. Then, finally, "Oh," he said. "I see." His entire body seemed to relax, and only then did she realize how tense he had been during his interrogation.

How very curious, she thought. Who on earth was he,

and what was he doing here? And why did she feel so suspicious of his motives? Toward the Carltons...and toward her, too.

"Connor," she said thoughtfully, wondering why she was even bothering to prolong their conversation. Perhaps she simply wanted to assuage her curiosity about him. Or perhaps she was hoping to uncover some explanation for his real reason for coming upstairs, should the one he voiced actually be some kind of deception, as she suspected it was.

Or perhaps, she thought further, it was for some other reason entirely, one she shouldn't be thinking about, let alone acting upon. Nevertheless, "That's a nice, old-fashioned name, isn't it?" she asked him.

He shrugged...and didn't seem to be especially interested in putting an end to their dialogue yet, either. Because he leaned one shoulder against the doorway now, crossing one leg over the other in a casual stance that seemed, somehow, in no way casual. "Maybe," he replied. He smiled devilishly—for truly, there was no other way to describe his expression then but naughty. "But I'm *not* a nice, old-fashioned guy."

Well, that was more than obvious, Winona thought as another thrill of heat rushed through her midsection, pooling in a place she would just as soon not be feeling heat right now—not in mixed company, at any rate. "Well," she tried instead, suddenly thinking that it might not be such a good idea to prolong this conversation after all, "as I said, the facilities are downstairs, so if you'll—"

"Mind if I just use your sink?" he asked impulsively, moving forward toward the washbasin in question. "I'm here, it's convenient, what the hell, right?"

Winona opened her mouth to object, but before she had the chance, he was shrugging out of his jacket, and his shirt was gaping open at the collar, and she was gazing at that dark hair again, and her imagination was igniting once more—oh, my goodness, was it igniting once more—and all she could do was stare as he approached.

Stare and take a step backward for each one that he took forward, gaping in amazement that he would be so bold and that she would be so passive. Just because she was a nice, old-fashioned girl didn't mean Winona Thornbury was a pushover. The one thing she did like about the twentieth century—and its ensuing new millennium—was that it had brought enormous freedom to her gender. So she had no trouble whatsoever putting her slippered little foot down, when times called for such a drastic measure. Usually. For some reason, though, with Connor Montgomery, all Winona wanted to do was retreat, as quickly as her slippered little feet would allow.

"It's probably just a little Jameson," he told her, as he stopped at the sink, seeming oblivious to her more-than-obvious retreat—she was, after all, fairly cowering in the corner by now. "It'll probably come right out," he added. He swiveled the spigot to the other side of the sink, then turned on the hot water and thrust his long, middle finger under the flow of water to test its temperature. "I'll just be a minute."

For some reason, as Winona watched the warm water rush over his finger, as she noted the way the stream parted so readily over that strong digit, as she remarked the way he crooked his knuckle and turned it first one way then the other, as she watched his finger curl and flex and curl again...

Well. For some reason she couldn't utter a sound. For some reason she couldn't move a muscle. For some reason all she could do was stand there and stare like an idiot, marveling at the dark, frantic ribbon of wanting that wound slowly, hotly, through her. Because behind that ribbon of wanting trailed a desire so keen, so querulous, it was unlike anything she had ever felt before. And Winona was utterly unprepared for it.

"Too hot," she whispered as she continued to gaze at the finger that cleaved the hot water with such finesse. Without even realizing she was doing it, she lifted a hand to her neck, curling her fingers loosely about her throat as she murmured further, "Much, *much* too hot."

Amazingly, Connor Montgomery heard her over the rush, because he glanced up to look at her as she uttered the brief, nearly incoherent, statement. His expression as he withdrew his hand from beneath the spigot, however, indicated that his mind was not on the temperature of the water, but instead was focused more on the temperature of...Winona? And strangely, her temperature did seem to be a bit...off.

For one long moment, they only stared at each other in a dazed sort of silence, neither seeming to comprehend the sudden sizzle of frantic heat that arced between them. Then Connor's gaze darted from Winona's eyes to her hair, then to her jaw, then to her mouth. Then lower, to the hand she had circled defensively around her throat, then to the bare wrist and arm above, then lower again, to her breasts, to her hips, to her legs and to her breasts again. Then back to her face, to her mouth, where his gaze lingered for a long time. His cheeks were growing ruddy now, presumably from the heat of the steam rising from the still-rushing water. Or, perhaps, that was the result of something else entirely.

"The water," Winona finally managed to clarify, the words coming out weakly for some reason. In fact, her entire body felt weak for some reason. "You're running the...the water...too hot. Cold water will work better for a stain on that fabric."

But he seemed not to hear her—albeit quiet—words, because his attention was still focused wholly on her mouth. His own lips were slightly parted, as if he were having a little trouble breathing, but his chest rose and fell a bit rapidly, so surely he was indeed getting enough air.

And then, without warning, without speaking, he turned off the water. Then, likewise without warning, without speaking, he took a small step toward Winona. Then another. And another. And another.

The soft scuffing of his shoes over the tile floor echoed wildly through her brain, making the silence surrounding them seem to come alive somehow. Winona told herself she should be frightened of him, reminded herself that she was up here alone with a man she didn't know, one who had been behaving rather oddly. He towered over her scant five foot two by a good foot, outweighed her by a good sixty or seventy pounds. He could easily overpower her. Could easily have his way with her. Could easily—

She told herself to scream, to run away. But her instincts, which had always been very good, assured her that she had nothing to fear. And she wasn't afraid of him, she was surprised to discover. She had no idea why. Somehow, though, he didn't seem at all dangerous. Not in the way she thought he should seem dangerous, at any rate. So she only watched him as he drew nearer. Nearer. And nearer still. Only when there was scarcely a breath of air separating them did Connor Montgomery come to a halt. But he said not one word to explain his actions. He only continued to gaze silently down at her face, studying her mouth as if he had some serious plans for it.

But that was all right, at least for the moment, Winona decided. She had to tip her head back to do it, but his nearness offered her a chance to study him in return. Only it was his eyes that fascinated her so, the way the clear-blue depths seemed to go on forever, starting off at the edges the color of a summer sky, darkening gradually to sapphire, then becoming darker still at the pupils, until the black and midnight hues merged into one. His sable lashes were long and thick, yet somehow they were in no way feminine. No, this man was masculine through and through.

His features, though elegant and refined, were sharp and virile. His build was lean and muscular.

Potent, she thought. That was what he was. Potent and narcotic and more man than Winona was accustomed to encountering.

She swallowed hard at the realization, and his gaze dipped instantly to her throat, his lips parting once again. She wondered if he could see her pulse beating erratically there, so quickly was her blood racing through her body by now. And then his eyes were fixed on hers once more, and Winona found it difficult to breathe. She felt his heat surround her, envelop her, calling to something wild and primitive inside her, something that wanted to answer him with an equally feral, uncivilized response. There was no way she could explain her odd reaction to him. But it was there all the same.

Somehow, though, she resisted his pull. She had never been one for spontaneity, nor was it her custom to succumb so readily to a complete stranger. Heavens, she didn't even succumb to men she knew well. And she certainly wasn't going to allow this bizarre episode to be her introduction to such an impromptu. Regardless of Connor Montgomery's peculiar, almost unearthly command over her, she reined in her inexplicable need to respond.

Until he repeated, "Too hot?" in the sweetest, most sensual voice she had ever heard.

And then she felt the rush of heat winding through her again, urging her to follow her desire instead of her reason.

She had to force herself to remain rooted to the spot. She nodded feebly as she softly replied, "Yes. Too hot." Then, in a final attempt to hang on to reality, she added, "The water, I mean. You had it running too hot."

His mouth crooked up at one corner. "Just the water?" he asked smoothly, his voice feeling like an erotic caress over her hot skin. "Or did I have something else…some*one* else…running too hot, too?"

This time she shook her head slowly, but somehow she couldn't quite pull her gaze from his. "I don't know what you mean, Mr. Montgomery."

He dipped his head just an infinitesimal notch closer to hers. "Don't you?"

She shook her head again, with a bit more fortitude this time. "No. I don't." She straightened some as she pulled back from him, telling herself not to be cowed by this man. And she stated more vigorously now, "As I said, the facilities are downstairs. I'll thank you to use those, instead of me. I mean, instead of mine."

But her correction came too late, as he had clearly heard her slip. Worse, he clearly understood it for the Freudian one it was.

"I see," he said softly, his mouth crooking up at the other corner now. But he didn't move away.

"Mr. Montgomery, please," Winona said, her voice breaking just the slightest bit on that last word.

And only then did the spell finally break, as if she had uttered a charmed incantation to drive the magic away. With one final perusal of her face, her mouth, Connor Montgomery stepped away, taking his heat, his influence, with him. And when he did, Winona felt as cold and alone as she had ever felt in her life. Her reaction was curious, to say the least, for her house was actually warmer than usual, and she was wearing two layers of clothing. But somehow, Connor Montgomery's withdrawal brought an uncomfortable chill behind it.

And that chill grew colder still as he moved completely away, turning to collect his jacket from the counter where he had tossed it some moments ago.

Moments, Winona marveled. Only moments had passed since she'd glanced up from her work to see *him* standing at her door. Yet somehow she felt as if decades had passed instead. As if she'd lived an entire life of love and loss and was now coming to the end of it.

"Well," he said casually as he shrugged the garment back on, seeming not to have been affected at all by their brief interlude. "Thanks for the use of your...facilities."

She expelled a soft, puzzled sound. "You didn't use my facilities," she reminded him.

He smiled in that intense, heat-inducing way again. "Didn't I? Oh. My mistake. I stand corrected."

Winona had no idea what to say in response to that, so she only kept silent.

"I can see myself out," he told her, grinning again.

"Yes, I daresay you can," she replied faintly.

He considered her again for a moment, once more seeming to focus his attention on her mouth. Then he turned around and exited her kitchen, without a single backward glance. She heard his muffled footfalls on the Oriental carpet that spanned her hallway, then the almost inaudible *thump-thump-thump* of his feet as he descended the stairs toward the restaurant. For long moments Winona only stood in her kitchen gazing out the door, wondering if she hadn't just dreamed the entire incident. Then she inhaled a deep breath and detected just the merest hint of his scent that had been left behind.

No, she hadn't dreamed it. Connor Montgomery was all too real. So now only one question remained. What on earth had just happened between them?

Holy Mary, Mother of God, Connor thought when he managed to make it back to his car in one piece. What the hell had just happened up there in Winona Thornbury's house? One minute, he'd been completely in charge of the situation, had known exactly what his next step would be, had, in fact, had Madam Winona right where he wanted her. In that minute, he had been *this* close to getting at least a couple of answers to the numerous questions floating around in his brain. And then the next minute...

Whoa.

The next minute, he'd had no idea what the hell he was doing, or where the hell he was—save some dizzying black hole of need and wanting, unlike anyplace he'd ever visited before. As he'd felt the rush of warm water streaming over his hand, he'd suddenly, as if from a very great distance, heard her murmur something in that soft, husky voice of hers. And when he'd glanced up from the sink, he'd found her gazing at him in a way he'd never seen a woman gazing at him before. Not a woman who was fully clothed, anyway. Damn, not even a woman who was naked and moaning and writhing beneath him had ever looked at him like that before.

But there had been Winona Thornbury, all buttoned up in that old-fashioned thing that hid every curve she had—well, as well as curves like that could be hidden—with her hair all neatly pinned around her head like some schoolmarm from the last century, looking as if she were about to come apart right there in her own kitchen. Her cheeks had been flushed, her full, lush lips had been slightly parted, her pupils had been expanded, and the pulse had been beating erratically at the base of her throat. She'd looked as if she were *that* close to going off.

And there had been Connor, ready to go off right behind her. Because the moment he'd seen her looking at him that way, he'd been hard as a rock and ready to roll. Never in his life had a hard-on come on that rapidly, or that fiercely.

It made no sense. Sure, Madam Winona was gorgeous and sexy and hot and luscious and delectable and... and...and... Where was he? Oh, yeah. Sure she was a sexy woman, but so were scores of other women in town. Connor was no stranger to looking at beautiful women—hey, what man was?—but something about gazing at Madam Winona had left him feeling hazy and stupid and helpless.

And *helpless* was a feeling Connor Monahan didn't like *at all*. He wasn't altogether fond of stupid or hazy, either.

Which was why he'd immediately had to step in and re-capture the upper hand, by stepping forward toward Madam Winona as if he intended to…to…to… Well, to do what came naturally. But that upper hand had eluded him for some time, because the nearer he'd drawn to Madam Winona, the hazier, stupider and more helpless he'd felt.

He still couldn't figure out what had happened, still didn't understand the torpor and fascination that had come over him just from gazing at her. She'd just looked so… And she'd made him feel so… And all he'd wanted to do was…

Holy Mary, Mother of God. He'd be better off not thinking about it.

And on top of that, he'd totally blown his chance to have a look around upstairs at the infamous Winona's, which had been what had lured him up there to begin with. When he'd seen that big party going up earlier in the evening, he'd realized he had an excuse for wandering up there himself later on, to have a little look around. So after he'd finished his dinner, he'd left the restaurant for a while, returning just before closing to tuck himself into a corner where no one would notice him. And then, when he'd seen Winona Thornbury climb the stairs, he'd realized his chance to get a better look at both her *and* her…facilities.

He'd been a little disappointed when her facilities had turned out to be what was clearly her private residence, filled with frilly, ornate antiques and flowered wallpaper and whimsical lamps and Persian rugs and other old, girly stuff. All in all, her decor hadn't been much to Connor's liking. He was a twenty-first-century guy of the first order, preferring clean lines and stark contrasts and few colors in his decorating schemes. Still, he supposed it shouldn't have come as a surprise that Winona's home would look like, well, a turn-of-the-century brothel. Nevertheless, he wished it had *been* a brothel. Sure would have saved him some time and trouble.

When he'd finally stumbled upon her, it hadn't been all that hard for him to play the ignorant dunce who had accidentally wandered into an area he wasn't supposed to be in. God knew he'd played the fool before—not so long ago, in fact—though it was definitely a role he hadn't relished, nor one he wanted to repeat. Still, Winona had fallen for it, hadn't she? She'd had no idea who he was or why he was in her house, except for having taken a misstep on his way to the men's room.

But Connor had completely messed up what was probably going to be his only chance to really investigate her digs, by fleeing in panic and confusion when he should have been pressing his advantage. Certainly he wished now he had pressed something in Madam Winona's kitchen. Like maybe Madam Winona herself. Yeah, like maybe he should have pressed her back against the counter there, even lifted her up on it to settle himself between her legs, thereby giving himself more freedom, freedom to run his hands up under her nightgown, over her bare calves and shins and knees and thighs, then higher still, to—

Enough, he told himself. He was just going to drive himself crazy if he kept this up.

And just why the hell *was* he keeping this up? he wondered wildly. Just what the hell *had* happened in there? Man. He really wasn't getting out enough. That much was obvious. Maybe he ought to call up that redhead on the Bloomington investigative team. What was her name? Lynette, that was it. Yeah, Lynette seemed much more his speed—fast.

Then again, how much faster could you get than a current-Madam-slash-former-pro? And why did Connor suddenly find it so hard to believe that Winona Thornbury was either? She *had* to be the ringleader of the prostitution operation, he told himself. There was no other explanation for it. How could any legitimate businesswoman not know what was going on under her own roof? Of course she was in on it. Of course she was the one in charge.

Even if she did still seem like a nice, old-fashioned girl. Even if no experienced woman blushed the way Winona Thornbury had blushed when Connor had suggested, none too subtly, that he wanted to make use of her facilities.

And what the hell kind of woman still used the word *daresay* in this day and age?

She was a puzzle all right, Connor thought as he turned the key in his ignition and heard the satisfying rumble of the little two-seater sports car's motor purring to life. A puzzle he couldn't wait to figure out. Because one thing was certain. Even if he'd blown his chance to get a better look around Madam Winona's digs, he still had every intention of getting a better look at Madam Winona herself.

Oh, yeah, he thought further as he sped out of the parking lot and into the busy street. He planned on being quite a regular at the restaurant for the next few nights. Maybe longer. At least as long as it took to uncover everything he needed to know. About Winona Thornbury's prostitution ring.

And about Winona Thornbury herself.

Three

———

Winona was thinking about how nice it was that Monday evenings were so slow, as if in apology for the velocity and insanity of the weekends, when her evening suddenly went haywire. And all because of a simple request relayed by one of her waiters.

"Winona," Teddy said as he poked his dark, shaggy head into the kitchen, where she was removing the last of her famous white-chocolate and raspberry tortes from the oven. "There's a gentleman sitting at table seventeen who's asked you to join him."

Her eyebrows shot up in surprise as she settled the confection gently on the counter, and she was certain her expression reflected the same astonishment that Teddy's did. "Don't you mean he's asked to *see* me?"

Teddy shook his head. "No, I mean he's asked you to *join* him. For dinner," he clarified further.

"But…but…but…"

Unfortunately, no other words except for that one, not

particularly polite one, would emerge from Winona's mouth. Certainly her patrons asked to speak with her from time to time, to ask about the menu selections or compliment her on one or two particular favorites. Once or twice she'd even had to field a minor complaint, though that, fortunately, was a very rare occurrence. However, none of her customers had ever asked Winona to join them, for dinner or anything else. What the man at table seventeen was requesting was quite unusual.

And if the man at table seventeen was who Winona suspected he was, what he was requesting was also quite exciting.

No, not exciting! she immediately admonished herself. It was unacceptable! *Completely* unacceptable. There was no way she would join *him*—for dinner or anything else.

"He was pretty adamant," Teddy added when Winona said nothing in response. "I mean, he was polite, but…you know…adamant."

Oh, yes, she could certainly believe that. After what had happened Friday night, Winona knew the man could be quite formidable. Among other things.

"Very well," she said softly, not knowing what else to do. She feared that if she didn't go out and at least talk to Mr. Montgomery, he might venture into the kitchen to find her. And the last thing she needed or wanted was for her staff to bear witness to…well…to whatever it was that seemed to burn up the air between the two of them whenever they were in the same room. It was unsettling enough that Winona had been witness to it herself.

Unsettling, she thought again. To put it mildly. She'd had trouble sleeping for the last three nights, thanks to Mr. Connor Montgomery. Because the moment she switched off her light and nestled herself under her covers, she was assailed by memories of him. Memories of how his heat had encircled her, of the deep, mellow timbre of his voice, of how handsome he was and how good he had smelled.

Memories of how very much she had wanted him, regardless of the mysterious origins of that desire.

And when she finally did fall asleep, it only grew worse. Because he invaded her dreams then, and, unconscious, Winona was helpless to stop those dreams from going too far. And in her dreams Connor Montgomery went beyond formidable. In her dreams he was relentless, towering over her, bending his head to hers, covering her mouth with his, his hands roaming over her entire, and often naked, body. In her dreams he said things to her, did things to her, that no man had ever said or done before. And in her dreams Winona, heaven help her, had only wanted him to do more.

Fortunately, upon waking in the morning, she had always been able to reclaim her sanity and good sense. She wasn't the wanton her dreams made her out to be. She was a decent, virtuous woman who had no room in her life for someone like Connor Montgomery. She'd allowed a man like him into her life before—completely ignorant of his wanton, licentious habits, of course—and had been left heartbroken as a result. She wasn't about to make the same mistake again. She wasn't about to have any more to do with Connor Montgomery than she absolutely had to.

"Tell him I, ah… I'll be right there," she said to Teddy, who nodded in response and disappeared back out into the restaurant.

Winona ran a quick hand over her hair, tucking a few errant strands of blond back into the chignon she had fashioned at her nape. Then she removed the apron she had tossed on over her calf-length, ruby-red dress—the one piped along the yolk and short sleeves with black velvet, boasting a black velvet collar and two dozen ebony buttons down the back. Then she inhaled a deep, steadying breath, and told herself not to panic.

She didn't have to actually *join* Mr. Montgomery for dinner, she told herself. She would simply explain to him how busy she was, regardless of it being a Monday night and the restaurant being nearly deserted, and he would just have to understand.

There. That was simple enough. It was settled.

Unfortunately, the moment Winona entered the dining room and saw Mr. Montgomery seated at table seventeen, she became decidedly *un*settled again. Oh, yes. Very unsettled indeed. Because his gaze immediately flew to hers and fixed itself there, and she was once more held in thrall by his intense blue eyes. And she realized then that nothing about her explanation would be simple at all. She'd count herself fortunate if she could remember even the most rudimentary vocabulary and enunciate her words clearly.

"Mr. Montgomery," she said as cheerfully as she could as she approached his table. "How nice to have you back at Winona's so soon. We must have made quite an impression on you the other night."

He smiled that wicked smile of his after she uttered the comment, which she realized, too late, carried a double entendre she hadn't intended for it to carry at all. Because had he taken one more step toward her in her kitchen on Friday night, he would have been making quite an impression on her indeed. One she sincerely doubted she would have forgotten.

"I mean, ah…" She began to backpedal.

But his low, meaningful chuckle halted her. Well, that, and the fact that she had no idea what to say to excuse her faux pas.

"Please, Miss Thornbury," he said softly, holding up a hand in a silent indication that she shouldn't even bother trying to explain. Probably, she thought, because he wouldn't believe her anyway. He swiveled his hand then to indicate the chair opposite his. "Join me for dinner."

Instead of sitting, Winona gripped the back of the chair with sure fingers and remained standing. "Thank you for the invitation," she said, her voice touched with irony, because Mr. Montgomery's edict had been anything *but* an invitation. "But I don't make a practice of joining my customers for meals. I'm much too busy."

"No exceptions?" he asked,

"No, I'm afraid not."

"Not even this once?"

"No. Thank you."

"Not even if I told you I can't stop thinking about what happened Friday night?"

Oh, dear…

"Mr. Montgomery—"

"Please, call me Connor."

"Mr. Montgomery," she reiterated, more forcefully than before, "I'm afraid that what happened Friday night—"

"And just what did happen Friday night, Miss Thornbury?" he interrupted. Again. "Have you figured it out? Because I thought about it an awful lot this weekend, and I'll be damned if I can even begin to understand."

Oh, dear, she thought. He had felt it, too. "I'm not sure I know what you mean," she said evasively.

"Oh, I think you know exactly what I mean."

"I—" She halted right there. This was nonsense. He was starting to behave like a teenager—which shouldn't come as a surprise, she supposed, seeing as how he hadn't aged much beyond the decade in question. And she wanted no part of such a thing. So she looked him squarely in the eye and told him, "Thank you again for the invitation, Mr. Montgomery. Have a nice evening. I hope dinner meets with your approval."

And with that, she spun on her heel and began to walk away. She was feeling rather smug, thinking she'd handled the situation fairly well, all things considered, when she felt confident fingers circling her upper arm, urging her to turn around. The gesture was punctuated by a softly uttered, "Winona, wait."

The gentle timbre of his voice surprised her, and hearing him utter her first name in such a way set her off-kilter. As a result, she stumbled a bit as she pivoted around. But Mr. Montgomery caught her other arm capably in his free hand to steady her. And then she stood face-to-face with him again—well, as face-to-face as one could stand to someone whose height was so...enhanced. But she was gazing into his beautiful blue eyes again, marveling at the fire she saw burning in their depths. Marveling, too, at the shiver of delight that shuddered through her at hearing him address her the way he had. And wondering at the tingle of heat that seeped through her sleeves where his hands were curved over her arms.

"Please wait," he repeated, even more softly than before. And then, even more surprisingly, he added, "I apologize. I suppose I was out of line."

"Yes," she agreed, every bit as softly. "You were."

"I'm sorry if I said something that offended you," he told her again. "I promise I'll behave myself if you'll agree to join me for dinner."

"And as I told you, Mr. Montgomery—"

"Connor."

"Mr. Montgomery, I don't join my customers for dinner. I'm even less obliged to join them for suggestive banter. I'd thank you to keep yours to yourself."

He said nothing for a moment, only continued to gaze down at her face, as if he couldn't quite make sense of what he beheld there. Then, "I really haven't been able to stop thinking about Friday night," he told her. "You're a haunting woman, Winona."

Again, her name on his lips. Again the shudder of heat that wound through her. Again the memories of Friday night assailing her. Winona closed her eyes for a moment, thinking maybe the gesture would help her drive them all away. But when she opened her eyes again, when she saw Connor Montgomery's face so close to her own, when she felt his heat, inhaled his scent...

"All right," she said. "I suppose it won't hurt to join you this once."

And she absolutely could not *believe* she had said what she had said. She simply did not join her patrons for meals. It wasn't professional. It breached the rules of etiquette. It blurred the line between social stations. Winona was a firm believer in all of these things. Yet she had just disregarded all of them for the sake of—

What? she wondered. What was she hoping to gain by having dinner with Connor Montgomery?

When he smiled at her again, she began to get an inkling of an answer to her own question. But she battled back the tide of pleasure that swelled inside her and reminded herself this was *not* a personal endeavor. No, she was only doing this because…because…because…

Well, just because. That was why. And it was a perfectly good reason, too.

Having justified—however feebly—her intentions, Winona allowed herself to be guided back to table seventeen, which, she recalled now, was one of their more romantically positioned tables. It was shaded on one side by a fat potted palm, by the fireplace on another and by a silk screen on a third side. The effect, on the whole, was one of seclusion and privacy—as secluded and private as one might get in a public building, at any rate.

In a surprising display of courtesy, Mr. Montgomery pulled out her chair for her, waited for her to be seated, then scooted her back toward the table. Then he seated himself directly opposite and reached for an opened bottle of red wine. Immediately Winona covered her glass with her palm, but he deftly moved it away, and, disregarding her silent protest, filled her glass with the ruby liquid before topping off his own. Then he sat back in his chair and eyed her with much interest, twirling his glass gently by the stem.

"So," he said. "What shall we talk about?"

Winona fingered the stem of her own glass, but didn't lift it. "I have no idea, Mr. Montgomery. You're the one who…invited…me to join you. In a manner of speaking," she couldn't keep herself from adding. "I assumed you had a specific topic in mind."

"Oh, I do," he assured her, smiling again. "But you won't let me talk about what I want to talk about. You run away when I bring it up."

She gaped faintly at him. "I did *not* run away."

"Didn't you?"

She straightened in her chair, her back going stiff, her derriere perched daintily on the very edge of her seat. "Certainly not," she told him imperiously.

"Hoo-kay," he told her, smiling in a way that indicated he didn't for one second believe her. "If you say so."

"I do."

He smiled again, then enjoyed a generous taste of his wine. "You're not from around here originally, are you?" he asked suddenly.

She arched her eyebrows at the swift change of subject. "Actually, I've been living in Bloomington since I came here to attend college twenty years ago."

His expression changed drastically then. "You went to college twenty years ago?" he echoed incredulously. "You're that… Uh, I mean… Ah…"

"Yes, Mr. Montgomery," she said, battling a smile— not to mention a few social conventions— "I'm that old."

"I didn't mean—"

"Didn't you?" she asked, taking perverse pleasure in being the one to interrupt him and set him off-kilter this time.

"No, I just… I meant… I mean… It's just that… Well, you sure don't look…"

Winona could scarcely believe it. She'd left him speechless. She had him feeling awkward. Well, my, my, my. Wasn't he just a bundle of surprises.

"Thank you," she said, sparing him from further discomfort. "I think."

He gazed at her for a few more minutes, as if he were looking for something, though she knew not what. Then, seeming satisfied with his perusal, he continued, "So... where are you from originally?"

"I grew up in Indianapolis with my sister, Miriam, and a maiden aunt who raised us."

Mr. Montgomery narrowed his eyes at her, as if in confusion. "Maiden aunt?" he repeated.

"Yes. Is there a problem with that?"

He shook his head. "No, it's just... I don't think I've ever heard the phrase 'maiden aunt' in, oh...my entire life."

"You heard it just now," Winona pointed out.

This time he nodded. But he seemed no less confused. "Yeah. I guess so. Gee, new experiences happen everyday, don't they?"

More was the pity, Winona couldn't help thinking. Oh, to be able to turn back time, she thought further, and to live in an age when things were so much simpler. Especially things between men and women. There had been specific roles back then, specific expectations, specific boundaries. None of the parry and thrust and ups and downs and confusing shades of gray that were so inherent in modern romantic relationships.

Of course, had she lived in those times, she probably wouldn't have been able to own her own business, she reminded herself. And she wouldn't have had the freedom to come and go as she liked, the way she did now. She wouldn't have been able to vote. Wouldn't have been allowed to own property. She would, no doubt, have been obligated, or even forced, to marry a man she didn't love. She may well have died in childbirth.

Oh, all *right,* she thought. So there were one or two things to be said for modern times. She just wished there could be more things said for modern relationships. Because Winona wasn't equipped to handle those. The one time she had tried, she had ended up with a broken heart. She wasn't about to wander into another one. Especially with a thoroughly modern man like Connor Montgomery.

"Really, Mr. Montgomery," she said, "if all you want is my biography, I can drop one in the mail to you tomorrow. As much as I appreciate your interest, I have work that I really should be doing, and—"

"Look, I'm going about this all wrong," he said, interrupting her. *Again.* "I just… I want to get to know you better, and I thought this might be the best way. You don't seem to take any time off from your job here."

He'd noticed? she thought, not certain whether that was a good thing or a bad thing. "Well, one does have to fairly well devote one's life to a new business, until it's well established, doesn't one?" she said.

"Yours looks pretty well established," he remarked.

And why did his voice carry such a wry tone when he said it? she wondered.

"I don't want to get complacent," she told him.

"I'll just bet you don't," he replied, in that odd tone of voice again.

Winona stood. She had no idea what Mr. Montgomery's game was, but even someone as unsophisticated as she in the give-and-take of men and women could sense that there was something fishy going on. And she wanted no part of it. Whatever it was.

"If you'll excuse me, Mr. Montgomery, I just remembered something very important I need to attend to right away."

"What's that?" he asked, clearly suspicious of her withdrawal.

"My good sense," she told him. There. Let him make of that what he would. Before he had the chance to pursue her comment—or her—Winona spun quickly around. Then, as much as she hated to admit it—she ran away.

Connor knew he was skirting the edge of ethical behavior—among other things—by trying to wheedle his way into Winona Thornbury's private life the way he had Friday night and again tonight. But he was so frustrated after so many weeks of hitting nothing but dead ends that he had arrived at, well, his wit's end. He'd worry about ethics later, he told himself as he watched her flee the scene. He would. At some point. Before it was too late. Probably. Right now, though, he had an illegal operation to break up, and he was determined to do it any way he knew how.

And he was still thinking about that later that evening, as he sat in an unmarked police car parked discreetly in the alley behind Winona's. But he also realized he was having a whole lot of trouble focusing on the illegal operation and his determination. Because all he could think about as he sat in that darkened car was the way Winona Thornbury had looked earlier that evening when she was seated across his table, as she'd told him a few rudimentary things about her past.

Naturally, Connor had already known most of those things about her past, because he'd read the police report the Bloomington PD had run on her as part of the investigation. He'd known when he went upstairs Friday that Winona lived above her restaurant—that had been the main reason he'd gone up there. In a word, duh.

Well, he'd gone up there for that, and also to see if maybe there was some kind of wild, illegal orgy going on in one of the rooms, with cash passing hands freely in exchange for deviant sexual behavior, and Winona ringing up unlawful acts on a cash register, one by illicit one. Hey, you never knew. He could luck into something like that. It wasn't outside the realm of possibility.

And he also knew that she'd lived in a small studio apartment three blocks away before opening Winona's, knew that she'd moved to Bloomington some time ago, knew she was a graduate of IU and that she had worked in a variety of restaurants in town before opening her own, knew she had no prior arrest record—not that that meant anything. Ted Bundy hadn't had a prior arrest record, either, and look how that had turned out.

But Connor hadn't paid much attention to specific dates in the police report as he'd scanned it, save those that pertained to the investigation itself. So Winona Thornbury's age, if nothing else, had come as a total surprise to him. She didn't look like a woman in her late thirties, no way. He would have pegged her in her late twenties, at most. Certainly he wouldn't have guessed that she was more than a few years beyond his own, recently acquired, twenty-nine.

Wow. Her sexual history must *really* be impressive, seeing as how she had almost a full decade on him.

Still, what difference did it make that she was nine or ten years older than him? he asked himself. It wasn't like he was interested in her. And hell, even if he was interested in her, he wasn't going to let a little thing like age difference come between them. Connor Monahan never let anything come between him and a beautiful woman. The less there was between them, the better, as a matter-of-fact—both literally and figuratively.

Still, he couldn't stop thinking about Winona.

He told himself it was only because she was so central to the investigation. Unfortunately, he wasn't very good at convincing himself of that. Because he was reasonably sure that the fact that she smelled like fresh lilacs after a summer rain wasn't integral to whether or not she was the leader of a prostitution ring. And neither was the fact that her skin had looked creamier and softer than a baby's tushie. And neither was the fact that her full, dewy lips looked sweeter than pink cotton candy.

Snap out of it, Monahan, he told himself. This is getting

you nowhere. Except more frustrated. Plus, it's embarrassing to see a grown man going on that way.

"You better be careful, Monahan," his borrowed partner, Glenn Davison, said from the passenger seat. He blew over the edge of a huge throwaway cup—one that, for noncaffeine addicts, might potentially hold a week's worth of coffee. "Calling her to your table tonight…that was pretty sloppy. Cap'n's gonna be ticked off about that when he hears."

"Yeah, yeah, yeah," Connor muttered. "I was just putting out some feelers—so to speak. We're getting nowhere on this case."

Davison snorted his derision in response to that. "Yeah, well, it's one thing to be feelin' a woman. It's another to get your ass hauled in on entrapment. If I were you, I'd be more careful."

"You're not me," Connor said simply, grateful for that particular reality. Although he didn't know his temporary partner well, Glenn Davison seemed to be the kind of man who wasn't into what most men were into. Like tidy dressing habits, for one thing. Like good dental hygiene for another. Or any hygiene, for that matter. As unobtrusively as he could, Connor rolled down his window a bit.

Hell, he shouldn't even be working on this case, he reminded himself. He was a member of the Marigold, Indiana, Police Department, forty-five minutes away. But the Bloomington boys had discovered during the course of their investigation that the girls working Winona's came not only from all walks of life, but all parts of the state, as well. It was yet another reason why they suspected that at least some of the girls were students.

There was even a girl from Connor's hometown of Marigold who had been working as a highly placed hooker in the organization. And that was something he simply could not abide. His hometown was one of the last vestiges of small-town life left in America, free of crime, free of poverty, free of strife. Hell, pretty much free of reality, truth be told. But he intended to do everything in his power to keep it that way.

Simply put, Marigold, Indiana was a "nice place." But not only was a Marigold girl tied up with the Bloomington prostitution ring, there were good indications from Connor's own investigation back home that she intended to start up a similar operation in Marigold. When his local investigation of her had overlapped the Bloomington PD's, they'd somehow found themselves all working together. Which was how he'd ended up with Davison as his current partner, and the Budget Motor Lodge, Bloomington, as his temporary home.

Damned bad luck.

"All I'm sayin'," Davison began again, after a couple of messy slurps of his coffee, "is that you better make sure you do this by the book. Cap'n's already steamed enough that you're even on this case."

"Yeah, well, that wasn't my idea, was it? Your chief called mine and insisted."

"Anyway, if I were you, I'd make damned sure I didn't do anything to compromise this investigation. You don't know Cap'n like I do."

"And as I already pointed out," Connor said, "you're not me."

He was about to elaborate, gleefully pointing out the many differences between himself and Davison, but his attention was diverted when a light came on upstairs at Winona's. Their vantage point in the car was far too angled for Connor to do much more than note the illumination, but he gazed up at that light as if it were the Holy Grail, in spite of his inability to see into the brightened room.

He knew her office was on the front side of the building, because he'd seen it during his brief foray into her humble abode. And although he hadn't pinpointed the location of her bedroom—he hadn't been able to make it that far before stumbling upon her in her kitchen—he decided the window at which he gazed now more than likely opened into that very room. Madam Winona would probably call it her *boudoir,* in that old-fashioned way of hers. To Connor's way of thinking, though, it was more along the lines of, oh…he didn't know. The words *pleasure dome* came to mind.

For long moments he only stared at the open window from which that pale-yellow light spilled, his mind's eye entertaining all sorts of possible scenarios that might be unfolding there. Winona striding into the room, her hands lifted to the scores of buttons that had fastened her dress earlier, unfastening them one by leisurely one, then shrugging the garment off her shoulders, pushing it down over her hips and thighs, tossing it onto a chair in the corner.

Beneath it, she no doubt wore some kind of nineteenth-century underwear, something manufactured of white cotton and whalebone, decorated with satin ribbons and frilly lace, with more buttons going down the front. Every time Connor got a load of Winona and her buttons, he was overcome by the desire—nay, the very need—to undo them all himself, one by leisurely one.

Don't think about it, Monahan, he cautioned himself. You'll just make yourself crazy.

And then she'd probably go to work on those buttons herself, he couldn't help continuing his mental picture, loosing each one with those delicate fingers of hers. Little by little the white fabric would open, revealing the dusky valley between her breasts, her ivory torso, her flat belly, the dimple of her navel. Then more, toward—

Connor squeezed his eyes shut tight and somehow willed his imagination to curb its wildly overwrought workings. He had to get a grip on himself. This was insane. There was no reason why he should be so fascinated by Winona Thornbury. No rational reason, at any rate. Hell, she wasn't even anything like the women he normally dated. He usually went for women who were sophisticated and modern, women who didn't use words like *daresay* and *maiden aunt*. He went for women who wore miniskirts and platform shoes and thong underwear, not whalebone and lace and buttons. Oh, and one more thing. He also tended to go for women who were *not* the leaders of prostitution rings.

That was it, he finally realized. That was the secret to Winona Thornbury's allure. She presented a paradox that no one with a Y chromosome could resist. Old-fashioned, prim and proper on the outside, a raging conflagration of coitus and debauchery on the inside. Every man's wildest sexual fantasies disguised as an innocent naïf. Virgin and whore in one convenient package. What man wouldn't be fascinated by that?

Just as the thought formed in Connor's brain, Winona Thornbury herself appeared at the open window, to push the sash down a bit, and to loosen a tie that held back one lacy panel. Connor's lips parted involuntarily as he homed in on what should have been an unremarkable action, one that lasted only a few seconds. He couldn't help it. He was stunned.

Because she *had* been dressed in a white cotton underthing decorated with satin ribbons and frilly lace. And as she'd freed the curtain, she had been unfastening the scores of buttons with her free hand, one by leisurely one. He had, for one scant instant, beheld the dusky valley between her breasts. And as the lace had fallen over the window, over Winona, obscuring her from his view, his mind's eye had seen again—all too clearly—exactly what he was missing.

And oh, boy. Was he missing a lot.

"This is gettin' us nowhere," Davison said then, dispelling Connor's licentious ruminations. "I don't know what you were hopin' to learn by staking out the place tonight, anyway. I told you we've done this before, probably a half-dozen times already, and we got nothin' from it. I told you this was gonna net you a big fat zero."

"Not quite a zero," Connor said, still gazing at the window from which Winona had disappeared. He had, after all, learned something very important. He'd learned that Winona Thornbury was every bit as lush and luscious as he had thought.

And he had learned it was going to be very, *very* difficult for him to bring her in. Not just because she was so elusive. But because he very much suspected that once he had her in his possession, he wasn't ever going to want to let her go.

Four

What followed Monday night felt, to Winona, like a veritable blitzkrieg of Connor Montgomery. Because he came into the restaurant every night that week. And he invited her to join him for dinner every night that week. And when she turned down his invitation—every night that week—he stayed late at the bar after finishing his meal. Every night that week. And he was still there at closing every night that week. She had to virtually chase him out of her establishment every night that week.

Or, more correctly, she had to ask whichever host or hostess was on duty that night to chase him out of her establishment every night that week. Because there was no way that Winona would get any closer to the man than she had to. *Any* night that week.

And that was due to the fact that every night that week he was dressed in his usual breathtakingly handsome way. Every night his blue eyes shone bewitchingly, and his full mouth crooked up playfully at the corners as if he knew something she didn't. Every night he became more and more overpowering, and more and more irresistible. And every time she turned down his invitation to dinner, Winona felt a curl of disappointment wind through her. But every time she turned him down, he became even more adamant when issuing his next invitation. And invariably her ensuing disappointment became even more keen.

By Saturday night she was at her wit's end. She simply could not understand why the man would spend so much time at the restaurant, or why he would continue to ask her to join him for dinner when she had made it abundantly clear that she wasn't interested. And she continued to not understand it on Saturday, when Connor Montgomery corralled her by the host stand just prior to closing and asked her, point-blank, "If you won't join me for dinner in your own restaurant, then how about joining me for dinner at someone else's?"

And then Winona had no idea what to say. Except maybe for, "I, ah…um…er…that is…ahem…oh…" Or stammerings to that effect.

Stammerings that must have been amusing to him for some reason, because the more discomfited she became, the broader his smile grew. "C'mon, Winona," he said. "Let me take you to dinner. You deserve a night off once in a while. All work and no play…"

"Makes for a very successful business," she quickly finished for him. Anything to change the subject.

But Mr. Montgomery was clearly resistant to such a change. "Yeah, but if you keep up at this rate, you're going to burn out. And burnout always leads to disaster." He smiled that toe-curling smile again. "C'mon," he murmured again. "Just one evening. Just one dinner. Where's the harm in that?"

The harm, Winona knew, was standing right there in front of her—six-feet-plus of raw, virile jeopardy. Connor Montgomery, she was certain, could very well be the death of her. And not in some sociopathic, serial killer sense, either. But simply because he was too handsome, too charming, too sexy, too modern, too confident, too masculine, too…too…

Just *too*. That was all. And that was a *very* big problem.

"Thank you, Mr. Montgomery—"

"Connor."

"Mr. Montgomery, but I really can't," she told him.

"Monday would be good," he countered immediately, as if he hadn't heard her. "How about Monday? This place seems to be pretty slow on Mondays. You could sneak off for a few hours."

She arched her eyebrows in surprise. "A few hours? Well, my goodness, Mr. Montgomery. Just how long do you plan on dinner taking?"

"Oh, dinner should only take an hour or so," he told her with much confidence. But he didn't elaborate, beyond smiling that devilishly wicked smile of his.

"I see," she said coolly. "Thank you. No."

His impish smile fell some then, and his arrogant posture eased. He expelled a long, weary breath and ran a restless hand through his dark hair. "Look, I'm sorry. What if I promise to be a perfect gentleman on Monday night?"

Winona couldn't quite prevent the chuckle that escaped her. Nor could she quite keep herself from replying, as politely as she could, "Oh, Mr. Montgomery, I sincerely doubt that."

His smile shone one thousand watts again. "You doubt that I would make that promise?" he asked. "Or you doubt that I could be a perfect gentleman?"

Winona weighed her answer carefully. There were times, she knew, when honesty had no place in courtesy. Yet she was the most honest, courteous person she knew. She strove to be honest and courteous above all else. Oh, dear. A dilemma. A paradox. What to do, what to do…

In the end honesty won out. Probably because she imagined Mr. Montgomery would appreciate that quality over courtesy. "I don't think you can be a perfect gentleman," she said respectfully. "It's nothing personal, mind you. I just don't think that chivalry is at the top of your to-do list, that's all. It's a problem that plagues many members of your generation."

That, too, made him smile. "My generation isn't so far off from your generation," he told her.

"That's what you think," she replied. "*I'm* not a member of my generation."

He narrowed his eyes at her, clearly puzzled. "What do you mean?"

But Winona only smiled in response. How could she adequately explain her old-fashioned tendencies to a man who was so firmly rooted in the here and now?

No explanation seemed necessary, however, because Mr. Montgomery nodded his comprehension. "Oh, I get it. You think you were born a few generations too late. That's why you dress the way you do and use words like *daresay*."

"Something like that, yes," she agreed.

"Still, Winona, even the most old-fashioned girls have one or two modern...needs. You can still be an old-fashioned girl and get...dated."

Winona feigned indifference to his suggestive remark, but she felt a ripple of heat undulate right down her spine. It was simply another indication as to why she shouldn't be anywhere near this man. All he would do was compromise her. Old-fashioned, indeed. "Do they? Can they?" she finally asked. "I wouldn't know."

But he only eyed her expectantly. "I'll bet you know more than you're letting on."

"Mr. Montgomery—"

"I can be a perfect gentleman, Winona," he interjected before she had a chance to say anything more. But he began to smile that naughty smile again, and she wasn't quite sure how to take his remark. "And I'll prove it to you. Have dinner with me Monday. If I'm not a perfect gentleman, then I promise I'll never bother you again."

Now that, Winona thought, was a proposition that interested her very much indeed. The thought of coming in to work without having Connor Montgomery watching her every move was really very…very…very… How odd. For some reason, the idea that he might stop coming in to Winona's once and for all brought with it a strange feeling of melancholy.

Oh, fiddle-faddle, Winona told herself. She was being silly. Coming to work without having Connor Montgomery there bothering her would make her life infinitely easier. She was more than a little tempted to take him up on his offer. Only to stop him from bothering her, of course. Because she was confident that there was no way he could behave himself as a perfect gentleman all evening. Even though she didn't know the man well, she could see that gallantry simply wasn't in his nature.

She considered him thoughtfully for a moment as she weighed the pros and cons of his proposition. "You won't pester me to join you for dinner here at the restaurant anymore?" she asked.

He shook his head.

"You won't waste my time calling me to your table so that you can indulge me in frivolous banter and insinuative innuendo?"

"No frivolous banter," he promised. "No, um, insinuative, ah…innuendo."

She eyed him thoughtfully for a moment more, until his good looks, devilish grin and sparkling blue eyes nearly overwhelmed her. "Do I have your word on that?" she asked as she turned her gaze back down to the reservations book on the host stand.

"My word as a gentleman," he told her.

She chuckled again. "How about giving me your word

as a rogue instead?'' she asked. ''I think that would probably be more trustworthy.''

When she glanced up again, it was to find him studying her with much interest. ''Fine,'' he said with a reverent dip of his head. ''You have my word as a rogue. It's as good as gold.''

''Yes, I daresay it is,'' she said quietly. And, for some reason, her comment made him smile again. ''All right,'' she finally told him. ''I'll have dinner with you, Mr. Montgomery, on Monday night. At an establishment other than my own.''

Now his grin turned positively wicked, and his blue eyes blazed with something almost otherworldly.

Winona narrowed her eyes at him. ''A *commercial* establishment other than my own,'' she emphasized.

His smile fell some. But he quickly rallied it again. ''Fine,'' he said. ''We can do that. What time Monday?''

She thought for a moment more. Mondays truly were slow at the restaurant. She could add another host to the mix—Laurel again, because the girl was amazingly efficient—and things should move just swimmingly. At the restaurant, at any rate. With Mr. Montgomery, however…

Well. Winona reminded herself again that there was very little chance he would behave like a gentleman, perfect or imperfect. And the moment he erred, the moment he said something he shouldn't say or touched a part of her he had no business touching, she would call an immediate halt to the evening and demand that he escort her home. And that, once and for all, should put an end to his…whatever it was he wanted from her.

''How about seven o'clock?'' she finally said.

''No problem,'' he told her. ''I'll be here at seven on the dot.'' But he punctuated the remark with a lascivious look, one that sent more heat shimmering through Winona from head to toe.

Oh, yes, she thought, considering his expression once

again. There was no chance that Connor Montgomery would *ever* behave himself. She was as good as rid of him.

It occurred to Connor as he rang the bell at the side entrance of Winona's—the one that led to her private residence, instead of the restaurant—that even the outside of her house seemed like something from a long-ago age. A white picket fence—a *white picket fence,* he marveled again—edged the yard along the sidewalk, and its gate had creaked in happy welcome as he'd opened and passed through it. A cobbled walkway bisected a garden buzzing with all sorts of insect life, a garden that nearly overwhelmed him with the mingling and narcotic aromas of lilies and lilacs and lavender. There was a small bench, perfect for two, nestled against the side of the white frame house, beckoning him to sit with someone special after dark and murmur sweet nothings—yes, sweet nothings, dammit—into that someone special's ears.

Man, he was really losing it, he thought. Not only was he skirting the edge of ethical behavior, but he was actually, well, stopping to smell the lilacs. And that wasn't like Connor Monahan *at all.*

Hoo-boy, was he in it deep now, he thought further as he awaited a response to his summons at Winona's door. Not only had he promised something tonight that he was reasonably certain was impossible for him to deliver—that he would behave like a perfect gentleman—but he was in violation, he was sure, of every ethical rule in the "How Not To Screw Up an Investigation" handbook, which he had somehow missed receiving when he was bumped up to detective. Probably, he thought, he had been in the men's room shooting dice when they handed the book out.

Yeah, that was his story, and he was sticking to it.

Of course, he'd be telling Madam Winona another story entirely tonight. All about how he was just a lonesome, solitary businessman who was new in town, a lonely guy with money to burn and no one to burn it on, because he didn't know a single soul, and gosh, it was just so nice to be out with someone for a change, and gee, wouldn't it be nice if he could just pick up the phone sometime and make arrangements like this and have a charming, beautiful dinner companion like Winona every night of the week—and damn the expense, anyway.

There. That was nice and vague—and not entrapmenty at all to Connor's way of thinking. And it was gentlemanly, too, dammit. But it was also still open enough that she could reply with something along the lines of, "Well, you know, Mr. Montgomery, I just so happen to know of a company that provides such a companion, and for a reasonable fee, too, and we take all major credit cards, and here's our list of services all spelled out in writing and their corresponding charges, and…"

Hey, it could happen, he told himself.

When there was no reply to his summons, Connor extended one hand to ring the bell again while he used the other to fiddle with his pale-blue silk necktie. He'd chosen his navy-blue suit tonight, because he'd been told a couple of times that it complemented the color of his eyes just so nicely. Mushy talk, to be sure, but he wasn't taking any chances. He wanted to bring Madam Winona to her knees tonight, to put it incredibly crassly—and not a little Freudianly, he couldn't help thinking further.

The thought was still lingering in his mind when the door opened inward and there stood the object of his, uh…the object of his, um…of his, ah…and there stood Winona Thornbury, on the other side. And as always he was astounded by the utter purity of her beauty.

Tonight, as usual, she looked as if she had just stepped out of the early twentieth century. Her pale-blond hair was swept up in the back, knotted atop her head by some invisible means of support, interwoven with tiny white, sweet-smelling flowers he was certain were real. Her dress was white, too, an amazing confection comprised of layers of lacy…stuff, and satiny…stuff, and sheer…stuff, and embroidered…stuff, and—dammit—pearly buttons. The garment fell to midcalf above white, ankle-high boots with—surprise, surprise—more buttons anchoring her down.

And gloves, he noted with surprise. She was wearing white cotton gloves that buttoned—of course—at her wrists, leaving her arms bare up to the lacy cuffs of her elbow-length sleeves. And for some very strange reason he couldn't begin to understand, Connor found those gloves, and that stretch of bare, ivory arm, to be the sexiest thing he'd ever seen in his life.

God, he had to start getting out more.

"Good evening, Mr. Montgomery," she greeted him softly. "So nice of you to be on time."

He nodded. "Pretty gentlemanly of me, wasn't it?"

"Oh, yes," she told him. "Quite."

"Is it okay for me to say you look beautiful? Or would that be too forward?"

It stunned him to see a patch of pink bloom on each of her cheeks, as if what he'd just told her honestly embarrassed her. Her. A woman who'd take a man around the world for eighty bucks. Okay, probably a lot more than eighty bucks, he quickly amended. But, hell, it would be worth every penny.

"No," she said. "I don't believe that would be too forward. Not in this day and age."

"Then you look beautiful, Miss Winona."

When she glanced up, she was smiling at him, a sparkle of something Connor couldn't quite identify making her blue eyes seem as rich and limitless as a summer sky. Something fierce and fast hit him hard right in the solar plexus, but for the life of him, he couldn't say what it was—other than powerful. And all he could do was smile back at her and hope he didn't look as goofy as he felt.

Somewhere he found the intelligence to crook his arm

toward her and dip his head in a silent bid for her to loop her own arm through his. "Shall we go?" he asked further, in the most gentlemanly voice he could muster. "I thought that since it's such a nice evening, we might walk to our destination. It's not far."

She pulled the door closed softly behind her, locked it up, then deftly threaded her arm loosely through his. "That sounds lovely, Mr. Montgomery," she told him. "By all means, do lead on."

Winona tried to keep her eyes forward as she and Mr. Montgomery strolled down the street toward the Garden Path Café, where he had said they would be dining. She had no idea how he'd done it, but he'd managed to select her second-favorite restaurant in town—well, what kind of proprietress would she be if she didn't choose her *own* restaurant as her favorite?

The Garden Path Café was located on the street level of a quaint little bed and breakfast called, well, the Garden Path Bed and Breakfast. Not surprisingly, it was decorated in perfect harmony with its name—rose trellis wallpaper, hand-hooked rugs in floral patterns spanning the hardwood floors, scores of blossoming plants cascading from baskets that hung from the ceiling and scores of more blossoming plants springing from terra-cotta urns settled all about the floor.

But best of all, the restaurant was quiet and slow paced and in no way demanding. It was perfect for getting-to-know-you type conversation and little else. There would be scant opportunity for Mr. Montgomery to indulge in sly remarks or stolen touches. Contrary to tradition, in this case, Mr. Montgomery was being a true gentleman for leading Winona to the Garden Path.

Which was all the more reason why she tried to keep her eyes forward as they walked toward the café. He looked far too handsome and was behaving much too courteously for her comfort. He made chitchat of the most benign form as they strode slowly toward their destination, complimenting her on her garden, remarking on the beauty of the sunset, soliciting her opinion on *The Scarlet Pimpernel*, as he had just started reading it himself the day before.

In other words, he was being a perfect gentleman. And the realization of such a thing distressed Winona greatly. The last thing she needed or wanted was for Mr. Montgomery to behave himself politely. Because the last thing she needed or wanted was to be attracted to him more than she was already. As it was, she was struggling with some odd fascination with him, and she couldn't understand why she had been completely unable to quell it. She didn't want to make it worse by finding him so captivating. So charming. So…gallant.

It made no sense, why she should be so enthralled by a man such as he in the first place. He was her opposite in virtually every way, and he claimed none of the most fundamental qualities she desired in a man. Yet memories of him compromised her every waking moment, invading her thoughts, her dreams, her very life. She had been relieved that such a great social—and yes, age—chasm lay between the two of them, because she had thought they would never be able to span it. Now, however…

She sighed fretfully. Now she was beginning to think that the two of them might perhaps have more in common than she originally realized. And that would only lead to trouble. Because, regardless of their present camaraderie, Winona had the feeling that Mr. Montgomery wasn't a forever-after kind of man.

He clearly still had too much growing to do—both in chronological and psychological terms—before he could make that kind of commitment. He was too young, too impulsive, too *au courant* for the kind of old-fashioned pledge of marriage that she wanted herself. Yes, he might very well commit himself temporarily—to exactly the kind of physical relationship Winona wanted to avoid—but he was obviously not yet ready to settle down in any matrimonial sense.

And Winona demanded nothing less than at least *potential* matrimony from any man with whom she might pursue a personal relationship. She wasn't about to involve herself with a man unless he could approach their relationship with the intention of possibly marrying, just as she would approach it herself. If that meant she remained single for the rest of her life, then so be it. There were worse things in life, she knew, than living alone. One worse thing was falling in love, giving oneself utterly and completely to a man, and then having that man betray and abandon one.

She should know, after all. It had happened to her.

When Winona Thornbury fell, she fell irrevocably. There had only been one man in her life to whom she had given herself sexually. And she had only done so after the two of them had been dating for three years and engaged for eight months and were just three weeks shy of their wedding date. And although she had found such a... succumbing...to be quite, well, nice, actually—certainly nice enough to let it happen several times over the weeks that ensued—she wasn't about to fall prey to her carnal desires again. Not until she had a solid gold band solidly circling the fourth finger on her left hand.

She would not compromise herself or her virtue in such a way again. Because once her fiancé had enjoyed her...her...her... Well, once he had enjoyed *her,* he hadn't felt the need to stay around for very long. Only two weeks later she'd awoken one morning to find a note from him in her mailbox and him completely gone. And his hastily dashed-off letter had only driven home, painfully, just how foolish a woman she had been.

That was why Winona couldn't let herself fall under Connor Montgomery's spell. Even after such brief intercourse with him—for frightful lack of a better word—she could see that he was the kind of man who would be quick to seduce, slow to satisfy…and gone in sixty seconds. And Winona was the kind of woman who, once seduced and satisfied, would be forever under his spell. She'd had enough trouble pining over her lost fiancé—not that she really pined that much for Stanley Wadsworth these days. Nevertheless, she would be foolish to add another lost lover to the mix.

She told herself that wasn't likely to be a problem and that she was worrying for nothing, because Mr. Montgomery was bound to stumble over dinner. He couldn't possibly have the table manners necessary for polite society, and with the first misstep, he would cease to be a gentleman and he would thereafter be obliged to leave her alone.

But once they arrived at the café, he surprised her again, holding her chair for her as she seated herself, ordering considerately for both of them—after consulting her about her choice first, of course. He chose exactly the right wine, used the proper fork at the proper time… He even knew correct napkin ritual. It was astonishing.

"You've been studying this weekend," she charged lightly after their server had left them to their tea and coffee and cheesecake.

When Mr. Montgomery glanced up from his cup, his expression indicated that he was genuinely mystified by her statement. *As if,* Winona thought. To put it in the vulgar, contemporary vernacular.

"Studying?" he echoed innocently. "For what? No one told me there was going to be a test."

She smiled as she stirred milk into her tea. "Oh, come now, Mr. Montgomery. You knew full well going into this evening that you were going to be tested."

He smiled back. "Am I passing?"

"That," she said, feigning primness—for truly, she was beginning to feel less and less prim around him, "remains to be seen. The night is still young."

"So it is."

She would have expected one of his more lascivious grins to punctuate the comment, but he only turned his attention—very politely, drat him—back to his coffee.

"So, Mr. Montgomery, tell me a bit about yourself," Winona said after a dainty sip of her own beverage. He had, after all been a perfect gentleman over dinner, steering conversation to topics that might interest her. And so modest he was in his gentlemanly manner, assuming that he himself might not be one of those interests.

Au contraire.

Because in spite of her conviction that she would not get involved with the man beyond this single, cursory encounter, the more time Winona spent with Mr. Montgomery this evening, the more her interest in him was piqued. And now she was going to seek some answers to the myriad questions circling about her brain. Naturally, though, she would do so in a ladylike fashion.

"Gosh, what's there to tell?" he asked.

"Well, I don't know," she told him. "That's why I'm asking."

He shrugged as he settled his cup back into its saucer. But he focused his gaze intently on her face when he said, "Basically, I'm just a new guy in town who's looking to make a few new…friends. Especially friends of the female persuasion."

Winona eyed him thoughtfully. Well, that was certainly a leading comment, she thought. One that might very well be construed as ungentlemanly. Was he about to err? Was he going to say something suggestive? Would this put an effective end to their time together? And why was she so disappointed to discover that it might?

"Well, you should find no shortage of those," she said carefully. "Friends of the female persuasion, I mean."

"No?" he asked. Politely, she noted, but there was something else in his voice that provoked suspicion. She just couldn't quite say what that something else was. "Do you perchance…have anyone particular in mind?" he asked further.

Winona narrowed her eyes at him. Well, that certainly was a very odd thing to say. He was, after all, having dinner with her, a dinner to which *he* had invited her. Was he hinting that he'd now like for her to introduce him to other women? Was that why he had hoped to make her acquaintance in the first place? Well. That wasn't very gentlemanly at all.

"No," she said cautiously. "I don't have anyone particular in mind. But there are a number of single young women in town, thanks to the university."

"Are there?" he asked, again in that strangely suspicious tone. "And how would you suggest a man go about meeting them? Provided a man wanted to?" he quickly added.

Part of Winona felt crushed that he would ask her such a thing, was surprisingly hurt by the realization that he had invited her to dinner only to use her as an outlet to meet other women. And truly, she couldn't understand why he would think her an appropriate candidate for something like that.

But another part of her—the rational part—reminded her that she shouldn't be at all surprised. Mr. Montgomery was a young, urbane, modern male. It stood to reason that he would seek out women of a similar nature. Clearly he had already seen the folly of asking out a woman such as she. She didn't play the singles game the way one was supposed to play it these days. Obviously, Mr. Montgomery was ready to move on to greener pastures. Still, she had no idea why he would think she might be willing to act as his…shepherdess…while exploring those greener pastures.

Ah, well, she thought, swallowing her disappointment. What had she expected? That he would be a perfect gentleman?

"I'm sorry, Mr. Montgomery," she said softly, avoiding

his gaze, "but you'd do better by yourself, I'm sure. I'm not socially linked to any of the young women in town, save those who work for me. If you're looking for introductions—"

"That's *exactly* what I'm looking for," he said, fairly pouncing on the comment. "Introductions. To women who work for you."

Something cool and heavy settled in Winona's midsection at hearing him spell it out so obviously. "Well, as I said, then," she told him, "you'd be better off on your own."

And as the cool, heavy weight grew heavier and colder still, Winona, having no idea what to say or do next, and wanting very much to escape from what felt like a bad dream, quickly stood. Hastily, she gathered her gloves and bag, which she had placed on the table.

"Good evening, Mr. Montgomery," she said as she turned away. "I thank you very much for dinner. But I only now remembered that I have a previous engagement I absolutely cannot miss. I do apologize for this frightful oversight, but I really must go."

And with those rapidly uttered words, even though she knew it wasn't very polite, Winona went. Quickly.

Five

Winona got as far as the exit before Connor, stunned by her reaction, realized she honestly meant to leave him sitting there all alone. Without thinking, he leaped up, hastily counted out what would pretty much cover dinner and about an 85 percent tip, threw the wad of bills on the table and ran after her.

He'd been so sure that he was being casual and discreet when he'd made his inquiry about introductions, but obviously, he hadn't been subtle at all. Madam Winona must have made him for a cop. She must have realized what he was asking for, where he was trying to lead her, and that was the reason why she was fleeing now—to avoid any further investigation into her illegal activities.

Or else, Conner thought further, she was fleeing because he'd just grossly insulted her, a perfectly nice woman who had no illegal proclivities whatsoever, by inviting her to dinner and asking her to introduce him to other women. This after promising to be a perfect gentleman, too.

Maybe she really did have nothing to do with the prostitution ring working out of her business, he couldn't help pondering further. Maybe she really would be shocked when she discovered what was going on. Maybe he was totally wrong about her. Maybe she really was just a nice, old-fashioned girl. A nice, old-fashioned girl who'd just had her feelings hurt by a mean, twenty-first-century jerk.

Nah, he quickly reassured himself, however halfheartedly. There was little chance that he was wrong about Madam Winona being *Madam* Winona. Connor Monahan's hunches always played out right. Always. His instincts were unimpeachable. And his instincts had told him from the start that there was something fishy about Winona Thornbury, and that she was indeed the woman in charge of the illegal operation working out of her restaurant.

Just because his instincts hadn't been quite so insistent since he'd gotten up close and personal with her, that didn't mean anything. He'd just been swayed by a pretty face and a killer body, that was all. And by a charming smile and a sweet demeanor. And by good manners and demure grace. And by inexplicably erotic little white gloves. Just because his instincts now were howling something totally different from what they had been howling before...

He expelled a growl of restlessness as he followed Winona Thornbury toward the exit. Dammit. He really was beginning to wonder if maybe he was wrong about her. Because the more he found out about her, the less there was that made any sense. Still, there was no evidence to indicate that she *wasn't* involved with the prostitution ring operating out of Winona's. Then again, there was no evidence to indicate that she *was* part of it, either.

Ah, hell. He didn't know what to do. Except go after her now and try to correct the blunder he'd just made. Whatever that blunder was. Whether it be that he'd just jeopardized the investigation—again—or insulted a perfectly nice—and innocent—woman.

"Winona," he called after her as he pushed open the café door and fled into the dark evening. The streetlights had come on during their time in the Garden Path, and now they cast a pale, bluish glow over the storefronts and passersby that lay between him and Winona. She was already half a block ahead of him, but Connor had no trouble finding her among the throngs of people crowding the sidewalk. There just weren't all that many people out tonight who were wearing turn-of-the-century gowns and gloves and marking their steps with a parasol. Go figure.

She didn't turn around when he called her name, though, despite his certainty that she'd heard him. He knew that, because a half-dozen other people *did* turn toward him when he called her name, some even farther down the block than she was herself.

"Winona!" he tried again, a bit louder this time. But still, she ignored him, increasing her speed in her effort to escape.

So he hastened his step, too, pushing his way between more than one group of people, gentlemanly behavior be damned. She had her back to him now. It didn't count. And within moments, Connor was close enough to reach out and cup a hand gently over her shoulder.

"Winona, wait," he said again as he gently spun her around. And the moment he did, every last breath left his lungs in a long, silent *whoosh*.

Good God, he thought when he saw her face. She had tears in her eyes. What the hell…?

"I'm sorry," he told her. Though for the life of him, he had no idea what he was apologizing for. If she *was* a madam, peddling flesh, she didn't deserve an apology. And even if she wasn't, he hadn't said anything all *that* insulting. Had he? Most of the women he knew would have laughed off his request to be introduced around, or else would have given back as good as they got. But none of them, he was certain, would have become teary eyed.

Yet Winona Thornbury had. Man, she was a hard one to figure. How sensitive could a woman be? Then again, maybe she was only crying because she knew Connor was on to her and was about to wreck her operation and throw her keester in jail.

Ah, hell, he thought eloquently again. He didn't know what to think. He only knew that at the moment he felt really, really lousy because he'd made Winona cry.

"I'm sorry," he said again, with more feeling this time—both in his voice and in his intention. He still wasn't sure why he was apologizing, but something told him he'd damned well better. Stranger still was the fact that he sincerely did feel sorry. For what, he had no idea. But he really did regret now what he had said and done.

Winona met his gaze levelly for a moment, silently, the unshed tears coupling with the blue tint of the streetlight to make her eyes appear huge and earnest and brilliant. The tip of her nose was tinted with pink, and her lower lip looked plump and bruised, as if she'd been biting it to keep her emotions in check. And it was with no small effort that Connor somehow prevented himself from dipping his head to hers and covering her mouth with his, in an effort to ease her crushed expression.

She seemed to sense the avenue of his thoughts somehow, because her gaze dropped to his mouth, too, and her lips parted some, as if she weren't quite getting enough air—or maybe because she was thinking about kissing him back. The electric moment passed quickly, however, as she suddenly gave her head a single, swift shake, as if she were trying to clear it of some troubling thought. Then she took a very thoughtful, very deliberate, step in retreat.

"I accept your apology," she said softly. Obviously *she* understood why Connor said he was sorry, even if he was still clueless himself. "Now if you'll excuse me," she added, "I really must be going."

And then she spun around again and began to scurry off

once more. This time, however, Connor was ready for her retreat, and he was right there beside her as she made it.

"I'll walk you to your destination," he said before she had a chance to object. "What kind of man would I be, after all, if I let you go traipsing off into the night all by yourself?"

"I'm scarcely alone, Mr. Montgomery," she told him as she strode resolutely forward, keeping her gaze focused straight ahead. "There are scores of people on the street," she added quickly, tilting her head back in defiance. Or maybe she did that not so much out of defiance as she did because she was trying to keep the tears in her eyes from falling.

Boy, did he feel like a first-class, see-exhibit-A heel.

"Still, it wouldn't be very gentlemanly of me to let you go off without an escort, would it?" he pointed out.

She sniffled a bit—in the most ladylike fashion, to be sure—then told him, in no uncertain terms, "I'm beginning to realize that my initial evaluation of you was correct." And she didn't miss one step as she then turned her head to look him squarely in the eye, adding, "You are no gentleman, sir."

And as if that weren't enough to send something chilly and awful blustering through what would have passed for a heart in any other man, one single, fat tear tumbled down her cheek as she made her pronouncement. And seeing it, Connor felt a frosty lash of self-loathing thrash his belly.

Instead of disagreeing with her—how could he?—he only turned his attention forward, shoved his hands deep into his pockets and kept walking alongside her. "You found me out," he concurred. "I guess you can't make a silk purse out of a sow's ear after all, can you?"

"Well, I wouldn't say that," she countered softly. She, too, turned to look ahead once more, her pace still clipped, but slowing a bit now. "I just don't think you *want* to be a silk purse, that's all."

"And you think I should aspire to that?" he asked. "I mean, what's so great about being a silk purse? They're small and flimsy—there's nothing to them. And they have strings attached."

"Indeed they do," she agreed, sounding sad again. "And you, I'm certain, would never go for having strings attached. Nor are you small or flimsy or insubstantial."

"Then why do you think I should be a silk purse?" he asked.

"I never said you should be one," she told him. "Frankly, Mr. Montgomery, I can't see you being happy as a silk purse."

"But I'm right at home as a sow's ear, is that what you're saying?" he asked dryly.

"No," she readily conceded again. "You're not that, either. You're somewhere in between, I should think. I'm not sure what you are exactly."

"Well, that makes two of us," he told her. "Because you sure are a mystery to me, too, lady."

She stopped walking then, so Connor did, too, turning to face her fully. She eyed him cryptically, but the tears were gone from her eyes now, her nose was no longer pink, and the bruising of her mouth had been replaced by the fullness and ripeness and lusciousness that he remembered. Nevertheless, he still wanted to kiss her. Wanted to kiss her and touch her and peel that chaste white dress from her ivory skin, then taste every last naked inch of her before burying himself as deeply inside her as he could, while she murmured his name into the darkness, again and again and again....

"Do you really have someplace else you need to be?" he asked her, the explicit image still raging in his brain. "Or was that just your polite way of dumping me?"

The merest hint of a smile curled the corners of her lips. "I suppose my appointment isn't all *that* urgent," she replied.

"It's a nice night," he remarked. "And it's still young. You said so yourself not long ago."

She dipped her head forward in acknowledgment, and the primness of the gesture only accelerated Connor's desire to…know her better. "I suppose I did," she said.

"We could take a walk through the neighborhood," he suggested.

"So that you might use the opportunity to make the acquaintance of a few young ladies?" she asked.

He shook his head and said, "No. So I can make the acquaintance of one young lady in particular. The one I'm with right now."

"I'm not particularly young, Mr. Montgomery," she reminded him matter-of-factly.

He smiled. "Gee, I didn't think ladies ever divulged their ages."

"I'd think that would be up to the individual lady to decide. As for me, I just think the years that separate us would be something you'd be wise to remember."

He eyed her thoughtfully. "Why?"

"Because there is more than a decade between us," she said.

He shook his head. "No there's not. I just turned twenty-nine. You're not quite ten year older than me."

"I wasn't speaking in chronological terms."

His eyebrows shot up in surprise. "Then what…?"

But Connor never finished his question, and Winona never answered it. She only smiled sweetly and held up her hand, silently indicating that she was ready to take his arm. Her forwardness surprised him, but he was happy to oblige, and deftly held up his arm. When she curled her fingers lightly over the fabric of his jacket, he noticed she had donned her gloves again, and something inside him tightened dangerously.

Those gloves. God. She'd taken them off once they arrived at the restaurant, and he hadn't been able to take his eyes off of her as she'd done so. Hell, he'd watched women remove their underwear with less passion than he'd felt as Winona had slowly, slowly, oh, so slowly unbuttoned those gloves and drawn them down over her wrists, her hands, her fingers. By the time she'd placed them gently on the table beside her little silk purse, he'd felt the stirrings of a hard-on and had thanked his lucky stars that the table between them had concealed his condition.

It made no sense. Here was a woman wrapped up tighter and more thoroughly than any normal human being had a need to be wrapped, and Connor was more turned on than he'd ever been in his life. Certainly he was more turned on than he'd ever been by a woman wearing far, far less. And he was beginning to suspect that his arousal had nothing to do with the fact that Winona might very well be a mistress of pleasure, who knew how to…do things to him that would never occur to other women—or else would thoroughly repulse other women.

No, Connor was becoming more than a little worried that his preoccupation with the delicious Winona was the result of something far more insidious that simple lust. Because he very much feared that he was beginning to—gulp—like her.

God almighty, he thought as they strode forward. Could it possibly get any worse?

Winona never, ever, under any circumstances, stayed out later than 11:00 p.m. It was, of course, helpful that in keeping with this rule she lived in the same building where she worked. But even had that not been the case, she simply wasn't the type of person to keep late hours outside those required for her job. She supposed that when all was said and done, restaurateur wasn't, exactly, the prime occupation for a woman of her bent, but it was what she loved, and it was what she did best, and since it did require keeping late hours in order to accommodate one's clientele, she had no objection to the late evenings, professionally speaking.

Socially, however, Winona was no night owl. Probably because, socially, she was, well, inert. Which made it doubly surprising when she and Mr. Montgomery returned to her home at just past two o'clock in the morning. She was amazed at how quickly the hours had passed and at how they had managed to fill those hours with animated conversation and spirited entertainment.

After leaving the café—and after that unfortunate exchange that Winona had decided to put down to misunderstanding and forget all about—they had forged a kind of companionship that had been surprisingly pleasant. They had stopped for ice cream at one point, and enjoyed it while seated at a small, outdoor table, watching the people pass by and indulging in agreeable conversation. Then they had stumbled upon, and been just in time for, a showing of Jean Renoir's *Beauty and the Beast*—in French with subtitles, no less—at a local art house. And there had been something so wonderfully intimate about sharing popcorn and lemonade with Mr. Montgomery in the darkened theater. She had no idea why. But it had been fun. Quite fun. Astonishingly fun.

They'd spent the remainder of the evening strolling through the streets of Bloomington, mingling with the college crowd where Winona had always felt so strangely at home, in spite of her propensity for another age and other customs. All in all, the night had been, well, lovely. To say the least. And all in all, Mr. Montgomery had been, well, charming. To say the least.

Now as they strolled through the gate that led into her garden, Winona realized that she had no idea what to do or say. The restaurant was closed, and her employees were gone for the night, so she and Mr. Montgomery were very much alone. Laurel had left the usual lights burning, but the sign was off, and the place was very clearly locked up tight. The antique porch light hanging over her front/side door was lit, but the twenty-five-watt bulb threw out only the merest puddle of light.

She halted just inside the gate and was about to turn to Mr. Montgomery, to tell him she was fine and could see herself in, but he stopped her by taking her elbow lightly and saying, very softly, "I'll see you to the door."

It was the very softly part that prevented her from objecting. Something in his voice was just…irresistible. So she only nodded silently and allowed him to lead her toward the door, then became inordinately interested in fishing her key out of her bag. But somehow the key kept eluding her, and she never could quite grasp it enough to withdraw it. By the time they reached her door, she was still fumbling for it. She heard Mr. Montgomery chuckle, but not in any way other than that he was mildly amused. So she let a few chuckles of her own escape, and somehow that eased the knot of tension that had threatened to tie the moment.

"It's the gloves," he told her as he reached for her bag. Effortlessly he located her keys, holding them up in one hand as if they were a trophy, giving them a triumphant little jingle as he smiled. Then he gestured her aside to unlock and open her front door, dropped the keys back into her bag and handed it back to her.

"Thank you. I'm usually not such a fumble-fingers, regardless of the situation," she told him. "It has nothing to do with the gloves, I assure you."

His smile grew broader, and as she gazed at him, Winona noted how the yellow glow of the porch light ignited amber fires in his hair, and how it made his blue eyes seem to glow silver somehow.

"Then it must be something else that's got you feeling nervous," he said quietly.

"I-I-I'm not nervous," she denied nervously.

"Aren't you?" he asked with much too much confidence.

She shook her head slowly but knew she wasn't being at all truthful. "Certainly not," she insisted anyway. "Why would I be nervous?"

He studied her in silence for a moment, then, "Maybe because you know how much I want to kiss you good night," he said quietly.

A runnel of heat splashed through her midsection at hearing his remark. "Do you?" she asked.

He nodded, his gaze never leaving hers. "I do."

"I...I see."

"So...may I?"

"K-k-k-kiss me?" she faltered.

He nodded again, still focused intently on her face, her eyes, her mouth. "I promise I'll be a gentleman."

"I...ah...well...you see...I mean...um...that is..." Winona swallowed hard and willed herself to be firm with him. Then she heard herself say, quite firmly, "All right."

Evidently, it took a moment for her consent to register with him, because for a moment Mr. Montgomery only gazed down at her face as if he were still awaiting her reply. Then her response must have finally dawned on him, because his handsome features went lax, his silver-blue eyes darkened to the depth and texture of storm clouds, and his lips parted the merest bit. Then he took a small step forward, bent his head to hers and brushed his lips lightly over her own, once...twice...three times, before finally pulling back.

The entire exchange lasted only seconds, and his body never touched hers save the scant, sweet seduction of his mouth on her own. Really, his kiss had been almost chaste. Yet somehow, Winona suddenly felt as if she were on fire. He might as well have just run his hands over every inch of her naked body, caressing, carousing, exploring, entering. Only when she opened her eyes did she realize she had closed them. And only then did she see that Mr. Montgomery had been as turbulently affected by the encounter as she.

And then she heard herself say the strangest thing. "Would you like to come in for a cup of tea, Mr. Montgomery?"

And he surprised her even more by replying, "No, thank you, Miss Thornbury. Perhaps another time." Then he quietly bade her good-night, dipped his head in farewell and turned to walk away. Only once did he look back, after closing the gate behind him. He lifted a hand in fond farewell, softly bade her good-night one final time and made his way down the dark street, toward the spot at the end of the block where he had parked his car.

And as she watched him go, Winona realized she had no idea whether what had just happened between the two of them was a good thing or not.

Connor drove straight back to his place after leaving Winona Thornbury's house. *His place* in this regard being *not* the Budget Motor Lodge, Bloomington, where he'd made his home for the past few weeks, but his real home—Marigold, Indiana. It was nearly 3:00 a.m. when he arrived at his apartment, but he didn't care. The last thing he felt like doing was sleeping. No, he was fairly sure that, thanks to his reaction to the little kiss he'd planted on Winona less than an hour ago, he'd never be sleeping again.

And that, of course, would be due to the fact that he was currently suffering from a state of consummate arousal heretofore unknown in the annals of sexual history. At least, that was probably how Winona Thornbury would have described his condition—had she not been too nice and old-fashioned to describe something like that. At least, she *acted* much too nice and old-fashioned to describe something like that. The jury was still out on whether or not she was, in fact, a nice, old-fashioned girl. At any rate, to Connor, his current predicament was more appropriately described as a simple raging hard-on that wouldn't go away. Even though he'd had almost an hour of boring driving to calm himself down. There would be no calming down for some time from this.

And that, of course, would be due to the fact that he had spent that boring almost-hour of driving thinking about Winona Thornbury and about the concussion of heat that had bolted through him with the first soft brush of his mouth over hers. It had been a punch of desire that had only doubled and then tripled with that second and third caress.

Just what the hell had gotten into him? he wondered as he let himself into his dark, silent apartment. His *too* dark, *too* silent apartment. Immediately he began prowling restlessly around the living room, turning on lights and the CD player and the TV and the radio, because he needed *some*thing to distract him, dammit, and take his mind off Winona. But even with everything blaring and shining at him, Connor still felt the subtle, quiet tug of Winona. Instead of his Spartanly furnished, Swedishly influenced bachelor's apartment, he saw himself, in his mind's eye, surrounded by the bounty and beauty of her house—herself—instead.

Why did she have him so tied up in knots? he wondered again. Was it some kind of game on her part? Had he been right about her all along? Was she a madam or a hooker or both, simply trying to hold on to the only business she knew, the only way she knew how? *Did* she know he was a cop? *Was* she trying to throw him off the trail? Because he couldn't think of any reason why a woman like her would be able to arouse such a rawly sexual response in him, unless it was because she knew some age-old, rawly sexual secret for seizing a man's libido the way she had his, and sending it through the wringer—the way she had his.

She had to be a madam or a hooker or both, Connor told himself. She had to be. It was the only explanation that made any sense. And she had to be working some kind of madam/hooker mojo on him to make him feel the way he was feeling now. He was burning up inside. He'd started burning the minute he began watching her taking off those little white gloves of hers, and he'd been on fire all night long. And that kiss...

Holy Mary, Mother of God. That kiss. He'd barely touched her mouth with his, but the minute he'd made contact, every desire, every need, every hunger he possessed had roared up inside him demanding to be sated. Had he taken her up on her invitation to come inside for tea—yeah, right—he was more than confident that, at this very moment, he and the luscious Winona would be tangled up in sweaty sheets, doing things with each other, doing things *to* each other, that he probably wouldn't recover from for days.

So why the hell hadn't he taken her up on her offer? he asked himself for perhaps the hundredth time since driving away from her place. Why wasn't he in her house right now, amid all that frilly, feminine stuff, showing her what a man could do?

Probably, he thought, because it would have compromised the investigation even worse than he had already compromised it. Especially if she *had* made him as a cop.

Ah, dammit, why couldn't he figure this thing out? he wondered as he freed his necktie from its loosened knot and tugged it rabidly from his collar. Why was it that the more he thought about it, the more confused he became, and the less sense all of it made?

The evidence was there, he reminded himself. They knew—they *knew*—there was a call-girl ring operating out of Winona's. All they had left to do was find out the particulars, and who was heading it up. The logical conclusion was that Winona herself was running it. But something inside Connor, something that was entirely new to him, told him otherwise.

He should have accepted her offer, he told himself. He should have gone into her house under the pretense of having tea and seen where she would lead him. If she had invited him into her bed, he would have known once and for all that she wasn't the nice, old-fashioned girl she pretended to be. Not that that would give him any more evidence that she was running an illegal operation, but it damned sure would have cleared up any confusion he might have about her as a law-abiding, morally upstanding human being.

Not that everybody who slept with their companion on the first date was doing anything illegal, Connor quickly reminded himself. If that were the rule, then he himself would be doing time for more than one offense. He wasn't even the kind of man who thought it was a matter of loose morals to jump right into bed with someone. Why should it be immoral to satisfy what was a natural, God-given urge?

He did, however, take exception to someone who pretended to be something he or she was not. He disregarded, for now, the fact that he himself was currently guilty of misrepresenting himself—he had a good reason, dammit. And had he been making Winona's sheets sweaty and tangled at that moment, he would have known that her prim, chaste, old-fashioned act was precisely that—an act.

Which still didn't provide him with anything about Winona Thornbury that he hadn't already known about her before tonight. Except, of course, that her mouth was every bit as soft and sweet and succulent as he had dreamed it would be.

He groaned with much feeling and made his way to his bedroom, switching on more lights, turning on more music in his wake. But all he saw then was another sparsely furnished room with lots of blond wood and stark designs that somehow seemed artificial to him. Odd, that he'd always liked the clean, uncluttered lines of his life before. And the rampant music assaulting his ears, music he had very much enjoyed previously, suddenly sounded disjointed and discordant now.

Shoving the troubling thought aside, Connor jerked off his jacket and tossed it onto a chair, then went to work on the buttons of his shirt. And all the while, he tried not to think about what it might have been like for Winona to be doing the honors instead.

She would have taken her time, he was certain, unbuttoning his shirt with all the unhurried patience she had shown for her gloves. Then she would have skimmed the garment slowly from his shoulders and dragged her fingertips leisurely down his chest, curling her fingers in the dark hair scattered there. Then she would have pushed her hands lower still, raking her fingers down over his rib cage and flat belly, to the waistband of his trousers, where she would free the button and zipper, and tuck her hand inside. And then she would cup her fingers lovingly, possessively over his—

Connor groaned again, with even more feeling this time, reaching down to unfasten his trousers himself, because they were becoming much, *much* too tight for his comfort. Then he left his bedroom to head for the bathroom instead. No way was he ready to go to bed yet. Not alone, at any rate. But a nice, cold shower seemed like a very good idea. And the more alone he was for that, the better. Because somehow he suspected that Winona Thornbury could turn even an iceberg into a steam bath, just like that.

And God almighty, he had no idea what to do.

Six

Winona didn't see Connor Montgomery in her restaurant the night following their, ah...little interlude, and she wasn't sure whether she should be delighted or upset about the development. Nor did she see him Wednesday night—and she had the same uncertain reaction then. He didn't come in Thursday, either. Nor did he make an appearance on Friday. Nor Saturday. And on all of those days that he wasn't there, Winona experienced a whirlwind of conflicting reactions. She was by turns relieved and worried, gratified and disappointed. Not once, however, did she feel content.

By Sunday morning she was beginning to wonder if perhaps she had simply imagined Connor Montgomery into existence, because he seemed to have vanished completely from the face of the Earth. She could find no evidence of him anywhere. Well, nowhere other than her fantasies, delusions and dreams, she was forced to confess. And in *those,* he most definitely had a life of his own.

Her dreams at night, especially, had been filled with him. During the day, whenever she caught herself thinking about Connor Montgomery, she was usually able to distract herself with thoughts of something else, or by keeping busy in the restaurant. But in sleep she had no such luxury. In sleep she was helpless to restrain her thoughts of him, and in sleep her thoughts of him were nothing short of tempestuous.

Even now, fully awake, as she sat in her office trying to clear up some paperwork she should have completed days ago, Winona couldn't quite keep memories of him at bay. Or, more accurately, she couldn't quite keep memories of her dreams of him at bay. Because those dreams, the ones that had come to her every single night, had been outrageous, ignominious, licentious, *scandalous.*

Well, all right, perhaps not ignominious, Winona conceded reluctantly. She certainly hadn't felt disgraced by any of her dreams. Not really. But she had most certainly been scandalized by them. Never in her life, *never,* had she entertained the kind of graphic mental imagery that her dreams of Connor Montgomery brought with them. Even when she had enjoyed her brief, ah…odyssey of sexual discovery…with Stanley Wadsworth, Winona hadn't come close to experiencing the sort of reactions she had experienced when she had been with Connor in a completely fantastical way.

Because she awoke from such dreams in quite a state, panting for breath, her heart raging wildly, her nightgown bunched about her hips, her sheets tangled between her legs, her body hot and dewy from the dampness of her perspiration and her own release. Never had she felt with a very corporeal Stanley the sort of things she felt with an illusory Connor. She had even ceased to think of him as Mr. Montgomery, which was thoroughly unlike her. But how could she use such a formality with the man when she had experienced such a…such a…such a *fulfillment* with him, if only in her dreams?

And what on earth was she going to say to him the next time she saw him?

Perhaps she *wouldn't* see him again, she told herself as she placed another sealed envelope atop the stack that had collected since morning. Perhaps, after spending such a moderate, unsophisticated evening with her, he had decided he wasn't interested in her after all. His kiss good-night had held anything but passion—for him, at any rate, even if that hadn't been the case with her at all.

And he had declined her invitation to come in for tea— though, truly, she still couldn't imagine now what had come over her to issue such an invitation in the first place. Not only had it *not* been teatime, but Winona was certain it was imprudent for her to suggest that she would have enjoyed his company in the wee hours of the morning. Because there was a very specific activity that men and women traditionally enjoyed at such an hour. And it most certainly *wasn't* tea. Why should she encourage Connor to think that she might have been interested in indulging in such an activity with him?

Unless, of course, it was because she very much wanted to indulge in such an activity with him.

Oh, dear, Winona thought. There she went again, thinking illicit thoughts about Connor in the light of day. Not only was that *not* conducive to good work habits, it *was* conducive to madness. Because it would only lead to frustration. Frustration and…other things she had no business inviting into her life.

But her worry over the whole situation was probably pointless anyway. He hadn't kissed her passionately. He hadn't accepted her invitation to…whatever. In fact, Connor seemed like the kind of man who would go for women of a much faster lifestyle than Winona practiced herself.

Which made her wonder again why he had asked her to go out with him in the first place.

She sighed heavily and stood, gathering up the assortment of mail on her desk. She had dressed that morning for work in a calf-length dress of pale-rose cotton. It was an unusually plain dress for her, in that the only decoration came in the dozens of pearl buttons marching down the front, the white lace trim on the three-quarter-length sleeves and a white lace collar that she had pinned at the throat with an antique cameo. But work was the last thing on Winona's mind today. Sundays were generally slow and leisurely at the restaurant, a limited brunch and an afternoon tea—a real tea, not the *whatever* kind of tea to which she had invited Connor last weekend—followed by an early closing before dinner, so that she could enjoy *some*thing resembling a weekend.

Perhaps no one would notice if she slipped out for a bit, she thought, gazing at the handful of mail. A short stroll to the post office up the street would do her good. It would be closed, of course, but she could drop the mail into the mailbox and have one less thing to do tomorrow. Right now, she felt restless, edgy and the day outside was lovely—clear and cool, with the mingling scents of apples and drying leaves vying for possession of the breeze. The fresh air, she was certain, would do her good and might invigorate her with a new sense of purpose.

Oh, yes. A new purpose. She definitely needed one of those.

After checking to make sure everything was running smoothly, and after alerting her host to her destination, Winona donned her gloves and draped an embroidered shawl fashioned of creamy white silk over her shoulders. Then she gathered up her mail and headed out into the street. She was halfway down the block when she noticed a familiar figure in a dark suit striding toward her. Her breath caught at the sight of him, her heart skipped an already erratic beat and she stumbled over an irregular brick in the sidewalk.

Connor Montgomery had returned to Bloomington. And, as was his habit, he was coming right at her.

Holy moly, Connor thought when he saw Winona striding oh, so casually up the street in his direction. To put it in much more polite—and much less panicky—terms than he was feeling at the moment. He hadn't meant to run into her just yet. He still had a whole speech to rehearse before he would be ready to see her again. He wasn't even sure he'd worked up the nerve to walk back into her life yet. Hell, he wasn't even sure he was ready to walk back into her restaurant yet. Even after a week of mulling things over, he still had no idea what he intended to do.

He had spent the bulk of the previous week holed up in Marigold, going over—yet again—every scrap of evidence he had in his possession regarding the Winona Thornbury case. He had called the Bloomington boys on a number of occasions to compare notes with them, had followed up on things he hadn't been sure about the first time, had, for the most part, reinvestigated the entire investigation.

His conclusion? Oh, that was an easy one. He was more confused now than ever.

Where before he had been absolutely convinced that Winona was not only involved in the operation working out of her restaurant, but spearheading it, after the evening the two of them had spent together, Connor had begun to have his doubts. Because instead of being an unctuous, opportunistic madam bent on making an illegal buck off the backs of young women, Winona really did seem like nothing more than a nice, old-fashioned girl who ran a successful restaurant for a living.

She hadn't seemed to have any hidden agenda, illicit or otherwise. She hadn't seemed to have anything to hide at all. Certainly she didn't seem to have as much to hide as

Connor did himself. So who was really the liar misrepresenting themselves in this relationship, hmm?

Best not to think about that one for now.

There *was* one thing he *had* figured out, however. He had figured out *why* he had begun to question his conviction that Winona was running an illegal operation. It was very simple, really. He shouldn't have been surprised by the discovery at all. But once he'd made the discovery, he'd been astonished.

He'd begun to question his conviction about her because, to put it in incredibly simple terms, he didn't *want* Winona to be spearheading an illegal operation. And the reason he didn't want her to be spearheading an illegal operation was because he *did* want *her*. Badly. And now he was afraid his attraction to her was going to color his opinion of her, maybe even blindside him completely. And if that happened, it would only jeopardize his ability to complete this investigation to its fullest extent.

Oh, right, Monahan, like you haven't jeopardized this investigation in a million other ways already.

The voice—not to mention the sentiment—was a familiar one, because Connor had been hearing both all week. Part of him was still confident that he hadn't done anything wrong where the investigation was concerned, that he hadn't crossed any lines yet, even if he'd maybe blurred a few. That part of him was sure that every action he had completed *would* hold up in court. Pretty much. With a good DA prosecuting. And a lot of luck.

But another part of Connor feared that maybe, just maybe, he was going about this thing the wrong way. And that maybe, just maybe, he'd done one or two things that were going to get him hammered. Hard.

Worse than that, though, was the fact that, the closer he got to Winona, the blurrier those aforementioned uncrossed lines became. And the blurrier those lines became, the easier they were going to be to cross. And once they were crossed... Well. Once they were crossed, there would be no going back over them. Connor just wasn't sure yet what would be considered crossing them and what would be considered blurring them a little more.

Probably, he thought as he watched Winona approach, her luscious body moving with all the grace and rhythm of a well-oiled machine, engaging in wild monkey lovin' with a suspect in a criminal case would be one of those once-crossed-never-comin'-back-over-the-line things.

Dammit.

And that, he knew, was what had really kept him in Marigold all week. He'd been reasonably certain Monday night—or, rather, early Tuesday morning—that if he didn't put some distance, both geographic and temporal, between himself and Winona, then he was most definitely going to cross that line. Because thoughts of Winona had just naturally overlapped with thoughts of wild monkey lovin' in Connor's mind. Day and night. Night and day. All. Week. Long. There was no two ways about that.

And now that he saw her striding toward him down the street, as he watched the subtle sway of her full hips and the way her pink dress swished about her well-turned calves, as he registered the little white gloves that he found so profoundly arousing, as he noted the long line of buttons down the front of her dress and wondered what it would be like to loose them one by one...

Connor sighed heavily and began to think that he hadn't put nearly enough time and distance between them. Maybe if he went to the planet Pluto for a couple of millennia, that might take care of it....

But instead of turning tail to hide himself to the nearest NASA facility, Connor continued to walk forward. He simply could not help himself. It was as if Winona had a string twined around her little finger whose other end was attached soundly to his libido. And she just kept coiling that string around her finger, little by little by little, pulling him closer and closer and closer, until he had no chance of escape.

And then, suddenly, she was tripping over something in the cobbled walk, and her stride became more hurried and less certain, and the next thing Connor knew, she was stumbling forward with real speed, grasping for something to hold on to that didn't exist and losing her footing and going down, and he was running forward to catch her, and just in the nick of time, he did.

Boy, did he catch her.

Because by the time all was said and done—or, at least, by the time all was done, since neither of them said a word, save Winona's softly uttered "Oops"—he was holding her in his arms, one roped protectively around her waist, the other across her back. And then he was pulling her entire body closer to his own, ostensibly to steady her, but actually because he really, really, really wanted to know what it would be like to have her that close. And because he'd really, really missed her this week.

Nice, he realized quickly. It felt really, really nice to have her close.

The soft aroma of lavender enveloped him as he drew Winona nearer, nearly intoxicating him with its sweet scent. Or maybe it was Winona herself who intoxicated him. All Connor knew was that he had his arms full of soft, warm, fragrant woman, a woman whose absence he had felt keenly all week long. And as that knowledge settled over him, he reacted the only way he knew how. He bent his head to hers and kissed her.

Not, however, the way his instincts were commanding him to kiss her at the moment—by opening his mouth over hers and consuming her in one big, greedy bite while he rushed his hands all over her body, unfastening her clothing as he went so that he could investigate all the soft parts he wanted to investigate. Somehow, in that moment, Connor knew—he just *knew*—there was going to be time for all that in the future. In the not-so-distant future, too. So, for now, he forced himself to be satisfied with another one of those innocent, chaste little kisses like he'd given her the other night. One that told her merely, "Oh, hey, it's good to see ya again."

Even at that, though, he was surprised when Winona did nothing to stop him. On the contrary, when Connor made himself pull away from her, when he lifted his head from hers to gaze down at her face, she only curled her gloved fingers more insistently into the lapels of his jacket, as if she had every intention of pulling him back down for more. For a moment her eyes remained closed, her lips slightly pursed, as if, in her mind, at least, she was still kissing him. Then, little by little, her eyes fluttered open, looking dreamy and uncertain and…and…and…

Connor caught his breath at the realization—and *not a little turned-on.*

So Winona Thornbury wasn't quite so nice and old-fashioned as she seemed, he thought. She wasn't quite as chaste and innocent as he'd begun to think she was. Because clearly there were fires burning behind that buttoned-up, battened-down facade. All he had to do now was figure out a way to…stoke them.

Later, he reminded himself. But *not* too much later…

Her eyes were even bluer than he remembered, he noted as he drank his visual fill of her, and her mouth seemed fuller, riper, more delicious. Her cheeks were stained with the merest hint of pink, though whether that was a result of the cool breeze circling them or something else entirely, he couldn't have said.

For one long moment the two of them gazed into each others' eyes, Connor with his arms still looped around Winona's back, she with her fingers still curled into the fabric of his jacket.

And then, suddenly, very, very softly, she said, "Why, Mr. Montgomery. How nice to see you again."

Connor smiled. Oh, she was so transparent. "It's good to see you, too, Miss Thornbury. You're looking well." *And you don't feel too bad, either,* he added to himself. Hoo-boy, was that an understatement.

Still focusing on his eyes, still speaking in that fanciful little voice, still held tenderly in his arms, she replied, "Thank you."

And still holding her tenderly, Connor responded quietly, "You're welcome."

For another moment she only gazed at him in silence, clearly still not realizing what a compromising position she was in. "I was beginning to think you might have moved away," she told him. "You were gone for so long."

"Ah…business trip," he said off the top of his head. "I, um, I had to be away for a business trip last week."

"I see," she said. Still dreamily. Still gazing into his eyes. Still holding firmly to his jacket. "You didn't mention that on Monday."

Connor nodded slowly. "Ah, yeah. Well. You see. About that. It was, um, sudden. Really sudden. I didn't have time to do much more than throw a couple of things into a suitcase and head out."

Boy, was that a lie, he thought. Not only had his trip had nothing to do with business, but he hadn't even taken time to pack. Just how much longer would it be before he could tell Winona Thornbury something—anything—that was the truth?

"Oh, my," she said, sounding a little breathless now. "I do hope everything is all right."

"It's great," Connor told her, smiling genuinely now because at last he could speak the truth. "Everything is just fine."

More than fine, he thought. In that moment, at least, everything was perfect. Because he was standing outside on a spectacular Sunday afternoon, beneath an endless blue sky and a canopy of trees kissed with scarlet and amber and gold. And he was holding Winona Thornbury in his arms and gazing at her in her pink dress and antique pin, with her blond hair escaping from the terse bun she had pinned at the back of her head, a few errant strands of gold being blown about her face by a soft autumn breeze. And what a face. Eyes that put the color and clarity of the sky to shame, cheeks as soft and ivory as porcelain and lips as dewy and red as roses after rain.

And Holy Mary, Mother of God, Connor had turned into a poet, and didn't even know it.

With much reluctance he steadied her on her feet and released her, cupping his hands over her upper arms until she seemed able to right herself. It took a moment for her to realize what was going on, to recognize how the two of them had passed the last few minutes, because she didn't release Connor right away, nor did she ever remove her gaze from his face. When she finally *did* seem to understand how she had just spent the last tiny bit of her life—being embraced by a man in the middle of the street on a leisurely Sunday afternoon—she *did* glance away from him. Very hastily. Very uncomfortably. Then she blushed furiously and bent to pick up some letters Connor just now realized she had been carrying and had dropped at some point during their embrace.

"Well," she said as she straightened, sorting through her mail as if she wanted very desperately to remind herself where each and every piece of correspondence was headed. "Well, well," she reiterated as she went through the letters a second time. And then, as she sifted through them a third time, she added, "Well…well…well."

"Well," Connor concurred, grinning. She was awfully cute when she was off-kilter. And if she got this nervous after a simple hello kiss, he couldn't wait to see what she would be like when she lost herself completely to her own passion.

Because in that moment, he became absolutely certain

that he would see her lose herself completely to her own passion. Better yet, he'd see her lose herself completely to his passion, too. And he to hers. And that was going to be even more enjoyable.

"Well," she said one last time. She finally lifted her gaze to his, then immediately shot it away once more. "It was, ah...it was nice seeing you again, Mr. Montgomery," she told him. She turned her attention then to a nonexistent smudge she seemed intent on erasing from her left glove. "I'm glad you made it back from your trip safely and soundly. Now, if you'll excuse me, I—"

"Have lunch with me."

Connor wasn't sure what had made him issue the invitation—or voice the edict, whatever—seeing as how he still had no idea what to say to her after giving her not one, but now two, kisses. He still wasn't sure how he felt, still wasn't convinced he hadn't compromised the investigation of Winona's restaurant, still wasn't certain he was doing the right thing. Hell, he wasn't even certain what thing he was doing.

But, somehow he just couldn't tolerate the thought of her walking past him, alone, and going about her life without him. It didn't seem natural for some reason. It didn't seem right. He wanted to be with her. In whatever way he could. And if that meant compromising the investigation, then... then...then...

Then he just wouldn't think about that right now.

Winona glanced back up at him quickly when he issued his invitation—or voiced his edict, whatever—and although she didn't look away this time, he could see she wasn't any too comfortable meeting his gaze.

"I'm sorry? What did you say?" she asked.

"I said, 'Have lunch with me,'" he repeated.

"But I...I...I..."

"At Winona's," he further prodded. "My treat."

She studied him for a moment in silence, her lips slightly

parted, as if there was something on the tip of her tongue that she needed to say. Naturally, Connor's instinct was to lean in again and press his own open mouth to hers, but he decided to wait until later. A little later, anyway. When they weren't standing out in the middle of Bloomington, for all the world to see. But not too much later, because, as always, after spending only a few moments in Winona's presence, he was burning up inside. And he suspected he was going to keep on burning—and Winona would, too—until the two of them did something to douse those fires.

"But I…I have to mail these," she said, holding her correspondence up for his inspection.

With a smile Connor plucked them easily out of her hand and strode exactly five paces back whence he had come, where a mailbox stood stoically at the edge of the walk. He pulled the metal door open with a soft *creeeeak*, dropped the letters inside, and closed it again with a muffled *clonk*. Then he recovered the five paces to stand before Winona and smiled some more.

"There," he told her. "All mailed. Now it's lunchtime."

"But I…I have to get back to work," she said.

"You close in less than two hours, don't you?"

She nodded.

He grinned some more. "I'll wait."

"But two hours—"

"Is nothing," he assured her. "Not when I think about how long I've been waiting for you already."

She narrowed her eyes some at his cryptic comment, and Connor hoped like hell she didn't ask him to elaborate on it. Not because he didn't want to have to lie to her again about the investigation. And not because he didn't want to lie to her about anything else, either.

But because he honestly didn't understand any better than she did why he'd said it at all.

Seven

By the time Winona closed her restaurant and locked up behind all of her employees, she was a nervous wreck. Because by then, Connor Montgomery had been sitting in the otherwise deserted bar area of the restaurant, sipping coffee and reading the Sunday paper—and watching her *very* intently every time she entered the dining area—for nearly two hours. And at the end of those two hours, thanks to the barrage of incendiary looks he had blasted her way, every nerve ending Winona possessed was *on fire*.

Well, thanks to those incendiary looks, *and* the fact that she kept replaying in her mind, over and over and over again, that lovely little kiss he had given her when she'd stumbled, quite literally, into his arms earlier that afternoon.

Yes, indeed, memories of that embrace had gone a *looong* way toward stoking the fires he'd set a week ago. Because memories of that kiss had inevitably reminded Winona—over and over and *over* again—of the other kiss she'd enjoyed with Connor the last time they had been together. And recollections of both had only doubled what had already become a strange, and almost intolerable, need for him.

She still couldn't imagine what had come over her to allow him such a flagrant liberty this afternoon, kissing her right out there in the great wide open. It was shocking enough that she had succumbed to him so readily last weekend, but at least then, his kiss had come about through a reasonable set of circumstances. The two of them had been out on a prearranged date, and traditionally, a kiss goodnight wasn't outside the realm of possibility at the conclusion of such an interlude.

Many women allowed their escorts a kiss good-night during such a state of affairs, Winona reminded herself. Though, indeed, perhaps *affairs* wasn't the best word to use in this situation. She hastily shook the thought off. No matter. From what she understood, many women even allowed greater liberties than just a kiss at the climax of a first date. Though, perhaps *climax* wasn't such a good word to use, either, she thought further, feeling flushed for some reason. Honestly, she had no idea why she was having so much trouble with semantics today.

At any rate, this afternoon, there had been no excuse for her outrageous behavior with Connor. Why, before she'd even had the chance to properly greet him, she'd been kissing him. And what kind of woman kissed a man before she even said, Hello, how are you, so lovely to see you again? Worse, she couldn't imagine what had come over her to enjoy such a scandalous kiss *so much*.

Never in her life had Winona experienced the feelings that Connor made her feel. Never had she known such feelings even existed for a person to experience. She had thought the height of her sexual discovery had come in the arms of her ex-fiancé, Stanley Wadsworth. But her brief time with Stanley had done nothing to prepare her for this…this…this explosion of sensation that erupted inside her merely by having Connor come near her. And if this was the way she felt after a few innocent kisses from him and a thoroughly benign embrace, what would it be like to completely give herself over to—

No, she assured herself. That wasn't going to happen. She would not succumb to the desires and needs that Connor incited in her. She would not. She wasn't going to give herself over to a man again without the benefit of matrimony to cement that giving. And Connor Montgomery was clearly *not* the marrying kind.

Still, she thought, it might be rather interesting to see what would occur if—

No, she told herself more firmly this time. It wasn't going to happen. Not until she had a firm commitment in the form of a wedding ring and church service. Period.

But maybe just once, she backpedaled. Just to see if he was really as—

NO! she proclaimed to herself more adamantly. She would not succumb. She wouldn't. She would *not.*

Winona repeated the vow again and again in her brain as she strode toward the bar to find him, as if in doing so, the words might generate some magical incantation that would ward off evil. Then she saw Connor seated where he had been seated all afternoon, gazing at her with that wicked, wicked smile, his blue eyes blazing with intent as he watched her stride toward him.

And she realized there was nothing in the world that would ward him off, once he set his mind to…whatever he'd set it to. All Winona could do was hope he had more willpower than she had herself. Because she very much suspected in that moment that, should Connor decided he wanted her—really *wanted* her—there would be no way she could possibly resist him.

Unfortunately, she also suspected in that moment that willpower was the last thing a man like him engaged in. Especially when it came to things like *wanting.*

"My, you've been patient today," she said as she approached him, telling herself she only imagined the breathlessness she heard lacing her words. Even if she was a little out of breath, it was only because she had been very busy today. Her breathlessness had nothing to do with the fact that Connor looked so…so…so…

Oh, my.

He stood slowly, his entire body seeming to grow and expand with every additional inch of space he claimed, in both height and breadth. At some point during the afternoon, he had discarded his jacket and necktie, and he'd unfastened the top buttons of his shirt to reveal a tantalizing wisp of dark hair beneath. He'd rolled back the cuffs of his white dress shirt, as well, to reveal sun-bronzed, brawny forearms, shadowed with more tantalizing wisps of dark hair, the masculine likes of which Winona had never seen.

Stanley hadn't been an especially virile man. Oh, he'd been masculine enough, and manly about the things most men found interesting. He'd enjoyed sports and had claimed a favorite brand of beer. And although Winona wasn't positive, she was reasonably certain that he had, on occasion, thumbed through her *Victoria's Secret* catalogues with an interest in something other than Christmas shopping for her.

But he hadn't been like Connor. He hadn't exuded a raw masculinity and potent toughness that defied challenge.

For the first time, Winona wondered what, exactly Connor did for a living. All this time she had assumed, thanks to the high-powered business executive suits he wore, that he was, well, a high-powered business executive. Now, however, she began to have her doubts. Wouldn't a high-powered business executive spend much of his day at a desk or computer, or on the telephone or an airplane, or having lunch with other high-powered business executives? And wouldn't such a lifestyle leave a man soft and pale and fleshy?

Yet Connor was hard and dark and lean. He had the appearance and demeanor of a man who spent a good bit of his time doing physical things, especially outdoors. And he didn't seem overly obsessed with the worlds of business and high finance, the way one would assume a high-powered business executive would. On the contrary, he never mentioned business or high finance at all.

Perhaps he thought such conversation would bore her, Winona told herself. Perhaps he was only trying to be polite by always steering the topic of conversation away from himself and what he did for a living. And perhaps he led a health-conscious lifestyle, she thought further. Maybe he spent his weekends outdoors, hiking or rock climbing, or performing some other physical feats of daring-do to negate the sedentary effects of his job. Perhaps that was why he was so physically fit.

Or perhaps he was deliberately misrepresenting himself to her, and pretending to be something he wasn't.

Winona had no idea why such a bizarre thought would leap into her head the way it did just then, and as soon as the peculiar idea materialized, she nudged it aside. It was silly. Connor couldn't possibly be misrepresenting himself or pretending to be something he wasn't, she assured herself. Why would he possibly need or want to? She was being ridiculous.

So, instead, she focused her attention fully on Connor, marveling at the way he seemed to suddenly fill her vision, the way he seemed to suddenly fill her very life. Her heart sped faster and more furiously as she absorbed the sight of him, until she feared it would rattle right up against her ribs and reveal to him just how badly shaken she was by his presence.

And she realized then, too, how very badly she *was* shaken by his presence. More so than she had ever been shaken by anyone else. Including Stanley—the man whom she had intended to marry. The man with whom she had thought she wanted to spend her entire life. The man she had thought she loved. Which could only mean that the feelings she had for Connor were...

Oh, dear.

She stopped herself dead in her tracks, but Connor seemed not to notice her sudden hesitation. Instead he only tossed the last of the Sunday paper onto the table, hooked his hands loosely on his hips and smiled at her. The most dazzling, heart-stopping smile Winona had ever seen.

Oh, yes, she thought as her heart began humming erratically again. She was definitely more firmly under Connor's spell than she had ever been under Stanley's. And something about realizing that made her feel not only panicked, but inexplicably sad.

"You think I've been patient today?" he asked, echoing the comment she could scarcely remember making now, and stirring her from her troubling thoughts. "That's funny, because I don't feel like I'm a particularly patient man." He waiting a telling beat before adding, "Especially not when I'm around you."

Oh, my, Winona thought. Not just because of the sentiment he expressed, but because of the glitter of purpose that ignited in his blue eyes as he said it, giving them the look of a man who fully intended to spend the rest of the day—

Oh, my.

"Right now, for instance," he added, "I'm feeling very impatient. And very..."

He inhaled a deep breath and, for a moment, he only continued to gaze at her in silence. Then, very, very slowly, he released the breath again. He said nothing, however, only kept his attention riveted on her face.

"Very...what?" she finally asked, her voice coming out a bit shallow and hurried.

"Hungry," he finished. "I'm feeling very...hungry."

And why did she suspect that his condition had nothing to do with the need for food?

"There's a, um…a, ah…a, er…" Winona swallowed with some difficulty before she finally managed to get out, "there are a few things left over from lunch that I put in the refrigerator upstairs for my own meals this week. If you're hungry—"

"*Very* hungry," he corrected her.

She nodded nervously. "If you're *very* hungry…" she began again.

"Oh, I'm *starved*," he interrupted her. Once more, though, he somehow made the announcement sound as if it had nothing to do with wanting food.

She nodded again. More nervously. "If you're starved, then…" she said, waiting a moment this time to see if he wanted to add any more clarification. Strangely, she found herself hoping that he would. But he remained silent this time, only continued to gaze at her—hungrily, she couldn't help thinking—and waited to see what she would say. "Then perhaps you'd like something like… Oh, I don't know. I have lovely pasty, for example."

His dark brows shot up in surprise at her announcement, then he rolled his tongue in his cheek. For some reason, Winona received the distinct impression that he was trying very hard not to laugh.

"A, um…a pasty?" he repeated.

She nodded, wondering at the glint of humor that suddenly appeared in his eyes. "Yes. A pasty. Well, actually, I suppose contemporary pronunciation would have the word rhyme with *nasty*. But I prefer the traditional pasty instead."

"Oh, I prefer pasties, too," he told her eagerly. Again, though, Winona felt as if he were laughing at her for some reason. How very odd. "Although there's a lot to be said for nasty, too," he added.

She narrowed her eyes at him suspiciously. What on

earth was he going on about? "All right then," she told him evenly. "Would you like one of my pasties?"

He did, quite literally, bite back a smile at that, and Winona's confusion grew. "Sounds, um…lovely," he told her. "I think I could probably really, you know, wrap my mouth around a pasty right about now. That sounds… really, really good."

And then, suddenly, for some reason, he had to clear his throat. A lot.

How odd, Winona thought again. She hoped he wasn't coming down with a sore throat. It wasn't the cold and flu season yet. Perhaps she should offer him some of the left-over soup, as well.

"There's soup, too," she said helpfully. "My lovely cherry tomato."

"Your…cherry…tomato?"

Goodness, his hearing must be clouded, too, she thought. He had to repeat everything she said, as if he were having trouble. And what a strange voice he was repeating it in, too.

A bit louder this time, she repeated, "Yes. Cherry. To-mato. Are you interested?"

He held up a hand, palm out, in a silent bid for her to stop, and now she could very easily see that he was indeed trying not to laugh. "No, thank you," he told her. "I'm just really looking forward to the getting that, uh, that pasty in my mouth."

Winona narrowed her eyes at him once more. He was doing it again, she thought. Making suggestive remarks that she didn't understand. She didn't know *why* they were suggestive, only that they *were*. She could tell by the way he was voicing them that he was thinking about something completely different from what she was thinking herself.

And, somehow she knew whatever was going through his mind was sexual in nature. She could tell *that* by the way her own body caught fire at hearing his roughly uttered words and seeing the spark of fire in his eyes. For all Winona's expounding on the importance of virtue and chastity and decency, sometimes, she thought, it simply did not pay to be sexually inexperienced.

"Fine," she said evenly. She turned her back on Connor then, and began to walk forward. Over her shoulder, she told him, "If you'll just follow me upstairs to my private quarters, then I'll ply you with the plumpest, hottest pasty I have at my disposal."

She heard him utter a strangled little sound at her announcement, but all he said in reply was, "Oh, Winona, my…mouth…is watering already."

Connor couldn't remember the last time he had enjoyed a meal as much as he enjoyed his Sunday dinner sitting in Winona Thornbury's abundantly decorated, outrageously feminine—and very private—quarters. Of course, it wasn't often that a woman like her offered a man like him one of her hot, plump pasties, or carried on about her cherry tomatoes, but that was beside the point.

The point was that she had been so innocent while voicing the offer of her hot, plump pasty and her cherry tomatoes. She really had been. Nobody could fake that kind of naïveté. And Connor just loved that. He loved her innocence, her ingenuousness. He loved that she'd been completely unconscious of the fact that she had been tossing double entendres his way by the handful. He loved it that she was obviously so inexperienced when it came to matters of a sexual nature.

And he loved her hot, plump pasties, too.

Okay, enough of the pasty jokes, he told himself as he sat back in his chair to watch Winona daintily pour tea from a dainty china teapot into his dainty china cup. His feelings for her, he knew, were anything but a joke, even if they were completely bewildering.

Normally Connor didn't go for innocent and ingenuous

and inexperienced. Normally, he liked his women to be as sexually sophisticated as he was himself. He had a strong sex drive. And he liked for that sex drive to be satisfied quickly and intensely and repeatedly. He didn't have the time or inclination—or the patience, for that matter—to teach someone about what pleased him. He wanted women who already knew how to do that—in spades.

But with Winona… For some reason he felt just the opposite. He liked it that she seemed to have very little knowledge of what went on between a man and a woman. He liked it that she didn't appear to have an extensive collection of lovers in her past. And he liked it that, in spite of all her innocence, ingenuousness and inexperience, she still seemed to catch fire whenever he came within a hundred feet of her.

Hell, he just liked Winona, period. He liked her a lot. And he was decent enough to admit, now, that he had been completely wrong about her from the beginning. Clearly, she had no knowledge of the fact that an illegal operation was running like clockwork right under her nose, in the very business whose reputation she strove to keep stellar. And she certainly wasn't the ruthless madam of a high-class prostitution ring.

What she was, Connor now realized, was a nice, old-fashioned girl. One who couldn't possibly see the illicit goings-on in her restaurant, because she was totally ignorant of the dark side of life. One who lived hopelessly in a world of manners and courtesy that was as old-fashioned as she was herself. One who celebrated a time when femininity and virtue were both highly prized attributes in a woman. One who honored her own femininity and virtue by being absolutely comfortable with both.

One who was being grossly taken advantage of by a man who was being anything but honest with her.

The moment the thought materialized, Connor pushed it brusquely away. He'd take care of that soon, he promised himself. He would. As soon as it was within his power to do so, he would tell Winona the truth, and explain why he had been forced to deceive her the way he had been deceiving her. The minute they wrapped up this investigation, he would spill all. Somehow he would make her understand that he'd had no choice but to mislead her. Somehow she would see his side of things, and she wouldn't be mad. Somehow everything would work out.

Because there was something else Connor had become aware of recently. He'd become aware of the fact that he didn't want his time with Winona to end. Not yet, anyway. He liked being a part of her life, enjoyed her company, wanted to get to know her better. Lots better. He'd never met a woman like her before, and he had a strange, inexplicable desire to learn more about her. Her. A nice, old-fashioned girl. An innocent, ingenuous, inexperienced—

The thought got stuck in his brain this time, because he finally realized what he was saying about Winona. Innocent. Ingenuous. Inexperienced.

Completely innocent? he wondered suddenly. Utterly ingenuous? *Totally* inexperienced?

As in…*virginal?*

Was that possible? Was it possible that Winona Thornbury had never been with a man? She was a thirty-eight-year-old woman, he immediately reminded himself. Of course it wasn't possible. What woman could arrive at the age of thirty-eight, in this day and age, and not have experienced that? Even a nice, old-fashioned girl had natural urges and desires. Hell, Connor could tell by the way she looked at him that she had needs. Profound needs, at that. Even all buttoned up and battened down, Winona was obviously a passionate woman. There was no way she would have let those passions go unsatisfied all these years, would she?

Would she?

Then again, there was no denying that she acted so…

And she seemed so… And she gave the impression of being so…

"So, Winona," he said suddenly, startling her enough
that a bit of tea sloshed over the side of the cup as she
poured some for herself, "tell me more about yourself."

She finished filling her cup, then sat down and reached
for her linen napkin, using it to dab at the small brown
stain that had appeared on the linen tablecloth during the
accident. For a long time she focused intently on removing
the immovable stain, and Connor wondered if she was going to pretend she hadn't heard him. He was about to ask
the question again—because, dammit, he intended to satisfy
himself one way or another tonight—when she finally sur-
rendered to the stain and refolded her napkin, placing it
carefully beside her plate.

Then, as she reached for the sugar bowl and took the lid
off, she asked, "Tell you what about myself? I told you all
about myself Monday."

Well, not *quite* everything, Connor thought. She'd totally
bypassed her sexual history, for instance. Of course, it had
just been their first date. Then again, lots of first dates covered past sexual history these days, due to the fact that sex
was a lot more dangerous now than it used to be.

He shrugged, feigning nonchalance. He couldn't very
well ask her point-blank how many lovers she'd had, could
he? Nor could he conceive of a polite way to phrase the
question, *So…anybody popped your cherry yet or what?*

So instead, he only hedged, "How is it that a beautiful,
vivacious, intelligent, virtuous—" okay, so he couldn't
quite leave the innocent thing alone "—woman like you
hasn't been snatched up by some guy a long time ago?"

Instead of being flattered by the question and responding
with a knowing little smile, Winona flinched so violently
that she shot a spoonful of sugar halfway across the dining
room table. And it was big table, too, Connor couldn't help

noting. Which meant she'd put some real effort into that flinch.

"I...I...I...I don't know what you...what you mean," she stammered. And she blushed furiously as she stammered, obviously *very* uncomfortable with the subject matter. The impression was only magnified when she hastily began trying to sweep up the sugar with one hand and succeeded only in scattering it about the table even worse than it was already scattered.

In spite of her obvious discomfort, though, Connor persisted. "I mean how come you've never been married?" he asked again, more specifically this time.

She glanced up at him quickly, then just as hastily dropped her gaze back down to the sugar she was so ineffectually trying to gather. "Who, um, who says I've never been married?"

Whoa, Connor thought. This was news. How had they missed a husband during their investigation of Winona Thornbury? And why did the realization that there was one—or, at the very least, had been one—bother him so damned much?

"You're married?" he asked, his voice sounding flat and empty, even to his own ears.

She threw him another one of those hasty glances, then went back to work on the sugar. This time, she actually managed to collect a few granules, which she flicked impolitely into her coffee, clearly so annoyed now by the conversation that she had completely forgotten her manners.

"No, I'm not married," she told him.

And just like that, the Earth began to rotate normally on its axis again, and Connor remembered to breathe.

She continued to focus on the sugar as she added, "Do you honestly think I would have been...kissing you...this week if I were a married woman? You did, after all, just say that I was virtuous."

Yeah, but are you a virgin? he wanted to demand. Instead he told her, "No, I don't think you would have been kissing me if you were married. You just threw me for a loop there for a minute, that's all."

"I do sincerely apologize for the loop throwing," she said, obviously trying to evade the subject. And she still wasn't looking him in the eye.

"Are you divorced?" Connor asked.

She didn't even look up at him this time. "No. I don't believe in divorce. I only believe in marrying out of love. Real love. True love. Love that never dies. Marrying for that kind of love makes divorce unnecessary."

Oh, man, he thought. That must mean... Very softly he asked, "You're widowed?"

She shook her head and sighed heavily. "No. I'm sorry. I didn't mean to mislead you. I've never been married, Connor."

He hesitated only a moment before asking, "Because you've never been in love? Real love? True love?"

Very, very softly now, she said, "I didn't say that." After a moment—and another one of those hasty glances in his general direction—she added, with a bit more fortitude, "I've been in love. I've just never been married."

"Then why...?"

"The not-being-married part wasn't through any choice of my own," she told him. "Had things worked out the way I'd planned for them to work out years ago, I would indeed be a married woman right now."

And why did she actually sound sad about such a prospect, instead of wistful? Connor wondered. She'd just said she'd been in love. Didn't that mean she wished she'd married the guy? Who else would she have been in love with? And why would it make her sad to be married to him now?

"I don't understand," he told her.

"I was engaged to be married once," she replied simply. At her frankly offered announcement, the Earth seemed to tip again beneath Connor. It was the strangest sensation. Although nothing in his immediate reality had shifted, at the realization that Winona had once loved another man and had intended to tie her life to his forever, everything seemed to change.

And then Connor's phrasing struck him. Winona had loved *another* man, he repeated to himself. That made it sound as if he considered her fiancé to be a rival of sorts. And that made no sense. Not only was the other guy obviously no longer a part of her life, but why should Connor consider him a rival? A rival for what? Her affections? He still wasn't sure he wanted her affections. Certainly not the way that other guy had had them. Yeah, Connor wanted Winona. But there was no way he wanted to *marry* her.

He shook the dilemma off quite literally and turned his attention back to her. "You were going to get married to someone?" he asked.

She nodded and gazed blindly down into her coffee. "That was my plan, yes."

"So what happened?"

She finally did meet Connor's gaze then, dead-on. But her expression offered nothing as to what she might be thinking or feeling, and all he could do was gaze back in silence.

"I believe," she said quietly, "that the colloquial phrase for what happened would be, 'He dumped me.'"

Connor's mouth dropped open in astonishment at that. *He* had dumped *her?* he thought. How was that possible? What the hell kind of idiot man dumped a woman like Winona? That was nuts. "He what?" he asked.

"Stanley left me for another woman."

The information still wouldn't quite gel in Connor's brain. What other woman? How could there even *be* another woman when a man had Winona Thornbury warming his bed? Then again, she still hadn't said anything to suggest she wasn't a virgin, so maybe she *hadn't* warmed ol'

Stanley's bed. Maybe that had been ol' Stanley's problem with the relationship in the first place. Still, even at that, a man would have to be crazy to let a woman like Winona get away. Hey, there was a lot more to a relationship than hot sex, after all.

And Connor could not *believe* he had just thought such a thing.

Even more amazing, he couldn't believe he believed it. But he suddenly realized that he did. He believed it most sincerely. For the first time in his life, Connor could honestly see how there might be more to a relationship than hot sex. Because here he was, having a nice time with Winona—having had a nice time with Winona on more than one occasion now—and they hadn't even come close to having sex, hot or otherwise.

Wow. What a concept. Who knew?

As he basked in this newly discovered knowledge, and before he could say anything else and without even having to ask for details, Winona suddenly started talking again, about the very thing Connor found most interesting—her relationship with the jerk who had dumped her. He settled back in his chair to listen. 'Cause this, he had to hear.

Eight

"**I** met Stanley when I was twenty-six," she said, turning her attention now back to her teacup. "We dated for three years before becoming engaged. Then, one week before the wedding, he left me."

Okay, so that answered one question, Connor thought. Probably. Because he couldn't imagine anyone dating for three years and not becoming physically intimate. Certainly they would have made love once they were engaged, wouldn't they? Even a nice, old-fashioned girl wouldn't have held out once she had a ring, albeit engagement only, on her finger, right? Winona must not be totally inexperienced, if she'd been engaged to the guy.

Still, this was Winona they were talking about, he reminded himself. So until she spelled it out for him, Connor couldn't be certain about anything.

He wanted to say something, at least offer some vague platitude in response, because he honestly wasn't sure what else to say. But Winona began speaking again, offering more details, so he only remained silent and listened.

"Stanley was very special to me," she said.

Okay, so maybe that was one detail he could have lived without.

"He was my…my first. Lover, I mean."

And maybe that detail wasn't as important as Connor had originally thought it, either, even if she had just spelled out exactly what he'd wanted to know. Because the thread of jealousy that wound through him at hearing it was a totally unfamiliar, totally unpleasant thing for him to feel. He'd never been jealous of any woman's previous sexual encounters. Not until now. But the thought of Winona with another man—yes, *another* man, dammit—even if she had met him years before Connor had even entered the picture… Well, it just felt lousy, that was all.

"I'd never…with anyone before him," she continued. "And I haven't…with anyone since, either. Even with Stanley, I didn't… I couldn't… Until we were practically married. It was three weeks before the wedding when I finally… When we finally…"

"I understand, Winona," Connor said. "If you're uncomfortable talking about it…"

"No, it isn't that," she said quickly, glancing up to look at Connor for the first time since she began talking about her broken engagement. And she seemed to be as surprised by her comment as Connor was. "In fact, I want to tell you about it," she told him. "I think I need to tell you about it. I think it's important that you understand."

"Understand what?" he asked.

She eyed him levelly. "How important that kind of relationship is to me. I can't be casual about…you know."

"Sex?" he asked frankly.

She squeezed her eyes shut tight, and two bright spots of color darkened her cheeks. "Yes," she said softly. "That. It isn't in my nature to be casual about it."

"I didn't think you were casual about it," he told her.

"I know. But you and I are of entirely different generations, Connor, and I know you feel differently about this than I do. Stanley and I were practically… We'd made a commitment to each other. What I, at least, considered to be a life-long commitment. I thought he and I were going to be together forever. Otherwise, I never would have…"

"So what happened?" Connor asked. He realized now that he very much wanted to hear the end of the story, even with the presence of that idiot Stanley in it.

"Stanley bought a computer," she said.

Connor waited for her to continue, to offer some kind of clarification for her comment, because he sure as hell couldn't see any connection. When she offered nothing more, though, he spurred gently, "And that would be significant because…"

Winona sighed heavily and turned her attention back to the spilled sugar. Instead of trying to clean it up, however, she only began to drag her index finger through it, making an idle design on the tablecloth. She watched the movement of her own hand blindly as she said, "He went online and found an entire world on the Internet that didn't exist in Bloomington."

"What kind of world?" Connor asked. Hell, what could ol' Stanley have found online that he didn't already have right here?

"He met a woman in a chat room," Winona said.

Oh, *that* kind of world, Connor thought. Yeah, a guy would be hard-pressed to find that world here in Bloomington. Unless he went to Winona's restaurant, of course, and picked up one of the phones. But that was neither here nor there.

"What I didn't realize when Stanley and I finally became intimate," she continued, "was that he had met this woman online, and was having… I guess you'd call it a cyber affair with her. I think it was what made him press for a more…"

She cleared her throat delicately. "A more…physical relationship with me. She brought out feelings in him…needs in him…that he wasn't able to satisfy with her, because she was in another state. So he turned to me for that, even though he knew I wanted to wait until we were married."

Something chilly crept up Connor's spine. "He didn't force you to…?"

"No," she said hastily. "It wasn't like that at all. I did want for Stanley and me to get more…to have…that. I was looking forward to it. I'd just really wanted to wait until our wedding night. But one evening he came to my apartment, and he brought me flowers, and he cooked me dinner, and he played soft music, and we danced, and…" She sighed almost wistfully. "He seduced me. It was actually very romantic. And quite pleasant."

That was another detail Connor could have lived without. But he said nothing that might have halted her story. Instead, he only waited to hear the rest.

"Oh, yes," she continued quietly. "It was very pleasant indeed."

Yeah, yeah, yeah, Connor thought. Just get on with it.

"In fact, it was *so* pleasant," Winona said, "that it happened several times after that, and really, I discovered so many things about myself during those two weeks. If nothing else, Stanley taught me—"

"So what went wrong?" Connor interrupted. There were just some details best left out, he thought.

Winona looked at him with some confusion for a moment, then, "Oh," she said. "Oh, yes. I'm sorry. As I said, by then he'd met a woman online and was carrying on with her. I suppose he'd hoped that when the two of us became physically intimate, it might satisfy the…urges…she had aroused in him. Evidently, though, he needed something more."

Idiot, Connor thought.

"He needed something I couldn't give him. I wasn't enough for him."

Idiot, idiot, Connor thought.

"Because one morning a week before the wedding, I woke up to find a note tucked into my mailbox. It was from Stanley. At first, I thought it was going to be some little love note from him, telling me how much he adored me, and how complete I'd made him feel. Instead, he told me that what he and I shared wasn't at all... Well, let's just say I didn't live up to his expectations."

Idiot, idiot, idiot, Connor thought.

"And he said he was sorry," she went on, "but he was moving to Racine, Wisconsin, to pursue a new life with his cyber love. I never heard from him again. I assume they lived happily—or something—ever after. As for me, I had to call nearly a hundred wedding guests and explain what had happened, then return sixty-five gifts that had already arrived."

"Oh, Winona..."

She closed her eyes for a moment, then opened them. "It wasn't a completely horrible experience. I learned some very important things from Stanley."

"Yeah, number one being that he was a complete jerk," Connor offered.

She smiled a bit sadly. "Yes, that was indeed the first lesson. The second was that what could...could...*ignite* between a man and a woman completely surpassed anything I could have ever imagined. And the third, most important, lesson was that one about the cow."

Okay, now Connor was hopelessly lost. "The, um, the cow?" he asked.

She nodded. "About how men don't buy it when they can get the milk for free."

"Oh, *that* cow," Connor said. "Actually, that's a misconception. Men will buy just about anything if you get them in the right frame of mind."

She said nothing in response to that, only gazed at the spilled sugar and her quickly cooling tea for several long, silent moments. Then suddenly, as if she were snapping out of a dream, she sat up straight and looked Connor right in the eye.

"Goodness," she said. "I don't know what's come over me tonight, to be discussing my relationship with Stanley. It's not exactly a polite topic of conversation, is it?"

Maybe not, Connor thought. But it was definitely an interesting one.

"I apologize for being so rude," she told him.

"You weren't being rude, Winona," he said, smiling. "You just needed someone to talk to."

She smiled back. "Thank you."

"For what?"

"For understanding."

Connor shook his head. "Hey, I don't understand anything about this. The fact that Stanley preferred some cyber babe over you, Winona... The fact that he preferred *any* woman over you..." He paid her the great honor of being completely baffled by Stanley's choice. "It makes no sense to me, that's all. And if Stanley felt that way," he continued, "then there was no way he was the right man for you. Hell, he wasn't a man at all."

She blushed becomingly, and her smiled brightened. "Well, I do agree that he wasn't the man for me. In hindsight, I'm glad I didn't marry him. He obviously didn't love me the way he should have. And it's not as though I'm pining away for him, is it? I've moved on."

But did she still love him? Connor wondered. She had, after all, said she would only marry out of real, true love. Love that lasted forever. Was that what she had felt for the dishonorable Stanley? It must have been, if she'd agreed to marry him. And if that was the case, was she lost for good?

But lost to whom? Connor asked himself. Once again, he'd chosen a strange way to collect his thoughts.

"Would you like to take our tea out onto the balcony?" she asked suddenly.

Her question dispelled the tumult of confusion that was wheeling through his head, something for which Connor was grateful, quite frankly. "I didn't know you had a balcony," he said. He had, after all, surveyed the exterior of her home quite extensively, and he couldn't recall a balcony anywhere.

"Well, I suppose 'balcony' is being generous," she said with a smile. "But I do have a little sitting area off my room that's nice for enjoying afters."

The word *afters* probably would have registered on Connor in a salacious way if it weren't for the fact that he never really heard anything after the words *my room.* As far as he was concerned, any chance to get a glimpse of Winona's more personal side was way welcome. And he did recall now a little decklike structure, barely big enough for two, extending from the back corner of the building. That must have been what she was talking about.

"Sure," he said agreeably. "That sounds great. There's supposed to be a full moon tonight, isn't there?"

She nodded. "It should be lovely."

It certainly should, he thought.

He followed her from the dining room through the rest of her home, glimpsing parts of it for the very first time. There was a generously sized living room—furnished in more of that Victorian excess style that she seemed to favor—a small office, only marginally cluttered, what appeared to be a sitting room of sorts, a spare room and, finally, Winona's bedroom.

Like the rest of the house, it was abundantly furnished with floral fabrics and hooked rugs with flower designs spanning the hardwood flooring, and lace curtains fluttering over the windows. The walls were covered with dried flower wreaths, and oil-on-canvas paintings of fair maidens gazing pensively out over grassy meadows. A small writing desk and stool were tucked into one corner, an ornate rocking chair sat in another. Two French doors on the opposite side of the room were closed and covered with more lace, but Winona promptly crossed to them and pulled them open, revealing what was indeed a small, covered sitting area beyond, just large enough for an economy-size wicker chair and settee, both covered with, inescapably, flowered cushions.

But that wasn't what caught most of Connor's attention just then. No, what caught most of his attention just then was the antique sleigh bed of indeterminate size that was, without question, the focal point of the room. At least it was Connor's focal point. Because for some reason, he couldn't quite bring himself to look away from it. Not quite double, not quite single, it would, nonetheless, accommodate two people, provided they slept closely together. Really closely together. Really, *really* closely together.

Gee, funny how the room had grown so much warmer after Winona had opened the doors onto a cool evening. Even though he could feel the kiss of an early autumn breeze on his face, Connor suddenly felt as if he'd walked right into an oven. How odd.

He realized then that Winona had already stepped outside and had placed her cup on the wide railing near the settee. She still stood, though, obviously reluctant to sit on either piece of furniture. Connor sensed her dilemma. If she sat on the settee, she might give him the impression that she wanted to be close to him, which he would naturally take as a romantic overture, and, it went without saying, he would take advantage of it. And if she sat on the chair, she might give him the impression that she feared being close to him, something he would naturally interpret as her desire to be close to him, which he would naturally take as a romantic overture, and, it went without saying, he would take advantage of it.

He smiled. Gee. The night was looking up. Big time.

As he silently crossed the bedroom toward the French doors, Connor couldn't help wondering if Winona were regretting her invitation to have him join her on her balcony. Gosh, he hoped not. Because he was really looking forward to seeing how things were going to turn out.

"It's nice out here," he said as he joined her outside. He couldn't help noticing that she jumped a little bit when he said it. Oh, he did so love having this effect on her.

"Yes," she said shortly. "It is. Nice. Out here, I mean."

Hmm, he thought. He'd reduced her to single syllables. This was getting interesting. Then again, he wasn't exactly being polysyllabic himself now, was he? He smiled. This was definitely getting interesting.

He set his own cup down next to hers, then turned his body to face her, leaning his hip on the railing. A good foot of space separated them, but he could still inhale the sweet lilac scent of her. And in the pale-yellow light that spilled out onto the deck from her bedroom, he could see the way the breeze plucked strands of gold from the tightly wound bun at the back of her head and danced them around her face. He could see the elegant line of her jaw, the blush of pink on her cheek, the berry sheen of her plump mouth.

She was exquisitely beautiful, he couldn't help thinking. Smart, funny, womanly and genuinely sweet. She was everything he should be running away from. Instead, he only wanted to pull her close.

Winona knew immediately after Connor joined her outside that it had been a very bad idea to invite him out here. Honestly, she had no idea what had possessed her to extend such an offer in the first place. This balcony was her private abode, the one place in her house where she could come and feel truly alone and at peace. But now Connor had invaded this place, at her invitation, and she didn't know what to do.

How could she have told him all those things about her relationship with Stanley? How could she have revealed such intimate details of her life to him? She'd never told anyone about her experiences with her ex-fiancé, had never even *wanted* to tell anyone about them. Yet she had spilled it all to Connor without the least provocation. And she simply did not know why.

She'd only known that she did need to tell him, that it was important for some reason that he know how seriously she took such a relationship. Perhaps, deep down, she knew where she and Connor were headed, knew the two of them were destined to end up in the same way she and Stanley had. She knew that, because the feelings she had for Connor made those she'd had for Stanley seem tepid and unreal. She had thought that she loved Stanley. She knew now that she had not. Because now…

Now she knew what it meant to love someone. As crazy as it seemed, at some point over the last few weeks, perhaps before she'd even spoken to him, Winona had fallen in love with Connor Montgomery.

There. She had admitted it. She knew it made no sense. She knew it was foolish. She knew it was unfounded. She knew it was mad. But she also knew it was real. And she knew it would last forever. And that was why she had needed to let him know what kind of woman she was. That was why it had been so important for her to make Connor understand what it meant for her to become as deeply involved with a man as she had with Stanley.

And now Connor did understand. She hoped. Surely he realized now that she would only make love with a man who was committed to her forever. And he knew she would only make that commitment to someone she truly loved. Therefore, if the two of them did follow what was happening between them to its natural conclusion, Connor would know that she loved him. Deeply. Truly. Irrevocably. And she knew—somehow, she *knew*—that he would be honorable enough to respect that.

He would be honorable enough to only make love to her

if he truly loved her, too. If she offered herself to Connor now, after all she had revealed to him, she would be telling him, without words, that she loved him and would remain committed to him forever. And because he understood that now, after all she had revealed to him, he would only accept her offer—would only make love to her—if he could make the same commitment to her in return. Surely he understood that now, she told herself. Surely, she had made that clear. Surely he didn't need for her to spell it out.

Surely, if he made love to her tonight, it would be because he felt the same way for her that she did for him. It would be because he loved her, too. Deeply. Truly. Irrevocably. Otherwise, he wouldn't accept her offer, and he would walk away.

She was still telling herself that when she suddenly felt a soft touch on her face, the merest brush of Connor's fingertips over her cheek. Startled, she turned to face him, and found him gazing at her intently, his blue eyes filled with something she was almost afraid to consider. He understood, she thought as she looked into his eyes. He really did understand everything she had told him, without telling him in so many words. He knew that she loved him. She could see it in his eyes. And she saw something else there, too, something that told her he—

"You are so beautiful," he said softly, almost reverently. "So…" But his voice trailed off before he completed the thought.

As Winona stood there gazing at him in silence, he lifted his other hand now, turning it to brush his bent knuckles along the line of her jaw. Involuntarily she let her eyes flutter closed, so that she might enjoy the sweetness of the gesture more keenly. And when she did, something inside her that she hadn't even realized she was restraining broke free.

A swirl of something wild and wonderful seemed to hum through her entire body as he touched her, coiling tight in some dark place deep inside. Her lips parted to enable her to better breathe, but instead of aiding herself, she somehow only felt more breathless. Again and again, Connor dragged his knuckles tenderly over her cheekbone, along her jaw, down along the column of her throat, until Winona didn't think she could tolerate the sensation any longer. When she finally opened her eyes, it was to find him gazing at her now as if she were the strangest puzzle he'd ever seen. A puzzle he couldn't wait to unlock.

Then he was bending toward her, dipping his head to hers. She knew he was going to kiss her, and she told herself to make him stop, because everything was happening much too quickly. Instead, she tipped her head back a bit and reached a hand toward him, meeting him a little better than halfway.

She knew immediately as she curled her fingers into the soft fabric of his shirt that this kiss wasn't going to be like the others they had shared. And the moment his mouth covered hers, she saw that she was right.

Where before he had only grazed her lips briefly once, twice, thrice, with his own, now he covered her mouth wholly with his in a kiss that was at once generous and possessive. Brazenly he pressed his entire body to hers, looping one arm around her waist to bend her backward as he deepened the kiss. The hand that had so gently grazed her face cupped her jaw firmly now, his thumb cradling her chin as he tipped her head back further still.

Winona gasped at the intensity of his embrace, but instead of retreating from him, she only tightened her hold on his shirt with one hand and pressed her other palm to his shoulder, grasping firmly the hard, heated musculature she encountered there. He was so large, so solid, so… so…so *much,* she thought. She told herself she should be intimidated by him, frightened of him, even. But she was neither of those things. In spite of the tumultuousness of the moment, a strange sort of calm washed over her, as if she were in exactly the place she was meant to be, at exactly the right time. In spite of her apprehensions, right here, right now, with Connor, felt like the most natural place in the world for her.

Unable to tolerate not touching him, Winona curved one hand around the warm skin of his nape, and threaded the fingers of the other up into his straight, silky hair. He seemed to like the sensation, because he accelerated the kiss even more, sinking his tongue into her mouth to taste her more deeply. Winona uttered a wild little sound at the invasion, curling her fingers more tightly over him in response. Connor responded by pulling her body hard against his own, then tilted his head to one side to facilitate his penetration even more.

He seemed to get lost in the kiss after that. Or maybe Winona was the one who got lost. She never was quite sure. Gradually, though, everything around her—everything inside her—seemed to shift and change and meld with Connor. There was only him. Only her. Only the two of them. She wasn't sure how long they stood so entwined, kissing, caressing, exploring each other more completely. But during that time, Winona felt as if she joined with Connor in ways she had never joined with another human being. He seemed to become a part of her, and she of him. And indeed there were times when she wasn't sure which of them was touching her, or him, or them, or…

And then she ceased to think at all, responded only to the myriad sensations unfolding in her mind and body. She dropped a hand to his chest, splaying her fingers open wide over his heart, and was comforted by the ragged, erratic pulse that hammered hard against her fingertips. He was every bit as shaken and tautly strung as she was herself, she thought. And somehow, that made everything all right.

She reacted instinctively after that, moving her hand lower, inverting it so that her fingers tipped downward, pressing the heel of her palm against his rock solid abdomen. She liked the way he felt, the way his body was so much different from her own. He was hard where she was soft, his body solid where hers was giving. They complemented each other so nicely, so naturally, so perfectly.

When she curled her fingers more insistently into his lean torso, he dropped one hand to her waist. He rested the side of his palm on her hip, hooking his thumb around front, settling it at the base of her rib cage. And all the while he kept kissing her, tasting her, consuming her. Winona told herself she should retreat, should pull away, should put a stop to things before they went too far.

But the way he was touching her and kissing her felt so good, she thought. Having him close this way generated things inside her she'd never felt before. She didn't want to retreat or pull away or a put a stop to things. Not yet. There would be time for that soon, she told herself. She would halt him—and herself—before things got out of hand. But right now she only wanted to know more.

His hand at her waist crept higher then, skimming lightly over her rib cage, until he settled his hand just beneath her breast, framing its plump fullness in the el-shape created by the position of his thumb and forefinger. Winona's heart raced at the intimacy of the touch, but instead of shrinking away from him, she automatically arched her body forward. Connor responded by growling something low and incoherent, then covering her breast completely with his hand, closing his fingers possessively over her.

Winona jerked her mouth from his at the contact, gasping her surprise. When she looked up at him, she saw him panting for breath, his cheeks ruddy from his passion, his pupils dilated in need. He met her gaze unflinchingly, but he didn't remove his hand. Instead he only closed his fingers even more possessively over her, pressed his palm more intimately against her. Winona's breathing, too, was rapid and irregular, and she imagined her face reflected her emotions as his did. For a long moment neither of them moved. Connor kept his hand right where he had placed it, and Winona did nothing to remove it.

Then, in one deft, smooth move, he opened his fingers and closed them again, more tightly this time, grasping her breast even more firmly. Winona's eyes fluttered closed, and she twisted the fabric of his shirt in her hands. Somehow she pulled him closer to her, when she'd thought he was as close as he could be. She sensed, more than saw, Connor dip his head toward her again, only this time he buried his face in the tender, fragrant skin of her neck.

As he palmed and petted her breast, he dragged his open mouth along the column of her throat, and Winona threw her head backward to facilitate his actions. The next thing she knew, he had his hand tangled in her hair, freeing the chignon she had taken such pains to arrange that morning. As her unbound tresses cascaded down toward her waist, she heard him murmur something low and lusty, words she couldn't quite make out, even if she understood their meaning instinctively.

The hand at her breast moved in a different way then, and through the haze of desire that had enveloped her, Winona gradually became aware of the fact that Connor was unbuttoning her dress. Without questioning her actions, she reached for the cameo at her throat and unpinned it, tucking the brooch blindly into her pocket before curving her hands over his shoulders once again. When he'd freed the buttons past her waist, he shoved the garment from her shoulders, skimming it down over her body until it pooled at her feet.

She should have felt shocked and embarrassed, Winona told herself. But the white cotton slip she wore beneath the dress covered nearly as much of her as the dress itself had. Nevertheless, it was one less barrier between them, and she felt the heat of his hand more keenly as he placed it over her breast again, grazing his thumb over the ripe peak in a slow, methodical, maddening, circle.

"Winona," he whispered as he pressed his forehead to

hers, "is what I think is going to happen really going to happen?" His voice was coarse and indelicate and needful and, oh, so very seductive.

She hesitated before answering, not sure what she should say. She wondered again if he truly understood what it would mean for her to let happen what he was suggesting. She wondered if he was willing to make the commitment to her that she had already made to him, however nebulously.

"I...I don't know," she told him honestly.

He pulled back a bit, gazing down at her face, his expression telling her nothing of what he might be feeling. There was something in his eyes, though, that made her feel hopeful. She wasn't sure why.

"Do you want it to happen?" he asked her.

Unable to lie to him, she slowly nodded. "Yes. I do."

"I do, too."

She swallowed hard. "You know what it means to me, Connor," she said. "You know what kind of woman I am."

His eyes never left hers as he replied immediately, and very resolutely, "Yes. I do."

"And you still want to..."

"Yes," he said. "I want to make love to you, Winona. Very much. More than anything I've ever wanted in my life. Do you want to make love to me?"

Her heart hammered hard in her chest, and the breath left her lungs in one long, low whoosh of air. He hadn't said it, she thought. He hadn't told her he loved her. He hadn't made any commitment to her. But he understood, right? she thought. He must understand. He must know that she demanded a life-long commitment before she would agree to—

"Yes," she said without thinking any further. One could only do so much thinking, she thought. Eventually one must act. And one must grab for one's happiness wherever it might lie.

So she lifted a hand to cup it over his rough jaw, and fastened her gaze to his. "Yes," she told him. "I want to make love with you."

Nine

For one long moment Connor only continued to gaze down at her in silence. Then, very slowly, he bent his body to the side, and reached his hand down toward the hem of her slip. Winona watched with a detached sort of fascination as he bunched the edge of the white garment in his bronzed fingers, wrapping the supple cotton resolutely around his hand again and again, until the garment was pulled taut against her skin. Then slowly, leisurely, oh…so erotically, he began to tug the fabric upward, until Winona could feel the caress of sweet September air on her naked calves.

Then yet higher, over her heated, sensitive flesh, until her knees and thighs felt the cool nuzzle of autumn, as well. When the fabric rose higher still, toward her hips, she turned her face to his, telling herself that this was insane, that they shouldn't do it, and that she must order him to stop. But he dipped his head to hers and kissed her, fiercely, possessively, druggingly, until Winona forgot entirely whatever she had intended to say.

In fact, as he deepened the kiss even more, invading her mouth with his tongue again to taste her as completely as before, she scarcely remembered who or what she was. She scarcely felt mortal at all. No, she was someone else, some-*thing* else, some sentient, fantastical being whose reason for existence was simply to feel the pleasure that Connor Montgomery wrought.

And what pleasure he wrought as he pulled her closer, drawing her slip higher now, up over her thighs and hips, until he had bundled it at her waist. With one arm roped resolutely about her middle, he hauled her close, until her body was completely flush against his. Winona gasped at the utter ownership in the gesture, but inside she thrilled at how desperately he wanted her.

She curled her fingers over his shoulders as he held her, then gasped once more when he dropped his free hand to splay it open over the soft cotton panties hugging her bottom. Then he began drawing rapid circles with eager fingertips over the thin fabric and her delicate flesh. The friction of the sensation sent something inside Winona churning uncontrollably. And when he curved his palm comfortably, confidently, over the lower curve of one buttock, she nearly lost her breath completely. *He shouldn't,* she thought, *he couldn't…he wouldn't…*

He did.

In that next moment, as he bent his body forward over hers, taking even greater possession of the kiss, of Winona, Connor tucked his fingers under the lacy waistband of her panties, spreading his fingers open wide over the bare flesh beneath.

The sensation that shot through her then was filled with fire, with need, with hunger. Never in her life had she experienced such an intense rapacity, such an acute urgency, such a profound desire. Never had she wanted anything—anyone—the way she wanted Connor in that moment.

The fingers cupping over her fanny clutched tighter then,

kneading her sensitive flesh intimately, emphatically, parting and exploring the sensitive cleft between before scooting lower still. Winona's knees buckled beneath her, and it was only with great effort—and the arm still roped around her waist—that she was able to remain standing. And all the while, his fingers crept lower, parting, pushing, invading, until they pulled down the chaste cotton panties to bare her bottom completely.

He dragged the scant garment down over her legs, and Winona obediently stepped out of it. Then he straightened, moving his hand this time between their bodies, skimming it up under her slip, over and between her legs, toward the very heart of her femininity. Before she could utter a word to object—not that she wanted to object, necessarily, but she thought that she probably should—Connor moved his fingers over her, into her, zealously fingering the damp folds of flesh he encountered there. Winona cried out at the contact, clutching him more fiercely, her entire body quaking as he creased her, stroked her, caressed her…and then penetrated her.

And when he did that, Winona knew it was over for her. Because the moment Connor possessed her in such a way, she knew it would never be enough. Not for him, and certainly not for her. With that skilled invasion, he unleashed in her something that had, until now, remained imprisoned, and there would be no way to corral the creature until she had received satisfaction. And satisfaction, Winona knew, would only come in the form of Connor. She would not be satisfied until the two of them finished what they had, perhaps foolishly, begun.

She parted her lips to say something, though truly, she knew not what, but Connor covered her mouth again with his and tasted her deeply, thoroughly, until she went limp in his arms. The twin penetrations of tongue and finger made her entire body shudder in response, and she could only cling to him, her fists curled in the fabric of his shirt, as he continued with his onslaught.

Again and again he kissed her, again and again he moved his fingers over her, inside her. A tight little coil of heat deep within her began to curl tighter still, then tighter, and tighter…and tighter…and tighter. And then, without warning, that coil burst free, blasting heat throughout her body. She cried out again at the eruption, convulsing against Connor. He held her firmly against him as she trembled in the aftermath, as the conflagration gradually quelled, as her body went limp against his. Little by little, her fingers loosened on his shirt, until she felt as if she would simply slide to the floor in a glorious puddle of completion.

But he caught her capably, wordlessly scooping her into his arms and carrying her into her room. She was helpless to stop him when he peeled her slip over her head and tossed it aside, pushed back the covers and laid her gently on the bed. But she felt strangely uninhibited as she lay naked before him. And she shamelessly drank in her fill of him as he stood beside the bed and undressed, his gaze darting over her body, from her face to her breasts to her hips to her legs, then retracing the visual journey all over again.

She let her own gaze wander, too, over every part of him that he revealed. Although she had known he was a big man, she'd had no idea how beautifully formed he was. His shoulders were broad and solid. And his torso was a landscape of rippling musculature covered by a rich scattering of dark hair that arrowed down into the waistband of his trousers. And then he was removing those trousers, too, and his briefs along with them, until he stood before her quite naked, his body gloriously silvered by the moonlight that splashed through the open French doors.

Even that part of him she knew a lady should never find fascinating, but from which she simply could not look away. He was quite aroused by now, she noted, quite... adamant, quite...inflexible, quite...

Oh, my.

"Why, Miss Winona," he said, his voice a velvet caress that parted the semidarkness and undulated over her nude body, "didn't anyone ever tell you it was impolite to stare?"

She smiled, but felt no obligation or desire to direct her attention elsewhere. "It isn't impolite to stare at a thing of beauty," she corrected him. "And you, Connor, are quite the magnificent specimen."

"Magnificent," he echoed with a chuckle. "Oooh, I like the sound of that."

"And I like..." But shyness overcame her sudden burst of boldness, and she found herself unable to finish whatever she had intended to say.

Connor, however, wasn't about to let her off the hook. "What do you like?" he asked when she declined to say. "Tell me, Winona. Tell me everything you want me to do to you."

She shook her head. "I can't."

"Why not?"

"I'm too...too..." But she couldn't even finish that statement. Being the kind of man he was, she was certain he would know exactly what to do.

He watched her carefully for a moment, then smiled. "All right," he finally said as he took a step forward, "then *I'll* tell *you* all the things I want to do to you."

"Oh, Connor, no," she whispered. "Don't do that. You'll embarrass me."

But he only continued to smile as he joined her on the bed. He lay on his side next to her, tangling his legs with hers, pulling her close, until not even the merest breath of air separated their bodies. His flesh was warm satin against her, shadowing her from shoulder to toe, and all she could think about was how much she wanted him. More of him. All of him.

"Will it embarrass you when I tell you I want to kiss you?" he asked softly.

She shook her head. "No."

"Will it embarrass you when I tell you that I want to kiss more than just your mouth?"

Heat seeped through her at his confession, but she shook her head again. "No."

"Will it embarrass you when I tell you that I want to fill my mouth with your breast?"

Now a burst of heat flashed in her belly, but she shook her head once more. "No. It won't."

"Will it embarrass you when I tell you that I want to fill my mouth with other parts of you, as well?"

His comment puzzled her. "Other parts?" she asked. "What other parts?"

Her confusion must have amused him, because Connor began to chuckle in earnest then, a dark, rich sound full of promise.

"You don't know what I'm talking about, do you?" he asked.

She shook her head, having no clue.

His smile grew broader. "You really don't have any idea?"

She shook her head again. "No. I'm sorry. I don't."

His grin now grew absolutely predatory. "Don't be sorry," he told her. "I'm sure as hell not."

"Connor..." she said, confused by what he was saying. Or, more specifically, by what he was *not* saying.

"Just wait," he told her. "You'll see."

And before she could ask him what he meant, he was kissing her again, rolling her backward onto the bed, until she felt the cool crush of the sheets on her heated back. As promised, he kissed her, deeply, masterfully, then he moved his mouth to graze her cheek, her jaw, her throat. Sighing,

Winona threaded her fingers through his soft hair, marveling at the silkiness. Connor dipped his head lower with every brush of his mouth over her skin, until she felt the flick of his tongue over the ripe peak of her breast.

And then he was indeed filling his mouth with her, sucking hard on her tender flesh. And then her heart was beating faster, and her breath was coming more raggedly, and her blood was racing through her veins at a dizzying speed. He held her breast firm in one hand as he tasted her again and again, each pull of his mouth more demanding than the one before. Winona tightened her fingers in his dark hair, holding his head in place as he nuzzled her, suckled her, consumed her. Then, suddenly, his mouth was gone, and he was moving his head lower, over her flat torso, tasting her navel as he passed it.

For a moment she wondered what he was doing. Then she felt his hands at the insides of her thighs, urging them open. He reached for a throw pillow that had been pushed to the foot of the bed and shoved it under her bottom, forcing her hips higher. When Winona finally glanced down to see what he was up to, she saw his dark head duck between her legs, and then—

Oh! Oh, *then!* Oh, good heavens! She felt the merest flick of his tongue against her, once, twice, three times, then a more thorough, more maddening taste. Again and again he stroked his tongue over her, even opened her with his fingers to sip at her more thirstily. And all Winona could do was gasp for breath and grip the edge of the headboard above her and hold on for dear life as he devoured her.

Just when she thought she would burst from the sensations spiraling through her, Connor pulled himself away and slowly moved his body back up alongside hers. By now, Winona could do little more than lie there, her body slick and slack from its response to his ministrations. But she heard him chuckle, felt him drop a kiss on her shoulder, and she smiled.

"I've never…" she whispered weakly. "No one's ever… I never realized…"

"Shh," Connor said softly against her ear. "We've only just begun, sweetheart. We have so many things to discover together."

She started to reach for him, but he brushed a brief kiss over her mouth and rose from the bed.

"Why…?" she asked.

"I need to take care of something before we go any further," he told her. Then he reached for his trousers and withdrew his wallet, digging in it until he located whatever he had been looking for. Winona watched with mixed feelings as he donned a condom before returning to her bed. But she said nothing, and neither did Connor, and perhaps that was for the best.

When he returned to her, he rolled her to her side away from him, then spooned his body close to hers. She was going to ask him why, then she felt the pressure of his shaft, so ripe and hard, pressing against her bottom, and she understood why. It was exciting this way. It was intoxicating. His hands drifted narcotically over her front as he kissed her shoulder and neck. Then he cupped one breast in sure fingers and slid his other hand down her torso, flattening it over her belly.

Instinctively, Winona lifted her leg and draped it over his thigh, and Connor took advantage of her movement, pressing himself more intimately against her. Before she realized his intention, he was entering her from behind, pushing her body back toward his to deepen his penetration.

Every bit of breath left Winona's lungs in a feverish rush at their joining. Never had she imagined herself capable of such an uninhibited response to a man. Never had she imagined herself making love this way to anyone. Yet with Connor, it all felt right and natural and good. So she nestled her bottom against his pelvis, reveling in the hiss of satisfaction he expelled when she did.

"Oh, yes," he murmured. "Oh, Winona. Oh, you feel so good."

A thrill of triumphant excitement shot through her when she realized she was having the same effect on him that he had on her. She felt powerful. She felt potent. She felt *alive*. Again and again she matched his rhythm, pushing herself backward with every thrust he made forward. And when he dipped his hand between her legs, burrowing his fingers in her damp flesh, she nearly cried out her need for more. His pace grew more rapid, and she reached back between their bodies, matching him, touch for touch. Then, just when she thought she would explode with wanting him, he withdrew from inside her.

She was about to voice her objection when he rolled to his back and pulled her astride him, thrusting up into her again. Winona bucked wildly, intuitively, against him as he filled his hands with her breasts and drove himself in and out of her. For long, wild moments, they coupled eagerly, until, with one final thrust, Connor went rigid beneath her. Winona's own release followed immediately on top of his, and she did cry out this time, because she simply could not keep her feelings inside any longer.

For one solitary, singular moment, they seemed transfixed in time and place. Then Connor's body went lax, and Winona crumpled over top of him. He rolled them both to their sides, facing each other, and pulled her closely, fiercely, to his heart. He buried his face in her hair and mumbled something fierce and incoherent into the tangled tresses. Winona wasn't sure, but she thought he told her he adored her.

And then, before she could stop herself, she mumbled against his chest, "Oh, Connor. I love you, too."

Connor never did fall asleep at Winona's house, even though she slipped into a blissful slumber at his side not long after their second coupling. Funny how panic and terror had a way of keeping a person awake.

He gazed down at the sleeping form beside him, noting the ease with which she cuddled against him, enjoying the warmth of her body pressed to his, marveling at the way he had bunched a handful of her silky hair in one fist, as if he needed to cling to her in whatever way he could.

And the only thought wheeling through his brain, over and over and over again, was, *What the hell have I done?*

Because as he gazed down at the woman who was sleeping so contentedly at his side, Connor realized something that shook him to his very core. He didn't want to let Winona go. Ever. And that, quite frankly, scared the hell out of him.

His first instinct was to bolt. To ease himself carefully out of her bed, get dressed as silently as he could and take off for parts unknown, never to return. He needed to think about this, needed to figure out what the hell he thought he was doing. How could he have made love to Winona when he had no business even talking to her? How could he have let her believe things about him that simply were not true? How could he have allowed her to think he was someone he wasn't? Hell, he hadn't even told her his real name.

Worse, by making love to her, after everything she'd just revealed to him, Connor had led her to believe he cared for her in ways he couldn't possibly care about any woman. He'd let Winona think he loved her. He'd let her believe that the two of them had a future together. A substantial future together. A permanent future together. Because he'd understood enough of what she'd told him about her broken engagement to know that she never would have made love with him tonight if she hadn't thought that was what he was offering her. Love. Commitment. Permanence.

Dammit.

He really was the biggest son of a bitch who ever walked the planet, Connor thought as his panic began to multiply.

He never should have allowed things to go as far as they had with Winona. She deserved a hell of a lot better than him. But he hadn't been able to help himself. He hadn't been able to resist her. When he'd seen her standing outside in the pale light of the rising moon, the wind nuzzling her hair around her face, her blue eyes filled with so much longing... When that ribbon of urgency and hunger had unwound so completely inside him, and he'd realized how badly he wanted her, how badly he *needed* her... When he'd understood that she cared for him the way she did...

Something inside him had just...snapped. He wasn't sure what or why. But in that moment, he had only known he had to make love to her. He *had* to. And damn the consequences, anyway. And now that he had made love to her...

Ah, hell. Now he didn't know what to do. He'd never responded to a woman the way he had responded to Winona. He'd never even come close. Making love to her tonight had been...

He couldn't even think of words to explain it. Indescribable, that's what making love to Winona had been. Her response to him had been incandescent, virtue mixed with desire, innocence mixed with eroticism. And an intuitive passion for which Connor had been completely unprepared. What Winona had lacked in knowledge, she had more than made up for in instinct and enthusiasm. Together, the two of them had generated an explosive reaction.

And that reaction scared him. Because he'd never felt anything like it before.

Damn. He would meet a woman like Winona right when he was living a big, fat lie. What was he supposed to tell her now? She thought he was someone else completely. Hell, she'd just made love with a man whose real last name she didn't even know. She'd all but told him before they made love that she loved him. And as if that hadn't been enough, she'd gone and spelled it out for him in the aftermath. She'd said it not once but twice. The first he might have been able to dismiss as careless words uttered in the heat of passion. But the second time...

The second time they had been cuddling and coherent, and she had looked him right in the eye and said, "I love you, Connor," before dipping her head to his chest and falling asleep.

And the thing of it was, he didn't *want* to dismiss her words. He was *happy* that she loved him. But God help him, he hadn't been able to say the words back to her. Because he just didn't know if he felt the words. He'd only been in love once before in his life. And it hadn't been anything like this. That time had been anxious and worrisome and gut-wrenching and even horrible at times. With Winona the things he felt were good. They were warm and tender and decent. He felt happy with Winona. So it couldn't be love, right? It had to be infatuation.

Hell, he honestly wasn't sure he was capable of feeling love anymore, not after what happened the first time. Not after his feelings had been trampled in the dirt the way they had. Certainly, he didn't see himself getting tied down to anyone anytime soon. Not even Winona. Even if she had done a damned good job of obliterating the image of nearly every other woman he'd ever known from Connor's mind. Even if he had absolutely no desire to see anyone else at the moment. Even if he couldn't really envision himself with anyone other than her for the rest of his life....

Run, he told himself again. *Beat it. Hie thee hence.* That was what he always did after he'd made love to a woman. He told her that what the two of them had just shared had been phenomenal, then he kissed her goodbye, and then he left. And those women never minded. They never expected him to hang around. A couple had flat-out shown him the door when they were finished, without so much as an "I'll call you."

But Connor had never minded. Sex had never been anything more to him than a way to let off steam and satisfy a few urges. A natural response to a natural instinct. And that was what it had always been to the women in his life, too.

Until now.

Now he'd gone and bedded a woman who had feelings for him. And for whom he had feelings himself. And he was shocked to realize that, with Winona, he didn't want to run. He didn't want to beat it. He didn't want to hie himself anywhere.

So instead, he only nestled his body closer to hers, pulling her nearer, tucking her head beneath his chin. He knew he wouldn't be sleeping tonight.

But he'd be damned if he would run.

Ten

As the fates—who were doubtless wetting themselves with laughter over Connor's predicament—would have it, the Bloomington cops got a very nice break in the Winona's prostitution case the following morning. A really good break, too, one that would enable them to close in on the restaurant perhaps as soon as the following day, once they got things organized.

But Connor had to leave the investigation to local boys that day—and that night. And in spite of all the hours he'd clocked on the investigation, he was perfectly happy to sacrifice the arrest. The last place he wanted to be when it went down was at Winona's, seeing her face as the cops rolled into her establishment like locusts, making arrests and closing her down until further notice. He wanted to be able to identify himself to her as a cop, and explain himself and his actions over the last few weeks, before she saw him wearing a blue windbreaker and wielding a Glock. Before she saw him busting people in her restaurant, and drew her own—erroneous—conclusions.

Especially since he still couldn't say exactly how erroneous her conclusions would be.

Because once Winona found out who and what Connor really was, she would conclude that he had been lying to her since the day they met. And, of course, she would be right. She would conclude that he was not the person she had thought him to be. And, of course, she would be right. She would conclude that many of the things he had said to her were grounded in total fantasy. And, of course, she would be right. She would conclude that he was a big, fat, lousy, son of a bitch heel. And, of course, she would be right.

She would conclude that he didn't care about her. And there, at least, she would be wrong. Dead wrong.

Because Connor did care about Winona. In ways he had never cared about anyone before. In ways he had never thought he *could* care about anyone. Those feelings had only multiplied after the night the two of them had spent together. Although he never had really slept the night before, he had dozed once or twice, and enjoyed some very nice dreams. And as the first rays of sunlight had spilled into Winona's bedroom through the still-open French doors, he had watched her awaken in his arms, bit by bit. And he had felt himself coming apart inside, bit by bit.

Because as he had watched her eyes flutter open and her lips part for her first conscious breath, as he had enjoyed the soft skim of her hair gliding silkily over his naked body, as he had felt the heat of her body suffusing his... Well. It had hit him in an almost blinding shock of awareness that he wanted to wake up in such a way every morning. Every morning for the rest of his life. And he hadn't known what to do.

So he had made love to Winona again, slowly, carefully, thoroughly. And then he had told her he needed to leave, to go to work, and she had nodded her understanding and smiled. She had asked if she would see him tonight. He had told her no, he had a previous engagement. Her smile had fallen some when he said it, as if she feared he might not be telling her the truth. Then she had told him that that was okay, she had an engagement herself that night, and wouldn't be home until late, anyway.

And something inside Connor had grown chilly then, when he realized just how many lies there were between them.

Ironically, though, Connor had been telling Winona the truth that morning. He *did* have a previous engagement tonight. A real engagement, too—the social kind. The kind you had to write on your calendar months in advance. The kind you only got allowed into with an engraved invitation. The kind that had fine food and wine. The kind where you had to wear a monkey suit. The kind where you had to watch every damn word that came out of your mouth to make sure you never said the wrong thing—because if you did, your great-aunt Pearl on your mother's side would whup you upside the head, but good.

The kind your great-aunt Pearl on your mother's side held once a year and expected *everybody* on your mother's side to attend *or else.*

Nobody said ''No'' to Auntie Pearl's invitations. Nobody. Which was how Connor now came to be wearing a damn monkey suit on his day off—his dark blue with a wine-colored tie, because it was his most conservative, and Auntie loved conservative. And it was how he came to be standing in a room filled with people, some of whom just so happened to be his four brothers and one sister and their assorted dates/fiancé(e)s/escorts/what have you. And it was how he came to be feeling restless and uncomfortable because he really wanted to be with Winona instead.

But he couldn't turn down Auntie's invitation—'cause *nobody* said no to Auntie Pearl. Or else. And he couldn't have brought Winona with him, either, even if she hadn't had a previous engagement herself, even though his engraved invitation had included the engraved words "and guest." Because if he had brought Winona as his guest, she would have found out that he wasn't really Connor Montgomery, Bloomington businessman, but was instead Connor Monahan, Marigold vice cop. And—call him an alarmist—that just might have caused her to start asking questions he still wasn't prepared to answer.

Oh, what a tangled web we weave, he couldn't help thinking. He would have finished the adage, but he wasn't sure how it went after that. He did know, though, that the last word was *deceive.* It was, after all a word with which he'd had more than a nodding acquaintance for quite some time now.

He sighed as he shoved the troubling thought aside and did his best to focus on the here and now. Ironically, both of his parents had been excused from Auntie Pearl's big bash, because even Auntie didn't expect them to get on a plane and fly up from Ocala for her annual Autumn Affaire. Well, Auntie *expected* them to, but she didn't get miffed when the elder Monahans weren't able to make it. Well, not *too* miffed, anyway. Not really. Just because she took it out on the rest of the Monahan clan by making them eat shrimp puffs and miniquiches and drink wine out of pansy little glasses, that didn't mean anything, right?

Right.

At any rate, now Connor found himself standing in the ornate ballroom of the expansive estate Auntie had called home since marrying his late uncle Holman nearly sixty-five years ago, at the tender age of sixteen. Auntie had been sixteen, at the time, not Uncle Holman. Uncle had been fifty-two. But that was another story. Now Auntie lived alone, save her personal trainer, Helmut, in the vast, Victorian mansion surrounded by towering oaks and maples, perched on a green, grassy hill in the middle of one hundred green, grassy acres of a green grassy farm, midway between Bloomington and Marigold…in the bog down in the valley-o.

A string quartet played in one corner of the ballroom, and scores of people mingled about, either dancing or drinking or snacking on canapés that looked as if they would make great ammunition when flung from the end of one of those little forks Connor had no idea what to do with. On one side of him stood his brother Rory, who was cooing softly to his fiancée things Connor was certain he didn't want to hear. On his other side, his sister Tess was murmuring something undoubtedly equally cloying to *her* fiancé. And Connor could think of nothing worse than being caught in the middle of so much mushy, gushy drivel. In a word, ick.

Man. The Monahans were dropping like flies. Tess had started it a few months ago by getting herself imaginarily knocked up with a nonexistent mob baby, something that had brought out the protective instincts in Will Darrow, who just so happened to be the best friend of Finn Monahan, the oldest Monahan brother. Then Will's protective instincts had turned into altogether different instincts, and Tess had just recently discovered that she was very truly pregnant with a very existent, nonmob baby—Will's baby, to be precise.

Fortunately, Will had done right by Tess. Not only had he had the decency to propose marriage to her, but he'd had the good sense to fall head over heels in love with her, too. Convenient, that, seeing as how the five Monahan brothers would have really hated to kick Will's ass after him being such a good friend for so many years. Now that wouldn't be necessary, because come November, he'd be making an honest woman out of Tess, and Tess would be making an honest man out of Will. And Connor was certain that the two of them would live happily ever after.

But then, no sooner had Tess and Will gotten things settled than Connor's older brother, Sean, had mixed himself up with Marigold's local "free spirit"—read "oddball"—Autumn Pulaski. Somehow Sean had lost a bet—or maybe he'd won it; Connor honestly couldn't remember now—and had ended up dating Autumn for longer than her proscribed lunar month—it was a long story. Now the two of them were planning to marry in December. And they, too, Connor was sure, would get completely mired down in all that happy-ending stuff.

And then the minute that had all begun to settle down, Connor's older brother, Rory—*Rory,* the epitome of the "absentminded professor" if ever there was one—had gone and fallen in love, too. Hell, Connor would have sworn Rory didn't even know *how* to fall in love. His brother's brain was so crammed full of historical dates and data, Connor wouldn't have thought there was room in there for him to even notice the existence of a beautiful woman, let alone end up proposing marriage to her. But in two months' time, Marigold, Indiana's, resident librarian, Miriam Thornbury, would become Mrs. Rory Monahan. Who would have ever tho—

Thornbury, Connor thought again as panic seized him. Oh, God. Rory's fiancée's last name was Thornbury, just like Winona's. At the very back of his brain, he'd probably had that knowledge for some time, but he honestly hadn't made the connection until now. He'd only met Rory's fiancée a couple of times, and he hadn't really paid attention to her last name, having enough trouble keeping women's first names straight in his head. Until now, he'd only thought about Rory's fiancée, Miriam, as either Rory's fiancée, Rory's fiancée, Miriam, or just plain Miriam. He hadn't thought of her in terms of Thornbury. But now that he did...

Oh, no. No, please...

"So, Miriam, can I ask you a personal question?" he

said suddenly, interrupting whatever maudlin little exchange she and Rory were still indulging in.

The cooing lovers halted their mushy stuff long enough to turn and gaze at Connor as one. Rory, dressed in a suit much like Connor's, peered at him through his horn-rimmed glasses, his black hair rumpled, his blue eyes only vaguely registering the fact that someone other than Miriam even existed in his universe. Miriam, dressed in a short, strapless, black velvet number with her dark-blond hair tumbling over her bare shoulders—and looking nothing like Connor figured a librarian should look—seemed equally perplexed by Connor's sudden appearance in her otherwise warm, fuzzy, Rory-oriented world.

"Hmm?" she asked vaguely. Then, with a brief shake of her head, she seemed to come around. "I mean…what question?"

Connor noted her blue eyes and the dark-blond hair again, the full mouth and high cheekbones, and boy, did he see a resemblance to Winona in that moment. Or maybe, hopefully, he was only imagining that, he thought. Maybe the two women didn't know each other from Adam. Or Eve. Whatever.

"Do you, ah…have any brothers or sisters?" he asked her.

Her expression would have been the same if Connor had just asked her to recite the Preamble to the American Constitution from memory. As did Rory's. Then again, Rory *could* recite the Preamble to the American Constitution from memory. But that was beside the point, and Connor pretended not to notice that his brother and his brother's intended were both looking at him as if he were nuts.

"Why do you ask?" she asked.

Connor feigned indifference, even managed to force a shrug that he was sure was sort of convincing. "Just curious."

"Well, I have a big sister," she said. "Her name is Winona. She lives not far from here, in fact. In Bloomington."

Oh, *dammit.*

"She owns a wonderful restaurant there," Miriam added.

Double dammit.

"One called, appropriately enough, Winona's," she finished with more than a touch of pride lacing her voice.

Dammit, dammit, dammit.

"Does she?" Connor asked, hoping nobody noticed that his entire reality was about to come crashing in on him. Hooboy. This was just what he needed. Until recently he had been looking to bust Rory's future sister-in-law for pandering and God only knew what other crimes. What were the odds on *that?*

Naturally Connor knew now that Winona was innocent of any crimes, which was mighty convenient, all things considered. But there was still that small matter of his current—and future—situation with Winona. No matter how things turned out with her—and truly, Connor still didn't know how things with Winona were going to turn out—he was going to have a tie to her for the rest of his life, in the form of her sister, his future sister-in-law.

Not to mention Connor's future sister-in-law was going to want to thump him, but good, no matter how things turned out, once she found out he'd initially been investigating her sister for pandering and peddling flesh and any number of other licentious crimes. Not to mention that, if Connor broke Winona's heart, his future-sister-in-law was going to want to thump him even better. Not to mention that Rory was going to be torn between the feelings of his new sister-in-law, Winona, or standing up for his blood relation, Connor.

Gee. Talk about being the family who put the *fun* in dys*func*tion…

"Funny you should ask about Winona tonight," Miriam piped up again. "Because your aunt Pearl hired her to cater this party. When she comes out from the kitchen again, I'll introduce you.''

Out from the kitchen? Connor thought frantically. *Again?* he thought even more frantically. Winona was here at his aunt's house? Now? He had simply lucked into missing her so far? He could stumble upon her at any minute?

Dammit, dammit, dammit, DAMMIT.

Without thinking, Connor grabbed his brother's arm and pulled him close, then steered him out of Miriam's earshot. ''Look, whatever you do,'' he whispered anxiously, ''do *not* introduce me to Miriam's sister, okay? And if Winona does see us together, you are *not* to introduce me as Connor Monahan, your brother.''

''What are you talking about?'' Rory asked, looking vaguely horrified by his brother's sudden attack of amnesia. ''Of course you're my brother. Of course you're a Monahan.''

''Not tonight, I'm not,'' Connor insisted. ''Not to the caterer. And somehow you've got to keep Miriam from mentioning me to her sister.''

Rory expelled a confused chuckle. ''What's Winona got to do with anything? Why are you acting this way?'' He reached for Connor's drink. ''I think you've had enough, little brother. I'm cutting you off.''

''Are you nuts?'' Connor asked, holding his drink close. ''I need this now more than ever.''

Rory eyed him with much confusion. ''You still haven't told me what Winona's got to do with anything.''

''She just can't know who I am, that's all.''

''Why not?'' Rory asked. ''She's not one of your criminals. She isn't…'' He halted abruptly, his expression changing drastically. ''Don't tell me you're investigating Winona for something.''

Connor said not one word, but only gazed at his brother solemnly.

Rory emitted another one of those strange, uncomfortable chuckles. "But she's…she's… Connor, she's as pure as the driven snow! She can't possibly be guilty of a crime."

"I know that," Connor said. "Don't you think I know that?" Before he could stop himself, and without considering the implication behind his words, he added, not a little frantically, "And even if I hadn't already known it, I sure as hell would have realized it after what happened last night."

Now Rory eyed him with much suspicion. "What happened last night?"

So much for being pure as the driven snow, Connor thought, biting back a wince. "I can't talk about it. Not now. Not yet."

"This is why you were in her restaurant last month, when Miriam and I were there, isn't it? Because you're investigating her. What on earth has she done?" Rory demanded. "No, wait a minute," he immediately backpedaled. "What is it you think she's done? Because I can tell you right now, Connor, the woman is harmless."

"I can't discuss it," Connor said. "I know she hasn't done anything. But right now, she can't know…"

"What?" Rory asked.

"She can't know her restaurant is under investigation."

"*What?* Under investigation for what?"

"I can't talk about it, Rory. Not yet. Just don't let her know who I am." He darted his gaze quickly around the room. "In fact, I have to get out of here. This place is crawling with Monahans. And if she finds out who I really am…"

"Auntie will never forgive you if you leave before dinner," Rory said.

"I know."

"If she gets hold of you, she'll whup you upside the head. But good."

"It's a chance I'll have to take."

"But—"

"Rory, I have to go. Give my best to Auntie, and tell her something came up. Something work related. She loves that cop stuff I do. She'll understand. Tell her it was a triple murder. She'll like that."

"You work vice," Rory reminded him.

"Then tell her it's the biggest heroin bust the state of Indiana has ever seen, and that I'll probably have to draw my weapon, and maybe even fire off a shot or two. It won't go over as well as a triple murder, but it'll have to do."

"But, Connor—"

"I have to go," he said again, cutting his brother off.

And then he made good on his assurance by bolting from the room without a backward glance. He didn't stop moving until he was seated at the wheel of his car, and realized belatedly that he was still gripping the cut crystal tumbler that held his Scotch and water. Hastily, he dumped the drink out the window and set the glass on the passenger seat. Then he ground the key in the ignition and threw the car into gear.

It was only when he hit the city limits of Marigold twenty minutes later that Connor remembered something very important. He remembered that Cullen was still at Auntie's party. Cullen Monahan. His brother. His *twin* brother. His mirror image. And Winona was going to see him there.

Once again without thinking, Connor slammed on the brakes and spun the steering wheel, wreaking a U-turn the likes of which the Indiana State Police would never see again. God willing, they wouldn't see it now, either. He had no idea what he was going to do. But one thought circled around and around in his head, like a great white shark honing in on a fat, naked swimmer. He had to get back to his aunt's house. Now. Because there was one thing Auntie hated more than not having her blood relations show up at her house for a party.

Auntie hated it when all hell broke loose in her home.

* * *

Winona was collecting the last of the canapés from Mrs. Greenup's buffet in the ballroom when she glanced up and saw Connor standing on the other side of the room, chatting with a small group of people. She smiled. Not just because she was delighted to see him, but because she realized then that he hadn't been lying to her, after all, that morning, when he'd told her he had a previous engagement.

He must know Pearl Greenup in some capacity, she thought, and Mrs. Greenup had invited him to her annual soirée, and Connor hadn't been able to turn her down, even if he might have preferred being with Winona tonight. She herself had seen what a formidable force Mrs. Greenup could be. Winona certainly wouldn't have been able to turn down an invitation from the woman. She got the impression that nobody said no to Pearl Greenup. Or else. So she couldn't fault Connor for telling her he needed to be here tonight instead of with her.

She was more than a little relieved to discover that he had told her the truth. Even after the night the two of them had spent together, Winona had been overcome this morning by the inexplicable feeling that he was hiding something from her. She had no idea why she should feel that way, or what he might *be* hiding, but she hadn't been able to shake the feeling, no matter how hard she'd tried.

So she was glad to know now that Connor had told her the truth. Her smile grew even broader as she watched him throw back his head and laugh at something one of the other people had said. He had the most wonderful laugh, she thought. Until now, she'd never heard it so robustly.

Then she saw him loop his arm around the waist of the woman at his side, and her smile fell. And then she saw him dip his head to brush a quick kiss over the woman's mouth and murmur something low that made her smile. And then Winona felt herself withering inside.

No, he hadn't lied about having a previous engagement, she thought again. But there were, evidently, a few other things he had kept to himself. She was beginning to understand now, what he had been hiding from her. She only hoped that the woman with him was a girlfriend and not a wife. Then again, what difference did it make? she thought. What mattered was that he had lied to her. Horribly.

Before she realized what she was doing, Winona found herself striding across the room toward him. She skimmed her hands nervously down over the skirt of her sapphire-blue, Victorian-era gown, then reached up to tuck a few errant strands of hair back into the bun she had fastened at the top of her head. She wondered why she was bothering with her appearance, then realized it was because the woman with Connor was so...so...

Honestly. The woman's attire fairly screamed, "Come and get it!" A brief miniskirt—and was that *leather* it was made of?—and an even briefer vest—with no shirt beneath—and high heels that were more heel than shoe. Her hair was an ebony cascade of silk that rolled down to her hips, and long jet earrings dangled nearly to her shoulders. And all Winona could do was wonder what, if this was the kind of girl he normally dated, Connor could ever have wanted with a nice, old-fashioned girl like her in the first place.

Winona was amazed at how numb and cold she felt inside as she approached the group of people. Somehow, she managed to keep her steps even and unhurried as she drew nearer, and she stopped when there was still a nice polite distance between her and Connor. And in a perfect display of well-bred courtesy, she did *not* wrap her fingers around his throat and squeeze the life out of him when she had the chance—and every right—to do so.

"Why, Mr. Montgomery," she said by way of a greeting. "What a surprise to find you here. I didn't know you knew Mrs. Greenup."

Connor turned at the sound of her voice, but he eyed her with some confusion. If Winona hadn't known better, she would have sworn he had no idea who she was. And in an odd way, he did seem different to her somehow, too. He'd gotten a haircut, she could see, but that was the only real difference she could discern. Nevertheless, he did seem a stranger in many ways.

"I'm sorry," he said, "but I think you must have mistaken me for someone else. My name isn't Montgomery."

She forced a laugh, but something inside her grew a little chilly, because his expression changed not one whit. Surely, he wasn't going to deny that he was who he was, she thought. Surely he wasn't going to deny that he knew her. Especially not after what the two of them had shared the night before. Perhaps this was some kind of morning-after— or, in this case, *evening*-after—game that lovers played with each other, Winona told herself, a game she would naturally know nothing about. She'd only played the game twice, after all. And she'd been terrible at it the first time.

Of course, viewing the evidence currently placed before her eyes, there was every indication to suggest that she hadn't been particularly good at it the second time, either. Because Connor had run right out to find himself a new playmate, hadn't he?

"Oh, stop," she said, hoping she was injecting the right amount of playfulness in her voice even though she was feeling anything but playful at the moment. "You know perfectly well who I am, and perfectly well who you are, too. *Mr. Montgomery,*" she added meaningfully.

But Connor still looked confused. "Well, I'll concede that I do know who *I* am," he said. "But my name is *Monahan,* not Montgomery. I'm Cullen Monahan, to be specific." And he said it with utter conviction and without a trace of humor. So much so, that Winona began to worry.

She couldn't understand it. Either Connor was flat-out

lying to her, or else he'd received a severe blow to the head that had left him utterly disoriented, or else he had an absolute twin wandering around out there in the world.

"Oh," she said, hoping she masked her own confusion. "I…I apologize. You look exactly like someone else. A man of my acquaintance named Connor Montgomery."

Now the man's expression did finally change. He smiled quite happily, looking more like Connor than ever. "I should have realized," he said. "You mean Connor *Monahan,* of course. He's what you might call my evil twin."

"I…I beg your pardon?" Winona stammered.

Now the man laughed. "Sorry. Old joke. No, really, I do have a twin brother named Connor. I'm sure that's who you've mistaken me for. Connor Monahan. Not Connor Montgomery."

Winona shook her head. "No, I'm certain his last name is Montgomery. I know him quite well. And he is most certainly your twin."

The man shook his head, now looking more bewildered than Winona felt. "That's odd," he said. "I've never known Connor to misrepresent himself. You're sure he said his name was Montgomery?"

"Quite sure."

"How strange…" His voice trailed off for a moment, then the man who identified himself as Cullen Monahan lifted his flattened palm to his forehead, and his expression cleared. "Of course. You met him in an official capacity. That would explain it."

"Official capacity?" Winona echoed. "What do you mean?"

"He's a cop," the other man said. "A vice detective for the Marigold, Indiana, Police Department. You must have met him when he was working on a case. He sometimes uses an assumed name for such things."

"A case?" Winona echoed. "A policeman? Marigold?

No, no, no. That's not possible,'' she insisted. ''The man I know is a business executive. He works in Bloomington.''

Cullen Monahan shrugged. ''Then he's not my twin brother.''

''But he is your twin,'' she said weakly.

Cullen Monahan gazed at her with much interest then, as if he thought her a bit…touched. Or perhaps, she couldn't help thinking, his expression was more in keeping with a man who was worried that he had said much too much about something he shouldn't have mentioned at all.

Oh, no, she thought as a heavy weight settled in her midsection. *Connor, please. Please, no…*

What on earth was going on? she wondered. This man said he had a twin brother named Connor. Winona had met a man named Connor who looked *exactly* like this man. They must be one and the same. But why would Connor have given her a false name for his last name? Why would he have told her he was a businessman, when he was, in fact a police detective?

Then Winona remembered something very important. She remembered that Connor Montgomery had never told her specifically what he did for a living. She had simply assumed he was a businessman, and he had never offered her any indication to the contrary, had never suggested to her that he was anything else. He'd never really told her *what* he did for a living, not in so many words. Yet he'd never contradicted her assumption, either.

But why the false name? she wondered further. Why would he lie to her about something like that? Unless…

You must have met him when he was working on a case.

But what kind of case would he be working on that involved Winona? That made no sense. She was the most upstanding, law-abiding citizen around. Might it have something to do with the restaurant? But her business was as upstanding and as law-abiding as she. Why, she never even cheated on her taxes. Never. What on earth could he have to investigate at Winona's? And why hadn't he simply identified himself as a police detective up-front, and asked her any questions he might have? It was almost as if he—

As if he were investigating *her*.

Something hot and unpleasant fired in her belly. That must be it, she thought. For some reason—who on earth knew why?—she was the subject of a police investigation. And Connor Montgomery—no, Connor *Monahan*—was the one who was doing the investigating.

Oh, no, she thought again as that heavy weight descended to the pit of her soul. *Connor, please. Please no…*

That was why he had initially come into the restaurant, she told herself. That was why he had watched her so intently for so long. That was why he had asked her out in the first place. It all made sense now. She'd wondered from the start why he would bother with a woman like her, when he was so clearly suited to another type of woman entirely. And she'd never been able to understand why he kept coming back, when they obviously had nothing in common. And last night…

Oh, heavens, last night. Last night couldn't have meant anything to him. Certainly not what it had meant to her. Last night, he'd simply seen an opportunity—an opportunity she had offered most freely—and had taken advantage of it. What man wouldn't?

Here she'd been thinking last night had been as special to him as it had been to her. Here she'd been thinking that the reason he had made love to her was the same as the reason she had made love to him. Because he loved her. Because he envisioned a future with her. But clearly, he hadn't understood anything of what she'd told him about her broken engagement. He hadn't understood the implications of her avowals. He hadn't realized she had fallen in love him. Not until she had *told* him, she thought. And even then, even after he knew how she felt about him, he'd made love to her again. He'd used her. Then he'd left her.

No wonder he'd had a previous engagement tonight.

Last night she would have done anything for Connor. Last night she *had* done anything for him. She'd given herself over to him completely, in ways she hadn't even known she could give. Because she had loved him. Because she had thought he loved her, too. Because she had been thinking—hoping—that the two of them had a future together. A future that would last forever. She had thought he cared for her. But clearly, he had simply thought what she was offering—and oh, my, how shamelessly she had offered it—was just too good to pass up.

Foolish, foolish Winona, she chastised herself now. When was she going to learn? When would she stop being such a…such a…such a *cow?* Such an easy-virtued, give-it-away-for-free cow?

Men only wanted one thing from women, she reminded herself ruthlessly. And when they got that one thing, they lost all interest in anything more. She never should have given herself to Connor the way she had. She never should have trusted him. She never should have let things go as far as they had.

One thing was certain, she thought. She would never give of herself that way again. Not when it hurt so much to lose it.

Eleven

Winona was so caught up in her sorrow and confusion that she barely heard the soft scrape of sound that heralded the arrival of someone else in the Greenup kitchen right after the guests had seated themselves for dinner. Thinking it was someone who was taking exception to the lack of a saltshaker because they had no idea what to do with a saltcellar, or some such thing, she was surprised to glance up and find Connor standing on the other side of the deserted kitchen, staring at her. Or was it Cullen? she wondered. What had the other man been wearing? She couldn't remember now.

This man—whoever he was—clearly did not have sartorial splendor in mind, however. Because his suit, although it had probably been impeccable when he had donned it, was now in a state of disarray that could only have come about because he had given up all hope of…something. Winona couldn't possibly have known what. Nor, she discovered, did she much care. All she knew was that this

man—whoever he was—had lied to her. Because she saw
then that it was indeed Connor, and not Cullen, who had
entered the kitchen. She knew that, because he gazed at her
with much familiarity. And because her body came alive
the moment she beheld him.

"Hi," he said a little nervously.

"Hello," she replied coolly, clasping her hands together
before her. Whether that was to keep her from wrapping
them around his throat to choke the life out of him or to
keep herself from reaching for him and clinging to him for
dear life she wasn't sure. Either way, though, her reaction
would have been troubling. So she only stood stock-still,
returning his stare, and waited to see what he would say
for himself.

He expelled a long, weary sigh. "Gee, judging by your
reception, I guess it's true," he said.

"What's true?" she asked, even more coolly than before,
clasping her fingers tighter.

Connor took a step toward her, and even though a wide
kitchen island stood between them, Winona instinctively
took a step in retreat. Her response made him halt in his
tracks, but his gaze never left hers as he hesitated, shoving
his hands deep into his trouser pockets. His mouth went
flat, and his eyes darkened angrily. Somehow, though, she
knew the anger was directed at himself and not at her.

"Word has it that you met my evil twin, Cullen, a little
while ago," he began. "And that he volunteered some information about me that he had no business volunteering."

Winona notched her chin up defiantly. "No, you should
have been the one who volunteered it," she said. "And
you should have done so long before now. Long before—"

"Last night," he finished for her.

"Yes."

He nodded almost imperceptibly, then forced a smile that
was in no way happy. "Leave it to an evil twin to mess

things up," he said. But neither of them seemed to find much humor in the statement.

"That's interesting," Winona told him, "because Cullen said that you're the one who's evil."

With his hands still buried deep in his pockets, Connor shrugged halfheartedly. "Yeah, well...tonight I guess I'm kind of inclined to agree with him."

She missed not a beat in rejoining, "So am I."

He studied her long and hard in silence for a moment, as if he were trying to impress her image upon his brain somehow. Then, very, very quietly, he told her, "Winona, I can explain."

"Oh, I don't doubt that at all," she replied, every bit as quietly. "I don't doubt that you'll explain it very well."

He seemed hopeful, eager, for a moment. "Then you'll give me a chance?"

"Of course," she said. "And once you've explained, then we'll part ways and never speak of this unfortunate incident again. In fact, we'll never see each other again. That will make it infinitely easier to keep from talking about it."

His face went pale and slack at her declaration. "That's not..."

He blew out another exasperated breath, then he took another step forward, removing a hand from his pocket, lifting it as if he intended to reach out to her. Winona stepped back in retreat again, but the kitchen counter hindered her progress, and she bumped against it with her fanny. Connor took advantage of the predicament to hasten around the kitchen island and position himself in front of her. Before she had the chance to bolt, he dropped a hand on each side of her, gripping the kitchen counter hard, and effectively penning her in.

His heat and scent seemed to envelope her, and she was immediately carried back to last night, when their naked bodies had been pressed so intimately together in an en-

tirely different fashion. She squeezed her eyes shut tight in
an effort to chase the image away, but it only grew more
graphic, more real. When she opened her eyes again, her
vision was filled with Connor, and, mesmerized, she found
that she simply could not look away. His face was only
inches from hers, and she fancied she could almost see the
dark turmoil swirling in his eyes. His lips parted fractionally, and it was all she could do not to push herself up on
tiptoe and cover his mouth with hers.

Heaven help her, even now, even knowing what she did
about him, she still wanted him. Still needed him. Still
loved him.

Her heart was beating frantically in her chest, and her
breathing had become heavy and erratic the moment he had
penned her in. But he was no less affected than she, she
saw. His own breathing was coming out in rapid, ragged
rasps, and she could see his pulse beating nimbly at the
base of his strong throat.

"We need to talk," he said intently, his eyes never leaving hers. "I mean, we *really* need to talk, Winona."

"Then talk," she said shallowly.

A burst of raucous, feminine laughter—Mrs. Greenup's,
if Winona wasn't mistaken—bled through the kitchen door
from the other side, reminding them that they were by no
means alone.

"Not here," Connor told her. "And not now. When will
you be finished?"

I'm already finished, she wanted to say. "I imagine I'll
have everything here packed up by ten-thirty, and then I'll
go home."

"I'll meet you there."

She shook her head. "No."

He looked panic-stricken at that. "But we need to talk.
Come to my hotel, then."

She expelled an incredulous little sound and said, "Oh,
I don't *think* so."

"It wouldn't be like that," he told her.

"No, you're right," she agreed. "It wouldn't be. I *won't* be. Ever again."

He said nothing for a moment, only continued to study her in that silent, desperate way. "You told me you'd give me a chance to explain," he reminded her.

So she had, Winona thought. "All right then," she said. "I'll meet you at my house at eleven. But don't think for a moment that there will be anything more than talking going on."

He met her gaze levelly, and her heart kicked up that funny rhythm again. "Do you think maybe there could be a little listening going on, too?" he asked softly.

"It depends on what you have to say," she told him evenly.

He nodded again, slowly, but didn't push himself away from the counter, or from Winona. Before she realized his intention, he dipped his head to hers and brushed his lips lightly over her own. The gesture almost undid her, so tender, so solicitous was it. And then he pulled himself away from her, taking a few steps backward, but never removing his gaze from hers.

"I'll meet you at your place at eleven," he said again.

Winona could only nod, because she had no idea what else to say. That seemed to be enough for him, though, because with one final, longing look at her face, her eyes, her mouth, he spun on his heel and departed the kitchen.

As he left, Winona couldn't help enjoying a good, long look at his back. Not because it was so beautifully formed and solid and sure. And not because she was remembering how it had felt the night before to curl her fingers so zealously into the hot, naked flesh that covered it.

But because she couldn't help thinking that she would be seeing it again very soon.

Connor didn't wait until eleven to drive to Winona's house. He went there immediately after leaving her in the kitchen at his aunt's house, without even explaining to his aunt Pearl where or why he was going. So Auntie would whup him upside the head next time she saw him. But good. At this point, whuppings from great-aunts were the least of his worries. Especially when he turned the corner onto Winona's street and saw the tumble of blue and red lights illuminating her restaurant.

Oh, God, he thought. The cops were already here. They were raiding the place. That was supposed to be tomorrow. How could they have pulled everything together so quickly? How could they be doing this tonight? How could they be here when he and Winona still had so much to do and say?

He pulled his car to a halt behind one of the marked police cars, then flashed his badge as he exited the vehicle. A uniform waved him into the fray, and Connor ducked under the yellow police tape to gauge the climate.

Not good, he realized immediately. Worse than a circus. Already they had busted four people—two women and two men—and had all of them seated in the back of several patrol cars. Another woman was being led out the front door in handcuffs as Connor approached. Inside the restaurant things were even more chaotic. Uniforms and plainclothes alike were swarming, talking to some of the patrons and employees, arresting a couple of others.

Looked like one of Winona's hosts, a guy named Bart, was right in the thick of it. He was the one who'd organized the hookers, the one who was orchestrating their activities. He and his girls had been plying their trades right under Winona's nose for God only knew how long. And tonight it was all coming down on their heads.

Hoo-boy, Connor thought. They could be here all night. Winona was going to be crushed by the time this was through.

He stepped back outside, to see if he could find the principal detective on the case and offer his help. Then, as if thinking about Winona had conjured her appearance, he saw a car, one he didn't recognize, roll to a halt near where he had parked his own. The driver, he saw immediately, was his brother Rory. Rory's fiancée Miriam was in the passenger seat. And then the back door opened and Winona jumped out. Someone from the restaurant must have telephoned her at his aunt's house, to tell her what was going on. Now she stood in the street, gazing at her restaurant with so much anguish and terror the place might as well have been going up in flames.

Then again, Connor thought, in a lot of ways, it was. It was going to take some doing for Winona to recover from this. And not just the prostitution bust, either. But a whole host of other messes. Naturally, he couldn't help but feel responsible for the bulk of them.

His instincts commanded him to go to her, to talk to her, to comfort her. But his damnable reason stepped in to halt him. She was with her sister and future brother-in-law, he reminded himself, and she'd probably rather have them than him to take on the role of comforter right now. Connor had other obligations, anyway. Later the two of them could talk, he told himself. Later, he hoped, he could comfort her. But right now, he had a job to do.

Hours later, when the moon hung high in the sky, and the restaurant had finally emptied of everyone except Connor and Winona, the two of them sat in her dining room upstairs, each with a neglected cup of tea sitting on the table in front of them. Neither had said a word after the last official had left. They had only turned to look at each other through their exhaustion and disorientation, and had come to the silent and mutual agreement that they should go upstairs.

Connor had followed her up automatically, had watched without speaking as she mechanically made tea and poured it for both of them. Neither, however, had shown any interest in drinking it. Both of them had far too many other things on their minds.

Now Connor leaned back in his chair and stared at Winona, who was perched on the edge of her own seat with her body turned away from his, so that she was gazing off in the other direction. He told himself to say something, anything that might alleviate some of the tension that was burning up the air between them. But for the life of him, he had no idea how to begin.

Fortunately, Winona seemed not to have that problem, because eventually she murmured, "I can't believe a ring of prostitutes was operating out of my restaurant, right under my nose, and I never even knew it. And I can't believe one of my employees was the one running it."

Connor couldn't imagine what she must be feeling at the moment. To be betrayed once was pretty horrible. To have it happen twice, in a matter of hours, no less, must be devastating. Of course, Connor was still of the opinion that he hadn't betrayed Winona. Nevertheless he wouldn't blame her for taking exception to his exception.

But she wasn't the only one who'd been overwhelmed tonight, he thought further. The last few hours had been pretty devastating for him, too. He'd learned a lot about himself in the last few hours. And some of it still had him reeling.

"If it's any consolation," he said halfheartedly, "Bart and the girls said they chose your place because of the high-class clientele."

She emitted a single, humorless chuckle. "Yes, well, thanks to Bart and the girls, my clientele will now be highly nonexistent."

"Don't be so sure," Connor told her. "Your clientele may very well double now, because of the curiosity seekers."

"Wonderful. Now I'll have an entirely new reputation. My slogan won't be 'At Winona's, everybody feels at home' anymore. Instead, it will be 'At Winona's, every-body gets felt up.'" She propped her elbows on the table and buried her head in her hands. "How could I have let this happen?"

Connor rose from his chair and moved to the other side of the table, seating himself beside her. He wanted to reach out to her, to touch her, but he was afraid that she would rebuff him. So for long moments he only sat with his hands doubled into fists in his lap, watching her grow more and more withdrawn. Then, unable to tolerate even the small physical distance between them, he lifted one and splayed it open gently over her back.

Amazingly, she didn't recoil. She only continued to sit silently with her head in her hands, as if she'd given up hope on everything.

"Winona, you couldn't have known," Connor told her. "You're too nice a girl to have ever suspected something like that was going on. It's no wonder they operated right under your nose without you realizing. In your world, things like prostitution and illegal behavior don't exist. In your world, there's nothing bad, only good."

"That may have been true once," she said without moving. "But not anymore."

He hesitated only a moment before replying, "Yeah, well, it sucks the first time it happens, but you learn to live with it."

She did move then, lifting her head slowly from her hands and turning to gaze at him fully. "What do you mean?" she asked.

He met her gaze levelly for a moment, not sure what to tell her, not sure if she would believe him, not sure if it would make a difference, anyway. Then he decided, hell, he had nothing to lose. Nothing but Winona. And he feared she was already halfway gone to him.

So, quietly, he began, "You're not the only person in the world who's ever been betrayed, Winona."

She said nothing in response to his comment, only continued to gaze at him in silence. But he had her attention, he could tell that much. So, reluctantly, he continued.

"Not long after I graduated from college, I met a woman. To make a long story short, she knocked me off my feet." He smiled sadly. "I'd never met anyone like her. She was…" He sighed. "She was just really special, that's all."

Winona arrowed her brows down as she listened to him, and Connor got the impression that her reaction now was similar to the one he'd had as he'd listened to her talking about her beloved Stanley the day before. Good, he thought. If she cared that much, then maybe they still had a chance to work things out.

"I fell in love with her, Winona. Totally, hopelessly in love with her," he said, heat seeping through his belly when he saw the stricken look that crossed her face. Oh, yeah. She cared. She cared a lot. "At least, I thought I loved her," he corrected himself quickly. "At the time I didn't think it could be anything but love. She had me tied in knots, never knowing if I was coming or going. I just… I was crazy about her."

"So what happened?" Winona asked, her voice low and rough. "Did you…did you ask her to marry you?"

Connor shook his head. "There were times when I thought about it," he said honestly. "But I could never bring myself to pop the question. Something held me back. Then, about nine months after we started dating, there was one night when she told me she couldn't see me because she had to work, and then that night, I saw her out in a restaurant with another man."

Winona's gaze never veered from his, and he wished like hell he knew what she was thinking. "She was two-timing you?"

"You could say that," Connor told her. "Turns out the man she was with that night was…her husband."

"Her husband?" Winona echoed incredulously.

He nodded. "She'd been married for years, and I never knew. Here I had made her the center of my life, and she had another life entirely that I knew nothing about. And as if that weren't enough, when I confronted her, she told me that all I was to her, all I had ever been to her, was a means to an end. Her husband had been unfaithful to her, and she wanted to hurt him the same way. His affair had lasted ten months, and that was how long she had planned to stay with me. After ten months she would have left me, because she would have used me for everything she needed, and she would have told her husband all about us. But I screwed that up for her when, by sheer dumb luck, I stumbled on her and her husband out that night."

Winona still said nothing, still only gazed at him in silence. Still only looked stricken and sad and confused.

"She got what she wanted, though," Connor continued. "The night I saw her with her husband, she introduced me to him as her lover. Told him all about what we had done and why she had done it. The guy then proceeded to escort me outside, where he then beat the hell out of me while she looked on. All that time I thought she had loved me the way I loved her. But I'd never meant anything to her. Nothing. She'd only been with me to hurt her husband."

Very quietly Winona said, "And instead, you were the one who got hurt."

He nodded.

"I know how you feel."

"Maybe," he said.

She studied him in silence for a moment longer. Then, very softly, she asked, "Why did you first come into my restaurant?"

Connor had already promised himself he would tell the total and complete truth about everything. He'd lied to her too many times, for too long, to be anything but honest now. So, in response to her question, he told her, "The local police received an anonymous tip that a ring of call girls was operating out of your restaurant, and when they looked into the matter, they found out that it was true. They just didn't know who was heading the operation up, and they didn't know how the ring was being run.

"I was working an investigation in my hometown of Marigold that overlapped the one here, and I ended up working with the Bloomington team. The local boys sent me in as a decoy, hoping one of the women would approach me and we could tie the matter up neatly. That was why I couldn't tell you who I was, Winona. Because I was investigating the place."

"Just the place?" she asked.

"No," he said. "I was investigating you, too."

She swallowed with some difficulty before asking him, "You thought I was a prostitute?"

He shook his head, and he could see a small flicker of relief ease her expression. Until he told her, "I thought you were the madam."

Her expression closed up again at his declaration, and her eyes filled with tears. Please, not that, Connor thought. He could stand almost anything, but he couldn't tolerate the realization that he'd made Winona cry again.

"And I guess after last night," she said, "you think of me as little more than a who—"

"Winona," he interrupted her. "After last night…" He sighed heavily. "I'm not sure what I think. Just that… You're not what I thought you were."

"And you're not what I thought you were, either."

"I'm *everything* you thought I was," he countered immediately. "I gave you a phony name, Winona. Not a phony person."

"I don't see the distinction."

"I couldn't tell you my name, because it would have jeopardized the investigation. But everything else I've showed you of me over the last couple of weeks… That was all real. It was all true. Everything you know about

Connor Montgomery is true of Connor Monahan. We are one and the same person. And anything that happened between you and me, *every*thing that happened between us, that was all real and true, too.''

She jumped up from her chair then, doubling her fists at her sides. ''I know it was real,'' she said. ''That's the problem. It doesn't matter who you are. I fell in love with you, anyway. And I'm going to be in love with you forever.''

''And I fell in love with you, too!'' Connor shot back without thinking. ''I'll be in love with you forever, too!''

He might as well have just told her he was a pod person from another planet, so profound was Connor's surprise at hearing what he'd just blurted out.

Winona, too, seemed stunned, because her mouth dropped open, her eyes went wide, and she whispered hoarsely, ''You what?''

Connor bit back the panic that welled up at the back of his throat, and he told himself he shouldn't be so damned surprised. He did love Winona. He knew that now, with all his heart and soul. He just hadn't recognized the feeling before now because it was one he'd never felt in the past. Even years ago, when he'd thought he was in love, love hadn't been what he felt at all. What he'd felt years ago for the woman who had betrayed him had been something else entirely. It had been passionate and emotional and intense, to be sure. But it had also been desperate and anxious and insecure.

That, he realized now, had been infatuation. This thing with Winona... This was something else. It was warm and loyal and boundless. It was constant and definite and certain. It was endless. And it went soul deep.

It was love. What else could it be?

''I love you,'' he said again, less frantically this time. He stood, too, cupping his hands on her shoulders. ''I love you, Winona, and I don't want to live my life without you.''

The tears in her eyes tumbled freely as she said, "I don't know if I can believe you. You've told me so many lies."

"I never lied to you," he countered.

"Didn't you?"

"No," he stated unequivocally. "Maybe I let you believe some things I probably shouldn't have let you believe, but I never lied to you."

"You told me your name was Montgomery."

"I had no choice."

"But it was a lie."

"All right!" he conceded. "That was a lie. But nothing else was. None of it. Oh, Winona, don't you see?" he pleaded. "I never lied to you about the important things. I never lied to you about this."

And with that, he looped an arm around her and pulled her close, covering her mouth with his. For a moment she struggled against him, fisted her hands loosely on his chest and tried to push him away. Connor told himself he would stop if she made him, that he would never, ever force her to do anything she didn't want to do. But he knew she wanted him. He knew it. He could tell by the way she had looked at him. He could tell by the way she had told him she loved him.

And he wanted her, too. He loved her, too.

The realization of that hit him square in the brain again, as if Aunt Pearl herself had just whupped him upside the head, but good. He loved Winona Thornbury. And he would never be the same again.

Her hands on his chest loosened then, the fists gradually uncurling until her fingers turned the other way and twisted in the fabric of his shirt. Connor deepened the kiss as she pushed her body closer to his, then moved his hand between them to close it over her breast. She sighed against his mouth when he touched her, then urged one of her own hands lower, down toward his taut abdomen. For long moments they only explored each other, kissing and caressing, until he thought he would come apart at the seams.

Those damnable buttons, Connor thought as he brushed his fingertips over the front of her dress. He was really going to have to talk to her about her wardrobe. Because he wasn't going to do battle with every dress she owned, every time he wanted to make love to her. After they got married, he'd just have to explain to her that—

He jerked his mouth from hers the moment the idea formed in his brain. Marriage. To Winona. Of course. Why hadn't he thought of that before?

"Marry me," he said suddenly, impulsively. Somehow, though, the statement didn't feel impulsive at all.

She stared at him as if he'd gone mad. "What?" she asked.

"Marry me," he repeated. "Please. Promise me you'll spend the rest of your life with me."

"But, Connor," she said, her voice laced with nervousness, "we have so many things to settle, so many things we need to—"

"We can even have a long engagement and settle things over it. But promise me, Winona, that you'll stay with me forever." He smiled. "Because I can't make love to you unless I know you're committed."

She smiled back. "I should probably be committed for this but… Yes. I promise I'll stay with you."

"Forever?"

"Forever."

"You'll marry me?"

"I'll marry you."

"When?"

She laughed. "I don't know, Connor. Can't we talk about that later?" She moved her hands to the buttons of his shirt and began to unfasten them one by one. "Right now I need you. I want you. I love you. Tell me again that you love me, too."

"I love you, too," he stated with all certainty. "And I want you. And I need you. Right now."

He closed his eyes for a moment, just to make sure he wasn't imagining things, just to be certain he hadn't been dreaming all this time. It shouldn't be this easy, he thought. It shouldn't be this simple.

Then again, they were in love, he reminded himself. What could be simpler than that?

Winona undid the last of his buttons and pushed her hands beneath the fabric of his shirt, shoving it from his shoulders. Connor released her long enough to let the garment slide over his arms to the floor. Then, without even thinking now about what he was doing, he lifted her by the waist and set her on the table, and moved himself immediately between her legs. She smiled wickedly as she curled her fingers over his bare shoulders, then bucked her hips forward as he drew nearer. Grinning mischievously back at her, he began to slowly push the skirt of her dress higher, over her knees, her thighs, her hips.

"These," he said as he moved a hand to the waistband of her panties and yanked hard, "have got to go."

Winona smiled as she leaned back on her elbows, and lifted her bottom from the table so that he could pull them off. Connor did so with rapt efficiency, tossing them to the floor near his shirt. Then he loosed the button on his trousers, tugged down the zipper and freed himself completely. He sprang out hard and fully aroused, and Winona continued to lie back on her elbows, opening herself to him completely. He took a step forward, lifted her legs and braced them over his shoulders, then positioned himself to bury himself thoroughly inside her.

They both cried out at the depth of his penetration, but he simply could not wait any longer to possess her and be possessed by her. Later they could make love again, and they could take their time and do all the things to each other that they wanted to do. Now though…

Hungrily, desperately, he thrust into her, again and again and again, the friction of their motion creating a delicious heat that seeped through both their bodies. Connor wanted to make it last, but there was too much welling up inside him for him to keep it all in. And in a near-blinding rush of heat and sensation, with a cry of both triumph and defeat, he spilled himself inside her.

For one long moment neither of them moved, both seeming too dazed by what they had just done to speak. Then Winona reached for Connor, and he met her halfway, linking his fingers with hers.

"Never lie to me again," she told him.

"I'll be as honest with you as I've always been," he replied.

"Take me to bed, Connor," she said with a smile.

And smiling back at her, he readily complied.

Epilogue

Spring was in full bloom the day of Winona and Connor's May wedding, and she was glad they had decided months ago to say their vows in her garden. Mother Nature had cooperated beautifully, and now the lilac bushes were brimming with fat purple blooms, lavender stretched from one shrub after another along the side of the house, and lily of the valley spilled abundantly along the line of the fence. Best of all, plump, heavy peonies of white and pink and violet dribbled petals along the walkway bisecting it all, as if acting the role of flower girl for the bridal party.

Of course, if she and Connor had simply waited a few years to get married, their brand-new niece Rosemary, whom Connor's sister Tess cradled close to her breast, could have played the part of flower girl. As it was, however, one month old, they had all decided, was just a tad early for such a role. And besides, there was no way she and Connor could wait years to get married. It had been hard enough waiting for months.

Still, they were delighted that the first member of the next generation of Monahans could be here for this occasion. Especially since Winona knew that the next member wouldn't be far behind. Her sister had sworn her to secrecy for now, but Miriam hadn't been able to wait to tell her a few weeks ago that she and Rory were expecting, too, with a due date in December. Winona wouldn't be surprised if Sean and Autumn shared similar news soon.

She turned her attention to Connor's twin brother, Cullen, and wondered when he and his new wife would make such an announcement. Who knew? Maybe she and Connor would even beat them to it. Not that Winona was in any hurry to become a mother, but there was that biological clock situation to think about. Certainly Connor made her feel ten years younger, in spite of the decade that separated them. Still, they had talked about having children soon.

First, of course, they would have to marry. She was, after all, a nice, old-fashioned girl. She wouldn't dream of having a child out of wedlock. As it was, she and Connor had been lucky she hadn't gotten pregnant that day in September when they'd made up so beautifully. It went without saying, though, that she'd moved past that pesky premarital sex hang-up she'd had for some time. Oh, my goodness, had she moved past that. Many, *many* times over the past several months. But they'd been very careful about taking precautions against pregnancy since that single time they'd gone without. Even if they hadn't been cautious about much else, sexually speaking.

Indeed Connor had proved to be a very adventurous lover, and Winona had been thrilled to learn all the tricks of the trade. So to speak. Surprisingly, though, she'd been able to teach him a thing or two, as well. About anticipation. About taking a leisurely approach. About making it last a long, long time.

Goodness, it was warm for May, she thought suddenly.

They should probably start the ceremony before someone succumbed to heat prostration. Or something.

The ceremony was to be a small one. Only immediate family had been invited, and she and Connor would have only one attendant each—Miriam would be her matron of honor, and Cullen, Connor's twin, was to be his best man. But a few of Winona's neighbors had halted on the sidewalk beyond the gate to greet the happy couple and murmur good wishes. And a few of her employees had stopped by to drop off some gifts. The restaurant was closed today, of course, but would be reopening tomorrow. Winona's business was so good these days, she didn't want to interrupt the flow. Even a few of Connor's friends from the Bloomington PD had stopped by to wish them luck. Winona wasn't about to chase any of the well-wishers away. She wanted as many people as possible to join her on this, the happiest day of her life.

Oh, no, wait a minute, she thought as she saw Connor approaching. This wasn't the happiest day. Not quite. The happiest had been the day she'd walked out of her kitchen and seen Connor seated in her restaurant for the very first time. She'd known nothing about him then, except that he'd made her feel something she'd never felt before. Over the last eight months, she'd learned more about him than she had ever imagined she would. But none of it—none of it— mattered more than how she felt about him.

They strode up the garden path together, arm in arm, toward the minister, who stood framed by the trellis upon which morning glories blossomed. Miriam smiled at her from one side of the trellis, her vintage lavender gown off- setting her blue eyes and dark-blond hair beautifully. Cullen, Connor's mirror image, stood on the other side in a pale-gray suit. Connor himself wore a dark-navy-blue suit, which enhanced the color of his eyes with breathtaking clarity. She only hoped her white Victorian gown edged with lace and seed pearls and buttons could hold a candle to him.

But judging by the appreciation that lit his eyes, she succeeded quite well in that candle-lighting business. In fact, judging by the way Connor was looking at her now, she'd guess that much more than a candle was burning. She hoped they didn't have to linger long at the reception inside. She couldn't wait to leave for their honeymoon.

"Are you ready?" he murmured as they drew nearer the priest. And she knew he was talking about too many things to list.

She nodded. "As they say in the vulgar contemporary vernacular, bring it on."

He grinned at her. "Oh, baby. Do I have plans for you."

They covered the final few steps together, clasping hands and gazing into each other's eyes, never once noticing anything else. Winona spoke her vows to Connor with utter conviction, and as he spoke them back to her, she was overwhelmed by how honest and honorable and decent he was and how he would love her forever and ever.

And as he slipped a perfect circle of gold over the ring finger of her left hand, Winona reveled in the knowledge that, in this day and age, she had somehow managed to find herself such a nice, old-fashioned boy.

*   *   *   *   *

ADDICTED TO NICK

by
Bronwyn Jameson

BRONWYN JAMESON

spent much of her childhood with her head buried in a book. As a teenager, she discovered romance novels, and it was only a matter of time before she turned her love of reading them into a love of writing them. Bronwyn shares an idyllic piece of the Australian farming heartland with her husband and three sons, a thousand sheep, a dozen horses, assorted wildlife and one kelpie dog. She still chooses to spend her limited spare time with a good book. Bronwyn loves to hear from readers. Write to her at bronwyn@bronwynjameson.com

Prologue

Nick didn't know what coming home should feel like, but he figured something ought to register on the nostalgia scale. Nothing major, mind you, just a touch of the warm and fuzzies. Hell, even a twinge of bitterness would be better than the emotional numbness that seemed to have settled over him during the long flight from JFK to Australia.

He hated the lack of feeling. It reminded him too keenly of the first time he'd stood in this drive gazing up at Joe Corelli's mansion, except that time he had deliberately schooled his eight-year-old heart to blankness. He hadn't wanted to feel anything—not fear or confusion, shame or hope—so he'd simply looked at the big house and wondered how long till someone realized they'd made a serious mistake.

Kids like Niccolo Corelli got arrested for being anywhere near houses like this.

But the stranger who introduced himself as some rela-

tive of his dead mother had looped a comforting arm
around his shoulders and said, "This is your home, Niccolo. Forget what came before—you're part of my family
now."

Part of a family.

Nick hadn't a clue what that meant, and, despite Joe's
best efforts, he'd never been allowed to forget his origins.

He stared a while longer at the big house and felt nothing. Maybe he just needed sleep. Ten hours, uninterrupted,
between sheets. Yeah, that was exactly what his jet-lagged
body and emotion-lagged mind needed, although they
weren't getting horizontal yet. With a barely stifled yawn,
he unfolded himself from the hire car and stretched his
limbs. Then, as he turned toward the house, he caught a
flicker of movement at an upstairs window.

Big Brother George watching from on high.

Just like that first time, Nick thought, although today he
raised a casual hand in acknowledgment instead of the
single-finger salute of fourteen years before. The curtain
shifted back into place, and Nick puffed out a derisive
laugh. Idly he scanned the ground-floor windows and wondered who else might be watching.

How many of the four women who had grown up as his
sisters waited inside the thick stucco walls? Sophie, no
doubt. At the faintest whiff of trouble, Sophie always came
running. She was the one who dobbed to her mother the
first time he bloodied George's nose...and to her father the
last time. It was Sophie who eavesdropped on the heated
argument between her parents before Joe brought him here,
and who spread the phrase "dirty whore's brat."

Yeah, he would bet money on Sophie turning up—if
George had bothered to let his sisters know he was coming.
His adoptive brother's communication record was some-
thing less than stellar.

He slammed the car door on that thought, but as he
strode up the drive, he could feel the tension in his jaw

and a stiffness in his muscles that had nothing to do with jet lag. He didn't want to be here—not here in Melbourne, nor at the country stables he had reportedly inherited.

Reportedly.

Wasn't it just like George to play petty games with the facts and to ensure that the solicitor handling Joe's estate played along, too? Nick blew out an exasperated breath. As soon as he learned the full story and slapped a For Sale sign on Yarra Park, he was gone.

This time for good.

One
___

If the night hadn't been so still, silent but for the occasional swoosh of straw under restless hooves, T.C. wouldn't have heard the faint creak of gate hinges.

Or the crunch of footsteps on the gravel path leading from the house-yard to the stables.

She could have made her way back to the stable hand's quarters at the far end of the barn and crawled back into bed, convinced her sleep had been disturbed by an unfamiliar and unforgiving mattress rather than the audible signs of a midnight intruder.

The footsteps paused, and a chill of fear shivered across her skin. "Turn around and go back the way you came. Get in your car and drive away. Please." Her entreaty was a whisper of breath that barely pierced the thick night air. She closed her eyes, counted to ten—slowly—but no car door clicked shut, no starter-motor engaged. With her heart lurching painfully against her ribs, she edged to the end of the stable row and peered out into the night.

Nothing moved except some ghostly strands of autumn fog—strands that seemed to slither up from the Yarra River to wrap the house in the promise of winter. T.C. retreated a step, drew a long breath. The air was cold enough to sting in her nostrils, but it was also rich with leather and horsehair, sweet molasses and fresh clover hay, familiar bracing aromas that lent strength to her weak knees.

Someone was out there—maybe the jerk who had dialed her number over and over these past weeks, only to hang up without speaking a word. She pictured him standing on the path, head lifted to test the air as his eyes adjusted to the darkness. Most likely a burglar who thought the place would be easy pickings with only a woman in residence, knowledge he could have gleaned in a casual chat with any of the locals in nearby Riddells Crossing.

Her fingers tightened around the gun in her right hand. It weighed next to nothing yet it felt curiously reassuring, considering it was useless. She switched it to her left hand and wiped her damp palm on her thigh…her *pajama-pants-clad* thigh, she amended. A semihysterical giggle bubbled up, and she pressed a hand to her mouth to stifle the sound.

Some scumbag was stalking her stables, and she intended taking him on dressed in oversize flannel pajamas and armed with nothing but a kid's toy cap gun. She would take him while he was rolling around the floor laughing!

The footsteps started again, approaching rapidly this time and without any pretense of stealth. She had no time to consider this, no time to consider anything, no time to plan. A dark figure came through the barn entrance less than a pace away, close enough for her to absorb the soft tang of his aftershave on a swiftly drawn breath.

Close enough to touch, in the ribs, with the toy gun.

"Don't move, mister, and I won't have to shoot you."

The phoney tough-guy line rolled from T.C.'s tongue

without conscious thought. She closed her eyes and grimaced. Had she really said that? With such cool calm strength, when her insides were quivering like half-set Jell-O? The quaver transferred to her legs and started them trembling. She prayed the hand holding her make-believe weapon wouldn't follow suit.

The stranger slowly raised his hands above his head. "Take it easy, sweetheart. Don't do anything stupid."

"*I* have the, um, gun, so *you* should be the one avoiding stupid moves!" T.C. hated herself for that stumbling pause, but before she could do more than wince, she sensed him start to move and jabbed him with the gun. Hard.

"I get the picture. I'm not to move, right?" He eased out the words in a deep, soothing monotone—the exact same voice she used to settle a nervous horse. That gave her pause. Why was he trying to mollify her? *She* wasn't the one creeping about someone else's stables in the dead of night.

"Right," she clipped out, irritated as well as confused. "No…wrong." She circled about him, transferring the gun from his ribs to his back, as she regathered her composure. "I *do* want you to move. I want you to turn, slowly, and put your hands up against the wall."

Surprisingly he complied, although his posture looked way too casual for T.C.'s liking. "You want me to spread 'em?" he asked. A hint of amusement colored the rich depth of his voice.

"That won't be necessary," she replied, absolutely unamused. The guy acted like having a gun—okay, a *toy* gun, but he didn't know that—pointed at his back was more an entertainment than a concern. She needed to assert some authority, but how on earth did she go about doing that? This was not a small man. At least six foot and, unless her night vision was severely impaired, most of it muscle.

Her only advantage was a handful of plastic imitation weaponry.

What if he had a real weapon?

The alarming thought caused her throat to tighten. She had to clear that solid lump of dread before she could ask, "Are you armed?"

"And dangerous?" he mocked.

T.C. cursed herself for expecting to learn anything from such a foolish question. In order to find out she needed to search him...to put her hands on him....

She steeled herself by drawing a deep breath but found the air edged with his disturbingly appealing scent. She let the breath go with a snort. So even bad guys can find their way around a bottle of Calvin Klein, she told herself. So what? Get on with it!

Plunging forward, she patted down his jacket, found two outside pockets and two sets of keys—nothing unusual there. Her hand stilled on the jacket. Not cheap vinyl but real, malleable, high-quality leather, which did strike her as unusual.

What kind of burglar was he?

"There's an inside pocket you'd better check. And one in my shirt."

Obviously a helpful one.

Stung out of immobility, she took another C.K.-imbued breath before sliding her hand inside the jacket. His shirt was incredibly warm and the fabric so fine that she could feel the muted texture of his chest hair against her palm. And beneath that...*holy toledo!* she felt the rippling curves and indents of some exceedingly fine pecs. It was like stroking the finest horseflesh, all supple and deceptively languid, while underneath the slow, steady beat of his heart pumped all that heat into her hand, her blood, her belly.

Stroking?

She pulled her hand back sharply, and a shimmer of

sensation skimmed across her fingertips, settled in her skin. "Static electricity," she muttered, shaking her fingers.

"Pardon?"

"I wasn't speaking to you."

"Then who?"

"None of your business." T.C. spoke through clenched teeth. "I'm going to search your pants now."

"Be my guest."

It was amazing how much amusement he managed to pack into that short statement. Enough to really rile T.C. She prodded him in the ribs with sufficient force to cause him to flinch. Good—maybe now he would show some respect!

His pants were jeans of the close-fitting variety. One rear pocket housed a slim leather wallet; the other contained nothing more than finely hewn muscle. She took a half step back and wiped her palm against her thigh, then scrubbed it harder. Somehow she couldn't erase the imprint from her skin.

She jumped clear off the ground when he drawled, "Don't stop there, sweet hands. There are more pockets around the front."

"I have a better idea. Why don't you just tell me where your weapon's hidden?"

He laughed, a low rich belly-laugh that did strange things to T.C.'s insides. "Why don't you slide that soft little hand around here and find out for yourself?"

Heat blazed into her cheeks. How dare he be so...so... Words failed her. She did the mental equivalent of spluttering and told herself the warmth in her cheeks was not due to his softly purred suggestion. She transferred the gun from left hand to right, stretched her tight tendons finger by finger, and inspected the hand that was indeed little but hadn't been soft for more years than she could remember.

"Don't," she said, her voice as crisp and chill as the

night air, "make the mistake of associating my size with softness."

And with the strength of those words ringing in her ears, she did exactly as he'd asked. She reached around and checked the front pockets of his jeans. Very quickly. Then she slid her hand up and checked the waistband. Neat fit, hard to hide anything there, she noted. She also noted when he drew breath. She could tell by the sudden tautness of his abs beneath her hand.

What she didn't realize was that the breath was taken in preparation.

His turn was quick, as was the hand that dislodged the gun. It clunked against the wall, hit the floor, then slid a long long way before clattering to a standstill. It took the stranger less time to twist her arm behind her back and right up between her shoulder blades.

"I'd like to think you were touching me up for the sheer pleasure of it, but something tells me that's not it. How about you tell me what *is* going on?"

He stood close behind her, close enough that the words washed over her nape in a warm wave. She shook her head to rid herself of the sensation, and he stretched her arm further.

"Ouch," she breathed. "You're hurting me."

"You think that piece of plastic you were brandishing hasn't bruised me?" He released the pressure on her arm, although he didn't let it go. Long fingers manacled her wrist. "Well?" he prompted.

T.C. frowned. If he knew the gun was fake, it explained his casual attitude, but why hadn't he called her on it? And why had he asked *her* to explain? She wrenched her arm and found herself hauled backward, right up hard against his body, so when he spoke his voice hummed close against her ear. "All right, sweet hands, if you don't want to tell me why you're skulking about in the dark, I'll have to start searching for clues."

His hand slid over her hip. T.C. yelped and tried to swat it away, but he pulled her nearer by banding an arm around her chest. Her back was pasted to his front, so close that when he laughed, the low sound vibrated from his chest into her body. It set up a resonant buzz along her spine, like a tuning fork perfectly pitched.

Or maybe that was in reaction to the hand cruising down one thigh then back up again, inch by leisurely inch. Omigosh, now it was inside her pajama coat, sliding across her belly. She wriggled frantically, needing to escape his touch—but wriggling was a big mistake. It brought her backside up hard against his thighs. All the breath left her lungs in a rush.

"What's the matter, sweetheart? Not used to having a perfect stranger run his hands all over you? Intrusive, isn't it?"

"My name's not sweet *anything!*" She kicked out, and the sudden flurry of legs and boots caught him unaware. The arm holding her slipped, and she swiveled sideways; his free hand grabbed…and closed over her left breast.

For a long second they both went completely still. T.C. heard the rasp of her own breathing, not quite steady, over the heavy thud of her heartbeat. Then she kicked out again, and this time her booted heel caught him in the shin.

He swore succinctly, and T.C. felt a rush of vindictive satisfaction. This was his fault. He shouldn't have been touching her at all, let alone in that deliberate way. She swung her feet again, and he grunted as he shifted sideways to avoid her heels.

He cursed again. "What are you, half mule? Stop kicking, for Pete's sake!"

"Then…let…me…go!"

"I'll let you go when I can see what you're up to. Where's the light switch?"

When she didn't answer his arm tightened. "Down there…straight ahead…last door on your left." T.C.'s instructions came out in reluctant grunts against the arm crushing her diaphragm.

He frog-marched her the length of the breezeway, pushed open the door to her quarters and flicked the switch. T.C. squeezed her eyes shut against the sudden brightness. Dazzling yellow figures danced across the backs of her lids. She heard Ug yap a greeting, the scratch of her nails as she scampered across the concrete floor, then felt the little dog bouncing around her legs...no, make that *their* legs.

Oh, great. First my dog doesn't even hear him arrive, then she greets him like a long-lost friend!

"Down. Sit." His instructions were so do-not-argue that T.C. almost sat herself.

Needless to say, her traitorous dog subsided.

The stranger's grip eased. His hands moved to her shoulders, swinging her around until she stood staring into his broad chest. Her nose almost touched the front of his shirt and the chest hair revealed by two open buttons.

She swallowed with difficulty and raised a hand to push against the solid wall of his chest. It didn't budge. Beneath her palm beat the steady pulse of his heart. She tipped her head back, found herself too close to see anything beyond a chin dark with regrowth and centered with a faint familiar-looking cleft.

Oh, no, it couldn't be....

She backed up until the full lips and long, straight nose came into focus; then she closed her eyes.

Oh, yes, it most definitely was!

"Tell me I didn't just kick Nick Corelli in the shins," she said on the end of a long tortured groan. *Tell me I didn't just run my hands all over Nick Corelli's body.* Except she knew she had—the knowledge still tingled in the palms of those hands.

She opened her eyes to find his focused intently on her, and for a long moment she could do nothing but stare back.

His eyes weren't obsidian dark like all the Corellis she had met but the pure cerulean of a summer sky. So unexpected, so unusual, so giddily, perfectly beautiful. Finally she remembered to take another breath, to close the mouth she feared had fallen open in gobstopped awe.

"You know me?" He sounded startled by that, and there was definitely surprise lurking in those amazing eyes. Surprise and something more. Interest? Or merely curiosity?

She shook her head, as much to clear her stunned senses as in reply. "We've never met, but I recognize you. From photographs. Your father showed me photographs."

"You recognized me instantly from a couple of pictures?"

More than a couple. T.C. felt herself color as she recalled how many...and how often she'd pored over them. Good grief, she had actually freeze-framed a video of his sister's wedding on one spectacular shot. It was a wonder she hadn't pegged him as Nick the Gorgeous One in the total dark!

"I take it you aren't a burglar. Do you work here?" He glanced down at where Ug lay at his feet—almost *on* his feet—and grinned. "Let me guess. You're security, and this is your guard dog."

T.C.'s heart did a slow motion flip-flop as the effect of that lazy drawl, the warmth of that slow grin, rippled through her body. She couldn't help her automatic response. How could she *not* smile back at him? How could she watch one quizzically arched brow disappear behind the thick fall of his hair and *not* think about combing it back from his face?

Belatedly she realized that the brow had arched in question. Asking what? Something about her working here? "Um...I'm the trainer. I train Joe's horses."

His expression changed from quizzical to startled in one blink of his dark lashes. "*You're* Tamara Cole?"

"That's me."

He inspected her with unnerving thoroughness, starting at her boots and working all the way up her legs and body. When he arrived back at her face, he let out a choked sort of snort that sounded like equal parts disbelief and suppressed laughter, and the warmth suffusing T.C.'s veins turned prickly with irritation. She knew she wasn't looking her best, but that was no reason for him to shake his head and grin as if he couldn't quite believe what his eyes were telling him. She folded her arms and regarded him as coolly as the hot flush of mortification allowed. "What are you doing here, Nick?"

"Apart from being attacked by a crazy little horse-training woman dressed in pajamas and boots?"

"I mean," she said tightly, as he continued to grin down at her, "I've been waiting to hear from someone for weeks and weeks, but I didn't expect *you*. Last I heard, you were lost in the wilds of Alaska."

The grin faded. "Who told you that?"

"George mentioned it. After the funeral." She shrugged off the memory of that short, unpleasant meeting. *Who-told-who-what* didn't matter when important questions remained unanswered. Like, what was Nick doing here, and why had he arrived unannounced in the middle of the night? "You should have let me know you were coming."

"I've been trying to do that for the last six hours." With disturbing accuracy he homed in on her telephone and picked up the receiver she'd left off the hook. "I don't suppose this has anything to do with the constant busy signal?"

"I must have bumped it. Or something."

He stared at her for a full ten seconds, then gestured with the instrument in his hand. "Is this on the same line as the house?"

T.C. cleared her throat, told herself it was ridiculous to feel such a sharp frisson of apprehension at the sight of a phone, at the thought of it being able to ring and ring and ring…. "Yes. There's only the one line."

"Then if it's all the same to you, I'd prefer we keep that line open." As he cradled the receiver, the meaning behind his words gelled. If he needed a phone, he must be staying.

"Why are you here, Nick?" she blurted. "I expected George, or that solicitor with the bullfrog eyes."

The corners of Nick's mouth twitched. "We used to call him Kermit."

T.C. tried to ignore the mental image of Kermit in pin-stripes but failed. And as they smiled in shared amusement, as she had done so many times with his father, T.C. knew why Nick was here. It made perfect sense that Joe would leave the place of his heart to the son of his heart, the one he had spoken of with such obvious love.

It also explained the delay. Nick—self-indulgent, free-wheeling Nick—had disappeared on some wilderness ski-ing jaunt the day his father was hospitalized. Joe lingered ten more days, but Nick didn't come home.

As she collected Ug from the floor and hugged the dog's furry warmth close against her chest, T.C. felt the tight twist of pain for the man who had been her boss, her men-tor and her savior—and the strong sting of resentment for the son who had let him down.

Nick watched as a sheen of moisture quelled the sea-green intensity of her gaze, and he felt a sharp kick of response, a need to ease the pain he glimpsed in those spectacular eyes. He actually took a step forward, but she nailed him to the spot with a fierce look that reminded him of his bruised ribs and scraped shin. He gave himself a mental tap on the head.

What was he thinking?

Jet lag must be kicking in if he thought she needed comforting. The pale cap of baby-soft hair, the cute little nose, the huge eyes—they were all a deception. This little firebrand had a tough streak a mile wide. His gaze slid to her lips for at least the tenth time since he'd flicked the light switch. Full and soft, with a distinct inclination to pout, there was absolutely nothing tough about them. They looked downright kissable…until they tightened savagely. Nick cleared his mind of all kissing-thoughts as he cleared his throat. "So, Tamara…"

"What did you call me?"

"Tamara. That *is* your name, isn't it? Or would you rather I kept on calling you *sweet hands?*"

"You can call me T.C."

"That's hardly a name, just a couple of initials. I think I'll stick with Tamara."

Her lush lips compressed into an angry bow, and Nick felt a sudden spike of stimulation. It was the kind of buzz he'd chased across continents, from challenge to challenge and from woman to woman. The kind he hadn't felt for too many years, and he didn't understand where the feeling was coming from.

Apart from her mouth and the way those big eyes sparked green fire, Tamara Cole didn't come close to his type. He liked women who slid out of bed with silk clinging to their curves. He liked women who knew they were women. Must be jet lag—that was the only explanation. That and the fact that George had got her all wrong. From his description, Nick had imagined big hair, a big blowzy body, an even bigger attitude. She surely had the attitude, but her blond hair was cropped boyishly short, and, frankly, there wasn't a whole lot of body.

Just a nice little handful.

He allowed that sensory memory to drum through his blood for a whole minute before he reminded himself how deceptive appearances could be. George was a prime example. Just because Tamara Cole didn't fit George's description of the shrewd opportunist who had wriggled her way into Joe's life as well as his bed—just because the very thought had caused his earlier guffaw of amusement—didn't mean she hadn't done just that.

"Why are you here, Nick?"

Her question cut into Nick's reverie, and he pretended to consider it as he strolled over to her bed, tested the mattress, sat and swung his legs up. He picked up her pillow and propped it between his head and the wall.

"Why am I here?" He regarded her bottom lip through half-closed eyes, and the low-grade buzz in his veins intensified. "I'm here to meet you...*partner*."

Two

"**P**art-ner?" T.C.'s voice cracked midword, so the second syllable came out squeaky. She tried to control her trembling legs but failed miserably, and the nearest storage trunk came up to meet her backside with an audible thump, jolting Ug from her arms. "What do you mean by *partner?*" Her voice sounded as weak as her knees felt.

"Standard definition. Two persons, sharing equally."

Oh, no. Joe, you didn't. You couldn't. You wouldn't.
"Sharing what…exactly?"

"This place."

T.C. swallowed, ran her tongue around her dry mouth. "You're saying Joe left me half of Yarra Park?"

"And everything on it, four-legged and otherwise. You have a problem with that?"

"Of course I do. It's too much, too…" Her throat constricted around the words, and she had to stop, to swallow twice before she could continue. "I don't understand. Why didn't he say something? Why hasn't *anyone* said anything?"

"There was a clause in the will.... Joe requested that I come here and tell you."

That made about as much sense as the rest of it.

T.C. shook her head slowly. *Oh, Joe, why did you do this?* She jerked to her feet and must have walked to the window, because she found herself staring into the aluminum-framed square of night. She forced herself to look beyond her stunned senses, beyond the thick emotion that constricted her chest and blurred her vision.

Why?

Her boss had been a steady, almost ponderous, thinker—this couldn't be some whim. He had also been devoted to his large family to such an extent that he had often lamented spoiling them with a too-easy lifestyle. Staring into the dark, she recalled their hostility the day of Joe's funeral, and for the first time she understood where it had come from. She had been in that same place. She knew how it felt to be overlooked in favor of a virtual stranger.

"I imagine your family has a problem with it," she said slowly.

"You could say they're less than thrilled with our little windfall."

T.C. whirled around. "Don't call it that! I didn't expect anything. I don't *want* anything." She spread her arms wide in an imploring gesture. "Why did he do this, Nick?"

"Gee, I don't know, Tamara. Some might assume it's because you were *very* good at your job."

Heat flooded T.C.'s cheeks, then ebbed just as rapidly. Surely he couldn't mean what that suggestive drawl implied...could he? Stunned, she stared at him, taking in his laid-back posture, the mocking half grin, and the heat returned in a flash of red.

"Yesss!" The word came out a long, low hiss as she

advanced on him. "I *am* very good at my job—that's why
Joe employed me—so I hope you're not insinuating I
earned this *windfall* doing anything besides training
horses." She reached down and wrenched the pillow from
behind him, then seriously contemplated koshing him over
the head with it.

"Hey, take it easy. I said *some* might assume."

The *some* most likely encompassed the rest of Joe's
family but apparently didn't include Nick—that was why
he had been so taken aback when he learned her identity.
What had he called her? *A crazy little horse-training
woman in pajamas and boots.* The thought of anyone
wanting to bed *that* must really have tickled him.

Not having to prove the nature of her relationship with
Joe should have delighted T.C., so why did she feel
so…slighted? Annoyed with her contrary feelings, she
tossed the pillow aside. It didn't matter what Nick Corelli
thought of her; it mattered that he was lounging on her
bed, treating Joe's bequest with a complete lack of respect.

"What about your part in this, Nick? What did your
family make of that?"

"They shared the rest of Joe's fortune." He shrugged
negligently. "I guess I got the consolation prize."

Hands on hips, she took a step forward and looked down
on him with all the scorn that comment deserved. "You
feel you deserved a prize?"

He tipped his head back against the bare concrete wall,
eyes narrowed, expression no longer amused. "Meaning?"

"Meaning where were you when your father needed
you? When your brother and sisters took turns sitting by
his hospital bed for days on end? It was *you* he wanted
there, Nick. *You* he asked for. And where were you? Oh,
that's right, you had some dinky mountain to ski!"

Slowly he unfolded his long frame and rose to his feet.
His eyes glittered darkly, a muscle ticked at the corner of
his mouth, and without conscious thought T.C. took a step

back. But when he spoke his voice was cool and flat. "George told you that?"

She swallowed, nodded, wondered what nerve she had struck.

"Did he tell you how much effort he put into finding me? That he didn't even bother leaving a message with my service?"

"He shouldn't have had to find you."

"I should have known Joe was sick…how?"

T.C. flushed. Joe hadn't told a soul about his diagnosis. No one had guessed until it was too late.

"I'm sorry, Nick." And because the words sounded totally inadequate, or maybe because the dark emotion in his eyes—the hurt, anger, regret—echoed somewhere deep within, she reached out and placed her hand on his arm.

"Yeah, well, it's history now." Nick shrugged off both her apology and the touch of her fingers. He didn't need her awkward attempt at sympathy any more than he needed his own sense of frustration at what might have been. Both were pointless. Abruptly he swung around, away from the mix of compassion and confusion that gleamed in her eyes. He needed something else to focus his frustration on, and he found it right before his eyes in the stark concrete walls, the uncarpeted floor and make-do furniture, the clothes discarded atop packing trunks.

"Why are you living here?"

She shook her head slightly. "What do you mean?"

"George said you used to live in the house but you'd moved out, I assumed to somewhere off the farm. Why the hell would you move out of the house into this rat-hole?"

"I didn't feel right staying in the house," she said stiffly.

"Couldn't you find anywhere better than this?"

"I didn't have any—" She stopped abruptly, changing tack with a forced casualness that didn't fool Nick for a second. "I needed to be here, near the horses. It's no big deal."

"George should have told me you were living here."

Except how could he, when Nick hadn't given him a chance? When he'd grown so frustrated by the man's smoothly evasive replies that he threw his hands in the air and walked out, jumped in his car and drove straight here?

He scrubbed a hand over his face and wondered what had happened to his logic, which seemed to have gone missing…probably to the same place as his usual even temper. He adopted a more reasonable tone before he continued. "If I'd known you were living here, I wouldn't have been surprised to see your light."

"So that's why you came down here." Her smile was edged with relief, as if she'd needed an explanation…or because the conversation had taken a safer turn. "Something woke me, but I wasn't sure what, so I turned the light out again. When I heard you outside, it scared about a year off my life."

"Sorry about that. I guess we both had the wrong handle on each other."

Whatever the reason for her smile, it sliced a swathe through Nick's irritability, made it possible for him to smile right back at her. And he found something in her expression, in the slow color that highlighted her cheekbones, that reminded him what sort of a handle they'd had on each other in the close darkness of the breezeway. Her hands sliding over his shirt, touching his jeans. His hand on her belly, her breast. Heat licked through him like wildfire, doing more than sear his blood vessels. It surprised the hell out of him.

Jet lag, he reminded himself as he shoved his hands in his jacket pockets and cleared his throat. "You want to pack a few things—what you need for tonight?"

She stiffened visibly. "I beg your pardon?"

"You're not staying here."

"I'm perfectly comfortable here."

Her mutt, which had fallen asleep on the foot of her bed, chose that moment to whimper and twitch. Nick snorted. "Your *dog* isn't even comfortable here."

"Must we discuss this now?"

"No. We can discuss it later...*after* we've moved you."

When he started toward her, she held up a hand. "Look, it's the middle of the night. I don't want to fight with you, and I don't want to have to make up another bed. Okay?"

Nick dragged a hand through his hair. Unfortunately he could see her point. "Fine," he conceded. "But tomorrow you're moving out of here."

"Shouldn't sorting out this ridiculous bequest be our first priority?"

Nick frowned at her choice of adjective. *Unexpected,* yes. *Unusual,* maybe. *Overly generous,* definitely. "You think it's ridiculous?"

"It makes no sense."

"You can't think of any reason why Joe would leave you a million-dollar bequest?"

All the color leached from her face as she stared back at him. In his world, a million dollars didn't turn a hair; to Tamara Cole, the figure was obviously staggering. Buying her out would be as simple as writing a check, Nick realized. So where was the satisfaction that always accompanied knowledge of a sure thing, a deal all but closed? As she continued to stare at him, wide-eyed and unblinking, he noticed she looked more than stunned. She looked as dead beat as he felt.

"Sleep on it, green eyes," he advised as he headed to the door. "We'll talk later."

"Nick."

He stilled, one hand on the doorknob. Now why should the sound of his name on her tongue cause his pulse to pound? All his responses seemed shot to bits tonight.

"I'm sorry about before, about mistaking you for a burglar."

Nick turned, caught her looking at him with that same expression as before, the one that made him think about hands in the dark and the sweet little body hidden beneath unflattering flannel. He stared back, a slow grin on his lips and a fast burn in his gut.

"I'm not."

After the door clicked shut, T.C. rested her overheated face against the cool windowpane and one hand against her overstimulated heart. No man's smile should be allowed to have such an effect, and especially not a man so out of her league.

It wasn't fair, but it wasn't unexpected.

From his photos, she knew the man was gorgeous, from Joe's stories she'd learned of his charm, but nothing could have prepared her for Nick Corelli in the flesh. Nothing could have prepared her for that blue gaze sliding over her like a silk blanket, warming her, sensitizing every cell in her skin, as he murmured "I'm not." As if he had enjoyed their tussle in the dark, as if the surge of attraction she had felt so intensely was mutual. As if a man who could take his pick of the glamorous, the beautiful and the smart, would be interested in her.

As if!

With a snort of derision, she turned her face against the windowpane and looked outside in time to see the house windows light up one by one, marking his progress through the entry hall into the living area, and then on to the bedrooms. A tug of alarm pulled her hard up against the glass. Which would he choose?

"Please. Not my room, not my bed," she breathed. "It's enough knowing you're in my home."

Whoa! When, precisely, had she started calling Joe's house her home? Sure, she had lived in it the past five

years, but only because Joe insisted, only because he was
the kind of man who brooked no argument.

"You think a house like this deserves to be empty? You
think I want to come here to an empty house after a whole
week spent with too many *idioti* for any one man's patience?"

The backs of her eyes pricked at the memory of Joe's
words, and she pressed her lids tightly closed. She hadn't
cried once in those god-awful months since she'd finally
learned of her boss's terminal illness, and she wasn't going
to start shedding tears now.

*If you don't want to be treated like a girl, don't cry like
one.* That came straight from her father's concise book of
lessons, right after *There's only one thing a man like that
could want from a girl like you.*

She had been young and reckless when she learned the
harsh truth of her father's words. She had given that one
thing to a rich, smooth-talking, heartbreaker named Miles
Newman, and after he laughed at her words of love and
moved on to the new stable girl, she'd dried the last of
her girl-tears and thrown away the handkerchief.

Never again would she trade her self-respect for something she mistook for love. Never again would she mistake
the flashfire of physical attraction for something more. Oh,
she wanted there to be somebody—a special person to
share her life, to love and to cherish—but she didn't need
the palpitations and the heartache and the tears. She needed
strength and stability. She needed respect and understanding and companionship. Until she found a man with those
qualities, she would make do with her own company.

Except at this moment her own company was making
her edgy and unsettled. She swung away from the window
and started to pace her room, but that activity did nothing
to ease her restlessness. The quarters she had accepted as
adequate now felt cold, dank and claustrophobic. The clutter she stepped over and around every day now looked like

a sad chaotic mess. She jammed her eyes shut and cursed Nick Corelli for this new perspective, then cursed herself double-time for caring. His opinion of her living conditions shouldn't matter one blue-eyed damn. But when she opened her eyes they were focused on her bed, and she could still see his long denim-encased legs spread across it. She could still imagine his body heat seeping into the covers.

With a growl of frustration she strode to the door and hauled it open. A horse whickered softly across the way, instantly easing the tightness in her chest. She pulled the door to behind her and moved surefootedly toward the lone equine head that loomed over its stable door.

"Hey, Star." She smiled as she rubbed the proffered jaw, then let her fingers dwell on the velvet warmth of the animal's muzzle. Warm, familiar, soothing. She felt her tense muscles relax another degree, felt her smile kick up a notch. "Don't you ever sleep?" she crooned as she ran her other hand along the mare's neck and under her blanket, automatically checking for warmth.

The mare stalked off with an impatient shake of her head, then circled the box with her long graceful strides. She, Tamara Cole, owned half of this fabulous animal. Shivering with a flash of intense excitement as much as the cold, T.C. shoved her hands deep into her pockets. "No," she told herself firmly. "You know you can't accept it."

And if she didn't accept it, what would happen? She wondered if Joe had considered that possibility and if he had made some provision, named some alternate benefactor. Nick hadn't mentioned it, but then, he hadn't mentioned much at all, and she had been too stunned to think coherently.

Now a whole crowd of questions scrambled for answers. Why had George told her to carry on as usual, knowing she was now a part-owner? Why had Joe made her a part-owner, knowing she would likely refuse the gift? Why had he specifically requested she learn the news from Nick?

Frowning, she turned to lean her back against the stable door. It didn't surprise her that Joe hadn't left Yarra Park to any of his Melbourne-based family. Neither George nor any of his sisters had ever shown any interest in the property—in fact, they had bemoaned their father's obsession with horses. An old man's eccentricity, George had called it, with a condescending twist of his lips.

Nor did it surprise her that he had singled out Nick, the only one who had chosen his own career path in preference to a ready-made position in a Corelli company. At first that decision had caused a rift, but ultimately Nick's independent success had earned his father's respect and admiration. It made sense that Joe would consider Nick worthy of his beloved property, but would Nick appreciate the magnitude of the gift?

T.C. snorted. He called it a consolation prize, for heaven's sake.

Frankly she couldn't see what he would want with a fledgling standardbred training establishment at the opposite end of the world from his New York base, and if he didn't want his half, what should she do about hers?

She blew out a breath and shook her head slowly. "Gee, Joe, it'd be really good if you could help me out here...if you could tell me what you were thinking when you drafted that will." Of course, no magical answer boomed out from beyond the steel rafters. "Seems like I'll have to do this the hard way," she told Star, knowing exactly how difficult that would be.

First she would have to deal with her treacherous body's intense physical response to Nick's presence, and then her awestruck mind might kick into gear and form some meaningful connection with her mouth. Maybe then she would be capable of asking all the questions that needed answering before she could decide what to do.

Three

—————

T.C. intended posing those questions the next time she saw Nick. She planned to stiffen her backbone, look him in the eye and say, "Nick, I need to know your intentions."

She was pleased with that forthright opener, composed the next morning while she and Jason, her stable hand, exercised the first half of their team. And when it was time for a coffee break, she took her mug to an upturned bucket in the breezeway, tilted her face toward the midmorning sun and fine-tuned her intonation.

"Nick, I *need* to know…Nick, I need *to know*…"

Then Nick sauntered into the barn, and her plans, her intonation and her backbone, turned to mush. He wore a polo shirt in the same azure-blue as his eyes, and faded jeans that hugged him in all the right places. The warmth that flooded her body had nothing to do with the sun. Her heart stalled, then bounded into overdrive. She felt all the same jittery reactions as when she stepped a horse onto the track before a big race, but she didn't look away. She couldn't *not* watch his lazy loose-limbed approach. Talk about poetry in slow motion. If he'd been a horse, she would have labeled him a fabulous mover.

"Is this the new boss?" Jason asked.

T.C. nodded, swallowed, inhaled once, exhaled once. By then Nick was close enough for her to notice his shower-damp hair and the rested look about his eyes. It was obvious *his* sleep hadn't been disturbed by spicy aftertones clinging to his pillow!

Somehow she managed to mumble the necessary introductions, and Nick shook Jason's hand. "You must own the one-two-five out front."

Very smooth opening, T.C. thought with a cynical twist of her mouth, seeing as Jason was mad-keen on his newly acquired dirt bike. They swapped notes in that rev-head shorthand T.C. had never understood, and when Ug snuffled noisily out of her morning nap, Nick hunkered down to tickle her behind the ears. With a fatuous look of bliss clouding her mismatched eyes, the dog promptly rolled onto her back.

T.C. snorted. She bet females did that trick for Nick Corelli all the time.

"What do you call her?" His gaze lifted from the prone dog and met T.C.'s over the rim of her coffee mug.

"Ug." Jason supplied the answer, which was just as well, because the smiling warmth in Nick's eyes had struck T.C. dumb. Behind the subterfuge of sipping coffee, she attempted to unravel the knot in her tongue.

"Strange name." He smiled right into her eyes, and that uncooperative tongue looped itself in a second half-hitch. Luckily Jason came to her rescue again.

"When Joe first brought her home—he found her down the road a bit—T.C. said she wanted to call her Lucky, because she was lucky Joe found her. But Joe says 'There's nothin' lucky about a dog that looks like that.'"

"So how did she get to be Ug?" Nick asked.

"Joe said 'I'd call her plain old ugly,' and it just sort of stuck. Except T.C. shortened it to Ug."

T.C. smiled at the familiar anecdote. She felt like she might finally be capable of speech. "You look like you slept well," she said, by way of a start.

"Like a baby." His smile deepened the creases on either side of his mouth, and it struck her that he must smile a lot. "Any more of that coffee around?"

"I'll get it," Jason offered. "Um, you want milk or anythin'?"

"The works." Somehow T.C. wasn't surprised. She figured Nick would demand *the works* in all kinds of ways. "Plenty of milk, at least two sugars. Thanks, Jason."

As the kid bustled off, Nick hoped the coffee wasn't already bubbling away in a percolator. He wanted some time alone with Tamara. He pulled up the bucket vacated by Jason and sat. "You know, I'd still be sleeping like a baby except the phone rang."

She stopped fidgeting with her mug and went very still. "I didn't hear it. I guess we were down at the track. Was the call for me?"

"I can't say. There was no one there."

She cradled the mug in both hands as if to steady it, declared, "Probably a wrong number," then swiveled around to peer down the alleyway. "I wonder what's keeping Jason?"

Nick gritted his teeth. Her evasiveness was already roughing the edges of his patience. "If it was a boyfriend calling," he suggested slowly, "I might have put him off."

"If I had a boyfriend, he'd know not to call when it's short odds I'd be down at the track."

When he met her hostile glare, Nick felt a perverse satisfaction, and it had nothing to do with the no-boyfriend revelation. Finally he had her attention. "Seems to me

there's something funny going on with your telephone. No
one there this morning, off the hook yesterday.''

"Geez, T.C.'' Neither had heard Jason's approach. He
stood there, shaking his head reproachfully. "Did you
leave it off the hook again?'' He handed Nick his coffee.
"She did that the other day, too.''

The warning glare she directed at Jason told Nick his
instincts were spot on. "Perhaps you had better explain.''

"Explain what? I knocked the receiver off the hook and
didn't notice. You got a wrong number. End of story.''
With a dismissive shrug, she turned to Jason. "You can
show Nick around while I finish the jogging.''

Nick stopped her intended exit with a hand on her shoulder. "Have you been getting nuisance calls?''

When she shuffled from foot to foot without answering,
Nick increased the pressure on her shoulder. Over the top
of her head he met Jason's worried look and smiled re-
assuringly. "How about you carry on with the horses while
I sort this out?''

As Jason set off, whistling cheerfully, he felt her tense
up beneath his hand. "You've been here less than twelve
hours and you're giving directions to my staff?''

"Our staff,'' he corrected.

She let out her breath in a soft whoosh. "We have to
talk about that.''

"Yes, we do. But first we're going to settle the phone
business.''

She bit her bottom lip, and Nick waited a count of ten
while she considered. "So, okay, there has been the odd
anonymous call.''

"How long has this been going on?''

She shrugged. "A couple of weeks. On and off.''

"A couple of *weeks!* Have you reported it?''

"Look, there's nothing to report. No threats, no heavy
breathing. Probably just kids mucking about. It's no big
deal.''

"No?" Nick swore beneath his breath, then out loud when the penny dropped. "That's why you attacked me last night. You thought I was the caller. What if you'd been right? What if I *had* been some stalker hell-bent on hurting you? Did you think of that before you confronted me with that damn fool toy?"

"I can look after myself. I've been looking after myself—"

"Is that what you think you were doing when you ran your hands all over me last night?" He grabbed her hand and pulled it to him, forcing her to touch him, then to stroke down his chest from collarbone to waist in one long, slow sensuous caress. "When you touched me like this?"

She recoiled as if she had contacted a live wire, then stood blinking her huge green eyes at him. She rubbed the hand he had used to demonstrate his point down her thigh as if trying to remove his imprint from her skin.

That notion was as powerfully erotic as her actual touch.

With a proud lift of her chin, she drew herself up as tall as her diminished height allowed and met his gaze. "I did not touch you like that," she said with quiet dignity.

"You might as well have," Nick muttered, and grimaced at the uncomfortable tightness of his jeans as she turned on her heel and walked away, her backbone rigid, head held high. He watched her until she disappeared out the front of the barn, and then he shook his head in disgust.

Well, hell, didn't that little demonstration come off a treat?

All he had managed to prove was how easily she could fire up his temper and heat his blood. He had come out here this morning to get the phone business sorted, to smooth over their rocky start with some getting-to-know-you dialogue, then to move her back into the house. After lunch he wanted to check the balance sheet valuations to ensure the offer he made to buy her out was fair. And after dinner, once business was out of the way, his getting-to-know-you plans were aimed purely at pleasure.

So far he had barely managed to tackle item one on his list—not exactly a grade-A start. Then he relived the touch of her hand, recalled the hot spark in her eyes and the soft color in her cheeks, and he smiled. He had some work in front of him to get to that last pleasurable item, but it would be worth the effort.

Yep, it would take both work and flexibility, and when Jason came by leading a horse, Nick saw an opportunity to adapt his plans. Chances were he would learn more from the kid in an hour than he could finesse from Tamara in a day.

"Need some help?" he asked as Jason tethered the animal to a hitching rail.

"You know how to bandage?"

Nick counted four rolls in Jason's hands and smiled easily. "I'm a quick study. You show me the first one, and I figure I can manage the rest."

T.C. eased Monte's leg down, stretched out the kink in her back and tried to prevent her gaze straying to the other end of the barn. What were they laughing about *this* time? They'd been at it for more than an hour, chatting easily, laughing with nerve-grating regularity, Jason obviously reveling in his role as teacher to Nick's student. Their rapport shouldn't rankle. Nick could spread his charm from here to the back of beyond, but as long as he didn't try it on her, what should she care?

With a last disgruntled glance in their direction, she stooped down, took Monte's leg again and eased it between her knees, determined to refocus on rasping a level surface for the horseshoe. She managed to concentrate for all of three minutes before she heard the slow tread of approaching boots, then the scrape of a drum against concrete. Looking back beneath her arm, she saw the out-stretched length of denim-clad legs as he took a seat.

Ignore him, she warned her body, but to no avail. Already her muscles had tightened in unconscious response to his proximity, to the notion of him watching her. So okay, she told herself, the man unnerves you, but he's right there, not six feet away, and it's about time you started on that list of questions. But as she shifted the words about in her mind, forcing them into some sort of logical order, her tension must have transmitted itself to Monte and he shifted his weight, almost overbalancing her.

By the time she righted herself and calmed Monte, she had decided this was neither the time nor the place for this conversation. Much too important for casual asides between hammer blows, she justified, attacking Monte's hoof with renewed fervor because she wanted the job finished—quickly. She could practically feel the touch of that warm blue gaze on her backside every time she bent into her task, but she clenched her jaw firmly, determined not to show how much he disconcerted her.

"What are you doing?" Nick asked after she had stead-fastly ignored him for several minutes.

"Rasping."

"I can see that much."

"Glad your eyesight's not a problem," she mumbled.

"Nothing wrong with my eyesight…fortunately."

She let the horse's leg down and tsked with disgust as she strode to the anvil seated on a nearby workbench and started bashing at the horseshoe. "Haven't you anything better to do than ogle my backside?" *Bash. Bash. Bash.*

"You think I was ogling?"

She stopped hammering long enough to cast him a long-suffering look.

"I hardly ever ogle a woman with a hammer in her hand. Too dangerous."

She almost smiled at that. Almost. Nick wondered why

she fought the urge, wondered what it would take to hear her laugh out loud. He had a feeling he would enjoy seeing her emotive eyes brimming with laughter even more than he enjoyed them sparking with irritation.

"I hope it doesn't bother you, me sitting here, watching you."

"Actually it does." Tossing the hammer aside, she turned around to face him. "I'm not used to having anyone watch me work."

"Joe didn't?"

"He…he didn't make me feel uncomfortable." And Nick did. He could see the uneasiness in her gaze, in the restless way she shifted her weight from one hip to the other, in the way she scuffed the toe of one boot against the ground.

"You must have gotten along pretty well with Joe," he said before she could turn away again. He didn't mind if her discomfort was due to her awareness of him, but he did want her comfortable enough to talk with him. Joe seemed like the place to start.

"Because he left me so much?"

"That's not what I meant."

One corner of her mouth curled cynically. "No?"

"No. You say you weren't lovers, but obviously you were closer than the usual boss-employee."

Their eyes met and held, and he saw a flicker of something—maybe surprise, maybe relief, maybe some kind of yielding—before she looked away. He saw her swallow, then take a deep breath, before she spoke in a slow, measured voice.

"Joe gave me this job at a time when I really needed it, and he did so against everyone's advice. I knew horses, but I'd never managed a stable this size. I was young and inexperienced, plus I was female. But he went with his gut instinct, and he gave me the job." A ghost of a smile curved her lips and touched Nick somewhere deep inside, somewhere he didn't even want to identify. "I made sure he never regretted that decision, and he appreciated the extra effort I put in. We weren't lovers, but we built a bond."

"Of mutual respect?"

She looked up then, and the intensity in her eyes smacked him hard, midchest. "I don't know about the mutual, but I do know how much I respected Joe. I admired him, I loved him, I wished he was my father." The last phrase came out in a breathy rush. Then, as if she regretted letting on so much, she turned her head and looked away.

"You said Joe gave you a job at a time when you really needed it. You were broke?"

"In more ways than you can imagine."

Silently Nick willed her to go on, to tell him something of the past that shadowed her voice.

"I won't bore you with the long story. Suffice it to say my esteem had taken a pounding and this job was exactly what I needed. I'm not talking about finding employment or the money—it was the responsibility and the trust. It was his belief in me."

She turned abruptly and stomped back to the horse, leaving Nick standing there weighed down by the intensity of her words and his own memories. He had experienced that same aching need. Hell, he'd spent the first eight years of his life with no one caring for him, let alone believing in him, so it had taken him a long time to recognize those gifts as the most precious Joe had given him when he took him into his family and called him his second son.

"Yeah," he muttered hoarsely to himself. "I wish he'd been my father, too."

He found her back at work, nailing the shoe with businesslike efficiency, as if she had already shed the emotion that still knotted Nick's gut. That irritated him almost as much as how she had walked away. He watched her swat a fly from the horse's belly, and with half an eye noticed the animal had worked its lead undone. It didn't seem to be going anywhere—in fact, it looked like it had fallen asleep. What was it with her animals and sleep?

"Why don't you get a farrier to do that?" he asked.

"Pay someone to do something I can do? I don't think so."

"Why do something so tough and painstaking when you can pay someone to do it?" he countered.

She looked up, her eyes sharp with disdain. "That's not my way of doing things."

Trying to prove her toughness, Nick guessed. Not because she was young and inexperienced, but because she was female. There was a story here, a history he suddenly needed to know. "What *is* your way, Tamara?"

No answer. Okay. He would try a different tack.

"How did you learn to farrier?"

"My father taught me."

"Your father's a horseman?"

"He was."

That was it. No further explanation, and, dammit, her reticence intrigued him as much as it irritated him. "So you followed the family tradition into horse training?"

In one smooth movement she turned, drew the horse's leg forward and rested the hoof on her thigh. "I chose this profession because I love it. Tradition had nothing to do with it."

Nick inspected her closely drawn brows, the flare of her nostrils, her tense grip on the hammer. "For someone who loves her job, you don't look like you're having much fun."

Eyes almost crossed with consternation, she glared up at him, but before she could respond the horse swung its head and nipped her neatly on the backside. She yelped and leaped sideways, and when Nick grabbed her shoulders to pull her aside and then to steady her, he noticed the tears flooding her eyes. He also noticed that she wasn't rubbing her behind but was sucking her thumb.

"Hey, what's the matter?"

She slid the thumb from her mouth, and Nick felt the most unexpected rush of heat. Unexpected and unwarranted, given the circumstances. It was those lips, that damn pout.

"Here, let me see." Gently he took her hand and inspected the blood oozing from the base of her thumb. The sharp end of an unclinched nail had obviously dug in. "Do you have first-aid supplies?"

"It's only a scratch."

He silenced her with a look. "Sit down and don't move."

His authority didn't come from a raised voice but a certain don't-argue timbre. It had worked on Ug the previous night, and it worked on T.C. now. She sat on the drum. She didn't move. And when she looked up to find him standing, feet spread, hands on hips, glaring down at her, she told him where to find the first-aid kit.

"It's in the lunchroom—in the cupboard next to the fridge." She indicated the general direction with her good hand. He nodded grimly, pivoted, then stopped short when confronted by the ugly end of Monte. T.C. watched in amazement as he smacked the gelding's rump to turn him around, gathered up the lead and retethered it to the hitching rail before striding off.

Like he did it every day.

She didn't want to admire the man's competence—she had spent the last half hour deliberately not admiring anything about him—so she turned her attention to her thumb. Gingerly she wiggled it back and forth, reminding herself that the pain was all *his* fault.

If he hadn't disturbed her sleep, she wouldn't be so fuzzy-headed. If he hadn't forced her to touch him, her senses wouldn't be chock-full of memories of his hands on her. If he hadn't distracted her with his questions, she would have noticed Monte was loose.

So let him play Mr. Competence if he wanted. Maybe then he would go off and do something else—like leave her in peace.

Unfortunately his idea of playing Mr. Competence involved hunkering down in front of her and steadying himself with a hand on each of her knees. She could feel every degree of his body heat radiating through his long fingers, through her jeans and her skin, all the way into her flesh. For a man who moved with such lithe grace, he seemed to take an inordinate length of time to regain his balance and remove his hands.

Not that T.C. gained much respite. She had scarcely recovered her equilibrium before he picked up her hand, placed it palm-up in one of his and bent over to inspect her injury.

She stared at her hand lying in his. How small and soft it looked compared with his—exactly as he had described it in the early hours of the morning. She disliked that thought as much as she disliked the hitch in her breath as his thumb stroked across the center of her palm, tracing her lifeline. Or was that her heart line?

She closed her eyes and dragged in a breath, but instead of badly needed oxygen, her lungs filled with his soft musky scent. Dimly she thought about leaning forward and burying her nose in his neck…but then something akin to liquid fire hit her thumb, and she rose clean off the drum.

Nick steadied her with a hand on her elbow. "Sting a little?" he asked as he reapplied the antiseptic-soaked swab.

"Try a lot," she muttered shakily.

He leaned closer, so close that when he looked up, she could make out tiny flecks of gold in the blue of his irises. Then he smiled that brilliant world-tilting smile, and she couldn't help but return it.

"Good girl," he murmured, and for some dumb reason the admiration intermingled with concern in his eyes brought a thick lump to her throat. Tears welled in her eyes. To her chagrin, one spilled over and rolled down her cheek. She scrubbed at it with the back of her free hand, bit her lip, chanced a glance from beneath her lashes.

The hand on her elbow tightened for a second; then he bent over the first-aid kit at his feet. "We need to get this covered up."

He took longer than necessary to fix a plaster to her wound, as if he knew she needed time to collect herself and that she would find her tears humiliating. The thought of such insightfulness threatened her composure all over again. She shut her eyes and tried to concentrate on the pain—except there didn't seem to be much of that anymore.

"All right now?" His thumb gently stroked the inside of her wrist.

T.C. nodded, although she wasn't all right. For a start, there was that thumb stroking fire across her oversensitive skin. She knew his intent was solicitous rather than sensuous, but her senses weren't listening to reason. He moved, or she moved, or maybe the air around them moved, for she caught another heady whiff of his scent.

Burying her nose in his neck suddenly seemed like the only thing to do. With eyes still closed, she must have actually leaned in his direction, because the drum tipped forward and she would have toppled right into his lap but for a last second reflex that saw both her hands curl around his upper arms, her injury forgotten.

"Hey, no need to throw yourself at me."

His quip should have defused the awkwardness. T.C. did try to smile back, but her lips wouldn't cooperate. The sensation of taut muscles beneath her hands had turned her mouth desert-dry. She tried another smile, considered removing her hands, but couldn't manage either simple task.

And when she moistened her lips, his gaze followed the movement. His smile faded. There was a moment of intense gravity as they studied each other, and T.C. felt as if she was suspended in time and motion. As if her senses were too packed full of everything-Nick to allow anything else in.

Nearby a horse snorted, breaking the spell, and one corner of Nick's mouth kicked up. She could have escaped then, if she had wanted to. She didn't. She sat still, completely enmeshed in the slow-motion sequence. His hand reached toward her. His fingers combed a slow path through her hair, to her nape. He drew her face to his, gradually and surely, until their lips finally met.

His were warm, their touch soft and restrained, as if he were savoring that first contact as much as she. It was no more than lips meeting, touching, retreating, returning, yet it was the most exquisitely sensual indulgence of her life.

She whimpered low in her throat. His hand tightened on her neck, drew her mouth closer, while he slowly—oh so slowly—tasted his way around her lips, enticing them open, inviting her response, causing a cascade of delight to ripple through her body. He was leisurely, almost lazy, but he was very, very thorough. Around the edges of her hearing something jangled vaguely, but she shut it out, focusing all her senses on the complexities of a kiss she had never known existed.

Until he pulled away from her clinging lips.

Then she recognized the metallic strike of shod hooves on concrete, heard a low tuneless whistle, the clink of a steel bit. Jason returning from the track.

Four

Like a teenager caught necking, T.C. jumped to her feet, stumbling over her boots—or Nick's—in her clumsy haste.

"Jason's back," she said, only because she had to say something, to drop some words into the ever-deepening pool of silence.

"I did gather that."

"Yes, well, I should go help him."

"I'm sure he can manage," Nick said reasonably.

"Manage what?" Jason asked as he came into view. He pulled up short and frowned at T.C. "Thought you were going into town to watch Dave do that bone-chip op?"

Thank you, Jase! T.C. checked her watch and tossed an apologetic smile in Nick's general direction. "I lost all track of time. If I don't get moving, I'll be late."

"I need to pick up a few things in town. How about I drive and we can talk on the way?"

T.C. shook her head vehemently. "No. That's absolutely not necessary." She needed to get away from him, to cool the suffocating heat from her blood, to talk some common sense into her muddled mind. She had no right to be kissing Nick. Those kinds of luxuries belonged in fantasies, not in real life. "I could be hours at the vet's, and then I have some shopping to do. I'm sure you have other plans for the afternoon."

His lips set in a stubborn line, and she could imagine him picking her up and tossing her bodily into the passenger seat. A tempting frisson of anticipation scurried up her spine, and she retreated quickly, holding up a hand, as if that might keep it at bay.

"Look, I'm happy to shop for you. I know there's nothing in the house unless you brought supplies with you, and I can hardly imagine you packing bread and milk and tea bags." She was prattling about as quickly as she was backpedaling. She took a deep breath and made herself stop. "I'm going to shower and change. Just write a list and put it in the Courier out front."

"You'll be gone all afternoon?"

"Unless Dave is called away on an emergency and has to reschedule the operation."

He seemed to give that considerable thought, and she wished for an insight into whatever was ticking over in his mind. Especially when she glimpsed a hint of wickedness around the edges of his quick smile. "And picking up a few things for me won't be any trouble?"

"None at all."

Despite an unsettling sense of *what-have-I-done?* she smiled brightly, turned and made it halfway down the breezeway before he called out to her.

"Tamara."

T.C. closed her eyes, which was a big mistake. Without vision, the impact of his voice drawling her name intensified about a thousand times as it curled around her senses. Slowly she turned to face him.

"About our unfinished business..."

Her gaze was drawn to the source of those softly spoken words, to the mouth that had moved with such sure sensuality over hers. Her lips tingled just thinking about it. Was that the business he meant? She shook her head slightly, dismissing the notion, but only until Nick spoke again.

"We *will* get back to it," he assured her. "Later."

Nick had just finished washing an afternoon's hard labor from his body when he heard the rattle of a vehicle crossing the grid into the house-yard. A silver flash sped past the window, and his pulse did a surprising little snap to attention.

Ignoring his body's response, he leaned in close to the shower-fogged mirror, rasped a hand over his six-o'clock shadow and reached for his razor as the front door slammed. The noise reverberated through every timber beam in the low sprawling house, setting the long bank of picture windows rattling.

Nick winced.

She sounded about as mad as he figured she should be, considering the shopping list he'd left on her dash. Possibly over the top—no, *definitely* over the top—but unavoidable. It had ensured that she would be gone long enough even if the veterinary operation didn't go ahead. Long enough for him to get his plans back in order.

As he carefully maneuvered his razor through the dip in his chin, he wondered how long her snit would last and how long it would take him to cajole her out of it. The notion set up a powerful thrum of anticipation. She could play tough and indifferent all she liked, but that kiss had given her away. He hitched a towel around his hips and headed into his bedroom to dress, his smile ripe with expectation.

The sharp tap of her boot heels on the slate floor must have masked his arrival, so Nick leaned back against a

kitchen bench and watched her crisscross the room, tossing
packages into the fridge, then the pantry, muttering to herself most of the while. She turned and took several more
strides before spotting him. Her gaze flicked from his face
to his fingers, which were still busy fastening shirt buttons.
Her stride faltered.

"Oh. You *are* here."

"Sorry I couldn't help you in with this stuff." He gestured at the grocery bags stacked on the island. "You
caught me just out of the shower, and I figured you'd prefer if I put some clothes on. Right?"

Her gaze followed his hands as he tucked his shirt into
his jeans. "Yes…um…right." Then, with a mental snap
to attention that was almost audible, she swung back to
the bench and buried her head in a grocery bag. "You
could help me put this away instead of taking up space."

"I could. But then I wouldn't have the pleasure of
watching you."

She rolled her eyes, clamped her teeth shut and continued stashing groceries.

It hadn't been a line—well, not entirely. The simmering
temper suited her almost as well as the sweet-fitting jeans.
There wasn't a lot to her top, so when she delved into the
next bag it rode up her back to bare an enticing sliver of
skin. He imagined sliding his hands over the silky warmth
of her skin and laying his lips against her smooth golden
nape.

As if his thoughts had been transmitted telepathically,
she jumped sideways to put more space between
them…and bumped her hipbone against a doorknob.

His attention was diverted by the hand rubbing her hipbone. It was the hand she'd injured earlier. "How is your
thumb?"

"I'll live," she replied, with an abrupt little shrug.

"Did you see a doctor?"

"It's a scratch, for goodness' sake. Get over it." She tugged a tattered piece of paper from her pocket. Nick recognized his shopping list. "I managed to find most of this stuff, *eventually,* but I had no idea what this—" she stabbed a finger at his scrawled handwriting "—this hieroglyphic was supposed to be. Some sort of schnapps." She delved into the last bag and slapped a bottle down on the counter. "This is the best I could do."

"Is it butterscotch?"

"Does it matter?" she spluttered, eyes wide and incredulous.

Nick rubbed his chin as if giving the matter deep thought. Of course it didn't matter. He'd added it to the list while still savoring the impact of that rich, sweet, heady kiss—a kiss with a kick at the end that had left him breathless. Exactly like butterscotch schnapps.

"Oh, for goodness' sake! When I offered to shop for you I was thinking basics, not exotic liqueurs and fresh pasta and bloody Atlantic salmon. Riddells Crossing doesn't exactly cater to gourmet tastes." She snapped the last bag shut, crumpled it into a tight ball and strode over to the bin.

He could actually feel the hot vibes of her anger blazing across the space between them, but he couldn't help stoking the fire. "In my experience, shopping *improves* a woman's temperament," he said, tongue firmly in cheek. "Makes her amenable."

She spun around, eyes spitting green fire. "Amenable to do what? Cook for you?"

"Some do," he drawled. "Others just skip that step and head straight for the dessert tray."

"I'm sure *they* do. Me, I've never had much of a sweet tooth."

Nick laughed out loud. She was about as thorny as a full-grown prickly pear, yet that didn't seem to matter. He couldn't remember the last time he had felt so thoroughly entertained.

"I'm all done here, so I'll leave you to it," she said.

With a little jolt of alarm, Nick straightened off the bench. She couldn't be leaving—not without giving him a chance at some heavy-duty cajoling.

"But I haven't thanked you for doing the shopping." He moved closer, trapping her in the right angle where two benches met. He leaned nearer still, until he could reach around her to snag a bottle of wine from the bench top.

"Oh," she said, as if she had expected something else from his proximity. She moistened her parted lips. "I really have to go. My own groceries are in the car. They'll be getting hot."

"Really? I didn't think it was that hot. Are you hot, Tamara?"

She shook her head.

Liar.

The heat softened the brilliance of her eyes and flushed her cheeks and throat. Nick focused on the rapid pulse beating in the hollow of her throat, and the need to touch his lips to that spot, to taste her heat, gripped him suddenly and intensely.

Cool it, he told himself. Despite the heat sizzling between them, instinct told him she wasn't ready for hot and heavy. With a wry half smile, he brushed the backs of his fingers across her throat. She swallowed convulsively and almost climbed backward onto the bench.

"Please, don't touch me," she breathed, eyes wide and panicky.

"You didn't mind earlier, down at the stables."

"That was a mistake. I was upset with the accident and—" she took a deep breath that trembled "—it won't happen again."

"Now that would be a pity."

"Oh, puh-lease! There's no need to patronize me."

"I'm not. I enjoyed kissing you. I absolutely want to kiss you again." He regarded her through narrowed eyes. "The enjoyment seemed mutual."

She looked away. "As far as kisses go, it was okay, but I'm not interested in taking this any further."

For a second Nick thought about pushing it, about proving that he kissed—*they* kissed—better than okay. Slowly he lifted a hand toward her face, but her swift intake of breath, the wide frantic eyes, made him pause. She was scared. Scared of letting him close? Scared of her own response? Scared of the powerful chemistry between them?

It didn't matter which.

He wanted her leaning into him, meeting him halfway, as she'd done at the stables. He didn't care to analyze why, so he simply moved away.

Even after his retreat, T.C.'s heart continued to hammer against her rib cage. Feeling weak and hot and breathless, she lifted an absent hand to her throat, to where she swore the brush of his hand had blistered a trail right through her skin. She gazed longingly at the door. If only her weak, trembling legs could carry her there. She shifted her weight from one foot to the other and decided to give them another minute before trying them out.

"I think it's time we had that talk, Tamara." With an expert twist of his wrist, he decorked the wine, then laid the corkscrew on the bench.

T.C. shifted her weight again. Left foot, right foot. Right foot, left foot. Her strength seemed to be returning. She should leave.

Except her gaze was drawn to Nick as he poured two measures of Shiraz. He picked one up, twirling the glass in his long fingers so the liquid shimmered ruby-red in the light. He lifted it to his lips, took more than a sip, and a shiver of longing vibrated through her body.

God help her, she wanted to taste that wine on his lips. On his tongue.

Her gaze darted to the door. She had to leave before she did something stupid, like drinking the wine he'd obviously poured for her. With alcohol dulling her defenses it would be too easy to let him touch her again, to kiss her again, to turn her to mush with less than a casual fingertip. By purring her name, damn his too sexy, overconfident hide.

The sudden flash of temper fortified her, and her legs held her weight when she stood up straight. "I'm going now."

"You don't want to discuss this partnership problem?"

"Of course I do."

"Then how about you take the wine into the front room," he suggested smoothly, "while I throw a couple of steaks on the grill?"

"No." She shook her head emphatically. No way could she eat with him, drink with him, and concentrate on business. "I can't stay."

"Can't or won't?"

"Actually I'm going out." Dave *had* asked her to stay for dinner. She had declined, but it seemed like the perfect time to change her mind. She cleared her throat. "I have a dinner date."

His glass paused midway to his mouth. "With your vet friend?"

"How did you know that?"

"Lucky guess."

T.C. considered his bland expression, the small movement of his hand that caused the wine to circle his glass in measured motion, and she knew luck had nothing to do with that guess. Indignation washed through her, hot and fierce. "Do I take it you spent the afternoon grilling Jason?"

"We talked some."

"And Dave's name just happened to crop up?"

"We were discussing your nuisance calls," he said evenly. "I asked Jason about ex-boyfriends, and the vet's name came up."

"Dave is not an ex-boyfriend."

"Do you mean not an ex, or not a boyfriend?"

T.C. ignored that. "You had no right to quiz Jase about my friends," she said stiffly, although she could have used the singular form, such was the sad state of her social life. "There is no logical reason for the calls. Like I said before, it's most likely kids mucking about."

"If that's the case, they will stop. I ordered a silent number, and it's already in place." He pulled a piece of note paper from his pocket. "Don't give it out to anyone you wouldn't trust with your life. Okay?"

As she took in his sober expression and his strong bold print on the note, T.C. felt something she hadn't felt in a long time. She couldn't put a name to it, but it had to do with someone watching out for her, and at that moment it seemed as scarily seductive as the soft touch of his lips. She grabbed the note and backed up, half afraid she might do something crazy—like leaning into his strength.

"Thank you." She swallowed, slid both hands along with the note into her back pockets. "That's something I should have done. I don't know why I didn't think of it."

"Perhaps you've had too much else to think about."

Perhaps. That certainly sounded better than the alternative that sprang to her mind. She'd done nothing because she didn't want to admit she felt scared and threatened, because she didn't want to appear weak. How stupid would *that* sound if she tried to explain?

"So, what else did you and Jason talk about?" she asked to change the subject.

"Mostly about the horses, the stable routine. He's a good kid. You did well choosing him."

"He was Joe's choice, actually."

His eyes narrowed. "I sense there's a story here."

"Not really. His mother used to do some casual work here as a housekeeper before her husband died. Jase got into a bit of trouble. Bad company, not enough to occupy himself. Joe gave him a chance, and he turned out to be a natural."

"He says he learned it all from you—that you're the natural."

T.C. laughed self-consciously. "I told you I was good at my job."

"Yeah, you did."

He was watching her with serious eyes and the smallest hint of a smile on his beautiful lips, and her heart slammed hard against her ribs. Oh, help! She couldn't think of a thing to say. Couldn't move.

"You know, I really enjoyed myself this afternoon. I'd forgotten that elementally satisfying thing about manual labor, getting dirty and sweaty for a purpose."

"You helped Jase clean out the yard?"

He laughed, probably at the expression on her face. "No need to sound so shocked. With two of us, we got it done in less than half the time."

"So what did you do with all that time you saved?"

His pause was infinitesimal—just long enough for T.C. to realize she wasn't going to like what came next. "We shifted you back into the house."

"You shifted me...? You moved my things?" She pictured his hands on her clothes, her underwear, and felt both hot and cold at once. She sucked in a long breath, tried to summon some indignation. Unfortunately, all she could summon was a wishy-washy, "I wish you hadn't done that."

"I told you last night you were moving. Jase agreed it'd be easier if we presented it as a fait accompli."

"Jase wouldn't know a fait accompli if it bit him on the butt!"

His laughter was quick and unexpected and, like everything else about Nick Corelli, infectious. T.C. couldn't help responding, couldn't stop herself from grinning back at him. With a slow shake of his head, he caught her gaze, arched that one brow and said, "Damn, but you are a surprising woman. I thought you'd be going for my throat by now."

Her gaze skidded to the throat in question, and she felt that same hot-cold, heart-slamming response. How surprised would he be if she went for this throat with her lips and her tongue and her teeth? She swallowed the heat, the thought, the incredible temptation, and looked away. "I should be mad at you. I suspect, after I've stewed on it a while, I *will* be mad at you. I hate people touching my things."

"Yeah, you have a right to be angry," he said slowly. Then, "How long d'you usually stew on these things?"

Huh? She looked up, blinking, caught that hint of wickedness on his lips.

"I'm wondering if I should lock my door tonight...."

T.C. blinked again.

"I'd hate to be attacked in my sleep with something else from your toy arsenal."

"I don't have an arsenal. Jase's cousin left that cap gun when he was here one day. I found it out back and put it in the tack room and forgot about it until the other night." And why am I bothering to explain? He's packed all my things. He knows exactly what I own and don't own.

"So I can sleep soundly tonight?"

Oh great! All night she would be imagining Nick behind an *un*locked door, Nick sleeping soundly with his arms wrapped around his pillow, his tanned back exposed by the low-riding covers....

Brrriiiinnnngggg!

The first buzz of the phone resounded through T.C.'s bones. She would have sworn her feet literally left the ground, and her gaze, wide and panicked, flew to Nick's before she could censure herself. And as he reached for the cordless on the bench, his eyes told her exactly what she wanted to hear. *Relax. You're not on your own here. I've got this.*

"Yeah?" he barked into the receiver. Then the expression in his eyes, still focused intently on hers, softened. So did his voice when he said, "Lissa, honey, how's things?"

A slow smile spread across his face as he listened to *Lissa, honey's* long-winded reply. T.C. noticed his whole body relax, and as if there had been some weird energy transferal, her own tension compounded until she couldn't stand still.

She mouthed "I'll be going now" and gestured to the door. With one hand over the mouthpiece, Nick called, "Hang on a minute—I want to talk to you," but she kept on moving. She didn't stop until she'd slammed the door on the voice and the eyes that demanded she stay, even while some other woman, a woman trusted enough to have their new unlisted number, hung on the end of the telephone.

Nick, honey, I don't think so!

"You gonna take that job over in the west now?" Big Will, who single-handedly ran the only licensed premises in Riddells Crossing, slid T.C. the beer she had ordered and the question she had not been expecting in one smooth motion.

"Did I miss something?" T.C. shook her head, not understanding where Will was coming from or, for that matter going to, with his opening gambit.

"Now the son and heir's finally shown up, are you gonna take that job you were offered?"

"Ah, so Jase has been in here already tonight."

"You got it." Will grinned. "Didn't stay long. Red's here."

T.C. scanned the bar and found Red Wilmot in the far corner, lounging against the silent jukebox. He had recently returned home from a lengthy stay in juvenile detention, and there was something about his cocky stance and sneering face that had her quickly turning away before he caught her looking. "Do you suppose he's learned his lesson?"

"I know Jase has, thanks to you and Joe."

"Jase is a good kid. Red was a bad influence, that's all."

"You could have done us all a favor and brought this Corelli bloke in with you." The loud, intrusive voice came from one of the tables to her right. Judy Meicklejohn, T.C. decided without turning around.

"She's going to dinner with Dave," someone informed Judy. "She could hardly bring another bloke along."

"No kidding? I didn't know you and Dave were playing kissy-kissy."

"We're not," T.C. replied. "We're just friends."

When someone, probably Judy, made scoffing noises, T.C. shifted uncomfortably on her stool. She had told Nick she had a dinner date with Dave. She hadn't bothered telling *him* they were just friends. And why is that, Tamara Cole? she asked herself. Because you wanted to scare him off, or because you wanted him to think another man found you desirable?

"What's the story, T.C.?" Will interrupted her thoughts with another of his questions-from-nowhere.

"Which story would that be?"

"Joe's son from New York," Rory Meicklejohn interjected. "Is he a big hotshot?"

"Or, more to the point—is he big and is he hot?" T.C. didn't recognize that female voice, and because her face had turned hot, she didn't turn around to see who had made them all hoot with laughter.

"Jase says he's cool."

"Which doesn't mean he can't be hot. Come on, T.C., spill it. What's he like?"

A good question. "He only arrived last night, so it's hard to say," she replied carefully.

"You think he'll keep the place?"

"Why would a city slicker like him want a place out here?" Judy scoffed.

"Joe wanted a place out here."

"That's different. He *bought* the place."

"This geezer might like it here, too."

T.C. shut her ears to the speculation that flowed back and forth across the bar. She was still stuck on the "What's he like?" question and discovering that she might have misjudged him a teensy bit. Today she had discovered a real man beneath the smooth talker. That man had tended to her injury with a gentle efficiency, had helped Jase shovel muck for half the afternoon, and had worried enough about her security and comfort to move her back into the house *and* to change the phone number.

And which man changed your perception of how a kiss should be, Tamara Cole? Was that the real man or the smooth talker?

T.C. frowned into her beer and hoped it was the smooth talker, the one she'd left smiling for *Lissa, honey.* The one who had tricked her into shopping for him, who teased her in the kitchen with his soft touches and smarmy lines. Yes, she decided, with a reinforcing nod, the kiss had to be Mr. Smooth Talker.

Because if it was the real man, she was in big, big trouble.

Five

"**A**nyone in particular you're trying not to wake?"

The amused question startled T.C. into dropping the boots she'd been carrying, and she jerked her head around so sharply something pulled in her neck.

Oh, great! Whiplash is exactly what I need.

She lifted a hand to rub at her stiff neck and glared at the man responsible. Propped in the doorway to the office, a mug in one hand and a sheaf of papers in the other, he looked far too awake for five-thirty in the morning.

"You want me to do that for you?" His velvet-coated drawl stroked her sleepy senses to immediate complete wakefulness; the thought of his strong, supple hands on her neck sent them into hyperactivity.

No!

No more touching. Last night she had decided that the best way to defuse the Nick-factor was to avoid all nonbusiness-related situations.

"I didn't expect you to be up this early," she admitted.

"My body clock's taking a while to adjust. I was awake before three, but then I crashed at ten."

So there had been no need to stay out late. Damn, she wished she had known that.

"Did you enjoy your evening?"

"Very much." Which wasn't so much a lie as a relative truth. When Dave had finally arrived after a difficult emergency procedure, they'd ditched the restaurant in favor of takeout. Dave fell asleep halfway through the combination of chow mein and cop show. T.C. had finished the food, channel-surfed into the early hours and worked on convincing herself that she preferred comfortable and stress-free to unpredictable and edgy. Like, say, the Shiraz-and-steaks-with-Nick alternative she had turned down.

Nick straightened away from the door frame and waved his mug. "Coffee's not long made."

Filling her nostrils with the strong fresh aroma tested her resolve, but she shook her head. "Thanks, but I'll just grab some juice and keep going."

She retrieved her boots and headed for the kitchen, remembering at the last minute to dispense with the sneaking.

"Do you always start this early?" he asked from close behind.

T.C. almost dropped her boots again. "Usually." As she grabbed a glass and swung across to open the fridge, she felt the warmth of his lazy inspection all the way to her toes.

"Sure you don't want coffee?"

Leaning further into the refrigerator's cooling depths, she mumbled a negative reply and tried to recall what she was looking for. When she slammed the door shut in exasperation, she found him still watching her, and the refrigerator's chilling effect immediately evaporated.

With a barely articulate "See you later" she dispensed

with the glass, snatched an apple from the fruit bowl and bolted.

"Is that breakfast?" he asked as he followed her to the back door.

"I don't like to eat early," she lied. "I catch up later, after fast work."

"Fast work happens to be my specialty."

With a mental eye-roll, she explained how her version of fast work referred to exercising the horses fast, in full race harness, as opposed to their slow work or jog days. "Jase and I usually do fast work first thing."

"Jase will be a little late today, but I'll—"

"What do you mean, a little late?"

"Ten. Eleven." He shrugged as if it didn't matter either way.

"It would have been nice to know this."

"I tried to tell you last night, but you bolted before I could finish."

True, but that didn't make it any easier to digest. "Please check with me before you go giving him any more time off," she said stiffly.

"Sure." His drawl sounded smoothly agreeable, but as she bent to pull on her boots, T.C. caught a coolness in his eyes. "In case you're interested in why, his mother wants him to take her to the cemetery."

The cemetery. T.C. closed her eyes as a cold wave of remorse crashed over her. It was the anniversary of Jase's father's death in a work accident, and she should have remembered. *She* should have given Jase the time off. He should have asked *her*.

As she followed Nick out into the predawn chill, her legs felt stiff and uncooperative, as if in physical response to her mental wretchedness. Jase had worked with her for more than two years, his mother Cheryl for longer, yet he hadn't come to her.

Had she become so unapproachable? So closed that he would prefer to ask a stranger?

She glanced at the stranger walking beside her, recalled his instant rapport with Jason, and her own bitter response. Shame burned through her, stopping her in her tracks.

"I wish I'd known—I would have taken them out there myself, or at least given Jase the day off."

"He only took a couple of hours because I insisted."

"I'm such a hard boss?"

"He thought he'd be letting you down."

She closed her eyes briefly, struggled against the savage lash of emotion, didn't know what to say. She didn't deserve such loyalty—lately, she had done nothing to deserve it.

"Come on. The sooner we get started, the sooner we get to eat breakfast."

T.C. didn't move. She needed alone; she needed composure. The last thing she needed was Nick's unsettling presence. "There's no need for you to do this."

"Yes, there is. I promised Jase."

She shook her head. "I don't have time to teach you what I want done. I'll be quicker on my own."

He stared down at her for a minute that seemed like ten. "It doesn't hurt to accept help, Tamara."

"I would accept your help—if it *was* a help."

He let out his breath in sharp exasperation and looked off into the distance. "We need to resolve this partnership bind. D'you suppose you can fit that into your busy schedule?"

His voice held all the warmth of a winter southerly, and it cut through T.C. just as surely. His approval didn't matter, she told herself, but the appointment did. "This afternoon? After I finish work?"

"Perfect." With that he turned on his heel and strode back the way they had come. T.C. held her breath until he disappeared beyond the bank of melaleucas lining the house-yard. He was gone, out of her hair for the best part of the day. She couldn't have planned it any better.

So why did she feel such an intense desire to call him back?

It took Nick all morning to deal with the paperwork Melissa had e-mailed, and finishing it was about the only enjoyable part of the exercise—that and knowing she would now get off his case.

His partner could be a real pain in the butt...when she wasn't being brilliant. With a wry grimace, he recalled the set down she'd given him yesterday when, in her words, she finally got him to answer the bloody phone. Dealing with her from this far away had its advantages. Like he could call her *Lissa, honey* without getting swatted around the ears. She hated endearments almost as much as she hated the way he abbreviated her name.

So why had he answered the phone that way? To get up her nose, or because he wanted to prove a point to Tamara?

The point being?

That he didn't give a flying fig about her decision to eat with the on-again off-again boyfriend. That he would be just fine on his own, thanks for asking.

With an impatient shove, he propelled his chair away from the desk and let it swing in a half circle. He stretched his arms high, cracked his knuckles and ignored the temptation to look out the window. He would not check up on her, even under the guise of seeing if Jason had arrived yet.

She had made it clear she didn't want his help. She'd made it clear she didn't want anything from him, and although she appealed to him on many levels—the courage she'd shown in confronting him that first night, her fierce loyalty to Joe, the incredibly stimulating touch of her hand…oh, and the way she kissed—she was way too prickly, too complex.

A thousand headaches in the making.

Just as soon as he had made a partnership-breaking deal, he would be on the first plane back to his life—the life he had made for himself. With a resolute nod he turned back to the desk and the box-file George had handed him before he walked out of their meeting.

"Crunch time, Niccolo," he muttered as his glance slid over the solicitor's label: Estate Of The Late Joe Corelli. Ignoring the sudden tightness in his chest, he slipped on his reading glasses and extracted the first wad of papers.

It was almost seven before T.C. forced herself to sit down in the living room—much later than she had anticipated, but by the time Jason had arrived that morning she had been way behind schedule. She had wanted to talk to him but couldn't find the words, and that sat badly with her throughout the afternoon, so every small task had seemed to take twice as long. Then she had needed a good long shower, and if she tried hard enough she could even justify changing her clothes three times before deciding on her usual combination of jeans, tank top and flannel shirt.

She could justify all night long, but when it came down to it, she was a coward. This conversation with Nick would likely decide her future—whether she stayed in the place she had come to accept as home, or whether she would be forced to ring that Perth trainer and take the alternative he offered. Yet she feared she wasn't up to it. It surprised her that she had found the nerve to knock at the office door, to push it open a fraction, to inform Nick she would be in the living room. She hadn't waited for his reply; she hadn't even looked in. She had pulled the door shut and kept on walking.

Maybe her father had been right. Maybe she was a little girl playing in a man's world.

Before she could sink into that mire of self-pity, Nick strolled into the room. Watching him move, so loose limbed and full of masculine grace, had the usual effect. Her pulse thudded, the air in her lungs turned hot and thick, and the soft denim of her much-washed jeans felt harsh against her skin, her buttoned cuffs too tight for her wrists.

"This is for you," he said without preliminary. "I think you should read it before we talk."

Read what? She blinked, noticed the guarded expression on his face before she noticed the envelope in his hand. The warm flush under her skin prickled with a strong sense of déjà vu.

Another letter from the grave.

She needed to run her tongue twice around her dry mouth before she could speak. "Where did this come from?"

"It was in the papers George gave me. I only went through them this afternoon."

"What do you mean…in the papers? Was it hidden? Didn't anyone know it was there?"

"I don't know. I'm sorry, but that's the truth." When she didn't take the envelope, he dropped it in her lap. "I'll leave you to read it in peace. Then we'll talk."

He left abruptly, leaving T.C. staring at the envelope until Joe's big boldly printed *T.C.* blurred into her father's spidery version. She sat up straight and shook her head.

"What is wrong with you? Why don't you just open it?"

There was no reason not to. This time there would be no bitter recriminations, no reminders of what a disappointment she had been as a daughter…or because she'd been a daughter. No terse words informing her that the family home, the stables and all the horses, had been left to an uncle she barely knew.

She squeezed her eyes tightly closed, as if that might

contain the hurt, stop it spreading from the deep-seated knot in her heart, and with a deep, shuddery breath she ripped into the envelope. Her trembling hands smoothed out the single sheet of vellum. Only then was she capable of opening her eyes.

Nick figured she needed privacy, and he wanted to try to reach George one last time. Not that talking to him would do any good—he would simply deny any knowledge of the letter. He had been obstructive from the get-go, but that was no surprise.

That was George.

Still, he jabbed out part of the number he'd dialed enough times in the past hours to know by heart, but then he pictured Tamara staring at the envelope, her face as pale as if Joe himself had appeared before her. With a harsh curse, he jammed down the receiver and went looking for her.

He found her sitting on the verandah steps, framed by the pale light cast through a foyer window. The dog clutched in her arms inspected Nick with solemn eyes, but Tamara didn't look up, and he knew she'd been crying.

Hell!

She sat hunched forward, body language screaming *keep away,* but whispering *hold me.* With a sense of fatalism riding him hard, he sat down next to her, close enough to feel her stiffen defensively.

"My shoulder's here if you need something to cry on," he offered.

"I'm not crying." She swiped the back of one hand across her eyes.

"It's okay. I don't mind a wet shoulder."

"It's not okay. Crying is weak and foolish and female."

Nick snorted. "Anyone who's tried to sneak into your stables in the middle of the night knows you're not weak. Definitely female, but never weak."

"You forgot foolish."

Nick smiled at her churlishness. "Yeah, well, some might consider what you did foolish. Others would call it brave."

When her tense posture relaxed fractionally, he felt a disproportionate degree of satisfaction. "You want to talk about what Joe had to say?"

"What did he tell you?" she asked carefully.

Nick shook his head, not understanding.

"In your letter… He did leave you a letter?"

"No."

She turned toward him slightly, enough that he could see the frown creasing her brow. "You're his son—you're family. Why would he write to me and not you?"

"Perhaps you were closer to him than any of his family."

She made a disbelieving little noise, then shifted restlessly, as if even considering that notion didn't sit well with her. "The first years I worked here, I didn't know him at all," she said softly. "He didn't stay over much, just came for a day whenever he could, rang maybe once a week. After his wife died, he started staying weekends, occasionally longer. I can almost see why people might have thought we were…" She cleared her throat. "It was only this last six months that he stayed most of the time."

"Did he know he was…?"

Dying.

The unsaid word hung heavily between them. To Nick, the air felt morbidly thick. That was why breathing was so damn difficult.

"I don't know," she replied in that same slow, considering voice. "He said nothing to me. I don't think anyone knew how sick he was."

No one had said a word, not to him at any rate. Big surprise! He had returned from a month in Alaska to a coldly formal solicitor's letter. The memory was as keen as the day he slit the seal on that innocuous looking envelope.

"I didn't know," he said, his voice so gruff he barely recognized it as his own. "I didn't know anything until it was all over."

When she placed her hand on his arm, Nick didn't shake it off. This time he accepted the firm, warm contact. He accepted it, and he waited for some cloying words of sympathy to break the peculiar bond he felt with this woman he barely knew, but who knew exactly how to touch him.

She surprised him by saying nothing.

They sat like that for a long time, their silence comfortable and comforting. Then her hand moved on his forearm. It was simply a shift in pressure, hardly a caress, yet it aroused his senses in a heartbeat. The sweet fragrance of some flowering shrub filled his nostrils, the hoot of an owl sounded preternaturally loud on the still night air, and she drifted closer, her eyes luminous in the ambient light.

His lips were only a whisper away when Ug bounded to life in her lap. T.C. turned her head sharply, and his lips grazed across her cheek. She laughed awkwardly, then sprang to her feet, dusting the backside of her jeans. "I have to go double-rug the horses. The nights are getting cold."

Before he could reply, she was steaming off down the path. He had to raise his voice to be sure it would reach her. "How are we ever going to organize anything if you keep running away?"

She slowed, her dark silhouette wavering against the silvery outline of the stable block. "I have to rug up," she insisted.

"We have to discuss our partnership."

She lifted a hand and rubbed it through her tumbled locks, and he heard her faint, frustrated sigh. "Then why don't you come help me?"

* * *

T.C. ran a hand under Monte's rug, then stepped back while Nick threw a second, heavier, blanket over the top. Accepting his help hadn't hurt, and he had been right on another account. She had to stop running away. They had to discuss how they would handle this partnership. Before she could change her mind or find another excuse to procrastinate, she blurted, "My half share in Yarra Park is Joe's idea of insurance."

Nick clicked the leg straps in place without missing a beat. "Insurance against…?"

"Selling up. Joe seemed to think you might not even consider keeping the place." She took a deep breath, found it rich with straw and horse and all things important. "Was he right?"

"Yes."

"You can't do that without my agreement. That's why Joe left me half." It was a sound reason, one she understood. She wished it was the only reason Joe had given.

Nick's blue gaze narrowed intently on hers as he approached. "I could if I bought you out."

"There isn't any offer I will accept."

He paused in front of her, eyebrows raised. "No?"

"No!" She stood her ground, lifting her chin defiantly.

"What if I offered you enough to start your own stables?"

"Money doesn't tempt me."

He smiled as she let him out of the box—a practiced smile that perfectly matched the calculating gleam in his eyes. So this was Nick the Trader, the financial whiz who effortlessly raked in the millions. Funny, but this version of Nick didn't scare her at all. *This* Nick wouldn't send her running.

"What if I threw in your pick of the horses?" he asked, his tone as slick and smooth as molasses. "Take any six you fancy."

"What if I told you I wouldn't take a million dollars and all the horses on this place?"

"I'd say you were bluffing...or crazy."

"This isn't about money, Nick. This place has never been about money."

"No?"

She looked him right in the eye, her message direct and sincere. "Joe built it from nothing. He must have looked at fifty parcels of land before he found the one that felt right. It had nothing to do with the price tag and everything to do with his heart. That's why it is so special."

And that was why she had to do all she could to uphold Joe's wishes—not only because she owed him, but because she understood how much it meant to him. She leaned closer to Nick, willing him to do more than listen. Needing him to *hear* her.

"This is no consolation prize, Nick. This place mattered more to Joe than anything. He loved Yarra Park, and he doesn't want it sold. You have to understand what it meant to him."

A fierce passion burned deep in her eyes. Hell, from this close Nick could practically feel her whole body resonating with it. What would it be like to taste that white-hot intensity? How would it feel to be buried deep inside it, to be wrapped in all that passion? He lifted a hand and placed it against the side of her neck, felt the leap of her pulse and the answering drum of his own.

"*You* understand. Maybe I should sign my half over to you," he murmured, watching her lips, thinking about them under his.

"I hope you're joking!"

She pulled back abruptly, his hand fell away, and he was left staring into her wide eyes. She was clearly appalled...and probably not only by his offer. The fact that he was putting a move on her in the middle of this conversation appalled *him*.

With a mental grimace, he leaned back against the door, shoved his hands into his pockets and considered her question. Was he joking about giving his half away? "He should have left you the whole caboodle. I have no interest in horses, and my home's in New York."

"Your home's been at least ten places in the last ten years," she countered hotly. Then, as if realizing she had given too much away, she bit her lip and looked away. A slow color suffused her face. "Not that anyone's keeping count."

Nick leaned more heavily against the stable door. He felt weird, off-balance, as he considered what she had let slip—not the one instance, but the whole picture. Joe talking about him, about his life, to this stranger who didn't feel like a stranger. And Joe singling him out, gifting him with his most precious asset. "Joe talked a lot, huh?"

She scuffed her foot against the concrete, shrugged one shoulder. "When he came up here he did. I guess he felt he could tell me things his family didn't want to hear."

"If it was about me, they definitely wouldn't have wanted to hear."

"You don't exactly get along with your brother and sisters, do you?"

It was Nick's turn to shrug. He shouldn't have said anything. He shouldn't have felt compelled to talk to her about something so personal, something he never talked about. "We've gotten off subject."

"Yes, we have." She fixed him with a straight look. "You don't have to sell up, you know. It's not like you need the money."

"What do you suggest we do?"

"Nothing. You go back to New York, and I continue to manage Yarra Park the way I've been doing."

Agreeing should have been a cinch. She was right—he didn't need the money—and he realized that despite only knowing her two days, he trusted her. Yet there was something about the way she held herself, as if on hearing his *Why not?* she would burst into a great whoop of delight.

"Well?" she asked, the one short word jammed full of impatient expectancy.

"Okay," he drawled, but when relief spread across her face with the startling brilliance of a perfect sunrise, some perverse part of his nature dug its heels in. "I'll consider it," he heard himself saying. "In the meantime, I'd like to help out. If I learn how things work it will make it easier to communicate after I leave."

Her sunrise smile dimmed about sixty degrees. "What do you mean? Aren't you going back to New York?"

"Not immediately. I prefer to do my considering on site."

"But what about your business?"

"I'll need to put in a couple of extra lines, but I can manage from anywhere with a modem and a telephone. That's the beauty of my business."

She swallowed, cleared her throat. "For how long?"

"As long as it takes."

A whole gamut of emotions flitted across her expressive face. Shock, horror, dread. And beneath them all burned the unasked question.

As long as it takes to do what?

To assess her competence as a stable manager, her integrity as a business partner?

Or for her to stop running?

Nick wasn't sure *he* knew the answer. An hour ago he had been ready to pack his bags; half an hour later he had sat with her hand on his arm feeling as if he never wanted to move, ever again. Ten minutes ago he had been contemplating hot, immediate sex against a stable wall.

Now, as he stared down at her, those thoughts of open-mouthed kisses and soft yielding flesh must have shown, for a panicky kind of awareness turned her skin soft and rosy. She took a step back and blurted, "I'm not sleeping with you."

"Well, I'm glad we cleared the air on that issue." And as if the air really had been cleared, he smiled negligently and arched a brow. "But wouldn't it have been polite to wait until you were asked?"

Six

Somewhere shy of midnight, T.C. gave up all pretense of sleep, swung her legs out of bed and pressed a hand to her grumbling stomach. Food had been the last thing on her mind when she had turned and walked away through the silence that followed Nick's humiliating jibe.

Operating on automatic pilot, she had come straight to her room and paced a path in the carpet as she replayed the evening's events over and over again. Of course she kept returning to that dreadful moment when her fears flew heedlessly to her tongue.

I'm not sleeping with you.

How could she have said that? Sure, she had thought about it. Often. What red-blooded woman wouldn't fantasize about Nick Corelli in her bed? But she had gone and *said it*—to his face—and now she would have to deal with the mortifying fact that she had completely misinterpreted the intent behind his kiss and those touches. Quite likely he treated all women the same way. A little flirting, a lot of charm. She would do well to remember the kind of man he was, and *that* kind of man she could deal with. Her experience with Miles had taught her that much.

Dealing with the man who had sat beside her on the verandah steps was not so easy. How tempting it had been to take up his offer, to lean into his strength, to let go of everything dammed up inside. Years and years and years of pretending she could cope, that she needed no one. Worse—how could she deal with the memory of his anguish and her own fiercely intense need to comfort him? That moment when something foreign and unexpected and dangerous had flared in her heart, something that went way beyond physical desire.

How could she work in partnership with him?

How could she not, knowing this was the only way of repaying her debt to Joe?

With a heavy sigh, she pushed herself to her feet and followed her stomach to the kitchen. She didn't bother with artificial lights—the full moon was bright enough to cast well-defined shadows as she poured a mug of milk and searched the pantry for something filling that didn't need preparation, finding it in the last of a batch of double-choc muffins Cheryl had sent over the previous week. She recalled Jason's goofy grin as he handed her the container, and how she had made her usual halfhearted protest, "She shouldn't have," while the sinfully rich aroma of fresh baking seeped into her pores.

"That's what I said," Jase replied, "but she reckons you don't look after yourself properly."

A week ago the caring behind Cheryl's gesture had settled pleasurably somewhere deep inside. Tonight, as she took her supper into the living room, that same place churned with regret. These past months she had been too wrapped up in her own loss to spare a thought for Cheryl's pain as she relived the events of twelve months before.

It hadn't surprised anyone when she grieved long and

hard for her husband. They had shared a special closeness, the kind visitors immediately felt in the open warmth of their home. Watching the exchanged glances and casual touches, as if they communicated in some secret shorthand, had never failed to move T.C.

Sometimes she would lie awake through the loneliest hours and wonder what it might be like to experience such intimacy; other times she would sternly reprimand herself for yearning after the unattainable. Better to be strong and insular than dependent on another for your happiness.

"Can't sleep?"

She turned her head to see Nick standing in the archway leading to the hall. Her heart quickened instantly.

"The full moon always unsettles me." It wasn't exactly a lame excuse, but it had a definite limp.

He came into the room, all rumpled hair and bare chest and long naked legs. She looked away, swallowed a hot gulp. *Holy jiminy.* He was wearing nothing but shorts, and he was taking a seat at the other end of the sofa, less than an arm's length away.

He gestured toward the remains of her supper. "You should have come out for dinner. You can't live on snacks."

"That's what Cheryl says." She could feel warmth in her cheeks, everywhere on her skin, and was as thankful for the low light as for the subject. Anything to distract her overactive imagination. "I was thinking about her just now, her and Pete. I guess that's another reason why I couldn't sleep."

"You want to know why I couldn't sleep?"

He tilted his head, and the moonlight slanted across his face, highlighting the sharp plane between cheekbone and jaw, making him look a lot less laid-back, a lot more dangerous. Her heartbeat kicked up another notch.

"I guess you have a lot on your mind," she said. "I know I have."

When he turned more fully toward her it was tough not to stare at all that bare skin, near impossible not to track the pattern of dark hair across his broad chest and down toward the low-riding waist of his shorts. Oh help, she had to concentrate on something else. Not those long athlete's legs…maybe his arms. One rested along the back of the sofa, and as she took in the strong curve of his biceps and the softer, almost vulnerable line of his underarm, the tug of attraction was so powerful she could barely breathe. She forced herself to look away. To breathe.

"I couldn't sleep because I was thinking about what you said down at the stables, and my knee-jerk reaction."

There was no reason to expound; she knew exactly what he was referring to.

I'm not sleeping with you.

"Is it because of your vet?"

"Dave?" She thought about taking the easy road, then rejected it. It seemed like the time for honesty. "No. Dave's a good friend. I wish it were more, but…" She shrugged.

"No fire?"

"Not even a spark. Look, it was a bit previous of me to assume…"

"To assume I want to get you into my bed?" Their eyes met and held. Spark, fire, inferno. T.C. felt her whole body combust. "It was a fair enough assumption."

It took a long time to assimilate that simple statement. What did he mean? And did she really want to know?

"You have that scared look in your eyes again. Why is that? The night we met, when you came after me with that cap gun, I thought nothing would scare you."

The tips of his fingers touched her hair, and she recoiled sharply, pulling her legs up under her in an unwittingly defensive posture.

"What are you so afraid of?"

"I'm scared of how far out of my depth I am," she

said, the words tumbling out in a breathy rush. "I don't know what you want from me."

"I think you do know. I think that's what scares you."

His voice was as soft as the moonlight, as dark and alluring as the shadows. T.C. felt a shiver run through her. Not cold, but heat. "Casual sex isn't something I handle well," she breathed.

"You think this would be casual?"

Her startled gaze flew to his and was immediately trapped by his intent expression. Her breathing grew shallow; her pulse pounded like racing hoofbeats on summerhard earth.

"I imagine nothing's ever casual with you," he said slowly.

"Yes, well, that's my problem. I take everything way too seriously."

"Funny, but that's exactly what I've been telling myself ever since I met you. That you're too serious and prickly and difficult."

How did he do it? How did he turn such an uncomplimentary description into flattery, just with a look?

"I don't know what to say to that."

"How about, 'I'm not usually this prickly but around you I'm on edge all the time. I can't sleep nights. I toss and turn until the sheets are as hot and twisted as the images in my mind'?"

A throttled sound rose from her throat. "I get your drift," she growled, shifting restlessly, feeling as hot and twisted as the images he painted. Needing to escape them but needing to set this straight. "I *am* attracted to you, physically, and there's been all this emotional drama drawing us together. The way we feel about Joe... But that's all this is. I mean, if it weren't for Joe, we would never have met. You are hardly the kind of guy I'd have bumped into at a friend's place. If you'd passed me on the street, you wouldn't have spared me a second glance."

"How do you know that?"

She rolled her eyes. "Believe me, I know. We don't live in the same world, Nick. We have nothing in common."

"Other than the fact that Joe tied us together."

Her eyes widened at his choice of words; then she quickly lowered her lids to hide her reaction. No way was she ever letting him know how closely she thought Joe wanted them tied.

"You want to know what I feel about this?" he asked.

She met his eyes with a heartfelt plea in hers. *Please, don't go there. Don't say it.* The deep breath she took seemed to shudder with tension. "I think it's best if we leave this where we were before. I'm not sleeping with you, and you're not asking."

"Best for who?" A hint of humor touched his mouth. "It sure doesn't feel like it's best for me."

And looking at him sitting there, so decadently beautiful—the bed-ruffled hair she yearned to smooth, the shadowed planes of his cheeks, that direct blue gaze—it didn't feel best for T.C., either. When she felt the temptation tingle through her nerve endings, she sat on her hands and bit down on her lip.

His last line, the delivery, the wicked glint in his eyes, called for a witty, teasing response, but she couldn't think of a thing. Better to change the subject.

"I've been thinking—" She had to stop, clear her throat, it was so husky. "I've been thinking about what I said earlier, about you going back to New York and me managing Yarra Park."

"Change your mind?"

"No." She shook her head emphatically. "But I don't think I was completely clear. I'm not comfortable with accepting this bequest."

"It's how Joe wanted it."

"Only in a de facto kind of way. It would have been

easier if he gave you all of Yarra Park with the proviso that you keep me on as manager.''

''You answered that one earlier. He didn't trust me not to sell up.''

''What if I gave you my half and we drew up an agreement that says you can't sell?''

''Hang on.'' Nick held up a hand. ''You won't take money for your half but you want to give it away? Am I missing something here?''

T.C. blew out a puff of frustration. ''Look, I don't want to own Yarra Park, I just want to live here, to work here, and the only money I want is wages. You don't want to live here, but surely owning the place doesn't bother you. Couldn't we come to some kind of agreement where we both get what we want?''

He didn't answer right away, and that gave her some hope. Then he shook his head. ''I don't think—''

''You don't have to think, you only have to agree.'' She leaned forward, imploring him to reconsider. ''Will you please think about it?''

He got to his feet and stalked to the window. For a long silent minute he stood there, his silhouette etched broad and strong by the frosted light, while T.C.'s whole being vibrated with a powerful longing that transcended the physical. She wanted to talk to him, *really* talk to him. She wanted to tell him all the reasons why she couldn't accept the bequest, yet she feared he wouldn't understand.

He turned to face her, his expression impossible to read in the tricky shadows. ''I have to be back in New York on the twenty-fifth. That gives me two weeks to think about this. How does that sound?''

About thirteen days too long.

He came closer and offered his hand, pulling her to her feet and not letting go. Suddenly the air seemed close with his body heat, redolent with his scent. She felt more than a little giddy and struggled not to lean on him for support, then struggled for something to ease the tension.

"Are we shaking on anything in particular?" she asked.

"Shaking?"

He looked down, seemed to consider her hand in his. She felt his grip tighten infinitesimally, and it felt as if something closed reflexively around her heart. Oh boy. Too much Nick at too close a distance. She tried to regain her hand and failed.

"How about we shake to mutual satisfaction?" he purred. Then he laughed in the same low, dark tone, probably at the confused heat in her expression. "You said we should both get what we want, and that sounds fine by me. Deal?"

T.C. blinked as he shook her hand; then she managed to tug her fingers free and back up until her knees hit the couch. If Nick hadn't been there, a solid anchor for her wildly flailing arms, she would have toppled right down, but once she'd regained her balance he stepped clear and yawned with a total lack of self-consciousness. "Seems like it might be worth giving sleep another try."

She managed to mumble something resembling *goodnight,* and he left as noiselessly as he had arrived, leaving her with three distinct impressions.

Number one—touching him was like absorbing his voice. Velvet over steel. Soft and harsh, darkness and light. Two—she didn't feel like she had shaken on anything resembling mutual satisfaction. Three—sleep would be a long time coming.

Nick wasn't sure why he had exercised such restraint during that moonlight meeting the previous night. The whole hour had been one painful exercise in self-restraint, and when she overbalanced and grabbed at his arms—hell, he'd been one narrow noble streak from following her

down onto that couch. From covering her head to foot,
skin against skin.

Noble streak? Huh!

He hadn't used that description for years, maybe a decade. It was Joe who had introduced him to the term—
said it was unusual to find a kid with such a noble streak.
Given his background, the irony hadn't escaped Nick, nor
had the impact of the compliment, and now Joe had gone
and topped it.

He had left him his most precious asset. The ultimate
compliment. He felt humbled, honored and, to top it off,
mighty confused. Why would Joe single him out? Sure,
he'd accepted him into his family and done his best to be
fair, to treat him as one of his own children, but they both
knew he was only distant kith and kin. That was why
George was being such a pain in the rear.

Tamara would know. Even without the benefit of that
letter, she knew more about Joe's thinking in those last
months than anyone else. But would she tell him? That
was the killer question. He had never met a woman so
closed, so unwilling to let anything of herself out, so afraid
to let anything of herself go.

Man, but he wanted to know what went on in her head.

As if responding to the power of that thought, she came
walking into the kitchen. Stopped. A faint touch of color
traced her cheekbones as her gaze met his, then slid away.
Then she seemed to gather herself, to take a strengthening
breath, and she kept coming. Nick felt breathless himself.
He couldn't figure out why she affected him so immediately, so completely. As usual, she was dressed to make
as little of herself as possible, yet something about the way
she moved, the way she looked at him, was all woman.
Yep, she only had to lean into the fridge at that certain
angle to jump-start his engine.

"You want coffee?" he asked, hoping for once she
would surprise him and say "yes."

"Yes, please."

Nick didn't do a double take. After all, she had been one surprise after another from the moment they met.

"What are your plans for today?" she asked as she brought milk and cereal to the table.

"Might as well start as I aim to continue. Down at the barn."

Her eyes widened. "You're serious about learning how the stables run?"

"Yes, ma'am."

"We'll see how long you last on the end of a pitchfork, city slicker."

Nick smiled back. He liked the teasing warmth in her eyes. Very much. "I don't mind getting my boots dirty."

He watched her munch her way through a hearty helping of cereal before he spoke again. At least if she bolted he wouldn't feel responsible for another missed meal.

"You mind if I ask you something personal?"

She paused, coffee mug suspended halfway between table and mouth, her face all big-eyed suspicion. "That depends."

"I wondered why you needed this job so badly." What caused that emotional pounding she had hinted at. "You don't have to tell me. I'm just curious," he said easily, as if he hadn't spent sleepless hours pondering the many possibilities.

"You know what happened to the curious cat." Still teasing, although more warily this time. At least she hadn't walked away. Yet.

"Are you a local?"

"Our family had a small acreage about an hour's drive west of here," she said carefully. "I lived there till I was seventeen."

"Was that when your father died?"

She took a measured sip of her coffee. "That was two years later."

"Your mother?"

"She died when I was little. I barely remember her."
She put her mug down with an abrupt click. "I don't know
if you're really interested in my family history or if this is
breakfast small talk, so I'll keep it brief. My father brought
us up—my brother and me—which wasn't so bad, because
we both happened to love horses and they were Dad's life.
Jonno was killed when I was fifteen, and things went
downhill from there. I stayed as long as I could, but when
I got a decent job offer, I left."

"Sometimes leaving's best for everyone."

"Well, my father sure didn't think so." She swirled the
remains of her coffee around the mug, a small sad smile
on her lips. "Obviously he wasn't as forgiving as Joe."

"He was tough on you?"

"Yes, but he also taught me how to work and about
self-discipline." She lifted her chin, defied him to take
issue.

"Seems to me you're too hard on yourself. Maybe you
needed someone to teach you about lightening up, having
fun."

"I've tried that. It's overrated."

Nick wondered if that was what her father hadn't for-
given—not the leaving home, but what she had done in
those years—and what his lack of forgiveness had meant
to her. "What happened to your father's place?" he asked
on a hunch.

She shrugged, but the gesture seemed awkward. And
telling. "He left it to someone else."

A father gutted by the death of his son, a daughter who
tried to fill the gap but felt she had failed, who maybe ran
wild for a couple of years. And her bitter, tough, unforgiving father gives away her heritage.

It explained a lot about the woman sitting before him.
Her self-contained strength, her vulnerability, how she
worked her butt off, as if paying some sort of penance.

Her reluctance to accept what she thought she didn't deserve.

"And this is why you don't want to accept your part of Yarra Park?"

Determination hardened her expression. "It's not right. Joe's family should have it. I know how they must feel about this."

"Joe's family is getting plenty. Believe me, this is nothing like the situation between you and your father."

"But…"

"Accept it, Tamara. It's what Joe wanted."

"But you said you would consider taking my half."

"I said I'd think about it, and I will. Are you this stubborn about everything?" Man, he hoped not. He had less than two weeks to change her mind, and he didn't mean about the inheritance.

"Stubborn?" She pushed herself off her stool, a faint smile curving her lips. "As a mule, Joe used to say, but only about things that matter. Now, let's go find you a pitchfork."

The next five days rolled out smoothly enough, with Nick dividing his time between the stables and the office. Although he made no overt moves or provocative comments, tension simmered beneath the artificial surface of civility, despite her attempts to keep the mood light and easy. The flame had been turned down to pilot, but one quick flick of the switch would kindle the inferno she had felt that night in the moonlight.

Eight more days, she thought with a resigned sigh as she let herself into Star's stall. Could she keep a grip on her twitchy fingers that long?

She waited while the big mare went through her you-can't-catch-me routine, prancing from wall to wall with a succession of disdainful head tosses. Collaring her was a game of skill, patience and acquired knowledge. "Fin-

ished?'' she asked when the pirouettes ended abruptly.
Timing was everything in this game. With a nimble side-
step, she intercepted a further halfhearted attempt at a pass
and slipped the head collar into place.

"Ready for some work?'' Star tossed her head with arrogant scorn, and T.C. laughed softly. "Silly question,
huh? You love to run.''

As she smoothed her hand down the mare's neck, a
sense of contentment settled in the pit of her stomach. This
was why she had chosen this profession, for this simple,
elemental feeling. Stooping down, she felt the mare's near
foreleg, checking for heat in the tendon she had injured
the previous season.

"Looking good, girl.'' Satisfied with the inspection, she
straightened to find Star nodding her head as if in agreement. T.C. couldn't help but laugh. "You are so full of
yourself!''

The sound of her laughter brought Nick's grooming mitt
to an instant halt. It had been like this for days. He would
be working away, limber and comfortable, when out of the
blue something would ignite his slumbering senses. The
soft lilt of her voice as she petted her dog, a wet towel
tossed negligently over a laundry basket, the lingering tang
of her apricot shampoo.

Or her laughter, unexpected and unrestrained.

He ambled over to the open half-door, watched her
hands skate lightly over the horse's glossy coat. Yeah,
those hands doing pretty much anything that involved
stroking turned him on.

He cleared his throat. "This one's Star, right?''

She turned slowly, unsurprised, as if she had known he
was there. "Her full name is Stella Cadente.''

"Shooting Star,'' he translated.

"You know Italian?''

"Enough. That name's a mouthful.''

"It is.'' She smiled. "That's why we just call her Star.

Most of them have some Italian in their racing names and a shortened version for at-home use.''

"Monte?" he asked.

"Is really Montefalco."

"Gina?"

"Lollobrigida." A softly inquisitive expression lit her face. "And I suppose you're really Nicholas."

"Niccolo. The Italian version."

Head slanted to one side, she considered it, considered him. And he knew he would do anything to hear that name, his full name, on her lips. *Please, Niccolo.*

"And what about you, Tamara?" He drew the name out lushly, saw her hand still on the horse's flank for an instant before she resumed stroking. Felt his own body pulse. "Why aren't you Tammy? Or Tara?"

"You have got to be kidding!"

He smiled at her melodramatic tone. "Why do you call yourself T.C.?"

"Your guess is as good as mine." With an abrupt click, she attached the lead and brought the horse to the door. He didn't open it. He wasn't letting her out of this quite so easily.

"My guess is you decided your name was too girly. You thought someone named Tamara should wear pretty dresses and high heels and a perfume that smells like a rich garden party—"

"Enough, already," she interrupted, but a smile lurked around the corners of her mouth, and when that incredibly sexy mouth smiled it did more for him than any perfume or floaty dress.

Intent on teasing her embryonic smile to full life, he leaned over the half-door to sniff at her unperfumed throat...and the horse lunged, eyeballs rolling, mouth open.

Seven

In a knee-jerk reaction, he hauled her out the door and out of the path of a set of extremely large and not very white teeth.

''Hey, what was that all about?'' She sounded breathless and slightly stunned.

''That beast masquerading as a horse would have taken a piece of your sweet little hide if I hadn't saved you.''

''Oh, no, she was definitely gunning for *your* hide.''

Her husky laughter rippled close to his throat, and when she shifted her weight, her hip rolled against his thigh. The fire on slow smolder in Nick's blood roared into full flame, but when his hands firmed on her back, she sobered instantly, pushing and twisting her way clear of his arms.

''She's never done that before,'' she murmured distractedly as the horse continued to stomp her hooves and toss her head.

''She's not the first female who's wanted to bite me.''

''I bet she's the first to take an instant dislike to you.''

"Ah, so *you* didn't."

A wry smile quirked her lips. "If you're fishing, Nick, forget it. I'm sure you've heard exactly how likable you are from plenty of people with far prettier words than me."

Yeah, but the thing was, he wanted to hear it from her. "If I was fishing, Tamara," he said slowly, clearly, seriously, "it wasn't for pretty words but honest ones."

Their gazes met and held, and Nick felt the heady rush of anticipation as keenly as if he stood strapped to his skis on a virgin Chugach ridge, about to go vertical. Then Star issued a shrill authoritative whinny that sliced right through the moment.

"That's her opinion," he said. "Now what about yours?"

"She's speaking for the both of us."

"If only I had a translator." He gestured toward Ug, who lay sleeping under the feeder. "Don't suppose she speaks horse?"

T.C. laughed. "Not so anyone would understand."

The mare stretched her long neck over the door in a gesture both elegant and eloquent, enticing Tamara to gather up the snaking lead *and* to scratch behind her ears.

Nick took a cautious step closer. Star rolled her eyes but kept her mouth closed. A promising start. Another measured step, a third, and she laid back her ears and kicked out at the wall. "Close enough, huh?"

The mare snorted.

"Seems I do speak some basic horse."

This time it was Tamara who snorted.

He rested a hand atop the door, waited. When the mare didn't take a piece out of it, he left it there, although he didn't take his eyes off her long black face.

"Can she run?" he asked.

"Like the wind."

"Is that how it feels, when you're driving? Like you're riding the wind?"

"Yes. That's it exactly."

He heard the smile in her voice, longed to see it on her lips, but when he started to turn, the mare bared her teeth. He kept his eyes firmly on those teeth.

"How did you know?" she asked.

"I'm guessing it's a bit like skiing. The wind, the rush, the sense of freedom. There are mountains like this beauty here, all mean and full of spirit, and then there are the rest."

She laughed softly. "Let me guess which you prefer."

He watched the big mare toss her head and swing her quarters around, left to right, as if impatient with the inactivity. "I'd like to try it," he said suddenly.

"You want to drive a horse?"

"I want to drive *this* horse. Will you teach me?"

"You're kidding! Was your first driving lesson in a Ferrari?"

Straight-faced, he looked down at her. "No. It was a Jaguar."

For a moment she simply stared back at him, eyes wide and incredulous; then she burst out laughing. The dulcet sound danced through his senses, filling him with a pleasure so pure it warmed him to the marrow of his bones.

"Well?" he asked when she finally recovered.

She glanced at the horse, who stood rolling her eyes at him. "When you can catch her, I'll teach you to drive her."

He took his time inspecting the horse, drawing out the suspense. Then he shrugged, pocketed his hands and stepped back. "Looks like I'll have to stick to the mountains."

"You're not going to try?"

He met the surprise in her eyes with a slow grin. "I know when I'm being had."

"Jase!" She sounded disgusted, but the look in her eyes approved his quick reading of the situation, and it warmed places Nick couldn't remember as anything but cold. "You could learn on another one. Monte's a real gentleman."

"Thanks," Nick said slowly. "But I seem to have developed a taste for the difficult, spirited type."

She met his unmistakable message head-on. And surprised him by not flinching. "Then it's a shame you have so little time. It could take months for a temperament like that to come around."

"Yeah?" His gaze skated from her face to the horse and back again. "Then it looks like we both lose out."

Despite his prior knowledge of Star's tricky temperament, T.C. had expected Nick to take up her challenge. She thought him arrogant enough to back himself in any difficult situation. Maybe he was, she thought consideringly, when she caught him standing at Star's stall door several days later.

Star took a tentative step forward and lowered her head to sniff at the hand resting on the door. Nick responded with a low laugh accompanied by some message of praise, and although distance muffled the words, T.C.'s body responded instantly to the mellow depth of his voice.

Exactly the same effect as he was having on Star, she realized. They had both started out kicking and snapping, and look at them now. Still wary, still inclined to take one step forward and two back, but both oh, so dangerously close to being seduced by a dark velvet voice and a steadily patient hand.

T.C. sighed with heavy resignation. Everything about the man—every damn thing!—was utterly alluring. His voice, the way he moved, that smile, the magic he made with a pot of pasta. Even his name was as exotically lush as the man himself. Niccolo Corelli. Why hadn't he turned out to be the conceited self-interested macho man she had imagined him to be? Why hadn't he been a carbon copy of Miles?

Heart in mouth, she watched Star toss her head and bare her teeth. Nick didn't move. He stood his ground, that one hand unmoving on the door, and she knew it was only a matter of time before the mare gave up the fight and came to him freely.

Did she stand any better chance of resisting?

She couldn't watch any longer, couldn't stand the apprehensive tension that churned in her stomach. Grabbing a head collar and lead, she strode to the door.

"I'm taking her out for some exercise," she said, more sharply than she had intended.

He didn't move, but she felt his steady scrutiny. "You want to take a passenger?"

What harm could it do? Maybe he would be as delighted by the experience as Joe had been on his first ride… although she doubted that. It seemed far too tame for a man who chased extreme adventure.

"Okay," she agreed eventually. "But this isn't a short cut to driving her. You're only the passenger."

"Yes, ma'am."

Ten minutes later, when she picked up the reins and swung herself into the jog-cart, she remembered why she had delayed this moment. Proximity. The bench seat was supposedly wide enough for three, but Nick took up an extraordinary amount of space.

So okay, she told herself, seated side by side there was bound to be contact, but that was no reason for her breath to hitch each time his sleeve brushed against hers. No reason for that bare whisper of sound to echo through her head, drowning out the cadent fall of hooves, the creak of springs, everything but the thunderous beat of her heart.

Annoyed by such a ridiculous state of hyperawareness, she clicked into a jog and edged to her right. A fat lot of good that did her. Nick simply spread to fit all available space, and now his thigh rested flush against hers. No big deal, she told herself, as she turned onto the track and settled Star into a steady relaxed pace. No bare flesh involved, a simple case of denim against denim.

All she needed was to redirect her senses.

Tipping her head back a fraction, she narrowed her field of perception, concentrating on the sun that touched her face, the strong wind that sifted through her hair and plastered her shirt against her skin. She absorbed the steady rocking rhythm of the horse's motion and felt herself start to relax.

"This is nice."

"Pardon?" She blinked, stared up at Nick.

"I said, I'm enjoying this." He nudged her with his elbow. "No need to look so surprised."

"I didn't think this would be quite your speed."

"You think I only like fast?"

Vivid images of all the things she had imagined him doing not-so-fast flashed through her mind. *Oh help, she did not need this now.* To hide the disconcerting wash of heat, she edged forward on the seat and pretended to reorganize the reins. She could feel his gaze on her, measuring, assessing.

"You love this, don't you?"

"Yes." She closed her eyes, felt the smile well up from somewhere deep within. "I love working with horses. I love how it makes me feel. It's hard to describe, but it's like…like this is where I belong."

"Did you feel that way about your father's home— where you were brought up?"

She thought about that. "I guess I did when I was younger. I know there were things I missed when I left, but there were other parts I couldn't wait to escape. But what I'm feeling here isn't about the physical things, it's about the spirit of the place and how it touches you. It's a sense of home." She laughed, more than a little self-conscious. "Do you know what I mean?"

When he didn't answer, she turned, caught the hint of a frown. "I can't say I've ever got that concept of home."

"What about Joe's Portsea house?"

"You've seen that place?" he asked with a mocking lift of one brow.

Not face-to-face, but she had seen pictures—it hardly fit the standard definition of home. But she wasn't talking about walls and lawns and manicured hedges, she was talking about feelings, and it seemed like he just didn't get it. She shrugged off an enormous wash of disappointment. Seems like she had been harboring a secret hope that he would fall in love with the spirit of Yarra Park as quickly and unconditionally as she had.

Only with Yarra Park, Tamara?

Do not go there, she told herself firmly. You'd do better to take this as a timely reminder of the footloose, uncluttered lifestyle he prefers...and of how little you have in common.

"You think I could do that?" he asked after a short, uncomfortable silence.

"I thought we agreed you were coming along as the passenger?"

He gave that lazy shrug he had down pat. "Worth a try."

T.C. snorted, then thought about it for another half-lap. "I'll let you drive if you agree to talk to a solicitor about me signing my half over to you."

"Don't you ever give up?"

"Worth a try," she countered with a mocking shrug.

His bark of laughter sounded like equal parts exasperation and admiration; then he surprised her with a casual, "Okay."

"Okay?"

"Yeah. I'll talk to my solicitor." He reached for the reins, but she didn't hand them over.

"When?"

"As soon as I can make an appointment."

She shook her head. "Not good enough. You're a Co-relli—they'll make time for you."

"Is tomorrow soon enough?"

"Morning?"

Laughing softly, he shook his head. "Can I have breakfast first?"

Still, she hesitated.

"Come on. It's not so hard, is it, handing over the reins?"

Yes, Nick, she thought. It *is* hard and it's scary, putting yourself into someone else's hands. Relinquishing control.

With a deep sigh, she handed them over. He assumed the correct hold like a veteran. He didn't ask any of the usual learners' questions: *Is this okay? Am I doing this right?* With the natural arrogance of someone who did everything well, he simply knew he was doing fine.

"You have good hands," she praised reluctantly.

"So I've been told."

By too many women, T.C. reminded herself. "Do you pick up everything this easily?"

"Everything?"

"All those action-man things you do—the heli-skiing and rafting and climbing. Were they this easy?"

"If they were easy, there'd be no sense in doing them. No challenge."

"What about the risk?"

He glanced across at her, his eyes as intensely blue as the autumn sky. Her heart flip-flopped. "It doesn't hurt to take a few risks, Tamara, to push outside your comfort zone. That's what makes you feel alive."

"No. *This* is what makes me feel alive."

Something in his expression as he took in her resolutely spoken words did strange things to her heart. She felt the compelling draw of his gaze but refused to meet it. The need to run, to escape, rode her hard, and she blew out a frustrated breath. "You want to try another gear?"

"Yeah. I feel like I could blow off some steam."

"Then I'd better take over."

As she took the reins, his fingers grazed across hers. Awareness charged through her system, causing her to fumble. Star reacted by grabbing the bit and plunging forward. For a while T.C. needed all her skill to restrain the horse's enthusiastic charge, but gradually the mare responded to her coaxing hands and soothing words.

As she came back into hand, T.C. realized Nick was laughing—not with reactionary hysteria, but with sheer unrestrained pleasure. His mood tapped straight into T.C.'s adrenaline overload. Unable to restrain herself, she let go her own wild tension-relieving whoop. The sound caught and lifted in the breeze, mingling with the thick red dust that rose in their wake.

Star picked up on the mood in a trice. T.C. felt her suppressed power shudder through the reins and let her run. They sped a full circuit on the very edge of control, and it was only as they eased back to a more sedate pace that she realized Nick had needed to grab hold of something during that helter-skelter spurt.

That something happened to be her leg.

She didn't need to look down to picture his palm spanning the width of her thigh, his long splayed fingers boldly defined by the near-white of her faded jeans. Desire, as wild and unruly as that mad dash, bit with vicious teeth. The only thing holding her in check was the sound practical fact that the reins in her hands prevented her reaching out and putting them on him.

Gradually Star came back to a jog, then a long, loping walk, and the air around them thickened with the sound of her elevated breathing, the sharp smell of exertion.

"That was…unexpected." Slowly, deliberately, he slid

his hand from her leg. "Kind of makes me wonder what else you're capable of when you let go."

His meaning should have sent her scuttling for cover, but it seemed like that high-speed ride had blown away more than steam and tension. It must have blown away a large dose of common sense, for she smiled as she said, "I guess it's lucky I've got these reins in my hands."

"Lucky for who?"

Lucky for me, T.C. responded silently as she turned Star back toward the stables and sanity.

Jason was waiting at the stables, full of questions. Had Nick really taken the reins? How fast did they go? Was it a rush? The necessary explanations—together with the mundane task of unharnessing—went a long way toward settling the smoldering tension.

They were both laughing easily at something Jason said when they reached for the girth strap at the same time. Their hands touched. The jolt—electric sharp, lightning fast—zinged through her, and she was instantly completely aware of him. The grave stillness of his gaze, his earthy male scent, the sheen of heat on his skin, the pulsing beat of his heart. If she closed her eyes, she swore she would hear the blood surging through his veins. But she didn't close her eyes. They had fixed on the sensual curve of his mouth, so near she could feel his breath on her face.

Oh help. If he kisses me, I'm sunk.

His fingers curled around hers. His thumb stroked once across the back of her hand, and her insides turned to liquid.

Oh help. If he doesn't kiss me, I'll die.

"Are you two going to undo that buckle or stand about holding hands all afternoon?" Jase asked with a disgusted snort.

T.C. reclaimed her hand and avoided meeting anyone's eyes. Jason gathered up the remaining gear and took it off to the tack room. Nick cleared his throat and asked if he should hose Star down. Star snorted and pawed at the ground, and Ug trotted in from an afternoon's rat hunting.

Everything back to normal, T.C. thought, although her pulse still skittered all over the yard like an unbroken colt. She watched Nick lead Star away and thought about the chores still to be done. She would rather watch Nick, or talk to Nick, or go take a long shower, then stretch out on her bed to think about Nick.

Everything definitely far from normal, she thought uneasily. What was wrong with her? She still hadn't moved several minutes later when a spray of water arced high above the concrete wall enclosing the wash-bay, closely followed by a muffled oath. By the time she arrived Nick looked about as wet as the horse with the hose clasped between its teeth.

At the sound of her strangled laughter, his head whipped around. "Are you here to help or for the entertainment?"

She folded her arms across her chest. "Oh, definitely for the show."

"Which is undoubtedly funnier from where you're standing."

At precisely that moment Star turned her head, gave him an innocent look and dropped the hose.

"Thanks for your cooperation," he muttered as the hose, still spurting water, snaked out of his reach. "Would you get that for me?"

She shouldn't have taken that call for assistance at face value. She should have noticed the narrowing of his gaze, the unholy light in his eyes. But she was too busy chortling at his predicament.

She gathered the hose and brought it to him at the front of the bay, and Nick casually stepped around her to block the exit. Snookered. Her eyes widened on the weapon she had unwittingly handed him. "Oh, no," she breathed, backing up the four steps it took to hit the wall. "You wouldn't."

"No?" he asked, and his grin felt more than smug. It felt positively feral. "Are you sure about that?"

No, she wasn't. He caught the furtive glances as she assessed her chances of making it to the tap before him.

"You can try, but you'll end up very wet."

"I have a feeling I'm going to get wet either way."

"You deserve to."

"If you'd been in my shoes, you'd have seen the funny side." A small bubble of merriment escaped her lips as she tipped her head back against the wall. Then she caught his unamused expression and lifted her hands in the traditional gesture of surrender. "Okay, I can take a little water. Do your worst."

Hell. She was standing there with her shirt pulled deliciously tight across her breasts, her green eyes glimmering a wicked challenge, daring him to do his worst? His *best* right this minute would involve nailing her to that wall with his body and his mouth and sucking the remnants of laughter from her full bottom lip. His *worst* would involve nailing her to the wall, full stop.

"Maybe you won't get wet if you ask nicely."

"You want me to say please?"

"I want you to say *please, Nick.*"

She moistened her lips. His body responded with extravagant haste—to the glimpse of her tongue, to her softly parted lips, to the anticipatory pleasure of hearing those two little words, her voice breathless and husky.

Please, Niccolo.

She struck with lightning speed, catching him at a distracted disadvantage…but not for long. With his superior reach and strength, it was never going to be a fair fight, although her tenacity ensured that they both ended up very wet.

Very wet and very close.

When Nick finally restrained her, he was achingly aware of how close. The second their eyes met, she stopped struggling. With her body wedged flush against his, he could feel her tightly coiled tension, could see both the heat of sensual knowledge and a familiar wariness in her wide green eyes, and wondered how long before she started running. He thought about begging.

Please, Tamara.

His fingertips trailed across her abdomen, stilled when they found the small gap where her shirt had pulled clear of her jeans. He rested his palm where cold wet cotton met warm satin skin, heard her sharply drawn breath and waited for her to snap at him, to pull away, to slap his hand.

She didn't move.

He looked down at the wet shirt plastered to the soft mounds of her breasts, at the clearly visible outline of her erect nipples, and his stomach clenched tight in an instant surge of need. He dipped his mouth and nipped at the earlobe that peeped through her softly mussed hair, at the smooth curve of her neck, at the point where that neck met her shoulder. He tasted the surface chill of cold water, then the fresh warmth of her skin, and, deeper still, the heat of pure desire.

He wondered if it was possible to drown in lust.

Everything about her aroused him, but nothing so much as the soft yielding in her eyes as her body swayed into his, as she cupped his face between her hands and muttered, "Will you please just kiss me."

"Please, Nick," he prompted, as his hands swept over her back. He bit her bottom lip, dragged it between his teeth, then slowly released it. A low frustrated moan built in her throat and resounded through his blood, stirring him, inflaming him...but it wasn't the words he needed to hear. "Say it," he demanded.

Eyes glittering, she moistened her lips, but they remained silent. Desperate hands slid into his hair, then held him steady as she stretched on her toes and planted her lips against his. She kissed him with openmouthed carnality, encouraging his tongue into the warm, moist cavern of her mouth with a boldness that sizzled to his groin. He gripped her more tightly, his hands curving over her behind, drawing her nearer, molding the softness of her belly to the pulsing heat of his arousal.

A groan rumbled deep in his chest as her hands stroked from his shoulders to his waist. He swore he heard steam sizzle in their wake. He did hear a low hiss whistle through his teeth as those hands continued their downward path, stroking over his butt, making him ache to be naked, skin to skin. Inside and out.

He walked her backward. Two steps and she was against the wall. Hands planted either side of her face, he bent his knees to bring himself down to her height, so he could look right into her sultry green eyes while he rocked his hips against her. Just once. Then he closed his eyes and struggled to control the primal need that pumped savagely through him.

Man, had he ever been so hard? So desperate?

She touched his face, her fingers a cool, gentle contrast to the furnace in his blood. "Please, Nick," she whispered as they locked gazes.

Finally.

"Please what?" he growled. "Tell me what you want, Tamara."

A shadow crossed her face. Indecision. She blinked it away, bit her lip.

Hell. Nick blew out a short, frustrated breath. His splayed fingers closed, curled into tight fists. "Right this minute I'm about as close to exploding as I've ever been with my clothes on. But nothing more is going to happen until you look me in the face and tell me what you want. Just so there's no mistaking. Your choice of words."

A slow flush bled into her face. "I can't say…that."

Imagined alternatives to *that* drove a thick groan from Nick. Weak with wanting, he rested his forehead against hers. He thought about prompting her, tempting her with more kisses. Rejected it. She needed to make this decision all on her own. In the morning, he wanted to turn his head on the pillow, open his eyes and look right into sea-green eyes softly glazed with desire, not clouded with regret.

He took stock of his surroundings for the first time in fifteen minutes. "I guess we're lucky Jase didn't walk around the corner. Or that one of your smarter animals didn't decide to break this up."

Her half-laugh, half-sigh flowed warm against his throat. "Thank you."

"For?"

"Not pressing me. Giving me a chance to get sane about this."

"Ah, that would be my noble streak."

He eased back far enough to look down into her face. The undertow of insecurity lurking in the depths of those amazingly expressive eyes grabbed him hard. For a moment he felt winded, as raw desire made space for a strong surge of tenderness. He brushed the backs of his fingers along her cheekbone, pressed a kiss to her nose, another to her lips, a third to her chin, then pushed himself away from the wall. Away from temptation.

"I think this would be a good time to go ring my solicitor friend, see if he can't fit a Corelli in this afternoon." He touched a finger to her lips, then stepped away. "Don't go getting too sane about this, okay?"

Slumped against the wall, T.C. watched him walk away. She wanted to call him back while she could still taste him on her lips and feel him on her skin, while the fever of need still burned in her blood. Before the return of sanity. But what would she say?

Yes, I want you to make love to me. I want your scorching kisses and velvet-cloaked caresses, your incendiary words and soft midnight whispers. I want to feel beautiful and strong and craved; I want to feel like a woman who is your equal. But how could she call him back when her insecurities cast such a thick shroud over her desire?

She feared the afterward, when his male hunger was slaked, when he tossed her a casual goodbye and a consolatory kiss, then sauntered off into the sunset. She feared the desperate ache of withdrawal from the loving she'd grown addicted to, and most of all she feared the loneliness of the nights that stretched ahead with only her hollow pride for company.

It was those fears that constricted her throat and dried her mouth as she watched him walk away. It would take less than a night of loving to become addicted to Nick, and despite the power of the attraction, despite everything he could make her feel, he was still a man who didn't know the meaning of home, a man who liked to move on. He was still perfectly unsuitable for her.

Eight

When he drove down the road less than an hour later, she should have been relieved, able to breathe again, but instead she thought about the day when he would head down that same road en route for the airport, and it felt as if her heart plummeted to her toes. And maybe it stayed there, because her feet seemed to drag heavily through every long drawn-out hour of the day, right up until the setting sun painted the horizon in multicolored dusk.

Then a sense of expectancy quickened her blood, and any noise prompted her heart to bound into her throat. She tried to distract herself with television, flicking indifferently past a score of channels, thinking that at least the volume would prevent her ears from straining for the sound of his vehicle. Fat chance. Minute by minute, her restlessness grew until she couldn't sit still any longer.

She punched the off button on a noisy sitcom and blew out an exasperated puff of air. How lame was she? Sitting here in the semidarkness waiting for him to come home, not even knowing if he would drive back tonight. And if he did, what would she say to him? Certainly nothing that he wanted to hear.

Tell me what you want, Tamara.

Well, Nick, I want what you want, with the same intense hunger I felt in your kisses, in that one grinding pulse of your hips, in your voice, so hot and tight. But I want it every day for the rest of my life.

No, she didn't think he would want to hear anything quite that honest.

That's it, she declared with savage purpose. I will not sit here torturing myself any longer. I need company. She tried Cheryl's number, but no one answered. Undeterred, she changed into narrow white jeans and her favorite lime-green stretch shirt, brushed her hair until it gleamed with life, touched her lips with gloss and headed out the door.

At the sound of an approaching vehicle, her hand stilled on the lock. Not his car, she realized after her pulse had done its first crazy stop-and-go, but the low throaty roar of a powerful bike. The sound resonated through her body and she didn't move—*couldn't move*—as a single headlight arced across the garden, then caught her in its searching eye. Seconds later the bike throbbed to a halt beside her.

It was a big, dark, dangerous beast of a bike, the kind that made her blood pump faster with reckless images of the forbidden. The kind that fit Nick as perfectly as his black biker's jacket and faded denim jeans.

He killed the engine, and the silence vibrated around her, keeping time with the accelerated beat of her heart. The sight of his booted feet, spread wide and planted on either side of the monster bike, made her own legs tremble. Her gaze floated upward, all the way to his full-face helmet, and even through the smokily opaque visor she could feel the intensity of his gaze.

Watching her.

She moistened arid lips, felt his gaze touch her, burn

her, as he removed his helmet. The contrast from smoky shades of darkness to pure light-filled blue was breathtaking. It was like looking into the center of the sun. Then he lifted a hand to rake the unruly hair back from his face, breaking the searing connection.

T.C. cleared her throat. "Where did you find this baby?"

Humor sparked in his molten eyes. "The stork sure didn't bring it."

"It would have had to be a mighty big stork," she mused, moving around the bike, compelled to look, to touch.

"You like her?"

"No way is this a feminine machine."

"No? She reminds me of Stella. All that brute power, scarcely contained."

She smiled. Yes, she could see that. Liked that he'd drawn the comparison, and the way he called Star the Italian version of her name. The less ordinary, the more exotic.

"Plus I don't much care for the notion of throwing my leg over anything I refer to as 'he.'"

Well, no. She could see that, too. She touched a fingertip to the handlebar, cleared the heat from her throat. "You asked if I like her.... I'm not sure anyone could simply *like* a beauty like this."

"You're right. I'd forgotten how it feels to ride one of these. To open her up and feel all that power surge through you."

He laughed, the sound low and throaty and as shockingly arousing as his words. T.C. rubbed her hands over her goose-bumpy arms. She felt his gaze follow the action, caressing her bare skin into complete awareness, brushing the length of her throat, resting on the curve of her waist. Touching the painfully tight thrust of her nipples.

"You're going out?" All the laughter was gone from his voice.

"Yes." *But if you ask me to stay, if you ask me to take a ride with you…*

He didn't ask, and in the awkward silence she found herself circling the bike again.

"So…did she follow you home or what?" She trailed her fingers across the back of the wide leather seat. It was sleek and surprisingly cool, a stark contrast to the rough heated edges of her own mood.

"Graeme loaned her to me for a couple of days."

"Graeme?"

"A partner in Kermit's firm. We were at school together."

"Your solicitor friend," she guessed. Then, "I can't imagine a suit riding one of these."

He shook his head. "There you go with your preconceptions again."

She leaned back against the door of her truck and folded her arms across her chest. "What do you mean by 'again'?"

"You'd made up your mind about me long before we met." He climbed off the bike, his expression unreadable. "That's why you've been so wary of me from day one. Because of who you think I am."

What could she say? That she'd been building a defense? That she feared she would fall for him totally, completely, inextricably? All she could say was, "I have to go."

He uttered a polite, "Have a nice time," turned and walked away.

T.C. was halfway to town before she realized she hadn't asked him what he'd found out from his solicitor friend.

Nick hadn't hesitated when Graeme offered to loan him the Ducati. He'd thought the ride home would help cool his simmering blood, but the moment he'd seen her standing there with her tight jeans and gloss-slicked mouth, he'd felt the burn like a flamethrower in his gut.

It had burned harder when she'd refused to talk to him—when she'd run away again—and hadn't let up the whole night, not even when he heard her vehicle cross the stock-grid into the yard. Not yet eleven, he noted. She can't have been having much fun. He tried to smile but barely managed a sneer.

Her soft footfalls sounded in the hallway. He heard them pause outside the office door; then he heard nothing but the wild pounding of his heart. His nostrils flared instinctively, and he swore he could smell her light enticing scent. He knew her essence filled his senses, had done so all week, ever since that first kiss.

He was instantly hard, intensely hard.

If you knock on that door, there'll be no more noble streak. There'll only be me and you and enough fire to incinerate this whole county.

He felt the sheen of heat on his skin and the coiled tension of every muscle as he sat, barely breathing, poised like some big cat intent on its prey. When he heard her footsteps retreat toward her room he almost howled with frustration. Instead he cursed whatever odd quirk of conscience or honor or pure male pride insisted he wait for her to come to him.

T.C. rose early and pushed herself hard throughout the next day, hoping to drive yesterday from her mind. "Might as well hope you'll grow wings and morph into Pegasus," she told Duke as she rugged him late in the afternoon.

The phone was ringing as she came into the house, tired from physical exertion and edgy with the prospect of facing Nick. She grabbed the receiver without thinking. "Hello?"

Her greeting was met with a beat of silence long enough

for her heart to bound and lodge in her throat. Surely not…not after a week of silence.

"Hello?"

T.C. pressed a hand to her chest and closed her eyes. Thank God! There was someone there. A voice. A woman.

"Hello?" the woman repeated. "Is anyone there?"

"Yes. Sorry. This is Tamara Cole. Can I help you?"

Another curious beat of silence. "Now I'm confused. I was sure George said you'd moved."

"Who is this?"

"Oh, how rude of me." The woman sounded more richly amused than contrite. "I'm Sophie Corelli. Could I possibly speak to Nicky?"

Nicky?

"I've been trying to reach him for days, and he never returns my calls."

"I'll see if I can find him," T.C. said weakly, although if he was in the office, he would have picked up Sophie's call. God forbid she would have to hunt him down in his bedroom or shower.

Cordless handset clutched to her chest, she peered around the partly open office door. No one home. Mind made up to take a message, she went in but found her purpose immediately overtaken by curiosity. Carefully she set down the phone and looked around. There wasn't much to see.

A blank computer screen, paperwork stacked in several untidy piles, a couple of notes scrawled even less legibly than his shopping list, a tray of computer printouts—charts of some kind—and sitting on top of them a pair of metal-rimmed glasses. She ran a tentative finger along one earpiece and told herself the strange little tug around her heart was the reassuring notion of Nick with an imperfection, not the incredibly endearing image of him wearing glasses.

"Looking for something?"

She turned quickly, backing away from the desk as if

she'd been caught snooping…which of course she hadn't. Luckily the bookcase provided support for her sudden weak-kneed breathlessness when he came into the room, wet hair flopping over his forehead, shirt untucked and hanging open.

All endearing thoughts evaporated in an instant haze of heat.

"Tamara?"

"Oh…a…um…call. For you." Four words, four syllables, yet she had trouble stringing them together. Swallowing, she looked away, focused on the phone instead. "It's your sister."

"That narrows the field to four. Any idea which one?"

"Oh. Yes. It's Sophie."

The corner of his mouth twitched—with irritation?—as he swung into the chair and swiveled it toward the desk. When he reached for the phone his chambray shirt stretched taut across the breadth of his shoulders, and her attention was drawn to several tendrils of hair curling over his collar.

Oh, help! This room is definitely too small and too poorly ventilated.

"Sophie? You still there?"

He propped the phone between his chin and shoulder while he buttoned his shirt. What was it with him and dressing in her presence? She edged along the wall until she heard his weight shift in the chair and felt the dark unsettling touch of his gaze. Ignore it, she told herself. But when she started to move, more overtly this time, he simply rolled his chair into her path.

Satisfied she wasn't going anywhere but incredibly irritated by her attempt, Nick turned his attention to the phone call. "How did you get this number?" he asked at the end of Sophie's introductory small talk. Sophie held a masters in small talk.

"From your partner, natch."

Nick swore. Sophie laughed. Tamara looked up from contemplating her toes, then away again just as quickly.

"George said you were only in the country for a day or two. Math was never my strong suit, but I can add. You've been there well over a week now. What gives, Nicky?"

"Ever heard of taking a break?"

"Didn't you just get back from a break—in Alaska, of all places?"

"Your point?"

"Hmm…wrong season for skiing, and I don't recall any decent climbs or white water nearby, so it must be a woman. Oh my God, is that why Joe's little woman is still there? You are too much, Nicky!"

"She wasn't Joe's—" He stopped himself right there. Swore silently when Sophie crowed with malicious delight. Willed Tamara to look at him, but she continued to stare fixedly at her toes.

"This is *soooo* priceless," Sophie cooed. "I can't wait to share."

"It's none of George's business."

"You think he hasn't made it his business? He's been in a hellish snit about your little bequest, and he can't bear to have you in the same country. What I can't decide is why he's still paranoid. Is it still about Emily?"

Nick scrubbed a hand over his face. "Don't call him to make trouble, Soph. Tell him I don't want anything of his, especially his wife, and I'll be out of the country this time next week. Will you do that?"

"Why not?" He could hear her shrug. "No skin off my nose."

After he recradled the receiver, Nick realized he had been gripping it with viselike intensity. Straightening his fingers was actually painful. Man, but he hated the way Sophie's troublemaking could still steam him…almost as much as George's paranoia. Was it any wonder he chose to live on the opposite side of the world? With barely contained frustration, he shoved his chair away from the desk and found Tamara eyeing the door.

"Thinking of running away again?"

Her fitful gaze jerked back to his. "It's not quite like that."

"Isn't it?" He slapped a hand down on the arm of his chair. "You'd have been locked behind your bedroom door ten minutes ago if I hadn't blocked your exit."

"I'm sorry. It's just…"

"Just what? Just that you don't have the guts to talk straight to me?"

She recoiled sharply, as if the words had stung, and Nick wanted nothing more than to back down, to apologize to her, and that only made him angrier.

"Stay, for once," he bit out. "Talk to me."

"I don't know how to talk to a man like you."

"A man like me?"

With a rough curse, he thrust his chair forward, startling her into knocking several books from the shelf at her back. Nick ignored their heavy tumble to the floor. He felt an insane urge to keep going, to surge out of the chair and demonstrate what sort of edgy, frustrated man he had become.

"Tell me, Tamara. What kind of man do you think I am?" he asked with dangerous calm.

"The kind I can't relate to. Joe drove me nuts with his stories. Nick's gone kayaking in Peru. Nick's joining an Everest expedition. To me your life is… I don't know…larger than life."

"What about this past week, Tamara? Don't you feel like you've been relating to me, cuz it sure as hell felt like we were relating down in that shower bay yesterday."

Hot color flared in her cheeks, hot memories in her gaze; then she looked away, and Nick cursed out loud. He hadn't meant to bring that up. *What was it with her?* She had a way of getting under his skin so damn quick he barely felt the pinprick, and right this minute she was so far under he could feel his skin stretched taut.

"Don't you think it's time you started judging me with your own eyes instead of on an old man's ramblings?"

That brought her gaze charging back to his, so heated it seared him with green fire. "How can you talk about Joe like that? He wasn't some rambling old man, he was your father!"

"He wasn't my father."

She stared at him, stunned into silence.

Gaze fixed on the ceiling, he rocked back in his chair and expelled a short harsh breath. "I don't know why I said that. It's not something I talk about." Not because he was ashamed, but because it didn't make any difference to who he was. Not anymore.

"Maybe you should." T.C. watched his lips set in a firm line as he rocked back to face her. Their gazes locked and held for five long seconds, and the guarded vulnerability in his expression squeezed her heart. She stood with the breath backing up in her lungs while her eyes willed him to explain. These next few minutes held the key to understanding Nick—not the Nick of her preconceptions but the real Nick—and that key would likely open the door on a whole new set of feelings. Strangely, the thought didn't scare her as much as it should have.

"You sure you want to hear this?" he asked.

"I *need* to hear it."

He scrubbed a hand across his face. "Where to start."

"The beginning's usually a good place."

"Not in my case." His smile was grim, humorless. "I don't even know much about my beginning. My mother was a hooker and an addict, or an addict and a hooker. Whatever. My father could have been anyone."

His gaze held hers, and the expression in the depths of his eyes was as harsh as his words, daring her to flinch or to look away. She did neither—she simply prompted him to continue. "What happened to your mother?"

"She was a distant cousin of Joe's, but they'd never met. They shared the same surname and that's about it. Apparently she saw his picture on the cover of a magazine, did some research on their family connection and decided to try blackmail. Joe didn't bite. A couple weeks later she OD'd. Joe's number was in her things, and the authorities thought he might be next of kin."

"So he took you in."

"What else could he do?" He shrugged, the gesture tense and self-conscious, and so unlike Nick. Her stomach twisted painfully.

"He could have done nothing." Except they both knew that wouldn't have been an option for Joe. "How old were you?"

"Eight."

She pictured a small bewildered child, wrenched from the familiar into a stranger's world, and she wondered if that was the reason he didn't get the concept of home. "That can't have been easy," she said slowly.

"It was easy enough on me. I got to eat regular meals and sleep in the same bed every night." His harsh exhalation didn't much resemble a laugh. "It was tough on Joe's wife, though. She already had five kids."

"I imagine she had plenty of help."

His gaze was sharp, almost hard. "Yeah, she had a housekeeper and a cook, but I wasn't talking about that."

No. She could see that. He was talking about the emotional side, the impact of a new kid thrown into that headstrong, spoiled, Corelli brood. It would have been tough on all of them, but especially so on Nick. She felt that as a dull ache in her heart.

"Joe talked so much about you, yet he never mentioned this. Never hinted, not even in the letter. As far as he was concerned, you are his son—that's why he talked about you so much. He was proud of you. He missed you. He *loved* you. He *was* your father, Nick.''

''Yeah, well, like you, I wished he was.''

He leaned back in his chair, his posture a negligent contrast to the tense lines of his face and the shadows that darkened his eyes. For a second she battled the urge to close the space between them, to wrap her arms around him and soothe away those shadows…but only for a second. Then she lost the battle. She went down on her knees, placed a gentle hand on his knee.

''He loved you as his son, Nick.''

A muscle twitched in his cheek. His gaze glittered with hard cynicism as it shifted from her face to her hand, then back again. ''What's this, Tamara? You can't put your hand on me in honest desire but you can out of pity?''

She shook her head, but he was already getting to his feet, stepping around her.

''I don't want your pity. That's not why I told you.'' He stopped at the door, blew out a harsh breath. ''I don't know why I told you.''

''It's not about pity, Nick. It's about understanding.''

''You think because I told you about my background you suddenly understand me?'' His voice was as hard as his eyes, as uncompromising as his stance. ''I'm the same man I was this afternoon. Nothing's changed.''

But as he walked away, she told herself he was wrong.

He was still the same man, but everything else had changed now that she knew the boy he had been. Now she saw reasons for a man to search for his place in the world, to prove himself better than his background, to earn everything he owned on his own merits and not from the benevolence of his adoptive family.

She only hoped that knowledge would give her the courage to go to him and put her hand on him in honest desire.

Nine

———

Sixteen hours later Nick watched a dark blue BMW glide to a halt outside the stables. He knew who would own such a vehicle even before the driver stepped out, smoothed an imaginary wrinkle from his jacket, then did an exaggerated backstep away from Ug's welcome.

On some other day Nick might have found that comical, but right now he wasn't in the mood for funny. He wasn't in the mood for visitors, either, especially unwelcome ones, although after Sophie's phone call, her brother's appearance wasn't exactly unexpected.

He pushed his wheelbarrow into the next stall and pitched a fork into the straw bedding. When the hair on the back of his neck stood to attention, he knew he had company.

"Lost, bro?" he asked without looking up.

"I heard you found yourself some dirt to play around in, but I thought Sophie was referring to something else."

Nick tightened his grip on the pitchfork. Told himself

the reality of wrapping it around George's puny neck wouldn't be nearly as satisfying as the imagining. He dug deep under a pile of soiled straw, lifted and tossed it in one deft motion, then raised innocent brows when it overshot the barrow to land square on a pair of highly polished Italian loafers.

"Sorry about that."

And in the silence that followed he realized he *was* sorry—not for sullying George's shoe leather but for succumbing to the moment. It was a puerile response, and it hadn't made him feel a whole lot better. Some, but not nearly enough.

George's thin lips pursed in distaste. "Could we continue our discussion in the office?"

"What, exactly, are we discussing?"

"I know of a party who's keen to buy into the horse business. He liked the sound of this place."

"You remember our meeting, the day I arrived? Which part of 'I don't want your help' didn't you understand?"

A quick flush stained George's skin. "I was approached by an associate of Joe's who assumed I was the new owner. I saw a chance to help you out."

"Well, thanks for driving all the way out here to help me out, bro, but I'm not looking for a buyer."

"What do you mean?" George's flush deepened to a dull red. "You live overseas. What would you want with a place here?"

None of your damned business. That was Nick's instant response, the one he would have given a week ago. Back then he would have grinned to show he couldn't care less, before he turned his back and sauntered away. But it seemed like his attitude had changed, probably because he had grown sick and tired of Tamara walking away instead of talking about whatever was bothering her. For the first time in fourteen years, he decided it was worth talking to George.

"Whether or not Sophie gave you my message, it bears repeating. I don't want anything that belongs to you, and that includes what you refer to as your help.

"Yes, I do live overseas—I made that choice because it was easier on everyone and it suited me fine. I wanted to make my own life. I proved what I could do without Joe's help and despite my background."

Flushed and tight-lipped, George opened his mouth to interrupt, but Nick held up a hand.

"I'm almost done. Hear me out, okay? My decision to keep Yarra Park has nothing to do with you. None of my life has anything to do with you. Not anymore."

"That's not much of an attitude toward family."

"You want to talk about attitude to family?" Nick's voice was as steel-sharp as the prongs on the pitchfork in his hand. "What about your efforts to contact me when Joe took ill? What about that solicitor's letter after he died? He might not have been my blood father, but he brought me up as his son and as your brother. Don't you think I deserved better?"

"You didn't deserve anything—" George said spitefully as he inclined his head toward the manure-filled barrow. "Except where you are right now. What you're doing here is a fitting job for you."

"I suggest you get the hell out of here before I do something fitting with this pitchfork."

"We both know you won't risk that," George sneered, but he edged out of Nick's reach. "This time Joe isn't here to stick up for you. This time I *would* press charges."

"He never took sides. He did what was fair."

"He might have tried, but we all know you were his favorite. That's why he left you this place."

"You got the Portsea house and the chairmanship and your share of the rest of it. Why are you so stuck on this one small thing?"

"Because it's not a small thing—it's the thing that mattered most!'' The words erupted from George's tight lips, as if the lid had been lifted on a pressure cooker of festering resentment.

"And you think that if I sell, it will make a difference to the way you feel? Hell, George, if I sent you Yarra Park in gift wrapping it wouldn't make a lick of difference. You don't know why Joe did it this way, and you can't change the fact that he did. It simply is.''

He met the bitterness in George's eyes, a bitterness he knew was burning the other man up from the inside out.

"Don't you think it's time you got over this jealousy thing? You're thirty-four years old. You have a wife and a family, the home and the job you wanted. Isn't it time you concentrated your energy on what you have instead of what you can't have?''

George had no comeback. First time in his life, Nick thought, as he watched him turn on his heel and stalk away. He wasn't sure if his message got through, wasn't sure if it ever would, but at least he had tried.

He would have returned to his chore, except a sense of foreboding niggled at his gut. He put the tool aside and walked out to the front of the stables as the sleek dark sedan pulled to a stop halfway down the driveway.

Hell. Tamara and Jason were on their way back from the track, but only one horse stopped as George climbed out of his car. Nick's shoulder muscles bunched and his hands curled into fists as he watched the short exchange, knowing that whatever George had to say wouldn't be pleasant. It also didn't take long. The car took off in a furious spurt of dust, while Tamara headed her horse to the barn at a sedate walk.

She swung out of the cart, seemingly unperturbed, but then she fumbled with the simple clasp on her helmet, cursed, and Nick noticed the tremor in her normally sure hands. He placed his on her shoulders, stilling her with gentle insistence.

"What did he say to you?"

"Nothing that bears repeating."

"That bad, huh?" He slid his hands down her arms, back up again. "He left here looking for a whipping boy—you just happened to be convenient. Don't take it personally."

"He said you threatened him with a pitchfork. If I'd had one handy, I'd have done more than threaten." Her eyes glittered with temper, and Nick felt relief radiate through his whole being. She wasn't shaking with fear; she was shaking with rage.

"Yeah, well, as tempting as that sounds, it would have done more harm than good."

T.C. snorted.

"I did hit him once, a long while ago. If Joe hadn't interceded, he'd have charged me with assault."

"I hope you hit him hard."

"Flattened his nose, but it wasn't nearly as satisfying as I'd thought it would be." He rubbed his hands over her shoulders and down her arms again, smoothing her brittle temper as quickly as it had flared. "Plus it gave him something else to hate me for."

Joe had told her his sons didn't get along, but he had never told her why—whether something specific had caused a rift or if they simply clashed on everything. Hate was a strong word, but that was exactly what she had seen burning in George's eyes when he stopped to hurl insults at her.

He took his hands from her arms, and T.C. immediately felt the loss of calm. She felt edgy and restive, as if *she* needed to run a few laps of the track. Returning to work wasn't an option. She turned and called out to Jason, "Will you finish up here?" before swinging back to Nick. "You want to take a walk?"

"Are we going to get wet?" he asked, inclining his head toward the clouds gathering on the southern horizon.

"Not for hours yet." She started walking and felt him beside her, matching his stride to hers. "Is getting Yarra Park one of the things George hates you for?" she wondered out loud.

"One of a long list. There's a whole heap of paranoia going on in his head that I can't begin to understand. He hated the attention I got when I first came to live with them, and I don't think he ever got over it. The older we got, the worse his jealousy got."

"What was he jealous of?"

"School reports, who made the football team, praise from Joe. Anything and everything."

"You know, I can almost see his point of view."

"Yeah?"

Feeling the curiosity in his gaze, she tilted her face to meet it. "Yeah. I have this picture forming of you two as teenagers. Nick, a couple of years younger but already bigger, stronger, better looking. I bet you made all the teams, got better grades, and every time George brought a girl home, she took one look at you and forgot big brother."

She smiled, wanting to ease the moment, but Nick didn't respond. And his words to Sophie came vividly to mind. *I don't want anything of his, especially his wife.* Holy toledo. She moistened her dry mouth.

"This fight you had when you flattened his nose…was it over a girl?"

"Yes and no." He paused long enough that she thought he wouldn't continue. Their initial get-me-out-of-here strides had slowed to a bare stroll, and the mood felt as ominous as the gathering storm clouds.

"Emily had been going out with George for a while when she told him she had this thing for me. I don't know if she really did, or if she just had some kind of agenda. I mean, I hardly even knew her—I'd met her a couple of times around the pool, but mostly I steered clear of George's friends. Whatever it was…" He lifted one shoulder in a stiff gesture of dismissal. "…it brought on the fight that had been brewing for years."

"Is that why you went away?"

"I would have gone anyway."

They stopped at the boundary fence. T.C. watched Nick rest his arms on the top rail and squint off into the distance, maybe studying the gathering clouds, maybe lost in the past. And suddenly she was gripped by the same restlessness as she'd felt back in the barn. Walking hadn't been enough. She blew out a swift breath. "I want to get out of here for a while. Will you take me on the bike?"

"Where do you want to go?"

"Nowhere. Anywhere." She laughed shortly. "You think we can race that storm?"

"Sounds dangerous," he said, coming around to face her, close enough that she felt the heat of his body and the solid beat of his heart. Not the larger than life figure of Joe's stories, but the real living, breathing Nick.

"Maybe I'm ready to take a few risks."

His gaze narrowed on hers, causing her pulse to flutter with nerves. Then he grabbed hold of her hand and growled, "Let's go," and T.C. felt anticipation gallop unfettered all over her body. Yes, she felt reckless and wildly impetuous, but more than that, she felt truly and wonderfully alive.

If T.C. had been in charge of the Ducati she would have ridden it hard into the storm, such was her mood. But Nick headed north, away from the threatening clouds.

At first the irregular acceleration as they twisted and turned through a tricky section of road honed her wildness to a sharp edge; then they hit the freeway, and the sonorous hum of the cruising engine smoothed those edges. She allowed herself to lean more deeply into the sheltering strength of Nick's body, to slide her hands into his jacket pockets and to rest her head in the hollow between his shoulder blades, which had seemingly been made for that purpose.

Instantly her mood eased from a little crazy to a lot sane. At her very core she tingled with a heightened awareness, but layered over it like the warm folds of a comfy duvet was another sensation she hadn't felt in a long time. She wrapped her arms more tightly around him and gave herself up to the feeling of absolute and total security.

They turned off the highway before they struck the border, tracking the Murray's wide river valley into the high country. Eventually they stopped at a rustic pub where they dawdled over a counter lunch and traded stories with the chatty barman.

Every so often their gazes would meet with a flash of awareness, or their knees would brush as one or the other turned on their bar stool, and the brief connection would sizzle through her blood. She was past fighting it, past analyzing it, past worrying where it might end. She simply enjoyed it.

When custom picked up, the barman drifted off and they continued to talk, skimming easily from thought to thought. He was talking about Graeme when she recalled the reason he had looked up his old friend.

"You never did tell me what you found out when you went to Melbourne."

"I found out Graeme owns a bike I covet."

She rolled her eyes. Nick grinned. Her heart rolled over.

"Okay, I found out there's nothing we can do until probate is finalized. It's a pretty complex setup, so that could take a while."

"What happens then?"

"Transmission papers are filed and the new title deed comes back in our names."

It sounded so final, so binding. A sudden anxiety churned in her stomach. "I really don't want that, Nick."

"And I don't want your half."

"Yarra Park belongs in your family," she continued doggedly.

"You want to give it to George? He'd like that. He has a buyer all lined up with a pen in his hand."

Of course she didn't want that. She didn't want anything to do with the man, especially after the things he had implied down by the track. Things she hadn't been able to walk off, or to outrun on the bike.

"What's the matter?" Nick took her hand and plaited his fingers through hers. "And don't fob me off with a 'Nothing' answer, either. I can hear the cogs turning."

"It's George. He said something earlier..."

"Did he threaten you?" His grip on her hand tightened almost painfully. "What did he say, Tamara?"

"I was too mad to make much of it at the time." She frowned, recalling the bad vibes that started afterward, as she walked Pash back to the stables. "He said I didn't belong at Yarra Park, that I should have left, and for some reason I wondered about those phone calls—if he might have been trying to scare me off, although that makes no sense. It's *you* he wants gone more than me." Spoken out loud, her concerns sounded ridiculous. She laughed self-consciously. "Forget it."

Nick didn't laugh. "He knew I'd want to sell out. You, he needed to convince."

"But those calls weren't threats, just silence." She shifted uneasily with the memory. "Why would that convince me to do anything other than not answer the phone?"

"Maybe he figured you'd be uneasy living there alone. That it would help you decide to take the money and leave." A deep frown furrowed his brow. She couldn't believe he was taking this seriously. That scared her a little. "Maybe he was building up to the threats, only then I changed the number."

"He would have been able to get the new number. Sophie did. When you've got that much money…"

He let out a long, ragged sigh. "You're right. It doesn't make sense, but then, George doesn't always function at a rational level. He proved that this morning."

"I'm probably dead wrong."

"Probably, but I'd prefer to be certain." There was a strength in the gaze holding hers, determination in the set of his jaw, and protectiveness in the hand linked with hers. He pulled her to her feet. "Come on. I'll take you home."

Nick eased the bike to a standstill inside the garage and killed the engine. Its throaty rumble continued to hum through her body, a perfect counterpoint to the rhythmic drumming of rain against the iron roof.

The storm had caught them on the road, lashing them with a cruel crosswind and buffeting squalls of rain. Despite the wild ride, despite that heart-stopping moment when the back tire lost traction on the slick bitumen, she had trusted Nick to deliver her home.

At this moment home felt like the solid strength of his big, warm body, smelled like a heady combination of wet leather and wet man. This was what she had been trying to explain that day out on the track—home wasn't so much a place as a sensation that reached inside, that took hold of your soul.

A spirit of rightness.

She felt the shifting of muscles as he lifted his arms to remove his helmet; then, in one smooth motion, he swung his leg over the tank and eased to his feet beside her. Rainwater trickled down his jacket, dripping from the hem onto jeans already so wet they were plastered to his hips and thighs. His teeth flashed white as he ripped the gloves from his hands, and something primal raced through T.C.'s blood, so hot and fast it blurred her vision.

Steady, she cautioned herself. Concentrate on *not* slithering into a boneless heap at his feet.

She focused on the zip of his jacket, then on a raindrop as it threaded its delicate path south via the jungle of metal teeth. She felt the soft scrape of his fingers against her throat as he released the clasp of her headgear, and her breathing grew shallow as he slipped the helmet from her head, unzipped her jacket and peeled it off.

"I'll get your boots. They're sodden."

"There's no need...."

"There's a need. You look like you're frozen to the seat."

She tried to move, but he stopped her with a hand on her knee, a hand so warm she swore steam rose from her wet jeans. No. She definitely wasn't frozen.

Carefully he worked the first boot off, then her thick sock. Tamara willed her senses to concentrate on something beyond the heated touch of his fingers on her ankle. Fat chance. She closed her eyes and luxuriated in the feather-soft stroke of his thumb over her anklebone. She imagined that same slow beguiling pressure elsewhere. Circling her navel. Teasing a nipple. Sliding inside her pants.

A drip of cold rainwater splashed onto the back of her neck, breaking her sensual reverie and her leaden immobility. Finally she was capable of swinging her right leg over the seat and shimmying around to sit sidesaddle.

Nick pulled the second boot off and tossed it unceremoniously behind him. Her sock followed. She noticed his eyes in the same instant that her boot thudded against the garage wall. They watched her with an intensity that would have knocked her socks off had she been wearing any.

"You need to get out of these wet jeans."

Yes, please.

The words formed, then seemed to stick somewhere between her mind and her tongue. If only she could say them. If only she could put that hand on him.

If only she weren't such a wimp.

He straightened suddenly. "You'd better go take a shower, warm yourself up. I'll see if everything's all right down at the stables."

A shower. Right. She slid to the ground, and her knees buckled, but he steadied her with firm hands.

"You *are* freezing," he murmured, and before she could reply he slipped a hand under her thighs and lifted her into his arms. The pounding rain seemed to intensify to a dull roar, although that could have been the roar of blood hammering through her veins.

The world tilted as he swung around and headed for the door, but Tamara had the distinct impression it wasn't shifting out of kilter but into perfect balance. As he struggled with the security lock, he tipped her closer to his chest, and her whole body sighed with extravagant relief. It had always known its rightful place—here, as close to Nick as the physics of matter allowed. Her slowpoke heart had taken more time to arrive at the same truth, but as he carried her inside the place she called home, it, too, caught up with the plot.

She loved him.

There was no surprise in the revelation, just a huge thickening of emotion in her chest, a complex feeling comprising as many parts pain as pleasure. She wondered if her heart was already foreseeing its broken future.

He set her down in the bathroom, on top of the vanity, and turned the shower on full steam. "Don't get out until you're properly thawed, okay?"

It was all she could do to unfurl her tongue enough to say, "Thank you."

"For?"

"Carrying me inside. Lunch. The ride."

"You had fun?"

She nodded.

One brow arched. "And I thought you said fun was overrated."

Fun. The word reverberated in T.C.'s head, seemingly in time with the water that beat against her skin. It was a timely warning, a reminder that fun was all Nick sought. Just like Miles...

No. She rejected that thought as quickly as it formed.

He was nothing like Miles. Her heart knew that truth as well as it knew the other truth. With Nick there would be no false words of love, no false promises. There would be respect and honesty, affection and attention.

Oh, and there would be heat. Firestorms of heat, for as long as this lasted.

Five days.

She had been trying not to count, trying to forget how little time was left. Only five days until he returned to New York, only five more days for her to...what?

To hesitate? To procrastinate? To hide her feelings?

Or five days to enjoy a brief taste of heaven, to embrace it with everything she felt? Could she do it? Would it be enough?

The questions pounded through her blood as she turned off the water and toweled herself dry.

What about the afterward? Could she kiss him blithely and tell him it had been fun, even while her heart was breaking?

She exited the bathroom as Nick came into the hallway from the living area. They both stopped absolutely still, her hands gripping the towel over her breasts, his fingers unbuttoning his shirt. As that first moment of stunned stillness passed, she noticed that he had shed his coat and boots, that he continued working on his shirt as he came toward her on silent feet.

That the tension in the air felt as electrically charged as the thick storm air.

In the gathering twilight gloom, she could barely make out his face. It seemed all sharp angles and shadowed planes, and with stubble darkening his jaw and his hair wildly mussed from the helmet and the rain, he looked dark and dangerous and primitive. And in that moment she knew that despite the heartache to come, despite the lack of future, she had no choice in the matter.

Her heart had made its own decision.

Weak with that knowledge, she slumped back against the wall, needing it for support, hoping it would give her strength as his gaze roamed over her flushed face, her hands gripping the top of her towel, and the length of her exposed legs beneath.

Without a word he moved past her, shedding his shirt with an almost violent shrug of his shoulders and tossing it ahead of him through the bathroom door.

So. The first move would have to be hers, and hers alone. She swallowed again. Then, with the newness of loving him full in her heart, she took that first step.

"Tight wet jeans and wet skin are a tricky combination."

He stopped in the doorway. One hand closed around the upright; the muscles across his shoulders tensed. His whole posture seemed expectant, waiting for her next words.

"You might want some help with them."

He turned, eyes glittering, a slash of color etching his sharp cheekbones. "What are you saying?"

"I'm saying I've changed my mind. And I'm asking if you've changed yours."

"Spell it out, Tamara."

Here goes nothing...and everything. She cleared her throat to make sure she enunciated each word very clearly. "Will you make love to me, Nick?"

Ten

For a long tense moment their gazes melded, his narrow, piercing, as if he needed to see into her very soul. Then he grinned, a pained lopsided quirk of the lips, but a grin all the same.

"Sure, but I'm going to need that help you offered. Feels like these jeans shrank in the rain."

"Really?"

"Why don't you come over here and see for yourself?"

Giddy with relief, with love, with nervous anticipation, she went to him. Stood close while he cupped her face in his hands and touched his lips to her forehead. The kiss was unexpectedly, exquisitely, tender. And when he breathed, "Thank God you changed your mind," T.C.'s heart swelled until she feared it would burst clean out of her chest.

Then his hands slid by her throat, over her shoulders, down her arms, and as they came to rest at her waist she imagined a faint tremor in his fingertips. She must have imagined it. Those practiced hands would never quaver.

Then he was kissing her, really kissing her. He tasted of the outdoors, chill and fresh and a little sharp, until his mouth settled more fully over hers, easing it open, and then she tasted only Nick—the absolute rightness of Nick under her lips, on her tongue, in her mouth. She could have kept on kissing him for hours—no, *days*—but then his tongue slid over hers, and the surge of desire was instant, and achingly intense.

She had to touch him, to feel him against her skin. Her hands slid around his back, urging him closer. He still wore those wet jeans, but there was nothing chilling about the contact between his powerful thighs, muscles bunched as he hunched down to her level, and her naked legs.

With a low, greedy moan she wrenched her mouth from his and buried her face in his neck. Her mouth tasted the rain on his skin; her tongue measured his rapid-fire pulse in the vulnerable hollow of his throat; her eyes drifted shut to better appreciate such a sensual smorgasbord.

His hands moved lower, cupping her hips, then lower still, until the tips of his fingers touched the backs of her thighs…and trailed a slow, deliberate course inward.

Holy jiminy! How could a touch so gentle burn as deep as a firebrand?

He eased away, and she felt the gentle tug, the drag of toweling over her skin, then nothing but cool air. The sudden chill goose-bumped her flesh, and for a moment she felt exposed and self-conscious standing naked before him. Then she heard his swift intake of breath, felt the first touch of his hands gently cupping her breasts, his dark velvet voice murmuring words of encouragement.

Eyes still closed, she felt the shift of air as he ducked his head, the cool brush of wet hair against her throat, then the rasp of whiskered skin on her breast. Her lids flew open as his tongue swirled around one fiercely distended nipple.

He drew her into his hot, moist mouth, and a tremor rippled through her body. And when he suckled deeply, hungrily, an arrow of stark desire shot straight to the core of her being.

Edgy with conflicting needs, she threaded her unsteady fingers in the cool silk of his hair, first holding him to her, then urging him away. "Let me touch you," she breathed.

"You can touch me all you like when you get me out of these cursed jeans."

She pressed herself against those cursed jeans and felt a soft shudder rack her body. Yes, it was definitely time to lose the jeans. As she reached for the button-fly, she felt his harsh inhalation, then the evidence of his desire.

Holy toledo. There was so much of him. Such a hard, pulsing, mind-blowing lot. Her head spun with an intoxicating feminine power she'd never experienced before.

Because Nick wanted her *this* much.

He drew a ragged breath. Swore softly. And suddenly he hooked his hands under her backside and lifted her. "Let's find a bed, sweet hands."

With rough impatience, he shouldered past a door. Six strides and she felt herself dropping; then the cushioning folds of soft bedcovers closed around her. By the time her head stopped spinning he had lost the jeans—without her help—and it crossed her mind that for such a leisurely man, he could move very quickly when he wanted to.

Naked at last, Nick came down to her, claiming her mouth in the way he ached to take her body, plunging his tongue between her kiss-swollen lips with undisguised hunger. He had wanted her—probably from the first touch of her hands on his body—but he hadn't counted on that desire grabbing him with vicious, clawing fingers.

Compelling him to forget slow, forget savoring the moment, forget everything other than driving himself into her heat.

Caveman tactics? Smooth, Niccolo. He hauled himself

back from the edge, slid his tongue more slowly against hers before easing away, wanting to look at her, then wanting to taste her. Everywhere. Her high, firm breasts, the curve of her belly, her soft thatch of curls. He slid a finger over her, felt her shudder, deep and strong.

"Please, Nick," she pleaded softly, her hips rolling in languid invitation.

"Yeah, sweetheart, I want that, too. Trouble is, I want everything with you, all at once." He slid a finger into her, swore urgently. "You're so wet. So tight."

Sweat broke out down his backbone as he felt her scorching heat screaming out to him. He closed his eyes, forced himself to still. He wanted to prolong the pleasure, to touch her, taste her, but when he opened his eyes, she was biting that full bottom lip, her eyes wild and hungry.

"Please, Niccolo."

Oh, man!

Protection.

He rolled with her, scrambled about in the bedside drawer, somehow managed to tear the package open and fit himself. Then he thrust into her in one long, fierce stroke, and as she closed around him, gripping him with sultry heat, he stilled, wanting to time-lock the exquisite pleasure of the moment. He gazed down into her eyes, was staggered to see tears, then humbled by the depth of wonder in her gaze. She placed a hand to his cheek and whispered, "Wow."

He had no response but to kiss away her tears. To touch her cheeks and her lashes with his lips and tongue as he started to move inside her, his strokes long and deep. He felt his control teeter when she wrapped her legs around him and tilted her hips, drawing him deeper. He moved faster, harder, compelled to completion by the rhythmical caress of her body. Then he touched her, once, and she exploded in a violent, quaking storm that shredded his control.

A savage feeling of possession burst inside him. He didn't wait; he couldn't wait. He had to pour everything of himself into her, and as she continued to pulse around him, he felt a similar clasp on his heart, squeezing him tight, as if it would never let go.

T.C. woke slowly, her brain at least a dozen steps behind her senses. They were already brimful of Nick. The steady beat of his heart against her cheek, the solid contours of his body fitted snugly against hers, the musky scent of lovemaking.

Her brain quickly found the right page.

Lovemaking...or sex? There was no doubt in her heart. In the cold morning light, she was even more in love, if that were possible. But what about Nick? Carefully she extricated herself from his arms. Had she imagined that intensity in his gaze, that feeling of once-in-a-lifetime connection? That immense sense of special?

She chewed on her bottom lip, then puffed out a breath. She had so little objectivity, and so very little experience. With a carefully covert wriggle, she put a little space between them in his big bed. Not that she was going anywhere; she just wanted some space to...look.

He lay on his side, covered to the waist. Her heart kerfudded against her ribs as she thought about pulling the sheet aside and taking her own leisurely time to drink in his beauty in the bright morning light. To look at him and maybe touch him some.

With her hands. With her mouth.

The wicked thought filled her with heat, sudden and breathtaking. How simple it would be to wriggle back over there and put her hand on his chest, to slide it over his flat hard abdomen, to lift the sheet and... She paused when voices infiltrated her secretive planning session—not the ones inside her head chanting ''Go for it!'' but others.

Her eyelids flew open. Had she really heard people talking? From the other end of the house came the definite sound of a door closing, and she catapulted out of the bed.

Nick rolled onto his side and regarded her with sleepy eyes. One dark eyebrow arched as he took in her flustered nakedness. "What's up?"

"You there? T.C.? Nick?"

T.C. whirled toward the open bedroom door.

"Jase," she breathed, dropping to the floor. She gathered and discarded random pieces of clothing with frantic hands, cursing when she hauled on a T-shirt back to front, fumbling to turn it around. Not an easy task when she was hunched down beneath mattress level, petrified of Jason appearing at any moment.

"He's come looking for us…. What time is it? I never sleep in…. Who else is out there? Do you have some shorts I can borrow?"

"Top drawer."

She rummaged, tugged on a pair of satin boxers, anxious eyes flicking from the door to Nick, who still lay there looking sexily rumpled and perfectly at ease. He'd probably been caught in this situation a dozen times.

"Anyone home?" This time Jason sounded closer—like out in the hallway—which meant he really was coming to find them.

"Be out in a minute," Nick called, but T.C. was already dashing around the bed and out the door.

She almost collided with Jason, whose cheerful grin froze as his eyes moved slowly from her strange attire to Nick's door, and then to some blank point on the wall behind her. His face turned a summer shade of red, which was likely a perfect match for hers. "Yesterday you said you'd be back by three, but I reckoned the storm must have held you up, so I wasn't worried. But when you weren't at the stables this morning, Mum reckoned I should come in and make sure you were all right."

"Mum?"

"She thought she'd come and see if you wanted a hand, like with the housework or anything."

Before she could do more than issue a silent groan, she heard movement behind her, then felt the gentle weight of Nick's hands on her shoulders, easing her back against his naked chest. At least he had pulled on jeans, although he wasn't doing anything to dispel the perception of why they had slept in.

"How about you go put some coffee on, Jase? We'll be right behind you."

They would have needed wheels and a motor to be right behind Jason, such was his haste to get away. T.C. sympathized fully. Awkward situations always made her edgy, and this rated pretty high on her personal awkward scale. What had she been thinking, lying there seducing him in her mind? She should have been aware of the time, aware that Jase would find her absence unusual.

Why *hadn't* she been thinking?

Nick smoothed his hands over her shoulders, down her arms, measuring her tension. "You're not okay with this, are you?"

This. Great descriptive term. Covered the undefined nature of their relationship about as all-inclusively as Nick's man-size T-shirt covered her. "No, I'm not okay, exactly." She blew out an unsteady breath. "I'm embarrassed, I'm not comfortable, and I have no idea what to say or how to act."

He pulled her resistant body to him, and his hands moved to her back, easing her closer still. Leaning on him felt very, very good. She felt his lips against her hair as he spoke to her, his voice low and soothing. "Jase was going to find out about us whether he came into the house this morning or not, so don't make a big deal out of it. Nothing has changed. Be yourself, okay?"

No big deal? Nothing had changed? The words felt like hammer blows to her heart.

And what were you expecting, Tamara Cole? Surely, after one night, you weren't expecting words of love and promises of undying devotion? You have been there. You've heard all the pretty words, and you know exactly how casually they can be offered by a satiated man. Better to know where you stand. Better to remember that this was about fun.

That hammer kept right on, beating a tattoo on her chest.

She felt him ease back far enough to place a finger under her chin and tilt her face to meet his reassuring gaze. "Okay?"

"Okay." Somehow she managed to dredge up a smile as she stepped out of his arms. "I'd better go put some more clothes on. I think I've scared Jase enough for one day."

A shower made her feel more human, less tragic—sort of like a wet reality check. No way would Nick Corelli fall in love with her. It was hard enough adjusting to the idea of him falling in lust with her. And when she came out of her bedroom and inhaled the aroma of sizzling bacon, she forgave Jase and Cheryl their ill-timed arrival. Her grumbling stomach reminded her how, in their greedy appetite for each other, she and Nick had neglected dinner.

Later they had been too exhausted to bother.

Lost for a moment in those memories, she walked into the kitchen and straight into Cheryl's spontaneous embrace. "It's so good to see you back in this kitchen," T.C. spluttered, holding on tightly as she battled the onset of tears. After Pete's death, Cheryl had stopped working, stopped going out anywhere. This was such a positive sign.

"I thought it was time this old tart got on with life. Joe's kitchen felt like a good place to start."

T.C. hugged the other woman for a moment longer before undertaking a narrow-eyed inspection. "Hmm, you're not looking too bad for an old tart."

"And you're looking too skinny. Looks like you need a decent breakfast." With that she turned back to the frying pan, completely at home with her self-appointed task.

Smiling through her tears, T.C. poured herself a mug of coffee and looked up to find Nick watching her from the doorway, a strange expression on his face. It was impossible to describe. Intense, but not with the usual heat of lust. Definitely softer and a little...punch-drunk.

Caught off guard by the impact of that look, she sank shakily onto a stool at the breakfast bar and buried her nose in her mug. Through lowered lashes she watched him come into the room with a wink at Jason, the smooth smile as he introduced himself to Cheryl. A casual arching of one brow as he came toward her, via the coffeepot.

Consummate Nick. Obviously she'd misconstrued that look, her vision skewed by tears and the high emotion of her reunion with Cheryl.

By keeping her mouth full, she avoided participating in the conversation that flowed from today's weather—gray and gloomy with the prospect of more rain—back to yesterday's storm and on to their firsthand experience of its perils. When Nick finished his telling of their hairy trip home, Jason said, "Guess I'd better get to work, then."

T.C. started to rise, but a firm hand on her shoulder kept her in place. "No need for you to leave halfway into your breakfast. Jason can start without you."

His steady gaze challenged her to disagree.

"Start with Gina and Push," she told Jason, although her eyes never left Nick's. "You know what to do."

The warm, steady approval in his eyes made her feel as if she had passed some kind of test. She felt inordinately pleased. Then he moved smoothly on to Cheryl, praising her cooking with a broad, white smile.

Time for another reality check, she told herself. This is Nick in full charm mode. Do not forget it.

"You want a regular spot on the payroll?" he asked Cheryl.

"One day a week would be nice. That's what I used to do for Joe."

"Done. Does your job description include shopping?"

"I noticed the cupboards were getting bare. I'll make a list."

Nick asked Cheryl if it would be easier to start an account at the supermarket or to get her a credit card; Cheryl wondered if he needed her tax number; Nick said they should discuss pay. They moved off toward the office, leaving T.C. feeling excluded and miserable.

Still, she couldn't afford to sit around feeling sorry for herself. In Nick's own words, nothing had changed. Nothing on the outside. There were horses to be exercised, boxes to be cleaned, all the things that would matter long after Nick had left.

She poured the rest of her coffee down the sink and took her miserable mood down to the stables.

Twenty minutes ago she had noticed Jason wince when he stretched to reach a saddle. Still self-absorbed, she had thought nothing of it, but this time she was standing right beside him, and the grimace on his face, quickly disguised, was undoubtedly pain.

"You've hurt yourself."

"It's nothing."

"It's not nothing if it makes your face twist in pain." He turned away, made himself busy, but she persisted, her voice full of stern authority. "Look at me, Jase."

The kid turned, face slightly flushed, eyes not meeting hers. Chastened, or still embarrassed? Hard to tell. "You think we can establish a little eye contact here?" she asked.

The pink in his cheeks deepened. She guessed embarrassment.

"Hey, Jase," she said softly. "If this is about this morning, then you've got to help me out. I'm the one caught out. I'm the one dying of embarrassment here."

"It's just…I wasn't expecting…" His gaze shifted, met hers briefly. "You know…you and Nick."

"Well, I wasn't expecting it, either."

Her wry tone stopped his nervous shuffle, and finally he met her gaze. "Do you s'pose Nick might hang around now?"

There was a hopefulness in his voice that echoed deep inside T.C. Oh, Jase, she thought, we are a fine pair, building secret expectations on a one-night stand.

Something of her thoughts must have reflected in her eyes, because Jase looked away. "Sorry. I shouldn't have said nothing. It's just been good havin' him around."

"Yes, it has. But his business is in New York. That's his life." A life as far removed from their rustic idyll socially as it was geographically. They were just a pleasant interlude, a holiday of sorts.

In the awkward, nervous silence, Jase lifted a hand to rub at his chest, and she saw the graze on his hand, the swollen knuckles.

"Your hand."

He pulled it out of sight.

"You've been fighting, haven't you?" The truth was in his eyes. "Oh, Jase. You know you can't afford to get into trouble again."

"I'm not in any trouble."

She recalled that night in the pub, Red Wilmot leaning against the jukebox and the bad feeling that had rattled through her bones. "It's Red, isn't it? Has he been giving you a hard time, because so help me if he has…"

"I can look after this myself." His jaw set stubbornly. "Geez, T.C., I already copped enough grief from Mum."

Yes, I bet you did.

She wondered if it was concern for her youngest child

that had jolted Cheryl out of her grief-imposed exile. If she was worried about Jason being led astray again by bad company. Red Wilmot was that and more. That same weird feeling gripped her again, as strong and as unfounded as her response to George yesterday, and she wondered when she had stopped thinking pragmatically and started listening to vibes.

About the same time Nick arrived to rock her rational world, she figured.

Like a thorn in her underblanket, her concerns kept nagging away long after she returned to work. The only thing that drove them completely from her mind was the sight of Nick walking toward her. At first she saw only his smile, warm enough to light both the gloomy interior of the stables and the deepest recesses of her heart.

Would she ever grow accustomed to seeing him, to the sudden breathlessness, the wild palpitations of her heart?

"Hey," he said in greeting.

"Hey, yourself."

Completely smitten, she smiled back at him. He lifted a hand, brushed something from her hair. "Straw in your hair."

A loud snort brought his attention to Star, tethered beside her. Nick leaned closer, stroked a hand the length of her sleek black neck and murmured, "Hello to you, too, beautiful."

Star flicked her ears benignly. No kicking, no head tossing, no teeth baring. Nick's brows shot up. "Would you look at that? Someone's had a change of heart."

"Maybe she's getting used to having you around."

"Is that so?" She felt his gaze resting on her face, felt her own extravagant response, and knew she would never get used to having him around.

Which was when she noticed his clothes. Crisp dark chinos, a soft fawn shirt, matching jacket. Town clothes. How could she have forgotten? One day very soon she would see him all dressed up in his town clothes, with a suitcase in each hand.

"You don't look dressed for work." She tried to smile, but it felt tight, forced.

"I'm going to Melbourne."

Was it possible to speak, to breathe, *to live,* with your heart lodged in your throat?

"I'm going to see George."

"Oh." He wasn't leaving…yet. Her heart resumed normal operations. "Is this because of what I said?"

"That's one thing." The hint of a frown touched his brow. "Yesterday I tried to talk to him, but now I realize I talked *at* him. He wasn't hearing me, and I have to make a better effort."

"And if he doesn't want to hear you?"

"Then I might have to flatten his nose again."

Aware of Jason hovering nearby, ears flapping, she shook her head. "Violence won't solve anything."

One brow arched. "Yesterday you wanted to take after him with a pitchfork."

"Not literally." She paused before plunging on. "About what I said, about the phone calls… I feel really funny about that. There's no logic to what I was thinking. You should leave it be."

With a gentle finger, he lifted her chin until she met his eyes. "I'll handle it. Trust me."

She swallowed, nodded, didn't feel a whole lot better, and she wasn't sure it was only because of the George business. Doubt bunnies were digging a huge hole in her smittenness.

"Why don't you come with me? Afterward we could have dinner somewhere."

"Like a date?"

"Yeah. Exactly like a date."

The first thing that came to mind was how she didn't have anything halfway suitable to wear, but she rejected that thought immediately. Worrying about clothes was so *not* like her. The next thing that came to mind was how the anxious churning in her gut felt as much like fear as doubt.

What on earth did she have to fear?

Not measuring up to the man at her side? Fear of falling in love with another of his many facets? Fear of facing George, knowing she had lived up to one of his snide insults? She *had* crawled into bed with her partner.

All of the above?

She shook her head, tried another of those tight, forced smiles. "It's probably a bad idea, the way George feels about me."

"That's the point. It's time he met you, sat down and talked to you. We need to clear the air."

"Can I take a rain check? I don't want to desert Cheryl on her first day back."

His gaze narrowed until she could see the light of argument in his pinpoint focus. Her agitation intensified to near panic. She did not want to go to Melbourne with him. She did not want to explain why.

Distraction seemed like the only solution.

Stretching up on her toes, she wound her arms around his neck and pressed her lips to his. It started out cool, lips to lips with a good deal of suspicion in between, but then she slid her fingers into his hair and made a low throaty you-can-do-better noise, and its whole purpose changed like wildfire. His hand closed around her nape, warm fingers that knew the exact way to touch her, and his tongue flicked against her bottom lip. Hot desire shivered into her veins, igniting her nerve endings so her skin felt too tight, her clothes harsh against her skin.

He broke it off with a low laugh that sang through her blood and rested his forehead against hers. "I gather you don't want to discuss this."

This time her smile felt natural.

"Last chance on the bike. I'm taking it back to Graeme." His hand slid down her back, pressed her closer. "We could park."

"On a bike?"

"It's a big seat. I'll manage."

She didn't doubt it, but still she straightened, touched his jaw regretfully. And shook her head.

"Jase could manage, you know that. The responsibility will do him a world of good."

"I know, but not today."

His gaze narrowed again; a frown tightened his brows. Irritated with his persistence, and more irritated with her own doubts and fears, she pulled away from him.

He took the hint.

Eleven

Despite the distraction of talking to Cheryl and worrying about Jase, the day seemed to drag on interminably. She didn't bother pretending it was for any reason other than waiting for Nick's return. She didn't bother pretending it would be any easier when he left for good. She had known that before she let herself fall in love with him.

When she couldn't stand seeing Jason hide his pain any longer—ribs, she figured—she insisted Cheryl take him to see a doctor. With twice the workload, the rest of the afternoon might prove less wearing. The phone rang around four, startling her so much she dropped a can of hoof oil. As she watched the greasy stain spread across the concrete like some brown alien slime, she wondered how long it would take before that first ring of a phone didn't lift her off the ground.

It was Nick. "Everything all right?"

"Yes."

"Are you sure?" He laughed, the sound oddly deprecating for Nick. "Forget it. I had this...feeling."

"Maybe it's catching," she murmured.

"Pardon?"

"Nothing." She twirled the cord around her hand. "How did it go? With George."

"Not so bad, considering. I don't think we'll ever be best buddies, but we made some headway." He paused, and she could picture that slight frown narrowing his gaze. "He says he knows nothing about the phone calls, and you know, I believe him. I don't know why, because he has one helluva way of bending the truth. But I do believe him on this one."

"You don't have to sound so apologetic. I told you it was only a feeling, and you've proven that they're not always reliable." She let that thought set before continuing. "There's been nothing since you changed the number, so likely it was kids. Let's forget it."

Forget it, but don't go, she willed. Stay and talk to me a while.

"You returned Graeme's bike?"

"Yeah, I'm back on four wheels."

"Damn."

"Exactly." He laughed, and she closed her eyes. Let the slow sensuous sound seep right into her, filling all those empty places. "You know you spoiled it for me."

"Me?"

"Yeah. My last ride on that beauty, and I didn't feel any of the usual. The whisper of freedom, of release. I didn't feel like I was going somewhere. I felt more like I was leaving something behind." The pause seemed chock-full of meaning, of importance. T.C. was sure her heart had stopped altogether. "I wanted you with me today."

"I know. I just... I'm sorry, Nick." She took a deep breath, wound the phone cord tightly around her fingers. "I wanted to be with you."

He swore softly, impatiently. "I'm about to leave, so I should be out there before six. You want to go somewhere for dinner?"

"We could stay in. Cheryl made something that smells like heaven."

"I'll bring wine."

"Hurry," she breathed, but she wasn't sure if he was still there. The dial tone sounded in her ear.

She showered, blow-dried her hair, slathered herself in skin lotion, even played with some makeup, although she removed most of that. She found her one set of matching underwear and agonized over clothes, eventually settling on a slinky knit top and cargoes that rode low on her hips, because, well, they were easy to get off. As far as being a seductress, it was the best she could do.

After she had set the table, she wandered about the house in an excruciating state of anticipation. Half an hour to go, even if he had heard her last urgent plea to hurry. She couldn't sit down, she couldn't stand up, and her palms were starting to sweat. In the end she took herself off to the stables, the only place likely to calm her, and as she walked the well-known path she was surprised to see a flash of movement cross the window of the tack room.

Odd. Unless Jason had come back, determined to finish cleaning today's work harness, which was exactly the kind of stunt he would pull. Shaking her head with resignation, she walked along the breezeway, calling his name.

No answer.

An uncanny warning tiptoed up her spine, and she whipped her head around, caught a flash of red hair, a twisted sneer and a raised arm. Heard two crude words, and then her head exploded in blinding white pain.

Hurry, she had breathed in that all-fire sexy voice. As if he had needed prompting. He checked his watch as the hired Land Rover bumped over the entrance grid. Grinned.

All-time new land record, Portsea to Riddells Crossing, despite stopping for wine. And flowers.

The wheels spun up gravel as he turned sharply into the yard, then lined up the garage entrance, braking sharply to park beside her Courier. He didn't know why he was in such a hellish rush. Once he was inside that door he intended to take it very slowly, and very slowly again. Maybe then they would open the wine and think about eating whatever Cheryl had cooked.

He forced himself to amble through the door. The kitchen light was on. The dining table set—with candles. "Nice touch," he murmured. Anticipation hummed through his veins as he walked the hallway. The bathroom door lay open, revealing her work clothes scattered where she had discarded them. He inhaled the lingering scent of her shampoo, pictured her naked, skin gleaming as she stepped from the water. His whole body pulsed.

Maybe the first time wouldn't be so slow.

Before he placed a hand flat against her bedroom door and watched it swing noiselessly open, he knew it would be empty. The whole house felt empty. Hollow, he realized, without her presence. He took a minute to digest the strangeness of that thought, strange because all the way back from Melbourne he had been feeling a sense of coming home. Now he was here, standing in the heart of that home, and feeling nothing but emptiness.

The stables.

He was already striding out, shouldering through doorways, and when he hit the path and heard the distant sound of Ug's shrill yapping, the anticipation in his veins turned cold with dread. He broke into a run and didn't stop until he came into the breezeway and saw her sitting there, propped against the stable wall.

"What the hell…?"

She moved her lips in a weak semblance of a smile, and

then Nick was there, hunkering down, taking her head between hands that trembled.

"Are you all right, sweetheart?"

"My head…exploded," she mouthed.

He looked into her glassy eyes, saw the flash of pain when his fingers tightened involuntary. Swore silently. "I'm sorry, baby." He swung her into his arms, and her head lolled against his chest.

She murmured "Better," and for a minute he couldn't move with the tremendous weight of relief.

She was all right. A concussion, he figured, but he was taking her straight to casualty to make sure.

Halfway to the hospital she turned toward him and said very lucidly, "I know who it was. I saw him."

If people didn't stop treating her like an invalid, she would scream…well, maybe not scream, since her head was still inclined to ache, but she would definitely whisper in a loud, aggravated tone. When the hospital released her after overnight observation she had breathed one mighty sigh of relief, but now she'd been home two days and it was worse than ward four.

Tired of her own company and daytime television, she had ventured down to the stables. Nick had picked her up and carried her back here, muttering something about her not knowing how to stop working.

"I had a bump on the head. I'm over it."

"Is it so hard to let someone look after you?"

He had been so angry that she'd let it be. Last night he'd insisted she sleep in her own bed, alone, which hadn't done anything for her head except make it spin with paranoia. Maybe that one night hadn't been as wondrous for him as for her. Maybe her encounter with the rough end of a shoeing rasp had provided Nick with the perfect out. Maybe one night was all she would have.

The notion had transfixed her with paralyzing force, so

when he'd come to say good-night, when he'd leaned down to kiss her lips with heartbreaking gentleness, when she'd longed to rope her arms around his neck and draw him down beside her, she had lain motionless and said nothing lest she blab about staying and loving her, not just for this night but forever.

When she woke, he had gone down to the stables, returning just before the police came to tidy up their investigation. They'd arrested Red the night he attacked her, and with several thousand dollars worth of Yarra Park harness in his trunk, he had little comeback. Drunk, belligerent and at odds with the world, he confessed to everything, including the phone calls.

That had started out as a drunken game aimed at unsettling the woman he blamed for turning Jason against him. The thought of robbery had just started to take shape when Nick answered the phone, putting him on the back foot. A woman on her own was the perfect prey for a coward like Red Wilmot.

After his fight with Jason, he had been seething with the need to retaliate, and he'd lucked out when he overheard Nick tell the service-station attendant he was heading into Melbourne for the day. He waited, watched and struck after T.C. went back to the house at the end of her day's work.

If she hadn't happened along when she did, he might just have taken what he came to get—anything portable and salable—or he might have had his fun trashing the place and turning the horses loose. He had done a little of that, she gathered, although both Nick and Jase shrugged it off as minor.

Don't you worry your poor aching little head about it, was the tenor of their response to her questions.

Now the police were long gone, and she had woken from an afternoon nap to find Cheryl had also left. She was alone, bored and gnashing her teeth. Somewhere in the distance thunder grumbled in sympathy, and she wandered onto the verandah to watch the approaching storm. A portentous bank of deep gray hung over the southern hills, split suddenly by a flash of lightning.

Had it been only three days since the last storm? It felt like so much longer.

The wild spirit of that day hovered around her, melding with her restless mood, until she grabbed her wind-cheater and took off at a brisk walk. This time she thought about her route, choosing a path that circled the property with an added loop along the river bank. At the farthest point the wind shifted without warning, blustering in from the south, and she knew she was about to get wet.

That didn't bother her. Instead she stopped to hold her arms wide and lift her face to the first heavy drops of moisture. With her eyes closed, the rain seemed to fall in slow motion. A plop on her forehead. A second striking the point of her chin and rolling down her throat. The next came in twin splashes on her cheeks, and then the heavens opened with a deafening roar.

A shout of laughter burst from her open mouth as she twirled in a wide circle and started to run. How long had it been since she had taken the time to run in the rain? Usually she was running *from* the rain, bustling to finish some chore or other, too busy to appreciate the freshness in the air, to breathe the rich scent of damp earth, or to jump the rivulets that trickled across the road. The other day she had wanted to outrace the storm; today she wanted to run with it.

By the time she collapsed on the edge of the verandah, she was panting hard from exertion. Behind her, the screen door opened, then clattered shut. She heard the firm tread of boots and smiled broadly as she straightened out of her restorative head-between-knees posture.

"Thank you," she managed to breathe as she looked up

past the denim legs and chambray work shirt into his set expression.

"What the hell have you been doing?"

Her smile froze. "Taking a walk. I needed the air."

"Couldn't you see it was going to storm?"

"It came in quicker than I thought." She laughed a little, determined not to let his attitude faze her. "Isn't it glorious?"

"What it is, is dangerous. You better get inside and out of those wet things."

"I am a bit soaked, aren't I?"

She felt the touch of his gaze as it flicked over her, but his mouth didn't lose its hard set. "If you hate being an invalid so much, you'd better get out of those clothes."

"I'll drip water all through the house."

"It'll survive."

Now he was starting to steam her, standing there with that grim look on his face. What had happened to the old Nick? The one with the easy smile and laid-back attitude. Poetry in slow motion, she'd labeled him that first day. Now he reminded her more of a funeral dirge.

"Come on, Tamara. Quit mucking about and get out of those wet things."

"Okay," she said affably, and she started undoing buttons. Her jacket came first, peeled off and dropped to the ground in a sodden heap. Next she wrenched off her boots, her socks. She had managed the pull her shirt out of her jeans when strong hands lifted her, swung her up and around in the one economical motion.

Déjà vu.

Except this time she didn't stop herself from looping her arms around his neck and angling her body closer to his. He stopped in his tracks, and as quick as a clash of lightning across the storm-darkened sky, the mood changed. She felt it in his extreme stillness, broken only by the small movement in his throat as he swallowed.

"I'm still furious, you know."

She smiled. "I know."

Twisting a little, she tried to see his face, but it was impossible from this angle.

"It was getting late. I didn't know where you'd gone." His arms tightened around her in strong contrast to the concern that softened his voice. Her heart bounded, lodged in her throat, and something hummed vaguely around the edges of her memory, something else he'd said that had caused the same leap of hope. Something about leaving her behind. She wished she could remember....

"What were you thanking me for?"

"Pardon?"

"On the verandah, when you came out of the rain."

"Oh. I wanted to thank you for making me stay home, for slowing me down and giving me the opportunity to run in the rain."

Said out loud, it sounded a bit loopy, until he bent his head and she felt a smile in the kiss he pressed to her forehead. "You're welcome."

He held her easily in one arm while he opened the door, but the redistribution of weight brought her breasts into contact with the hard wall of his chest. They responded immediately, hardening, shooting desire into the depths of her body, and she wanted no impediment, no barrier. She wanted to be skin to skin.

Impatiently she grabbed his shirt, pulling at the buttons and silently bemoaning her clumsiness. As he maneuvered them through the door a button popped free, then a second, and she slid her hand inside to rest against his heartbeat momentarily before moving restlessly on, touching the fine smattering of hair, measuring its harsh texture over the smoothly muscled flesh beneath, sliding over a nipple and back again.

One bare foot swung down and skimmed the front of his fly. His extremely distended fly. He stopped stock-still in the center of the kitchen as she pressed her bare toes against him, as her whole body shimmered with heat.

He drew a harsh breath. "Easy, sweetheart, there's no rush. If you keep that up, I won't get past the table."

T.C. imagined the glossy patina of polished cedar sliding against her naked skin and gave a dreamy little shiver of pleasure. "And that's a problem?"

He laughed softly as he resumed walking, the fall of his boots loud against the slate floor. For the boots of a man urging *her* to slow down, they seemed to be moving in a mighty big hurry. She smiled her approval as he carried her into his room and lowered her to his dresser.

"These wet jeans will have to go." His words were a statement of fact, but his voice…oh, the glorious things that dark velvet voice could do. Then his hands skimmed under her shirt, his long fingers tucking into the waistband of her jeans. The pleasure reached so deep she swore it stroked her very soul, and she knew only Nick had the power to touch her so deeply.

She smiled a siren's smile. "Be my guest."

His eyes darkened as he unsnapped the waistband and eased the zip open. Then the back of his hand brushed against her bare belly, and her swift intake of breath sounded loud and harsh. He drew back a fraction, so when he touched her again it wasn't only with his hand. She felt the heated caress of his gaze trailing his fingertips as they dipped into her navel, as they pressed lightly against the soft curve of her belly, as they slid lower to trace the lace banding her bikini panties.

A delicious heaviness pooled low in her body and flowed through her like liquid heat. Her throat closed around a soft moan—of pleasure, encouragement, hunger—as she willed those teasing fingers to push away the scrap of material, to touch the core of her need, so hot and wet and demanding.

Oh, how she craved that touch.

"Lift up," he growled suddenly, startling her out of her sensual lethargy. Obediently she lifted her backside so he could peel the wet denim over her hips and down her legs.

Then he picked her up again, lowered her to his bed. Eyes closed, she heard a click she recognized as the lamp.

"Hell," he swore softly. "The storm must have knocked the power out."

"We need power because…?"

"It'll be dark soon." He touched the backs of his fingers against her cheek. "And I want to be able to see your face when I'm inside you."

The words, spoken so slowly, softly, definitely, painted the most erotic images. Her fingers curled instinctively, gripping the covers. "There are candles," she managed to say. "In the pantry."

"Perfect." He ran his knuckles lightly over her cheek again, her softly parted lips, whispered, "Don't move," and headed for the door.

"Hurry back."

She felt his eyes on her, burning her. "Oh, I'm running."

With a frustrated groan, she turned her face into the covers. Closing her eyes, she rubbed her cheek languidly against the cool, crisp linen, nostrils flaring as she inhaled his scent. She stretched her limbs and frowned when her rucked-up shirt tightened uncomfortably across her shoulders. God, her shirt… She fumbled with the buttons, tearing one off in her haste to rid herself of the cumbersome old thing.

"Tip one in seductive technique. Lose the flannel work shirt," she muttered as she tossed it aside, revealing her plain practical cotton chemise.

For the first time in her life she wished for lacy, diaphanous underwear of the kind Nick would be used to. Exotically scented skin and voluptuous breasts to fill the lacy, diaphanous underwear would be nice, too, but she saved her breath on wishing for them. And oh, for the confidence to strip, to arrange herself artfully on his bed wearing nothing but a sultry come-hither smile.

Her decidedly unsultry snort of laughter destroyed that image. "Who am I kidding?" she muttered.

Tamara Cole doing sultry was as likely as Tamara Cole enticing Nick to stay, and for all the heat in his eyes, for all his concern and caring these past few days, Nick was leaving. The knowledge should have cooled her ardor, but it didn't, for she knew that loving Nick, even for this brief time, would be worth the heartache that followed.

He returned on silent feet, and she sensed him moving around the bed, heard the faint clunk of a candleholder placed on the bedside table, then the scratch of match against flint. The distinctive smell of burning candlewick reached her nostrils a second before she opened her eyes to find him standing over her, his eyes glittering with golden shards of reflected candlelight.

Such a beautiful man. Far too beautiful for her.

She eased herself forward and sat on her haunches on the very edge of the bed. Then she looked way, way up. What she saw there made her weak and strong at once. His eyes had fastened on her breasts, on the nipples she felt budding tightly against her chemise, and they smoldered with banked heat. His nostrils flared, and he swore softly, almost reverently, as his gaze slid back to hers.

The air seemed to thicken with sultry heat; her whole body vibrated with it. Her focus narrowed to this moment, to the image of her and Nick isolated from the rest of the world by the rain that cloaked the house like a thick gray curtain, and even more by the strength of their desire.

Breathing heavily, she lowered her gaze to his bare chest, then tracked the dark hair that arrowed down to his jeans. She sat back on her heels and ran her tongue around her dry mouth. Oh boy, she wanted to touch him. Right there, where his jeans stretched so tautly. The need prick-led in the palms of her hands.

"It's time you delivered on that offer, Tamara." God, how she loved the way her name rolled from his tongue. She closed her eyes and let the lush syllables wash over her. "Take my jeans off."

His hands cradled her face for a moment, then slid into her hair, drawing her closer to all that broad, hard man.

"Okay," she breathed, "but first I have to touch you."

"Be my guest," Nick murmured, but his attempted grin felt tighter than a grimace, and at the first tentative touch of her hand he damn near rose off the floor. It was no more than a brush of fingertips against denim, but he hauled in a tight breath and told himself to get a grip. The caress of a woman's hands was one of life's greatest joys, and on the joy-scale, Tamara's touch equated to pure ec-stasy. Not pain, he lectured himself as her fingers spread over his stomach.

So why did that almost shy caress cause his chest to feel as if it was being gripped in some giant vise?

He heard her draw a tremulous breath before sliding her palms to his waist and up his sides. Her thumbs traced the line of his bottom rib, then hesitated again. His whole body screamed in need. It felt as if every cell was clamoring for her attention, until he could no longer stand the suffocating tension. His eyes flashed open and focused over her head—on her reflection in the mirrored wardrobe door.

The candlelight danced over her as she knelt before him, a burnished canvas of shadow and pale shimmering light. From her golden halo of hair down the long straight line of her back, from the dip of her waist to the feminine fullness of her buttocks, her beauty stunned him. Nick hadn't actually run to get the candles, yet that picture caused his chest to ache as if he'd covered the distance at world-record pace. At altitude.

"Beautiful," he murmured, his voice so husky it was barely audible.

She shook her head.

"Yes. You are incredibly, amazingly," he pressed his lips into her soft hair, "arousingly beautiful."

Her expressive sigh whispered against his chest as his hands slid onto her delicate nape. *Delicate.* He smiled at the unbidden description. His strong, independent Tamara wouldn't like it. His hands slid over her shoulders and down her arms, taking the straps of her chemise with them. As he peeled the thin garment from her skin, he heard the sharp little hitch of surprise in her breath and knew he'd uncovered her breasts. That she sat before him bare to the waist.

He didn't look.

Resolutely he concentrated on the erotic image in the mirror. His hands slowly skimming the length of her arms and back again. His hands so big and dark as they spanned her waist. His fingers playing along her spine, pushing under her rolled-down top and into those sexy little dimples above the curve of her buttocks.

Then he felt her hands on him, sliding from his chest to below his navel. He fisted his hands in her hair as if that might help him hold on to his thin thread of control. His absolute concentration on their reflection had somehow removed him from the present, or from his body, but the touch of her fingers brought him back to the here and now with a clattering force.

He forced his hands to gentle, to ignore his rampant need to haul her forward. The very thought caused him to pulse with a hardness akin to pain. She touched him again, tracing his length with a fingertip he shouldn't have felt through the thickness of denim. But he felt it, all right, like a scorching fire-trail.

"Take them off, Tamara."

Ignoring his tight-lipped demand, she touched him more

boldly, and when he caught the look in her eyes, of awe, fascination, excitement, his knees almost buckled. When she wet her lips, Nick groaned violently and jammed his eyes shut.

Momentarily her hands left him. Then she started to pull his jeans down, leaning forward for more purchase. She was so close that he could feel her breath on his skin. A wisp of hair brushed the inside of his thigh, and his hands clenched into tight fists to stop himself from dragging that warm, moist mouth to him.

Hell, if he allowed her that, that lush mouth closing over him, he wouldn't last beyond the first sweet touch of her tongue. The thought wrenched a tortured sound from his throat, and she sat back on her heels.

"Sorry," she breathed, her big eyes staring up at him, her teeth biting down on her bottom lip, and such a look of remorse on her face.

"Oh please, sugar, don't ever be sorry for making me feel like this."

He reached for protection, held it out for her. "You want to do this?"

And oh man, she did it so well.

He struggled to slow his hands, hands too eager to strip the rest of her clothes from her body. In one motion he peeled both pieces of underwear over her hips and down her legs, legs that trembled under his touch. Her beauty stunned him anew as his hands and eyes and mouth skimmed over her nakedness, loving the lushness of her mouth, the length of her neck, the soft flesh of her inner thighs, and those breasts, even more perfect than he'd remembered.

With one hand splayed across her belly and his mouth at her breast, he stroked her sensitive swollen bud with light sureness, teasing her and pleasing her until she whimpered and arched and cried out to him. For him. Only then did he give her what she craved, first with his mouth; then, while the cries of release still broke from her, he lifted her hips and drove himself home.

Home. Not a place but a woman.

A woman of satin skin and tender hands, of lean strength and soft curves, of immense strength and fragile ego. A woman whose sultry heat drew him deeper into her body while her heat-hazed eyes drew him deeper into her soul. A woman whose soft keening moans drove him higher and harder until pleasure burst, pure and true, in a Technicolor shower of sensation that spiraled out of control, even as her name exploded from his lips.

Tamara.

Spent, he sank into her curves, covering her with his body, fingers entwined, foreheads touching, limbs aligned.

He was home.

Twelve

One candle burnt out before Nick could move. The rain had stopped, and he supposed it would be dark but for the weak glow of the remaining flame. Following the rain, it would be cold outside, but here in his bed it was warm, thanks to the woman in his arms.

Bathed in flickering light, she lay limp and satiated, her face nestled between his shoulder and chin, her legs still intertwined with his amid the tangle of sheets. He smiled and pressed his lips to her forehead, traced a finger down the line of her nose. She murmured something sleepily that might have been his name, and the soft, sweet sound whispered across his skin and eased its way into his heart. His arms tightened around her, held her more closely.

The woman he loved.

He lay perfectly still and absorbed the intense sense of satisfaction the knowledge brought…and wondered when his hunger for her had ceased to be merely a painful groin-based one and spread to fill his whole being. He wanted to wake her, to tell her. He wanted to see that sunrise smile spread across her face as she heard those three little words.

Words he had never before thought, let alone uttered.

Except that this was Tamara, and there was no guarantee she would accept his love easily or quickly. What was it she had said down at the stables? *It could take months for a temperament like hers to come around.* He'd known then, as he knew now, that it wasn't Star's disposition in question.

No, he needed to be patient and careful in handling Tamara. He needed to ease her into the notion, to give her time to arrive at the truth herself. Problem was, he didn't have the luxury of time, not with his return to New York only days away.

Something twisted tight in his gut when he thought about leaving her, as he remembered his fear when he'd found her in the stables, and again when he had come home to an empty house this afternoon.

The solution seemed simple. She would come to New York with him. Together they would do what had to be done to pack his things, to sort out his business; then, together, they would return to Yarra Park.

It sounded simple, but nothing was really ever simple with Tamara.

"Come with me."

The hand resting languidly on his chest tensed. "To New York?"

"Yes." He slid down the pillow, turned his head to better see her face. "I don't want to leave you here alone."

She traced the line of his collarbone with one gentle finger. "I have a dog and twenty-three horses. I'm never alone."

"Okay. Then, how about I don't like being alone?"

"Alone in New York? Now there's a novel concept!"

Nick didn't smile.

"You're serious." She rolled onto her back and let go her breath in a long, serious-sounding way. It made Nick hold his own breath. "What would I do over there while you're working? You know how I can't stand doing nothing. And I really hate cities."

"You hate being out of your comfort zone."

As soon as he said it, Nick regretted it. He saw her tense, felt her withdraw another notch. *Hell.* He needed to do better, much better.

"Remember I said I needed to be back by the twenty-fifth?" He waited for her small nod of acknowledgment. "There's a fund-raiser the next week for a charity I support."

"What kind of a charity?"

"A foundation to help disadvantaged kids. It relies heavily on this annual bash for its running costs. This isn't something I can miss, Tamara, and I want you there, too."

A mixture of curiosity and apprehension, a hint of yielding, softened the green of her gaze. Nick smiled. This was better.

"It's a dinner and an auction, and a few celebrities always turn up."

"Sounds like a big deal."

"It is for the foundation. But for you, green eyes, it'll be fun. What do you say?"

Wrong choice of argument. Nick saw it in her face a full second before she shifted her head on the pillow in silent rejection.

"Do me a favor and think about it, okay?"

This time she shook her head more resolutely. "I won't change my mind."

"You want to tell me why?"

She fixed him with those big expressive eyes. "You remember the Tamara you described to me, down at the stables one day? The one in the floaty dress and the heels and the perfume? Well, *she* is the kind of girl you would take to a New York fund-raiser, not me.''

''It's you I'm asking.''

''I'm sorry, Nick.''

She turned away, her chin set in that inflexible way he had come to recognize. But then he considered her curiosity about the foundation and his own determination. Just like the horse she called Star, Tamara needed time and the right kind of handling. He still had a couple of days to work on her, and, just like Star, she would come around to his way of thinking.

The next afternoon he was closeted in the office trying to catch up on some of his recent neglect. Both mind and body wanted to be elsewhere, and while he could park his body in a chair and tell it to stay put, he couldn't stop his mind from wandering.

Its natural inclination was to wander all over the past thirty or so hours and the fact that he hadn't been able to change Tamara's mind. Perhaps he shouldn't be pushing the fund-raiser thing, but, hell, he wanted her there. Tonight may well be his last chance to talk her into it.

If he couldn't change her mind, then it would be one of his last nights with her for weeks...at least two, maybe three, maybe more. Either way, tonight had to be special.

The idea grabbed such a firm hold that he didn't hesitate before calling Sophie. He wanted the best, and Sophie knew nothing else. To hell with any consequences.

It was coming up to five when Tamara stuck her head in the door. ''I have to go pick up some feed. Want to come?''

''Do you have to leave right away? I have to finish this report.''

She came in and sat on the edge of his desk. ''Type quickly. The feed store closes at five-thirty.''

While he labored at the keyboard, she picked up a slip of paper. Sophie's restaurant list, he noticed, wishing he had put it out of sight. He wanted this to be a surprise.

"Ooh, fancy," she commented with a hint of a smirk. "You know these places?"

"I know *of* them. They're hardly the kind of places I'd *know* know."

He lifted a brow.

"These are the kind of places where they check the labels on your clothes to make sure you can afford the prices, which, incidentally—" she leaned toward him as if confiding some great secret "—they don't put on the menus."

Nick didn't return her smile. "I can afford their prices."

"Hey, I know that, although I can't see why you bother. The food's overrated." She gave a dismissive little shrug as she put the list down. "Now, are you coming to town? We could grab a pizza from Dom's."

"I gather they're neither overpriced nor overrated?"

She blinked, looked a little confused by his terse answer. "No, *and* you don't have to dress up."

Nick knew he should leave it there, but he couldn't. He leaned back in his chair and regarded her through narrowed eyes. "How is it you know so much about these fancy restaurants if you've never been to one?"

"I didn't say that. I only said I haven't been to these particular ones." She slid from the desk, her face blank of all expression. "I have to go if I'm going to catch Weale's."

"Hang on a minute." Nick was on his feet, a hand wrapped around her arm before she could take another step. "We haven't finished this discussion."

"First you'll have to tell me what the discussion is about."

"What it is about," he ground out, "is a date. You and me."

"Oh."

He studied her for a second, the slight flush in her cheekbones, the strangely vulnerable look in her eyes.... With a muttered oath he pulled her into his arms. She came, stiff and resistive. Unyielding. "I'm leaving the day after tomorrow, and I want to take you out somewhere nice."

"You don't have to do that. I like Dom's pizza."

Her hands pushed against his chest, forcing him to release her. That bit at the already frayed edges of his temper. "That's not the point."

"What *is* the point, Nick?"

"The point is...*hell!*"

The point was, he needed tonight. He needed to show her what he couldn't tell her. That he loved her, respected her, wanted a relationship with her. That he wanted to do things for her, to cosset her, to protect her. That he wanted her with him...beside him.

"I want you to come to New York."

He hadn't meant to say that, not so forcefully. She actually took a step backward, then another. And for once the expression on her face, in her eyes, gave no clue as to what was going on in her mind. He felt a chilling sense of dread deep in his gut as she took a long, measured breath.

"Don't you think it's best if we leave it here?"

The dread turned icy in Nick's veins. For the first time it struck him that she might not share his feelings about their relationship. That she might be happy to wave him goodbye. That this might have been only about sex...or about softening him up. To get her way with Yarra Park.

"You want to expand on that?" he asked, and his voice sounded about as cold as he felt.

"Look, Nick, it's been nice, and as you said, fun."

"Spare me the platitudes. You've been using me? Is that what you're saying?"

Taken aback, maybe by his words, maybe by the sharpness of his tone or the harshness he felt in his expression, she shook her head almost fiercely. ''No.''

He watched her face as she struggled to make sense of his accusation.

''Are you saying I slept with you to change your mind about the inheritance?'' she asked slowly.

''Did you?''

Wariness returned, wariness and uneasiness, peeping out at him from between her thick lashes, and Nick laughed harshly. He didn't want to hear her answer, not if it wasn't honest.

''Forget it. It doesn't make a lick of difference to my decision,'' he said.

''You have decided?''

''Yes.'' Nick couldn't remember when he'd reached that decision. Maybe he hadn't until this moment. ''I'm keeping my half, but I'm not taking what's been given to you. If you want your name off that deed, then you can take the money I offered you for it.''

He turned to the desk and scribbled out a check.

''This is for your half of the land. We'll have to work out a better valuation on the horses. I don't believe the one the solicitors gave me is fair.''

She didn't take it from his outstretched hand. Her face was very pale as she shook her head slowly, a little stunned. ''I don't want your money.''

He tossed the piece of paper on the desk. ''Then give it to charity.''

As they stood there facing each other in that strange state of standoff, the cold infiltrated Nick's bones. He could talk all night long, but he wouldn't change her mind—not about picking up that check, not about coming to New York, not into believing they had a future.

''Hell, you could give stubborn lessons to a mule.''

"I'm not trying to be difficult." Her eyes pleaded with him to understand. "You know how I feel about this."

"You want to have another try at explaining? Because I don't believe I do. I don't believe you've ever told me the full story about anything. About how you came to work for Joe and why it meant so much to you. About why Joe left you a piece of this place. About why you slept with me, or about why you won't come to New York."

He stared at her for a moment, as she stood there wearing her tough, insular, independent armor, but with some kind of silent plea in her eyes. He knew he only had to open his arms and she would be there, but he also knew if he didn't stand tough, she would never talk to him. Never tell him the whole story.

"I'll be catching the earliest flight I can get a seat on tomorrow. You want to talk between now and then, you know where to find me."

T.C. did find him the next morning, down at the barn, standing outside Star's stall. With her pulse thumping double time, she stilled to watch him, to drink in the completeness of his male beauty. He was everything she wanted in a man, everything she longed to hold in a man...but could she tell him?

Heart in mouth, she watched Star's tentative approach, saw the mare hesitate, head lowered but steady. No head tossing, no eye rolling, no foot stomping. It would take nothing more than a few words of reassurance, a certain tone of voice and a confidence-giving straight look, and she would come to him, put herself in his hands.

Silently she willed him to extend his hand, to say those words, to make it easy. But he stepped away, turned and moved on to the next stall.

Saying his goodbyes.

The reality of the moment rocked her to her very core. He was about to leave. This was her last chance to speak her heart. Oh, she longed to lay it all out for him, all those true stories he had encouraged her to tell, yet he had given so little away, had admitted nothing of his feelings for her. And she still felt so much like a first starter tossed into a match race with a stakes champion.

If only he had turned and found her standing there. If only he had offered some word of encouragement, some sign. If only he had come and kissed her in that way he had, that way that made her feel as if *she* were the champion.

But he kept on walking out the far end of the barn. She took a deep breath and found the air rich with leather and horsehair, sweet molasses and fresh clover hay…and found none of her usual bracing reassurance in the familiar scents.

She wondered if she ever would again.

Life after Nick left was exactly as T.C. had expected. Hollow, colorless, lonely, as gray as the skies that kept her misery company. Even Cheryl's fresh batch of double choc-chip muffins was doing little to lift her spirits.

"Something on your mind?" Cheryl asked.

Not on my mind, on my heart. "This ugly weather's getting to me."

"Only the weather?" Cheryl shook her head, a soft smile of understanding on her lips. "You miss him. It's okay to admit it."

"That's ridiculous. He's only been gone a few days."

"A few days is a long time when you're in love."

T.C. laughed softly, self-consciously. "Is it so obvious?"

"To another woman." She paused tellingly. "Have you told him?"

"Three weeks ago he was just a larger-than-life character in Joe's stories."

"I knew Pete was the one after two hours."

"Really?"

"We met on holiday in Queensland, and that first day I didn't know anything about him other than how he made me feel. Turned out we lived at opposite ends of the country, and we both had our families there, our lives. When I went home, I was so miserable I knew I had to do something about it."

"What did you do?"

"I gave notice at work and started packing all my things, and then Pete turned up at my door. He had fewer things to pack."

"I couldn't go to New York. I couldn't live there."

"Did he ask you to?"

T.C. shook her head. "He asked me to go with him, to be his date at this charity thing."

"And let me guess—you turned him down cold?"

"I couldn't just leave on a few days' notice."

Cheryl lifted her brows. "You could've if you'd wanted to. You know Jase and I would have managed, or you could have got someone in to help out—old Harry or Gil's brother."

"But I don't know how he feels about me, what he expected of me if I went to New York. I couldn't put myself through that. Not again."

"Nick's not like that other bastard."

"I know, but he could hurt me so much worse."

"Oh, sweetie." Cheryl came to her then, embraced her with arms full of compassion and reassurance. "There's lots of things hurt, but you know what hurts most? Regrets."

A thick haze of tears clouded Cheryl's eyes as she released T.C. She wiped them unselfconsciously on the edge of her apron.

"I've been pretty miserable this past year, and it's only been the kids that have kept me sane, them and the memories of all the happy times me and Pete had together. You don't want to grow old with only regrets. Memories make much better company."

T.C. shifted restlessly on her stool. "Are you saying I should go over there?"

"You make up your own mind on that, but I *am* telling you it's time you stopped looking behind you and started looking toward your future."

"If only it were that easy," T.C. said heavily. "But we were never starting from scratch."

"What do you mean?"

"Joe left me a letter to explain his will. He wasn't only giving me half of Yarra Park. He was giving me Nick."

"Matchmaking." Cheryl shook her head, then chuckled with rich amusement. "And doesn't that sound just like Joe?"

"Yes, but strangely enough, I can't see the funny side. I don't want the inheritance or Joe's matchmaking or anything else between us. I just want it to be about him and me."

"I take it you never explained this to Nick?" Cheryl regarded her through shrewd eyes. "And why not? He's a good man, sweetie. You should talk to him."

"I know he's a good man, Cheryl, but how do I know I'm a good enough woman for him?"

"Joe must have thought so. He picked you out for his favorite son."

Sure, Joe might have thought so, but Joe had been biased. How long could she hold the interest of a man who craved excitement and challenge? Whose life was devoted to moving from one adventure to the next?

She wanted Joe to be right. She wanted Nick, but she wanted to hold him for life, not just until he moved on.

As she selected a search engine, T.C. told herself she was doing the research out of interest. She simply wanted to know more about this charity Nick supported.

The Alessandro Foundation.

After a frustrating ninety minutes she stumbled across it in a magazine article, and as the facts unfolded line by line, she found herself creeping closer and closer to the computer screen, drinking in every snapshot of the boy Nick had been and a new understanding of the man he had become.

She saw a young Nick in the character sketches of the youths the foundation helped. Kids they took from a dead-end existence to places and experiences they could never have known existed. Wilderness camps and cattle drives, kayaking trips and mountain climbs, places that would challenge their boundaries, tackling tasks that would build their self-esteem.

The foundation aimed to prove that, with courage and commitment and a positive attitude, they could do things they'd never dreamed possible.

T.C. sat back in her chair. The kind of courage and commitment and positive attitude she needed to go after her future.

Without looking any further, she knew Nick's involvement far transcended that of a passive supporter. She knew why he had undertaken so many adventure expeditions over the past years, why he had been in Alaska when Joe died, and her heart tightened painfully in her chest.

How could she have so misunderstood him?

How could she not have seen the man he was?

It was a long time before she could go on, searching with more purpose now, needing to find out about the charity auction, if there was still time to do something that would take courage, that would show commitment and strength of character.

Something that would take her way outside her comfort zone. But if she succeeded, if she could do this, maybe she would also have proved to herself that she was worthy of Nick.

Thirteen

Finding out about the fund-raiser was the easy part. Finding out that Nick was the prime lot, that a gaggle of rich, beautiful and savvy women would be bidding for a weekend adventure with him as their private guide…that was the hard part.

Because she knew instantly what she had to do.

She picked up the check Nick had tossed on the desk, and the sight of all those zeros caused her eyes to cross.

"You said to give it to charity. I suppose it might as well be your favorite one."

Resolutely she folded the check and tucked it into her pocket; then she leaned back in her chair to consider the practicalities. They were so much easier to focus on. She had two days. No, a day more, she realized, thinking about the time difference between the two continents. She blew out a long breath and tried to ignore how it quavered.

Not much time, and beyond booking a plane ticket, she didn't know where to start. If she called, Nick would either arrange everything or he would tell her not to bother. And/or he would demand to know why she had changed her mind, why she was coming. He would demand to hear all those full stories.

He would have them soon enough, but not over the phone. This was about proving her love, about proving herself worthy. It was not a coward's task and would not be done the coward's way. No, sirree.

She pictured the stunned silence in the room when she made her bid, the spotlight falling on a lone woman…a small blonde wearing the wrong kind of dress and tripping over heels she couldn't manage. For a moment her resolve weakened. Those old insecurities clawed their way back to the surface and dug in with sharply honed talons.

They screeched, *Remember your last sad attempt at sophistication? Miles laughing as he told you to stick to your boots. Remember the patronizing laughter of his friends?*

And then she remembered the look in Cheryl's eyes when she spoke of regrets. No, she didn't want to grow old with regrets. She wanted a chance at the memories.

She slapped her hand down on the desk with a purpose that belied the enormity of what she still had to do. Get her hands on a ticket to a fancy New York society fundraiser, get herself to that city, find something to wear.

Fifteen minutes later, she heard a car pull up.

A compact European sedan sat in the drive, and when T.C. came out the door, a vaguely familiar looking woman slid out of the driver's seat and pushed designer shades to the top of her sleek dark bob.

"Hello, you must be Tamara." She smiled across the roof of her car. "I had to come and meet you. Curiosity is my middle name. That makes me Sophie *Curiosity* Corelli."

She came around the car, at least five foot eight of elegant taste and exquisite grooming, and extended a perfectly manicured hand. T.C. took it in her smaller unmanicured one. "Hello, Sophie. I've heard a lot about you."

Both perfectly shaped brows shot up. "Is that so?"

T.C. felt a betraying warmth in her cheeks. Sophie *Troublemaker* Corelli, Nick had called her. The sister with too much time on her hands. She glanced down at Sophie's Italian sandals, then up at her artfully applied makeup. She couldn't recall praying for a fairy godmother, but it seemed as if one had arrived behind the wheel of an Audi 4.

"Would you like a coffee?" she asked with a tentative smile.

"No, but I'd kill for something cold."

T.C. took a deep breath and ushered the woman she hoped to make her ally into the house.

Two nights later, she stood trembling in the lobby of one of Manhattan's most exclusive restaurants, wondering what had possessed her to undertake such a foolhardy scheme. Slinking away and leaving the country undetected suddenly seemed mighty appealing.

Is that what you really want? Is that why you went through all that tedious primping and preening? The hairdresser and the beautician and the exhausting shopping trip? If you chicken out now, how will you face Sophie? And Cheryl and Jase?

Worse...how will you face up to yourself?

Despite the stern words, her knees kept knocking and her mouth remained so dry she knew for sure and certain it would be incapable of uttering a sound. The doorman looked across at her for perhaps the twentieth time, and again she avoided eye contact. If she didn't move soon, he might have her arrested for loitering.

A man in a tux came out of the dining area and stopped to say something to the doorman. Security? She didn't think security would wear dinner-suits, but then, what did she know? This was a very high-class venue. The thought of being thrown out onto the street without a chance of explaining had her heading for the ladies room. She had already used it twice. Halfway there, she caught sight of herself in a huge mirror.

Herself?

What she saw was an elegant blonde wearing moss-green layered georgette that floated in all kinds of interesting ways in response to her body's undulating motion. Beneath the softly flowing fabric she saw long, smooth legs and little sandals that sparkled as they caught the light. Their high heels were what caused her body to undulate.

As she stopped, absorbed anew by this miracle of Sophie's creation, she noticed the man in the tuxedo eyeing her again. She recognized that look. He wasn't checking out a suspicious character—he was checking out the blonde in the mirror, the woman named Tamara.

Her glossy lips curved into a smile just as her admirer caught her eye. She gave him an apologetic shrug, tucked the little evening bag under her arm, and, with a new confidence in her step, she turned toward the doorman.

This was the third time Nick had participated in this auction. The other times he hadn't minded the attention, had even played up to the crowd, given them his best smile and encouraged them to do their worst.

Tonight he simply didn't want to be here.

Get it over with, he thought as he stepped into the spotlight on the small raised dais in front of a well-fed—and equally well-lubricated—audience. That was all part of the plan. The more champagne they drank, the more deeply they dug into their wallets.

Dutifully he responded to the welcoming applause and the odd wolf whistle, but by the time bidding commenced, his face ached with the effort of smiling. He supposed he was out of practice.

Prompted by the celebrity auctioneer's prodding, the bids came helter-skelter, past ten, then twenty, thousand.

"Do I hear twenty-five?"

"You betcha," rang loud and clear from an ancient supporter in the front row, and the crowd roared with delight.

Nick tuned out. Get it over with, he repeated silently, so I can get the hell out of here. And go where? Back to that cold, hollow apartment, to pace the floorboards well into the morning hours?

He knew the restlessness in his spirit couldn't be fixed as easily as it had in the past. None of the traditional challenges—no mountain, no river, no glacier—could do it. Only Tamara could.

Tamara. He was so lost in thoughts of her, of feeling her in his arms again, that he imagined he heard her voice, raised as if to attract attention.

"I don't think I could have heard you correctly, madam." The auctioneer was peering toward the back of the room. "Would you mind repeating your bid?"

"Five hundred thousand dollars."

He hadn't imagined her voice. She was here, in this room, repeating her killer bid on the last lot. On him.

Nick wasn't the only one stunned. The laughter and chatter subsided to hushed murmurs, accompanied by the swish of fabric and creak of chairs as people turned to stare. Nick stared with them.

"That's a serious bid, madam?" the auctioneer asked.

"Lock the doors so she doesn't escape," a heckler called. The laughter seemed a little strained, expectant, as if the joke might fall flat.

"It's a serious bid, but I can't go any higher."

"In that case…" The auctioneer did his usual *Any more bids? Going once, going twice* patter, before bringing his gavel down. Someone up back started to clap. Gradually the rest of the crowd joined in, the applause rising to a thunderous crescendo that pretty much matched the beating of Nick's heart.

He still couldn't see her, still couldn't be sure he hadn't imagined this whole scenario. Still wasn't sure how he felt about this whole ridiculous scenario.

He stepped off the stage and out of the light...although not out of the spotlight. The auction coordinator had her arm through his, wanting to complete the formalities. Others on the organizing committee gathered around, slapping him on the back and shaking his hand as if he had just performed some amazing act of benevolence.

Some of the crowd were standing, forming an informal guard of honor as they applauded the winning bidder's progress to the front of the room.

And finally he saw her.

T.C. felt her knees start to wobble and was grateful when a woman stepped from the group surrounding Nick to take her arm. That kept her upright. "Well, here she is. Our mystery bidder. I suppose you would like to meet Mr. Corelli?"

"We've met."

His voice sounded as reserved as the first touch of his gaze, and T.C. felt it like a physical blow. What had she expected? Open arms and melting smiles? Maybe not, but a touch of warmth, of encouragement, even of surprise, would have been nice.

The organizer was trying to draw her aside, talking sotto voce of paperwork and the chance of publicity, and T.C. appealed to Nick—to those cool blue eyes.

"Can we handle the formalities later, Yvonne?" he asked.

The woman tutted something about *unknown quantities,* and something definitely unreserved sparked in his eyes. "I can vouch for this lady's check, Yvonne."

"Are you certain?"

"I believe I wrote it myself."

Yvonne's raised eyebrows almost disappeared off her forehead as she added up the score. T.C. felt the weight of a dozen calculating gazes, but there was only one that mattered. It had turned intent, serious, questioning. Her smile was tentative as she held up his check.

"You said if I didn't want it I should give it to charity. I liked the sound of this one."

"It does good work."

"Yes, you do."

Yvonne cleared her throat, and impatience or irritation flickered in Nick's eyes. But he turned to her and smiled. "We will handle the formalities tomorrow. All right?"

But it wasn't a question, not really.

"And could we have a little privacy right now?"

That wasn't a question, either. The group dispersed amid some unsettled muttering, and finally they were alone…alone with a room full of curious onlookers pretending not to watch.

Nick turned his impatient, irritated gaze on her, and T.C. felt her stomach dip. "Now, you want to tell me what this is all about?"

"Well, according to the catalogue, I have bought an adventure weekend with you as my personal guide." She took a deep, nervous gulp of air. "Now, I know it's rather short notice, but I was wondering if you would have this weekend free?"

"You have something in mind?"

She held nothing back when she looked right into his eyes. "I believe I owe you some backstory."

"You needed to come all the way over here, to pay an exorbitant amount of money, to talk to me?"

"I hope it will be worth it."

He gave nothing away in the next moment—a long breath-held moment that meant more to T.C. than any single moment that had ever come before.

Then he gave a swift nod of his head, murmured,

"We'll see what you've got to say, then," and his voice sounded as dark and compelling as the hour before dawn. Then he took her hand and drew her in his wake across the room, through the crowd that parted before them and closed ranks behind them. A crowd that applauded their departure as they would stars leaving the stage.

T.C.'s head was still spinning long after they climbed into the back of a cab and started for whatever address Nick had given.

She felt his gaze on her from across the cab and the distance he seemed to have put between them again. "There were easier ways of doing this, you know."

"I know." She took a deep breath. "But I decided I didn't want to do this the easy way. I decided I should do something right outside that comfort zone."

"Coming to New York wasn't enough?"

"Not to get rid of that check."

"It always comes back to that!"

"Yes, it does, and you want to know why?" She didn't wait for him to say anything, for him to turn any further away from her. "I didn't want Yarra Park or what Joe wanted for us to come between us. I wanted this to be about us, Nick, with no inheritance and no expectations interceding."

Her impassioned plea seemed to fill the enclosed space, to suck up the very air until she felt giddy with lack of oxygen. "Expectations?" he asked slowly.

"Yeah." She smiled, wryly. "Joe wanted us to be together. His wanting you to come over to Australia to tell me about the inheritance, his wanting me to talk you into caring for the place so you would keep it—it was a match-making thing. He wanted us tied together."

He took a long time to digest those words, to turn them over and to formulate his response. And all the while Tamara's heart beat a heady tattoo in her chest.

"And so you wanted to get rid of these ties. You didn't want to be tied to me?"

Here it was. The moment when she put it all on the line. She took a deep breath. "I didn't want to be tied to you by other people or by property. That doesn't mean I didn't want you."

"And you couldn't tell me this before I left Australia?"

"Ridiculous, huh? But I needed to sort it out in my head first, and I needed to take a huge dose of courage, and I needed Cheryl to talk some sense into me."

For the first time he smiled, and it was as if that simple action released an unbearable pressure in her chest. "If she talked you into paying half a million for a weekend with me, then I'm not sure we're talking sense here."

"Oh, I think it might be worth it."

He sobered instantly, and she could feel the intensity of his gaze from across the cab. "You still haven't answered my question. Do you want to be tied to me?"

"I do." She smiled hesitantly. "But only in whatever way you want that to be. I know that I'm difficult, and I know I don't like change, and I know I'm not always courageous."

He stopped her by taking her hand, lifting it to his lips. "It took a whole lot of courage to do what you did tonight, Tamara."

"Maybe, but I'm no prize, and I don't want you to think you owe me anything."

This time he stopped her by kissing her lips.

"Will you stop prevaricating and get to the point? Do you love me? Is that what you are trying to say? Because that sure as hell is all I want to hear from you, sweet lips."

But the look in his eyes gave the lie to the frustration in his words. They were smiling and offering exactly the right dose of encouragement. They invited her; they coaxed her; they gave her courage.

"I love you, Nick, but that doesn't mean you have to—"

"I love you, okay? Now will you stop trying to let me off the hook?" His touched a gentle finger to her lips. "You're what I've been searching for."

"The ultimate challenge?" she asked wryly.

He laughed, the sound low and sweet and jammed full of his feelings for her. "Well, sweetheart, I figure you are looking like one hell of a lifetime challenge." Then his eyes turned serious. "But I meant I'd been searching for the place I belonged. You are that place, Tamara. You are my home. I love you, green eyes."

Tears pooled in those eyes and spilled over, sliding down her cheeks as Nick took her mouth, as he kissed her in the way only he knew how, and she didn't bother hiding them. She let them fall as she kissed him back, as she touched his cheeks, his hair, as she breathed against his lips, "Welcome home, Niccolo."

* * * * *

DESIRE™ 2 IN 1

AVAILABLE FROM 18TH OCTOBER 2002

WHEN JAYNE MET ERIK Elizabeth Bevarly

20 Amber Court

Jayne Pembroke hadn't planned a marriage-of-convenience to millionaire playboy Erik Randolph. He set her heart racing; but was it a good thing to fall in love…with her own husband?

SOME KIND OF INCREDIBLE Katherine Garbera

20 Amber Court

When her gorgeous boss, Nicholas Camden, made love to Lila Maxwell, right there in his office, she wondered if that night of passion could be the start of a lifetime commitment…

BILLIONAIRE BACHELORS: RYAN
Anne Marie Winston

The Baby Bank

Ryan Shaughnessy married his best friend, Jessie Reilly, to save her from the sperm bank! But did Jessie see him as *more* than just the father of her twin babies?

JACOB'S PROPOSAL Eileen Wilks

Tall, Dark & Eligible

Jacob West needed a wife to secure his inheritance and Claire McGuire was the perfect in-name-only bride. But she awoke a deep passionate possessiveness in him. Had the powerful tycoon been overpowered…by love?

DR DANGEROUS Kristi Gold

Marrying an MD

Injured doctor Jared Granger hated being a patient! That was, until he found himself in the healing hands of physical therapist, Brooke Lewis—part seductress, part saint and *all* woman.

THE MD COURTS HIS NURSE Meagan McKinney

Matched in Montana

Dr John Saville suspected that Nurse Rebecca O'Reilly's saucy defiance hid a secret innocence--and desire. Would he resist the ultimate temptation—or surrender and claim Rebecca, now…and forever?

AVAILABLE FROM 18TH OCTOBER 2002

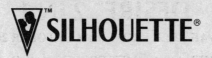
SILHOUETTE®

Sensation™

Passionate, dramatic, thrilling romances

CAPTURING CLEO Linda Winstead Jones
HOT AS ICE Merline Lovelace
RETURN OF THE PRODIGAL SON Ruth Langan
BORN IN SECRET Kylie Brant
THE RENEGADE STEALS A LADY Vickie Taylor
PROMISES, PROMISES Shelley Cooper

Special Edition™

Vivid, satisfying romances full of family, life and love

SURPRISE, DOC! YOU'RE A DADDY! Jacqueline Diamond
COURTING THE ENEMY Sherryl Woods
THE MARRIAGE CONSPIRACY Christine Rimmer
SHELTER IN A SOLDIER'S ARMS Susan Mallery
SOLUTION: MARRIAGE Barbara Benedict
BABY BE MINE Victoria Pade

Superromance™

*Enjoy the drama, explore the emotions,
experience the relationship*

JUST AROUND THE CORNER Tara Taylor Quinn
ACCIDENTALLY YOURS Rebecca Winters
LAST-MINUTE MARRIAGE Marisa Carroll
BABY BUSINESS Brenda Novak

Intrigue™

Danger, deception and suspense

SECRETS IN SILENCE Gayle Wilson
SECRET SANCTUARY Amanda Stevens
SOLITARY SOLDIER Debra Webb
IN HIS SAFEKEEPING Shawna Delacorte

1002/51b

DELIVERED BY
Christmas

Linda Howard
Joan Hohl · Sandra Steffen

Available from 18th October 2002

*Available at most branches of WH Smith,
Tesco, Martins, Borders, Eason, Sainsbury's
and all good paperback bookshops.*

THE
COLTONS

FAMILY   PRIVILEGE   POWER

*Look out for our fabulous brand
new limited continuity series*
THE COLTONS,
*where the secrets of California's
most glamorous and talked about
dynasty are revealed!*

Available from 16th August

THE COLTONS

FAMILY   PRIVILEGE   POWER

BOOK FOUR
THE DOCTOR DELIVERS
JUDY CHRISTENBERRY

Burdened by fame and family secrets,
Liza Colton seeks refuge in Saratoga Springs.
Meeting Dr Nick Hathaway makes her
feel whole again, but poisoned by his past,
the cynical doctor cannot see her for
who she really is.

Until one night of passion changed everything.

Available from 18th October 2002

COL/RTL/4

SHERRYL WOODS

about that man

It was going to be a long, hot summer...

On sale 18th October 2002

On sale November 15th 2002

*Available at most branches of WH Smith,
Tesco, Martins, Borders, Eason, Sainsbury's
and most good paperback bookshops.*

SILHOUETTE®
SENSATION™

proudly presents

Ruth Langan's

fabulous new mini-series

THE LASSITER LAW

*Lives — and hearts — are on the
line when the Lassiters pledge to
uphold the law at any cost*

BY HONOUR BOUND
October 2002

RETURN OF THE PRODIGAL SON
November 2002

BANNING'S WOMAN
December 2002

HIS FATHER'S SON
January 2003

1002/SH/LC43

SILHOUETTE®

proudly presents

five wonderful, warm stories from bestselling author

SHERRYL WOODS

The Calamity Janes

Five unique women share a lifetime of friendship!

DO YOU TAKE THIS REBEL?

Silhouette Special Edition
October 2002

COURTING THE ENEMY

Silhouette Special Edition
November 2002

TO CATCH A THIEF

Silhouette Special Edition
December 2002

THE CALAMITY JANES

Silhouette Superromance
January 2003

WRANGLING THE REDHEAD

Silhouette Special Edition
February 2003

1 FREE

book and a surprise gift!

We would like to take this opportunity to thank you for reading this Silhouette® book by offering you the chance to take ANOTHER specially selected title from the Desire™ series absolutely FREE! We're also making this offer to introduce you to the benefits of the Reader Service™—

- ★ FREE home delivery
- ★ FREE gifts and competitions
- ★ FREE monthly Newsletter
- ★ Exclusive Reader Service discount
- ★ Books available before they're in the shops

Accepting this FREE book and gift places you under no obligation to buy, you may cancel at any time, even after receiving your free shipment. Simply complete your details below and return the entire page to the address below. *You don't even need a stamp!*

YES! Please send me 1 free Desire book and a surprise gift. I understand that unless you hear from me, I will receive 2 superb new titles every month for just £4.99 each, postage and packing free. I am under no obligation to purchase any books and may cancel my subscription at any time. The free book and gift will be mine to keep in any case.

D2ZEA

Ms/Mrs/Miss/Mr ....Initials.......................................
BLOCK CAPITALS PLEASE

Surname ....

Address ....

....

....Postcode..................................

Send this whole page to:
UK: FREEPOST CN81, Croydon, CR9 3WZ
EIRE: PO Box 4546, Kilcock, County Kildare (stamp required)